# Kingdom Come

By the same author

*Fiction*

For Want of a Nail
The Second Inheritance
Without a City Wall
The Hired Man
A Place in England
The Nerve
Josh Lawton
The Silken Net
A Christmas Child
Autumn Manoeuvres

*Non-fiction*

Speak for England

Melvyn Bragg

# Kingdom Come

Secker & Warburg
London

First published in England 1980 by
Martin Secker & Warburg Limited
54 Poland Street, London W1V 3DF

SBN: 436 06714 5

Set, printed and bound in Great Britain by
Fakenham Press Limited, Fakenham, Norfolk

To Alice

# PART ONE

# I
# Going Back

Lately, Betty had begun to wake up much earlier than she
needed to. It was not traffic which disturbed her—for although
the bungalow was in the middle of the town it was situated in a
quiet side street, one of the old streets. Nor was it any animal
which brought her alive. It was just past midwinter, the early
mornings were black, dogs were kennelled, cats indoors, the
farms, which had once probed deep into the centre of the
market town, were now denuded of barns and beasts, overrun
by the new estates. She just woke early, that was all, there was
no reason she would admit to: dreams to a woman of her age and
background were of no account and she kept her restless night
visions private. It would not do to talk about them, or even to
confess they existed.

Her husband, Joseph Tallentire, slept heavily and, he
asserted, very badly. He did not stir when she got up, and the
sudden creak of the door—so loud and suspicious that she
paused like a child—did not disturb him either. She went
through to the kitchen with a clear conscience.

It was very pleasant, she thought, this early morning time
alone in the neat pine kitchen. Her son had helped to pay for it.
It was as near as she would ever get to those American kitchens
she loved so much in the nice films they used to make once upon
a time. It was something, anyway, at the end of a lifetime. She
put on the water for the tisane which eased her asthma and drew
open the curtains, even though it was dark.

There were three men who would come to see her that day.
One, her son, she loved but increasingly worried about, as he
seemed to lose himself in preoccupations foreign to her.
Another, her adopted son, she saw every day, he lived in the
town, he was a great comfort. Sometimes she thought that she

3

liked him more than her natural son. The third, whom she had also helped to bring up, she feared, he had the power to terrify her. All of an age, brought up in the same town. All bearing the same surname. Like her own. Given to her by the man she had married thirty-seven years ago. Now upstairs asleep— almost a stranger.

She had taken the snout off the kettle so that it would not whistle. When the steam came out of it, she found pleasure in just looking at it. A light frost on the window panes. Scalding steam within. For a few moments she felt herself suspended between the two, the ice and the heat. There was a pleasure in it which she could not articulate—just being there, alone in that minute space on the planet, darkness, frost, glass, steam and the electric light. Once she had feared being alone—now she found herself savouring the condition in which memories and impulses rose into her mind like the scent of the tisane breathed in to soothe her weary lungs.

In this solitary time she found that she was thinking and organizing her thoughts as there had never been the leisure to do before. At a time when she ought by custom to have been thinking more of death, she surged at life. She read more, now that all the boys were well away from her home. She listened to the radio, liked the plays and enjoyed the drama and the documentaries on television. At the end of her life she had found the time and opportunity to begin to educate herself. In a quiet, indeed a secretive way, she grasped this. But she kept it tight to herself, as if she were ashamed of it, and in one way she was. She would have hated any of her life-long friends to have thought that she was "putting on airs" or "getting above herself". She had cleaved to the norm, the average, the anonymous, the decent, the tolerant, amused and only apparently passive role assumed by many of those of her class, age and sex. Bingo, shopping, an occasional trip, film, outing, "dance", "do"—that was the camouflage. But inside her was this secret store, this hive where she fashioned patterns out of the books she read and carefully laid up stocks of knowledge and perceptions which she longed to have released. It was as if there was a place, late formed in her mind, which needed just the touch of a sympathetic nature to open it and bring it to life, like a lost

4

garden in a fairy story. Douglas, her son, could have done it if
he had wanted to; if he had noticed; if he had tried. But she
would never bother him with such silly ideas. She would go
further and overact the safe old mother she thought he wanted:
safe and plain and without complications. That was what he
needed. She knew what all of them needed, she thought, and
she was prepared to be wax to their impressions of her. Without
regrets. It was too late, at her age, for regrets.

(2)

Cumbria was 39,000 feet below. So definite and clear, it
seemed, full of strength, ancient and enduring. Up in the jet,
Douglas was incubated like a sickly infant—a body in a capsule,
babied with piped pleasures, instant food and drink—totally at
the mercy of a machine he did not understand.

He leaned forward for a better view and the stranger beside
him gave a gentle, sensuous groan as the light disturbance
rippled across her mind. Douglas let her settle herself and then
concentrated on the sight beneath him. He had spent half his
lifetime down there and half out of it. The two halves nowadays
appeared to cancel each other out. He was uncertain, fragile, in
a state of violent self-distrust and high as a kite. After a slight
pause to register his awareness of the sentimental nature of the
gesture, he raised his glass to the scene below and drank to it.
No one was watching.

All his family had been born there, even his son. His grandfather's life, save for the interlude of the First World War, had
been totally circumscribed by those hills and plains, by the
crops and beasts which fed off them and the coal and iron under
the tough crust of earth. It was not the earth, though, but the
waters which caught his glance. The sea, a final tongue of the
Atlantic, licking a firth between Scotland and England, and the
lakes, scattered so poetically about the bare fells, glistering
brightly on this clear morning of the year. From his god's-eye
view, it was all like a charming model in a natural history
museum, this place which had borne and supported so many
lives and contained so many deaths of his name and kind. He
himself, he thought, would probably die in a motorway car

5

accident, an aeroplane crash or of a heart attack in a side street of a foreign city. With luck.

He had begun to think about his death. Most mornings now, when he woke up, he found himself counting the years, weighing up the odds, trying to sift the worthless from the desired, and, as yet coolly, contemplating the sure fact of that return to the dark.

Douglas thought that he spotted the town of Thurston, his home town, to which his parents had returned for their retirement. "The last lap" was what Joseph, his father, sportingly called it, "the last lap". They would be waiting to see him that evening and later he would take his grandfather a bottle of whisky, as he had done the last few years, just after midnight, to celebrate another New Year's Day. His wife and son might be there too, although there was no guarantee, no agreement had been arrived at. Had he finally hurt her too much? He strained to pick out the fell village in which he had recently bought a small cottage, but snow had fallen on the tops, making the landscape unfamiliar.

As the Jumbo dipped towards London, Cumbria was pulled away from under him and she murmured, "That's right, that's right," in her sleep. She put an arm around his neck. He let it rest. Her brown hair smelled rich and sweet from some herb he could not identify. He loved it pressing so lightly about his face and took care to move gently as he drank yet more of the stiff spirit from the plastic glass. Home again, home again, jiggety-jig!

He still found some wonder in this flying. He had drunk champagne after the massive plane—carrying more people than lived in that Cumbrian village where he had his cottage—had hoisted itself up from Los Angeles. Over the North Pole, at 600 m.p.h., he had eaten *Boeuf Stroganoff* and taken two half-bottles of claret. Into a 160 m.p.h. headwind, above Greenland, he had watched a movie about a shark while listening, on headphones, to Beethoven's Fifth and then the Best of the Beatles. Now, with the temperature outside at less than zero centigrade, he was keeping warm on his fourth large scotch, mulling things over, and trying to remember the name of this woman who was half embracing him.

6

To his grandfather, John Tallentire, at this moment brewing his tea in the cold council Old Age Pensioner's flat in which he insisted on living, though alone, Douglas' whole trip would have appeared as an hallucination or a marvel. To his son, John Tallentire, at this moment banging the buttons of an empty television in a centrally heated metropolitan Victorian living room, it would all be as commonplace as travelling on a bus. Douglas was between the two; between the earthbound life of his grandfather, whose work linked him directly to the shepherds in the Old Testament, and the space-age of his son, who would see God alone knew what.

Douglas was half-cut—in that cradled, voluptuous state (which always had to be paid for) in which life seems either slow motion slapstick or a penetrably profound drama. He found the button and successfully employed it. Then he readjusted his neighbour about his left arm and shoulder and neck. His nose dipped deeply into her hair and he lingered. Why could he not identify this herb? He had helped his grandmother make herb puddings. He had followed her down the lane beside the old Jacobean cottage, so cosy and redolent in his mind (recently bulldozed to the ground—"unfit for habitation"), and helped her pick the herbs. She had patiently told him all the names in those sweet, unharassed days. He had prided himself on learning them. So why could he not identify this strong, delicious smell? His knowledge of nature was now so slight. So much forgotten, ill learnt, jettisoned by his memory—a trail of lost information forever trickling out of his brain, an invisible thread which would lead him back only to ignorance. Danger! Soulful Celtic twilight approaching! The new drink came just in time. Johnnie Walker, a brisk confident Briton on the label!

"C'mon," he encouraged himself, the blood and alcohol in equal and still companionable competition (one of his observations on travelling: capacity increases in direct proportion to length of flight). "C'mon. Pull yourself together and go to pieces like a man."

"I left my heart in San Francisco," the song said, on a sudden loop in his head. What had he left there? He had spent only three days in the place this time: little sleep, tense work, drink, the exhilarated exhaustion of that irresponsible hedonism which is aware of retribution. What had been left in L.A.? As he hummed he tapped his right foot and it nudged the airport toyshop present which was crammed under the seat in front of him. A clockwork whale for John's bath: it squirted water half a metre in the air. He had resisted a large rubber shark—though John would have preferred it, he guessed—but it would not have fitted under the seat. She moved again, snuggled even closer and murmured "Yes ... well ... yes ... hmm." To whom was she talking?

He had promised himself he would make some resolutions on this trip. After all, the last day of the year was the time for it. That long abortive litter of diaries begun, drink stopped, exercises taken up, reading lists copied out ... At the very least he could sum up the decisions waiting to be taken. Decadence was breaking promises to yourself. A message came from the steward—"Please refrain from Smoking." He finished the scotch.

She woke up and stretched herself most amply. She was a fine figure of a woman, as they used to say, very satisfactorily, and she knew it. By the time she was through with the long, loosening yawn, the arched back and the plunging heave of bosom, Douglas was powerfully aware of it. As she intended. Straight flirtation, Douglas thought, was the purest sex, undeniably.

"I slept?" she asked, throwing him a long, perfectly dentured smile, with just a tremor of helplessness about it. Douglas felt as if his feet were being skilfully tickled by a feather.

"You did," he confirmed.

"Are we here?"

"We are here."

"Is it raining?"

"No. Clear but cold."

"I thought it always rained in England."

"Mostly in summer."

"You made a comfortable pillow."

"Thank you. I did my best."

"Do you always drink so much?"

"Not always."

8

"I need the john."

"I'm afraid you'll have to wait until we land."

"What if I can't?"

"I hate to think."

"Do you really?" She smiled and turned full towards him and the chat they had enjoyed before she had settled down to sleep rose up from the immediate past nostalgically, somehow hinting at intimacies long past, brushed by this feeling of latent flirtation. They knew enough about each other to become a phone number in the book of future possibilities. In the moment she smiled and her lazy-merry eyes flicked over his face, both knew and were aware, and Douglas decided that his New Year resolutions might as well begin here. He would not, in any way, follow this up.

"Why don't we exchange telephone numbers?" she suggested. Her face was a perfect oval: healthy, open, American and unreadable; he had no idea what she might do or not do. She smiled again, this time with less teeth, more purpose.

"I was hoping you'd say that." He lobbed a return grin.

"I'll be in London a month. Maybe more. *Saint* John's Wood. You know it?"

"Quite well."

"Nice, huh?"

"Nice, very." He hesitated. "Can I ask you something—it's rather personal?"

She looked perturbed. A pace, an order and a progression had been established—the phone call in a few days' time, a good dinner—he could see she feared that he was going to be clumsy and spoil it. Her reaction stripped away the flirtatiousness—and added a few years to her age—and he saw a tough cookie inside the American pie. But the question had to be asked.

"Go ahead." This time her smile was on Automatic. He paused, drew it out.

"What shampoo do you use?" he asked. She grinned.

"It's pine. Pure pine." She ducked her hair into his face. "Take a breath."

"Of course! Damn! *PINE*!"

"Pardon me?"

9

"I should have known." The pine woods next to the shore where all his childhood treats had taken him—and the tentative walks with girls, nesting on the prickling ground, hurried kisses, fumbles, heads pressed in smell of pine. And he had forgotten even *that*! Thinking too much of Grandmother's herbs: too much piety over Cumbria.

"Can I ask *you* something?"

"Of course."

"Are you married?"

"Yes." He felt happy admitting that.

"Children?"

"One." There had been another, a girl; now dead.

"I like to know the score," she said, and her businesslike assumptions put him off her for ever. But politeness rolled on.

"We could share a taxi. I live near St. John's Wood."

"I'm being met. I hope." She showed him her perfect teeth, but it was not a smile this time.

"I'll keep out of the way."

"I'll expect your call." She tucked a small piece of paper in the top pocket of his jacket, kissed him lightly on the cheek, and then utterly devoted herself to preparations for the landing. These included wrapping herself up in highly unbecoming ski-clothes, which made her look like an Eskimo. He would not have recognized her.

Later, as the taxi screwed itself irritably into a long morning traffic jam on Hammersmith flyover, Douglas recalled that for three days now he had slept little, eaten little, drunk a lot and been in a state of almost constant enervation. Twelve thousand miles had come and gone: half way around the world since Monday, and now he was stuck in London W.6, beside a sign advertising Lucozade. He could have sunk the monstrous advertiser's bottle. His system might not have noticed. It was odd how these vast leaps across the globe could see you refilled with energy as quickly as you were drained of it. The taxi moved somnambulistically in the slow traffic and Douglas, suspended between sleeping and waking, experienced a rush of tranquillity.

He was calmly aware of being embarked on a course which would change and possibly ruin his life, and yet his instincts urged him not to resist that course. The outward pattern was much as it had been over the last few years; reasonable employment as a television freelance producer and reviewer; some writing. Yet he was isolating himself inexorably—from his friends, and from his ambitions in preparation for an action for which he despised himself—leaving his family.

When he was most alone and most respected himself, he thought that he wanted above all things to be a good man. But his character was against it.

Often he would tell himself that this was no more than a pose or a vain attempt to dignify the pointless scramble of his life. He suspected himself so critically that anything which tasted of piety appeared false. But the desire remained, however derided or dismissed. He accused himself of evasions and ill-thought-out reasoning. But the urge remained, and whether this was a hangover from an adolescence intoxicated by Christianity, an insurance, an affectation, a superstition, a counterfeit of strength, a lie to himself, a way to ennoble his life without doing much—no matter—it persisted. And however many darts he pitched into it, it kept bobbing to the surface of his mind. Why did it matter?

Sometimes it seemed to Douglas that his life was not so much punctuated as punctured by questions which were either unanswerable, or meaningless, or both. The question was, what was the question? It was important to know.

The taxi was hauling itself towards Chiswick and soon the driver would be able to leave the commuters, boring themselves into the city, and dodge through the cross routes which would take him to North London through all those Victorian side streets built for a colonial empire and now filling up with Commonwealth citizens come to roost.

He looked out of the window as the cab bounced him through St. John's Wood. He would have liked one of those villas once. Now he knew he would likely never be able to afford one and the longing to own one had left him. Which one, he wondered, would take in the pine-crowned American beauty? He touched the slip of paper inside his breast pocket and stuffed it deeper down. Forget it.

Back onto a big road now, with flats and shop-frontages and

traffic patterns like that of hundreds of other large cities the world over, and up the Hill. There would be no time for sleep. He went back into gear, the metropolitan man took over.

Letters to answer, calls to make, check back at the B.B.C. "The filming went well—yes—well enough—needs careful cutting—yes," pay one or two of the bills—those printed in red—that was the rule—how could he be broke on what he earned? How did you accumulate the capital to take the time to do what you wanted to make the money to live by what you wanted to do? Answer that! There would be, what—three days—about thirty letters to answer: lectures (no), talks (no), requests for charity (yes and no), and bills. One or two particular phone calls to make, a review to write: good clean work. John's whale was safe. Cigarettes for her—a poor gift, though welcome. Then the launderette. Set off for Cumbria immediately after lunch. Go to Bank. £9.50 taxi fare. For a ride from the airport! The pavement was littered as usual: the dustmen must have been.

He paid up, using his money as if he owned it, turned and there she was, at the top of the steps, in her old maroon dressing gown, watching him critically.

"Home?" he asked. She smiled a little wearily and nodded. "Yes. This is it," she replied and came to help him with his cases.

(3)

"You think you're *so* bloody marvellous."

Lester did not reply. He was getting dressed rapidly and he was concentrating on the job.

"You think you're *so* bloody marvellous."

Emma's voice was full of despair and self-pity. She sat up in the bed, the expensive hair-do (she was blonde again) collapsed about her tired, mussed face, pecking at the ivory-imitation plastic holder which held the first of the fifty cigarettes a day she depended on for dear life and feared were killing her.

She's like a great fat doll, Lester thought, stepping smartly into his new trousers. A monster doll. One of those you see at the big fairs. Walks, talks, blinks, squeaks. He smiled to him-

12

self. That was it! *And*—she was like one of those blubbery big sex-shop dolls, "the sailor's friend", they were selling up and down Tottenham Court Road. Yes! She was a half-breed between one of those Kewpie Dolls that blinked (*her* eyes were blue as well) and one of those rubber gals the poor sods carted off to bed with them! The thought cheered him up. He laughed.

"What's so funny?"

It drove Emma mad the way he refused to answer. She felt her head choking with anger as, physically, her throat choked when she vomited. The comparison was easy to make because she was often sick these days. Little food, lager, vodka and lime, cigarettes, no exercise: and the baby. Slowly being formed, silently, secretly there, stalking her relentlessly. She thought of the baby now: she saw it curled and peaceful somewhere deep in her large stomach, safe, slim, white, sucking its thumb. Although she knew that Lester hated it, she began to cry and the mascara came down her cheeks like the markings of a clown.

"You don't even *like* me," she cried.

He speeded up. But all his clothes were new. He had to be careful.

"You don't even *like* me." Emma thrashed around the bed, truly in despair.

Lester looked at himself in the mirror. Not bad at all. Late thirties, but you would take him for late twenties by the body. (The lined face was the giveaway, despite the youthful cut of the hair—still thick, thank God.) Good quality clothing. No more than three or four extra pounds on him since he'd stopped racing—when?—half a lifetime ago. He could still run, though, he kept fit. He examined himself carefully. He inspected himself as if he were about to go on-stage —professionally, without self-consciousness.

"How do I look?" he asked her.

"Pig."

"C'mon. I want an answer. I'm serious. Do I look all right?"

"Give us a hug. Just a hug."

"I've just got dressed up."

The look of distaste on his face almost made her howl—but, by making a great effort, she repressed it. He really did hang on

13

her approval and she had never been able to resist him, or refuse him anything, though he had come and gone like the wind and treated her like dirt.

"You're beautiful," she said passionately; but to Lester it sounded like mockery. He was impatient with her.

"I'm *not*—what you said! Have some sense! C'm*on*!" Lester's need was serious.

"The clothes fit very well. Brown suits you. Give us a hug. Please, Lester."

"What else?"

"Your hair needs a shampoo—but it's just the right length."

"I'll wash it on the train. Shirt?"

"Lovely!"

"Goulding House. Twenty-eight quid!"

"It suits you. Just a little squeeze then?"

He turned back to the mirror and pushed his hair this way and that. She was right about the shampoo. He went to the bathroom to see what he could find. What a pigsty it was!

As soon as he left the room, Emma did what she could to restore herself. She licked her fingers and wiped her face, using the sheet to dry it off. She rolled over and hung over the bed to look for her brush which she, was sure, was on the floor. The action lifted her shortie-sexy pure nylon pink and black lace nightie and revealed the full and tender moons of her large, firm, innocent bottom, trussed about with a suspender belt. She had slipped that on when she woke up to help him along a bit in the morning but he had not even reached out for a quick feel. Lester came in with his egg shampoo as the huge bum juddered with the strain of reaching out for the brush. It was one helluva bum. He went across to it, took a cheek in each hand and gripped very fiercely, digging in his short, newly manicured nails. This was extraordinarily satisfying: he had not a clue why. From beneath the edge of the bed, a happy face screwed round and beamed at him from under the hair-stack which now looked like a drunken Restoration wig, but was, in fact, like everything else about Emma, all her own.

"Jig-jig?" she said in that baby voice which turned him right off. "Lesty jig-jig wif Emmy?"

He dropped her: the red finger marks were as clear as paint.

14

"I'm late for the train."

"Just a liddle-iddle jig-jig for auld lang syne wif Emmy? Emmy-wemmy."

The middle-class nursery endearments—so gentle, so nicely silly, so sweetly harmless—thudded into Lester like insults. That was a sodding vicar's daughter for you! They were all the same.

"I'm off."

He had already packed his case. It was rather battered but covered with airport tickets and labels. All authentic. That would also impress them in Thurston. After they had digested the story of his travels, Majorca would seem like Morecambe. He still had something to play with.

"Take me." She swung upright, again reminding him of an object with clockwork inside.

"I'm all dressed up."

"I mean to Cumbria. To see the New Year in with you. You and me. I can't stay here. Can I?"

The last two words were rapped out. She gazed tragically around the bed-sitter. It was a small first floor room in a terrace of mid-nineteenth-century jerry-built houses in Kentish Town. Emma had draped it with the debris of her progress and, latterly, her decline. Revolutionary posters from what she called "my student bit" (which had been rudely aborted). Psychedelic posters from what she called "my flower-power bit". Cheap Eastern mats, junk and joss-sticks from "my transcendental bit".... and all the records, paperbacks, cast-off furniture and small, personally precious objects of a lifetime's utterly careless accumulation. Most things in the room looked as if they had merely drifted in for warmth, as Emma herself had. She had come down a slothful, selfless and, as most of her friends thought, stupid spiral which had gradually drawn her from a good university with good pals and good prospects to this, as they saw it, trashy, out-dated "bohemian" existence on National Assistance. Lester used her as a hideaway and boarding house. She was also, he would tell her honestly from time to time, "one staggering screw". Whenever he said that, the little girl inside her wriggled mightly and the large eiderdown of underprotective flesh shuddered.

15

He would be gone in a moment.

She took her life in her hands.

"Lester." The word was marred in its delivery as she had automatically and compulsively begun to light another cigarette. The smoke was huffed out of her rather thin mouth like steam out of an old railway engine—a little instant cloud. "Lester." She found the exact jolly tone. "What would you say if I said I was pregnant?"

"You're not, are you?"

"If I said I was?"

"Are you or are you bloody not?"

"What if—"

"I haven't time for this crap."

Emma was as brave as she could possibly be.

"But what if . . .?" she whispered.

Lester did not hesitate.

"I'd say for one—whose is it? For two—get rid of it. And for three—it won't be the first time you've done that."

She was very still. She said nothing.

"There's a fiver on the sink," Lester said. "I'll see you."

He was gone.

She paused for a moment and threw back the grubby sheets decisively. In her shortie nightie and the black suspender belt, she walked over to the sink, picked up the fiver and tore it into four pieces. She went across to the phone and rang Geoffrey's number. He was a solicitor. She had known him since they were children and he wanted to marry her. Despite it all, he had stayed loyal and, equally important, he did not laugh at her and use her for amusing anecdotes. He was not in.

"If you stay here, old girl," she said in her real voice, a surprisingly firm, English Home Counties, old-fashioned, ruling-class voice, "you'll go potty. Can't do the wee 'un an injury, can we? *Right*!" She marched across to the fridge, took out the open bottle of Pouilly Fuisse and had a very good swig. "Better." She had another for luck. And then, because why not, she finished the bottle. "Must remember to cut down on it for baby's sake," she said. "O.K., girl. Pack bags. Back to Daddy and Mummy." The ugly, gaunt, unheated vicarage in Suffolk which her mother hated so much that, winter and summer, she spent every possible hour in the three acre garden. "Be a sensible Emma now. Deep breaths. You're keeping this one. God! Help me this one last time. Please."

She burst into tears and then looked for the sellotape to stick together the five pound note which would take her home.

As Lester paid with the Barclaycard he noticed that it would run out at the end of January. He had done quite well off it. Two complete new outfits—choosing his shops shrewdly, as he had done in the old days, never going for the most expensive garment, not buying on Fridays or Saturdays, which made them nervous. Fewer shops were taking credit cards without other identification these days. This annoying mistrust had caused one problem but he had walked out of it: literally. For cash, he had had a stroke of luck at the dogs when he most needed it. He was set up for about a month. That would have to do.

"Sign," the ticket man said. He put the card on a little turntable and spun it round.

Lester Tallentire signed the name James Harrison, with a flourish. He had never given a thought to who this man might be. He'd bought the card from a friend.

"Twenty-six quid for a Second Class return!" said Lester.

"Robbery," the clerk agreed. "Soon all the trains'll be for the Shah of Persia and his missus—nobody else."

"Happy New Year," said Lester.

"Watch the Scottish lads," the clerk said, gloomily. "They generally wreck the trains on the way up to Glasgow this time of year. It's a Scottish thing, isn't it, New Year, with the haggis? They're all on it already. Drunk."

Lester felt a lurch of fear. He smiled, stepped away and walked slowly, considering whether or not to go back and change to a First Class ticket. This would put him out of reach of the drunken Scotsmen, who would inevitably go on the rampage up and down the train, which only made one stop on its three hundred mile journey to Lester's destination. He was in a bad enough way already and needed peace to work things out. As he went over to the First Class ticket window, though, he veered away. It would cost more than thirty pounds, which he thought was the upper limit on a Barclaycard. Besides, it might draw attention. He would get a seat a long way from the buffet and bar. He would set himself up with some beer and sandwiches here in the main hall, which they were trying to look and run like an airport lounge. Lester disliked the style: too modern for trains, he thought. He was worrying too much, wasn't he?

No. There was little point in denying it. Lester attracted trouble as he attracted sex. For about ten years now his life had swooped from one to the other, as he had hung around the Pop world and a few smalltime criminals with increasing desperation, trying to get his hands on some of the bullion. Even now, though he had been part of it, though he had managed five groups, one of which had almost got into the Top Thirty, though he was thought of, back in Thurston, as a Mr Big-Shot who knew all the Superstars—even now to give himself a profound and cathartic thrill all he had to do was close his eyes and think of the money to be made in the Pop Business. Five hundred thousand pound advances: two million dollar recording contracts: old pals from tacky clubs on Merseyside pulling in seven hundred and fifty thousand dollars per man per year for zero. Oh God! He sweated over his lust for it. Flat, sodding broke, with a bunch of Glasgow hooligans on the way to the cold North for the New Year! And reduced to stealing again!

No miracle intervened. It was just as Lester had feared. The Scots, determined to get to their hameland skin-full of Scotch, were soon carousing and then merely yelling: the real aggravation started at the worst possible time, as the train was going up Shap Fell, which would take it into Cumbria. The next station to be made for, where there would be any possibility of getting some police onto the train, was Lester's station, Carlisle. There were about forty-five minutes when the driver's only option was to drive on.

Lester knew he had been picked out. They had passed down his compartment as they moved up and down the train—Hoplites, Cowboys, Warriors in their own eyes: vandals to the mothers who clutched at their children and herded together their possessions: castrators to the men, most of whom, like Lester, had the sense to burrow intently into their papers or paperbacks and attempt to blot it all out. But they had picked him out. No wonder. He was, after all, one of them. And, however much he tried, when that "hard man" stare came at him—he did not flinch but returned it. The leader—in filthy, baggy jeans, clown's boots and a pink, thin shirt, slit to the waist—had turned to the five others with him and said, "He's our boy! He's our pal. Hello, Jimmie. Remember us? He's our friend. Eh, Jimmie?" The gang honked with laughter and stampeded back to the bar for more fuel.

Six to one was hopeless. Even one to one now . . . you got soft. He was in no shape. He looked good, but he was soft. Exercises kept you fit but not tough. There'd been all that trouble with the Law in November. Then the boys around Fulham. Big Emma had been very useful over the last two months. None of his kind knew her—neither the mob from the time he'd first hit London—a hard man on the run from a Liverpool gang—nor the scene he'd crashed into—the Rock lot—Emma wasn't somebody you could take around. Besides, he thought, you had more chance to find a winner if you were on your own. A lot of the Rock lads were bi- or right out gay and there was no point not obliging, Lester believed.

Lester was known to the Rock sophisticates as a scrubber, a tart, bad luck and an ageing joke. To the criminals, he was a fringe labourer. He was unaware of this.

He had run to Emma because he had been scared. He had been scared often enough in his life, but this time it went on for days and then for weeks. He had been out of luck before, and on the run before, but never so frightened. That was why he had treated her so badly. She understood that, even though he did not.

The long train went steadily up the mountainside, steadily hauled over the rock, away from cities, towns, even villages. These hills were quite bare. And inside, half a dozen youths, fighting drunk on about a quarter of what Douglas had absorbed on the aeroplane, looking around for an excuse to start smashing up people and things and themselves.

Lester, tuned in tensely, had awaited the change of tone since the first visitation. He heard it when they were two compartments away and moved fast.

He took his case with him but left newspaper, beer can and uneaten sandwiches there. That might gain him some minutes.

The thick sods might even wait for him to come back for his sandwiches. Which they would have eaten.

He got into the toilet at the very front of the train just as it reached the top of Shap and cruised for a few moments before it plunged down to the plain, averaging about 90 m.p.h. It was due at Carlisle in thirty minutes.

Lester tore off the lavatory seat for a weapon and jammed his suitcase between the locked door and the basin. He opened the small window and looked out at the snow-draped hillsides. Once upon a time he had run up and down those hills—raced to the top of them and back again. His career as a professional runner had failed, like everything else—but there had been one year—with his Uncle Joseph's backing ... He tried to keep himself calm by this thinking of the past. He had taken off his new jacket and folded it carefully on the top of his suitcase. He jogged on the spot and did some isometric exercises to warm himself up. The wind from the snowy hills was bitter. The train rocked from side to side like an old piece of fairground equipment. They went through Penrith and the train leaned over to the right. Only fifteen minutes to go.

Somebody knocked on the door.

He did not answer. Caught, stupidly, unawares. If he had answered, he realised, a moment too late, he could have gained another minute or two. He put his shoulder to the door, dug his feet against the opposite wall, set himself, then relaxed, and waited.

"We know you're in there, Jimmie, you wee bastard!"

There was only one voice. A boot made the thin door shake.

"We'll get you, Jimmie!" The Glasgow city slang, the gang cutting whine of menace, spun out the words sadistically. "We're goan tae hurt you, Jimmie. Eh? Eh?"

Lester had seen the guard. A cheerful old man, coming up for his pension by the look of him. A handsome grey moustache, clean uniform, deferential manner, a loud "Thanking You" for everyone; and panic in his eyes at the sound of this mob. He would be locked in his own cubby-hole, praying, as Lester did, for the train to hurtle down yet faster to the city.

"He's in here! The wee bastard's in here! Pissin' hissel', eh, Jimmie?"

The Scots drummed along the bare compartment floor and then came the blows and kicks and the almost insanely repetitive oaths which accompanied the kicking and hammering and built up the rhythm.

Lester did not say a word. He braced himself but he did not yet begin to spend every effort he had. They were uncoordinated and, though the door was splintering and bulging, no serious breach had been made. Yet.

He was even starting to think he might get away with it when the regular thud jarred the door. They had got together and were ramming it rhythmically. He anticipated it and strained against it with all his force. His insides were dissolving, he felt the stink coming out of him, he was starting to shake from the stress: he must not lose his nerve.

"Together—c'mon lads! Don't say the Glasgow lads were beat!"

*Thud*! The locked door shuddered.

"Aa' together. Aaaa . . . eee!!"

*Thud*! The obscenities disintegrated into a howl for blood.

"We're on our way, lads! Stand back—and now!"

*Thud*! The hinges buckled. The suitcase slid down to the floor.

"We are the champions! Celtic! Cel-*tic*! Cel-*tic*!"

*Thud*! *Thud*! "Cel-*tic*!" *Thud*! *Thud*! "Cel-*tic*! We are the chaaa-mpions!!"

The door was smashed but he held against it as the brakes came on and the train slowed down for the station. Fists came in to punch his head. A hand grabbed his hair and pulled until the tears raced down his face but he kept his shoulder down, his feet against the wall. "Mother," he heard himself gasping, "Christ!"

"Bastard! Bastard!!"

They were screaming now, scrambling among themselves to get at him, scuffling and slithering in the small space, hysterical with violence at being denied their victim, who was as rigid as a corpse in his small keep.

The train drew into the platform in a leisurely fashion. A bottle, its edges jagged, suddenly appeared a few inches from Lester's face. He jerked back his head and the door fell. They

21

stood there. Teenagers, faces bloated with hatred, screaming to destroy this stranger before them.

Lester picked up the lavatory seat and scythed it at their faces, catching the leader square on the bridge of the nose, which broke. So exhausted he had little sense of what he was doing, Lester managed to lever up the door with his right foot so that they had an obstacle to get over before coming to him and he stood in the corner, between the lavatory and the small window, swinging the seat with all the strength he had. He wailed and gasped as he fought. He was kicked in the groin. His shirt was ripped off him. He was smashed in the head. He felt blows on his chest and bootcaps bruising his legs.

The police came. He was standing on the platform. They told him to wait to give his story. He went in one side of the Gentlemen's—cleaned himself up desperately—put on his coat—came out of the other entrance and quickly left the station. He wanted no trouble.

(4)

Harry was badly winded. He felt embarrassed, bent over like a collapsed marionette, while the trainer pumped him up and down. He did not like drawing attention to himself.

It was a big crowd for a Thurston rugby match—getting on for three hundred and fifty. New Year's Eve was the date of the traditional fixture with the nearest town, Aspatria. There was always needle in these Derbys. Harry had been late-tackled. Around him, the other twenty-nine players waited without fuss. It would take a miracle to change the result now. Thurston was winning twenty-seven–eight and there were only ten minutes to go. The only tension now came from the fear in the Aspatria side that Thurston's backs would gallop over for more tries and run up a cricket score; and the fear in the Thurston side that they might not do so. The men—lightly clad—moved around to keep warm, this freezing midwinter afternoon.

The evening was closing in. Grey deepening to charcoal, drawn tightly across the sky. The rugby pitch was outside the town, built, characteristically, away from the centre, in that short burst of Sixties affluence and self-confidence, when there seemed limitless room for both expansion and exclusivity. The land was owned by the Rugby Club and most people came there by car. It was not handy for those who had to walk from the old town centre or the new council estates. The new Club had changed the social life of the town. Squash courts had encouraged a host of fanatics for this previously minority sport. There were tours of France with the rugby team and, at the Saturday dances, visits from nationally known jazz bands and up-and-coming Rock groups. Wives and girl-friends came to those dances in expensive dresses, the latest styles. The Clubhouse was purpose-built, open plan, rather like a ski-lodge in the Alps, people said. There was talk of building tennis courts and the plans were being drawn up by one of the architects who played for the team. Scruffiness was discouraged and a full-time barman had been hired. An ex-President had unearthed a Seventieth Anniversary and a short "History of the Club" was on the cards. Someone had suggested butts for archery.

Half a dozen brief handclaps acknowledged Harry's return to the game and the players spread out for the penalty. Beyond the pitch were open fields; rich farmland stretching to the sea on the north and the same distance, about eight miles, to the mountains on the south. The young men in shorts, bright shirts, hooped socks, fit and with intent faces, looked as if they had been sketched onto the landscape. It was the light layer of snow, perhaps, which made everything a little fanciful. The penalty was missed: too short.

"Come on Thurston!"

"Come on Aspatria now, lads, there's still time. There's still time, lads, now." The voice was clear: like a farmer calling to his dogs in the neighbouring fields. There was a lot of shouting, but it came from individuals. On the whole, most people liked to savour these games privately or with their friends. Only very rarely did the crowd call out as a unit and then it was soon over.

Harry pressed his fingers into his waist, bent forwards and took some deep breaths without, he hoped, anyone noticing. He had almost scored his second try.

The kick-off again. Thurston's neatly drilled pack took the ball, held it, brought in the Aspatria forwards and then let it out. A long pass to the stand-off. Harry was a few yards outside

23

him, running steadily, gathering speed. The stand-off dummied, almost got through but was caught by the wing forward. A ruck collapsed as the ball refused to come out cleanly. Harry trotted back into position on his diagonal line. He was the inside centre three quarter.

He loved this game. He loved his team-mates. He could think of no better way to spend an afternoon than this. None! Other people could take anything they wanted. Just give him this. "Come on Thurston!" he said, under his breath. The players moved across the field in patterns and formations which delighted or frustrated the initiates.

The ball came at him rather high. He was forced to check his stride but he caught it, turned out of the tackle and made straight for the line. One of his faults as a player was that he was a little over-eager to pass the ball. He did not like to appear to hog it or to appear selfish in any way. But this early passing was often unproductive. No one doubted his courage, so they put the fault down to poor tactics and agreed that it was the chief reason for his not being picked for the county side. He had always played well for Thurston though: or, as the committee phrased it, grown into new authority as organizers of the most successful side in the district, he was, "a splendid servant to the Club".

Harry was now travelling fast, reaching out with the ball between both hands—he would have to dive, the defence was coming in quickly. He began to fling himself forward. A big wing forward lifted him with his shoulder, hoisted him into the air and Harry was grounded. Sixteen pairs of studded rugby boots scrambled above him as the two packs of forwards foraged for the ball. To anyone unused to the game, it must have appeared that the life of the fallen man—whose rugby strip included no protective padding whatsoever—was in real danger. But Harry wriggled out, sound but for a few scratches and bruises, preserved by the conventions which somehow drew a line between ferocity and brutality.

"You should have got that one," the stand-off said dourly as Harry ran back into his position.

Harry nodded. He would have got to the line a couple of years ago. He had lost half a yard. Thirty-three was ageing for this game. Still, he would play for as long as they wanted him to, in whatever team, in whatever position. The Thurston side was still pressing. The ball came out again, the pass low, awkward, fumbled: he dropped it.

"Wake up, Thurston!"

Harry cringed a little and chivvied himself harshly. He was getting slack. The Aspatria side won the ball from the set scrum and tried a break around the blind side. Harry crashed their winger into touch with a hard tackle and then helped him to his feet. He felt better. Defence had always been the soundest part of his game.

The whistle blew. Three cheers from each side. Handshakes. Clapping the visitors into the Clubhouse. On the note of polite and formal amateurism these thirty players finished the game which had absorbed so much of their skill and energy—teachers, accountants, shopkeepers, one or two farmers, civil servants, a couple of mechanics, local government employees, young engineers and junior management from the big factory, a firm stratum of that rising generation which was well entrenched in well protected and well supported jobs, responsible, affluent enough for all immediate purposes, as secure, apparently, as could be imagined. They were a group to whom the words "privileged" and "middle-class" would be anathema. All of them were convinced that, in *their* world, class distinction had dissolved. Yet, perhaps unwittingly, they were building up once again the old structures of exclusivity which they would swear were over and done with forever, and of no interest at all.

Singing in the steaming showers. All the talk of Rugby, Rugby, Rugby. Harry drank a quick pint of shandy in the bar, which was bulging with supporters and players, who were conscientiously putting down a foundation for the drinking which would go on way past midnight and well into the New Year's Day. In Thurston they prided themselves on the way they brought in the New Year—"Scottish style," they said—the Border was only twenty miles away—and bagpipes were at a premium. Harry bought his round and then slipped out. It was dark.

He was going to see John, his grandfather, who was not his

"real" grandfather, just as Betty was not his "real" mother—but they had adopted him so completely that it was only recently, on the plateau of his adult life, that he had faced it as a possible problem. His conclusion had been to love and respect them even more for what they had done. He felt no pain or anger at the implications of his adoption. After all, he had had a real home, real love and "to all intents and purposes" (this was the phrase he used to himself) "a real family". He was glad that he could do something in return, these days, truly pleased at the opportunity to show his gratitude.

Though he had a car—he needed one for his job on the "Cumberland News"—Harry enjoyed walking. He liked to look around the place. It was as if he were checking up on it, or rather, giving it his care and attention. He had lived in the town all his life, he was perfectly contented there and had only once wanted to leave it. That was when he had considered emigrating to Canada with three of his friends who had moved to Toronto. He had joined them, spent six months happily finding his feet, come home for a holiday and somehow never gone back. Now he was settled in Thurston, as he told himself, "for good".

He walked along Low Moor Road, glancing at each of the new bungalows and houses which formed one of the latest little suburban tentacles of the town; noted the still unmended crack in the large end wall of the secondary modern school, which had lately become part of the Comprehensive; looked in the two farmyards which had, even in his lifetime, been separated from the town by fields and seen their fields suddenly sprouting bungalows; went through the Kissing Gate up towards Highmoor, where the old mansion had been turned into luxury flats and the Deer Park was now a private housing estate and the council had made adequate provision for old people. He liked visiting old John and knew his visits were welcome, which was pleasing.

The compound of old people's flats was built, three storeys high, around a small green (once a walled rose garden). The Warden's House had a dining room and a television room to be used by the pensioners if needed. Old John preferred to eat on his own (except on Fridays—a compulsory communal supper was imposed then) and watch television alone. He was a little deaf, hated to show it, and would rather miss a programme in the Common Room than ask his neighbours to be quiet. Joseph had bought him a nice little portable for his own flat.

Harry went in without knocking.

John was mending a shoe. There was a fire in the grate, the television was on with the sound well up, the apparatus of high tea made a trail from the larder-cupboard to the armchair—an open biscuit tin, the bread tin, the pan in which the beans had been cooked, a plate, a bag of fancy cakes—everything looked in disarray—an old man's careless domesticity—and yet the overwhelming impression was of calm, a rather bleak tranquillity, as the old man huddled over his shoe, hammer very carefully tapping in little bright nails which he took one by one from between his teeth.

He nodded to Harry—indicated that he should help himself to refreshment—and continued with his job. Harry poured himself some tea and sat down on the hard-backed chair beside the table.

"You can knock that damn thing off!" The television vanished to a pinpoint and that too went out.

The sudden silence made them smile at each other, then John nodded and went back to the delicate tapping of the short slim nails into the sole of the shoe. Harry waited and unobtrusively massaged the bruise on his thigh.

When he had first left school and gone to work on the farm, Harry had been recommended by his "grandfather", who worked on there long after Harry left for journalism. Eventually the old man had been laid off—well after his eightieth birthday. John had taken to the idea of retirement very badly. However, as always in his hard and unyielding life, he had settled for what was inevitable. There were hedges to be trimmed around the lawns of nearby private houses. He established a routine—his own meals, his own shopping, a drink on certain lunchtimes and certain evenings and a visit to Joseph and Betty for Sunday dinner.

Above all, though, at the end of this enormous life, which had taken him down the pits and under the sea to hack coal in conditions known to Roman slaves and onto the land to plough with horses and work like one, into the First World War, to be

27

used as indifferently as any footsoldier in history, and back to his hero's home to face the death of his first wife, the breaking up of his family, the death of his favourite son, more hardship, more labour, unemployment, eventually drifting up to a ledge of affluence on the mid-century tide, John found pleasure in what had previously seemed nothing but a chore: walking. He walked along the River Wiza and noted the banks where the trout might hide; he walked around the few remaining lanes in the middle of a gutted and modernized Thurston; he walked to the park to watch the children on the swings. Once, near his ninetieth birthday, he had walked to the village in which he had been born. It was three miles off. He had gone without telling anyone. But someone from town had seen him, offered him a lift in their car, been gruffly refused, and reported the curious incident. Curious, because John was beginning to be widely known as "old" (ninety in a man was quite rare) and also because, as the motorist said, "You could tell he was tired out, flaked, jiggered, you could tell—but the old bugger wasn't going to have a lift—'No thanks!' he said, like he was telling me off—just 'No thanks!'" John had gone to look at the cottage in which he had been born. It had been painted and improved and embellished, after the taste of a couple of dentists who commuted from the village to their practice in Carlisle. "They made a smart job of it," he said, approvingly. He had passed it by once and then returned alongside it, not wanting to stop and stare in case he was seen and caused alarm.

His barrel-bellied father, who always wore a hat—bullying—his mother—distant now, an anxious lock of hair on her brow, blue, bluebell eyes, slim face, quick shy smile, red knuckles—his numerous brothers and sisters—they had played beside that stream . . . there used to be an orchard where the new double garage stood . . . all the shops were gone and the forge where he had first worked . . . and Emily, his wife . . . he could not find the place where she had lived . . . there were too many memories, he thought, too much crowded in. What was he to do with it all?

That had been in the spring.

Harry idolized the old man and idealized him. When John was silent, as now, Harry would respect it, know that silence was preferred for a while, be happy just looking at John, small, very lean, still a head of hair on him, though thinner, and still the unexpected blue eyes that struck out of the browned face. John kept his head low, being more than usually careful over the job. Shoes were expensive, Harry thought, approving the thrift; they had to be looked after.

"Did they find out who that lad was?" John asked the question without looking up.

"Yes. He was local. He'd been to school with Douglas."

"Do they know why?"

"Nobody knows."

A young man had just been found dead in some woods a few miles from Thurston. All the indications were that he had lived there for some weeks, until he succumbed to hypothermia. One or two people now thought they had seen him about the woods. Nobody had reported him. His body had been found by a couple looking for a place to lie.

"Those two must have had a queer shock," John said, and he turned his face up to Harry and smiled grimly, the remaining two nails in his mouth giving him a rather bizarre appearance. "Tea's cold, I'm sorry."

"I didn't come for tea. It's all right, anyway." He took a large mouthful.

Awkwardly in his pocket there was the ounce of twist Harry brought up every Saturday. It was always a problem, getting it out of his pocket and onto the mantelpiece where he always left it. Whichever way he manoeuvred seemed flashy, somehow, as if he were throwing charity in the old man's face.

"You won then."

"How do you know?"

"You haven't said anything."

"It was a bit scrappy."

"Aspatria used to hammer Thurston. Used to be miners, Aspatria, all of them. Up from the shift at dinner-time— into their togs and on with a game. I never played a game, young fella, never once. We worked Saturdays. There. That should hold." He held the shoe before him and examined the neat job.

Harry was uneasy. There was an inflection in John's voice

29

which perturbed him, but he was unable to diagnose the source of his apprehension. He waited.

"They should see you through a few more hundred miles. Eh?"

There was no answer. Harry was uncomfortable now. For some reason, the proportions of the small room had changed. The single light in the middle of the ceiling appeared to illuminate a much more limited area. The undrawn curtains, flower-patterned, green, appeared short, doll's house curtains. The few pieces of furniture were so cramped Harry could have stretched out his leg and touched John, who sat very still, vulnerable. The young man could not bear that vulnerability.

Harry glanced about him as if some visible threat were in the room. His throat was dry. He could not understand why the old man's mood was so fiercely silent and sorrowful. Once again he took refuge in cheerfulness.

"Joseph was telling me you used to make all their clogs when they were little. He said you used to shape the wood to a bit of paper you made them stand on—and then buy the wood and leather to cut for yourself. He said he's never worn anything more comfortable in his life! He can still feel them on his feet, he says, when he puts his mind to it."

John did not react to any of this. As the silence began once more to grow and thicken, Harry felt panic come over him. He feared things that were unclear. He could not endure them.

"What's wrong?"

There was a slight shake of the head.

"C'mon, Grandad! You can tell me."

Without glancing up, or moving at all, John spoke, pausing between almost every sentence.

"I was coming along that bit of field just behind here. Just now. Just walking. I hadn't done much. I hadn't gone far at all. And my legs gave way." Here he hesitated for a full minute, wondering at his own words. "They buckled. They just packed up. It's happened before but I took no notice. Except, this time—I had to crawl back here like a baby." He repeated the sentence, amazed. "I had to crawl—like a baby. If anybody'd come up I was going to say I was looking for a button. I got myself here along by the fences and using the walls." He looked up, quite suddenly, and the blue eyes stared through the swell of tears. "I can't walk, Harry." He paused. "It's all finished. It's all over." He wiped his eyes with his shirtsleeves. "You won't tell anybody," he said harshly, and Harry nodded.

Finally, they looked at each other directly, and Harry was pierced by the old man's terror.

## (5)

It was not at all as Betty had hoped. She had wanted them to meet up as a happy family. She wanted there to be easy pleasure and harmony. She wanted cheerful bustle and companionable-ness—the spirit of Christmas and a New Year. Instead she got a fraught assembly which crashed and jarred through the bun-galow, uncaringly, she thought, uncaringly. They made it seem small when it could have seemed *warm*. Even Harry was not reliable, not his usual self.

Lester had arrived first, looking "dreadful", she said to herself, and vowed to say it to no one else and to contradict flatly anyone else who said it. His mother, good old good-time Helen (Joseph's youngest sister), had not left the key under the stone and Lester was in no state to go around the early evening pubs looking for her. He wanted something to eat and he wanted a wash. Betty gave him a clean towel and asked him where he had got the cuts and bruises. Silently, she absorbed the lie about falling down the stairs at the station and went to make him, on request, egg and chips.

Joseph, of course, was pumpkin-packed with curiosity, but he too had the manners not to ask directly. Remarks like, "They should see to those bloody stairs" and, "You used to be quick on your feet" and, "Maybe he needs a breathalizer before being put in charge of egg and chips—just joking! Just jok-ing!"—these and one or two other searching, intimate invita-tions to confidences were ignored by Lester, who locked him-self in the small but well appointed bathroom, relaxed for the first time in hours, opened his coat, removed his ripped silk shirt, stripped off his battered trousers, shivered violently, felt the cold sweat on his forehead and was noisily sick. The sound travelled through the thin walls and silenced Joseph.

31

There was a desperate merriness about Joseph now. Either that or he was crushed in unfathomable melancholy. His life, it often seemed to him, had come, in all senses of the word, to nothing. He used activity to beat down thought.

As Lester came out of the bathroom—to a fully laid table—the meal all set out—Douglas, Mary and John came in. The lounge was instantly overcrowded. They grouped in the middle, the backs of their knees pressing against the arms of the three piece suite. Betty pushed the few pieces of furniture here and there to make more space. Joseph immediately engaged Douglas in the intense interrogation least likely to be tolerable after a three hundred mile drive—what was he exactly doing? What was Hollywood like? Who did he meet? How was the film going? Betty herself swung between irritation at Joseph's relentless tactlessness and amused sympathy for his understandable curiosity. She too wanted to know those things and Douglas would tell her in his own good time: in time, he would lay his adventures at her feet. But now—tired and fussed after the car journey—he fretted and strained, half wanting to satisfy his father, half aching to be let off the leash of this paternal-proprietorial interest. Between her husband and her son there could still be a tension as competitive and bare as between two boys. Lester watched them with exaggerated interest, as if he were at a ping-pong game: he had always taken Douglas for a fool and, despite Douglas' success, Lester had not changed his mind. Indeed, he had added another dimension to the son of the man who had helped him more than his own father: Douglas was a phony. All that highbrow talking! Phony, Lester thought, junk! Yes: that was about it. He went on with his meal, virtually ignoring the new arrivals.

Betty noticed that, too.

Douglas and Mary had come to leave John for the night, so that they could go out on the New Year's Rounds. Betty insisted on this, even though Mary thought it unfair on her, but—"enjoy yourselves while you can," Betty said, urging others to the self-indulgence she had always denied herself. "Besides, I like having him to stay, don't I, John?" She smiled at the boy and hugged him, but he did not make much of a response. With his hands in his pockets he was staring moodily

32

at the large print of Constable's "Hay Wain" which dominated one wall, and yawning. He had slept in the car and Douglas and Mary had been able to argue undisturbed. "Have some tea," Betty suggested, although she felt, surely and sadly, that her son and his wife wanted to be away as fast as they possibly could be. "Lovely," Mary said, summoning real enthusiasm to sink the scum of selfishness and ingratitude which floated above her mood. She wanted to stay with Betty for a while. "Lovely; let me get it." "We'll get it together," Betty countered, "leave the men with a bit more space."

Harry came in.

By this time, Douglas and Joseph had edged, thankfully, into talk of local news. Joseph was sometimes a little impatient of Douglas' interest in this; Lester thought it was just another example of Douglas' phoniness: the "I've kept my feet on the ground bit", as Emma would have said. (He smiled as he thought of that big bare bum—and the smile hurt his face. Thank God Betty and Joseph liked him for what he was and no questions asked.) But Harry, who loved Douglas as a brother should love a brother, even though, or perhaps because, they were not related in blood, saw that this concern was genuine and was happy to join in and feed it. He respected Douglas a lot. He could imagine how hard it was in London.

Yet, when Douglas was there, Harry felt that he had to alter his behaviour. Although this bungalow was more familiar to him than it was to Douglas, although it was he and not Douglas who had helped Betty and Joseph move in, and although he came regularly and did the heavy work of turning over the garden, re-siting the fence, planting the fruit trees (the garden was disproportionately large)—yet, despite all these daily bonds of help, loyalty and affection, Harry felt it right and natural that Douglas assume precedence in all things whenever he crashed in from London for a few hectic or strained hours. Douglas recognized that and deliberately held back from over-much family attention when Harry was there.

"There was this business of Alan Jackson's death in All-hallows Woods," Harry offered, and gave the same brief details he had given his grandfather, ending with the lonely self-destruction in the woods. "You knew him, didn't you?"

33

"Yes." Douglas felt suddenly desolate, full of pity for Alan Jackson. "I suppose I knew him as well as anybody, once."

Alan had been a peculiar man. In one illumination, it seemed as if he saw the whole of the life of this man he knew so little and yet, in truth, *did* know "as well as anybody, once". There and then he felt a powerful, instant sense of loss. He wanted to go over it privately. The man was gone from the earth: a man his own age—school—a man he had shadowed in some way in his childhood.

"It seems he was rather the solitary type," Harry suggested.

Douglas nodded. He wanted to concentrate in silence on this death. It was almost as if he needed to be left alone, to grieve over it. And yet the man had been a stranger to him in the years since school. And even then there had been no shared sport or dances or girls, they had not even been in the same form. But Douglas felt that he knew the man to his soul; he could sense the sad parabola of the life which had taken him back to those particular woods; he could understand, he thought, why this lonely individual had died in the way he had. He wanted time to think about it. It marked him out in some way he could not fathom. It was as if the man's death met a need in him.

"Thanks!" Lester shouted his appreciation, pushing aside his empty plate. "Just exactly what I needed." He burped but kept it inside his mouth. "Any apple cake?" He tilted back his chair and took out a cigarette.

"There's always apple cake in this house," Joseph said, sentimentally. "I love apple cake. So does Douglas."

It must be possible, Douglas was thinking, to envisage a soul, or a life after death, when he himself—though in this over-crowded room—could now be so heavily, almost wholly, engaged elsewhere. His thoughts, his imagination, his sympathies were with Alan Jackson—he saw the clumsy young man stumbling about in those damp, thin woods, blindly trying to fend off the in-crushing world—and yet he was also here, in the flesh, in the touchingly spick and span lounge, brightly lit, newly dusted and polished, here he was, one of four men of the same name. What was this sudden cessation of existence?

"If you would take your apple cake on your knees across in

34

that easy chair, Lester, we could organize everybody else around the table." Betty was making the best of it.

With Mary's help the table was set out once more, this time for four—Douglas, Mary, John and Harry. Betty had wanted to have a proper High Tea for all of them and she had cooked and prepared all day for this. But it was clear to her that Mary and Douglas were impatient to be gone. They had arrived so much later than they had said they would. Then Lester and Harry being here as well made it impossible. So she postponed the High Tea, with the crackers and the sweets, the best crockery and the napkins. There would be another time, perhaps.

Even so, there was enough on the table to feed the four of them three times over. Tongue, veal pie, ham, a salad, fresh bread, teacakes, scones, rum butter, cheese, jams, apple cakes, gooseberry tarts, trifle, cream, "to keep you going until you can get something," Betty said, stubbing the rising cries of appreciation, putting the meal in its place as she poured the tea and hovered, watching them eat.

"I'll just have a bit of that apple cake," Joseph said from his chair beside the fire.

"You've had yours before."

"Well, I'll have some more again, thank you. This is my house."

"Oh dear," Betty smiled: she knew it irritated him when her tone implied his absurdity, but sometimes there was nothing she could do to prevent it. Joseph felt the ice in the silence of Douglas and thought, mistakenly, that it was a comment on himself.

"Well, it is," he insisted. "And I've always been fond of apple cake, now, haven't I? John knows that."

The small boy was appealed to in a situation where the cross-currents were far too many and too charged for him to be at all able to disentangle them. He sensed that there was an argument going on—indeed, sadly, one of the better learnt lessons of his life was the understanding he now brought to the many different arguments between his parents. He could gauge their level of seriousness as well as the adults themselves. Most often he forced himself to appear calm, and the effort of repression often gave him a misleading appearance of being indifferent to what was around him.

"Don't you, John?" Joseph wheedled away at his grandson. "John and me's mates," he announced.

"Oh, have some apple cake and be quiet!"

"I won't if you feel like that."

Douglas chewed very slowly, counting the number of times he was chewing this thankfully thick home-cured ham. Why was it that over such trivial exchanges as this one about a slice of apple cake he would feel that he wanted to kick the house down?

Harry ate as if all life but the digestive system had taken time off. He was unhurried but thorough, going from plate to plate like a platoon engaged in a scrupulous mopping up operation. Lester, sprawled in the chair opposite Joseph, felt himself totally relax for the first time since he had got in the train. Now that he was through it, he felt almost lightheaded at his survival. Douglas would have been pulverized. And Harry?

"What weight do you carry now?" he asked Harry.

"Twelve-six."

"A hundred and seventy-four pounds," said Lester in his Mid-Atlantic drawl. "You carry it well, pal."

"We train three times a week now. Commando courses and weights, they're all very keen, these days."

"We got our training digging ditches," said Joseph, suddenly grim.

"Win today?" For the second time since he had arrived, Douglas deliberately heaved the conversation into a local area. But this time it was to give himself space, so that he could freewheel inside his head. When had he last seen Alan? Had he wanted to die? What did it mean, this plunging helplessly about the woods?

"Yes." Harry admitted the victory reluctantly.

"Who's in the team now?"

"The First Team?"

"Yes."

"The lot?"

"Yes."

"Well . . ." Harry had pronged a piece of tongue, a piece of

36

pie and a pickle; he put them into his mouth and crunched them up before he settled down to list the team.

"Apart from you, there's only two others I know," Douglas said.

"You're lots past it, lad," Joseph said, standing up to hand his empty plate to Betty, "past it. Thank you for the apple cake. I enjoyed it."

"Football lads stay the same," Lester announced, obscurely feeling that this got in a dig at Douglas. "Younger brothers, or lads who are the sons of the lads I played with. Mind you—football lads always did stick together. Didn't make as much of a song and dance as you rugby toffs."

"They don't play football now." Joseph was suddenly angry. "It's all kissin' and pussy ball. Nobody can dribble today."

Douglas wondered where his father's lurches of anger came from. They were like clouds appearing in blue skies—up they came, these black moods, and clearly he could not cope with them. He must, though, he resolved, be more patient. When he criticized his father he was very often criticizing himself: he had realized that only lately.

"What was different about it in your time, then?" Douglas asked, by way of making amends.

Pleased to be able to preach, the floodgates opened and out came a list of great footballers of the Thirties and Forties—a knowledgeable and comprehensive list which ended in a discussion of the respective merits of Stanley Matthews and Tom Finney. Lester and Douglas had just been old enough to see these players and appreciate them and, for a few moments, with the three men jostling opinions good naturedly and Harry and John appreciating it all, Betty felt that there was this thing called a Family, that it did wrap you around in warmth, that it did make sense of everything. If only Mary had not seemed so distant and so tired. She looked worn out.

"There was one Thurston lad," Joseph said, now sure of himself and in command, "now this is true, this. It was just before the War. What a player! All the talent scouts used to come and watch him. Archie Robinson. What a player! I've seen him beat a man and then take it back, just to beat him

37

again. That ball was tied onto his boot with a bit of string. But he wouldn't move from Thurston. He-would-not. He wouldn't go to any of those big clubs. He-would-not. And do you know why? Eh?"

They all did. He had told the story many times. Nobody spoke up.

"Because he would only get changed in his own house! He would only change in his own house!" Joseph began to laugh loudly at the idiosyncratic nature of the man. For him the story was rich in meaning. It meant that individuality still existed: it meant that the Big Money Boys (his idealization of the few sad ex-professional footballers in flat caps who travelled Third Class to remote towns looking at "prospects" in the rain) had been spurned: it meant that the ordinary person had gifts on a level with the highly applauded. It meant he knew a great man known to few. "He wouldn't change," Joseph explained, aware that his own enjoyment of this story was not as infectious as he had hoped, "anywhere else except in his own house. You see? That was the sort of lad he was. Only in his own house. And *that* was why he wouldn't join any of those other clubs, see, John? It would have meant him travelling and then he wouldn't have been able to change in his own house. What a dribbler!"

Douglas choked a little, held it back and tried to catch Mary's eye. She was far away, though, eating her meal as placidly as could be, he thought: perhaps a little tired, that was all. Could she switch on and off like that? In the car on the way up they had all but agreed to a trial separation. Yet there she was, deftly collecting the plates, helping his mother, taking part, more part than he was.

Harry was finding it difficult to carry out old John's request that he tell nobody about the collapse. It seemed to him that Joseph and Betty and Douglas had much more right to know than he had. Yet how could he let them know without breaking the old man's trust? He felt as if he were telling a lie by omission, keeping something hidden which should have been open: it was a rare and most unpleasant sensation and it made him subdued.

The conversation died down again. Mary was too exhausted

to make any effort—but she wondered at these lulls, this recurring blankness. She was a stranger to their class, their town, and their private and shared memories and yet she felt that between them there were sometimes such chasms that she could not imagine where they had come from. Douglas occasionally claimed to derive such a tight and fruitfully cosy strength from this background of his—and indeed he was loyal to it and it was as clear on his life and work as the print of ferns on ammonites—yet, here they were, all met together after months of different lives in diverse places—stone silent. She let it be, saving herself.

"Tick-tock. Tick-tock. Tick-tock," Joseph said and then, staring at John, he began to sing:

> "My grandfather's clock was too tall for the shelf
> So it stood ninety years on the floor.
> It was taller by half than the old man himself
> Though it weighed not a penny-weight more.
> It was bought on the morn of the day that he was born
> And was always his pleasure and pride.
> But it stopped, short, never to go again
> When the old—man—died."

He sang it to the bitter end, waving his arms before him as if conducting the massed bands at Wembley; when he finished, the silence resumed.

Harry made his effort.

"I just called in to see Grandfather," he began.

With relief, all of them turned to him.

"He seemed a little bit under par," Harry replied, in answer to their enquiries after the old man. Surely "under par" wasn't breaking trust?

"He's a marvellous old man that," Joseph said with a full sweep of sentiment. Here at last was an opportunity to unite the room in that deep good-fellowship which the presence of all these loved people made him yearn for. "Do you know: that old man. Once ... do you know? He was down the pit, Number Nine Pit, I believe it was ..." Another familiar story, another respite.

It was no surprise, Douglas thought, that they should be at sixes and sevens. He was hung-over, sucked into self-concern and oddly upset by the death of Alan, his old schoolfriend. Mary, he thought, was in neutral, engines off; no wonder, poor love, the hammering they gave each other. Lester had clearly been in a fight and had rushed here, probably to hole up: he had crash-landed on Douglas several times in London for loans and cover, until the last time, when Douglas, who admired his reckless cousin, had summoned up the sense to say "no more". Harry was in a world of his own, Douglas thought, which was not uncommon. He envied Harry, whom he saw as somewhere out there with the Good and the Contented, in a land he himself would yearn for all his life without being able to visit. John, his son, was not looking forward to being without his father yet again. And Betty—the centre of the family—was disappointed. Douglas wanted to go and put his arms around his mother to cradle away the years of hurt and fill up the emptiness, live up to the expectations ... and, on top of that, Joseph, who was sensitive to all, fully realizing the unevenness, the disinclination and the fatigue, determined to bury it all with those blasts of anecdote which somehow, unfairly, set Douglas on edge.

"And so this other fella and your grandfather," Joseph pointed almost accusingly at Douglas, "were in this shaft."

"The accident," Douglas said, referring to the pit-fall which had gravely injured his grandfather. "When he walked out of hospital bandaged up."

"*Not* the accident! *Not* the accident! This is another time. An old fella told me this, that I met at a hound trail a few months ago. I haven't told you this. It's to show how *strong* they were then, do you see?"

"More tea anybody?" Betty had gone out to brew a fresh pot: she stood at the kitchen door, unaware that she had arrived like an actor on a false cue, smiling hopefully at the roomful, still prepared to work at it.

"I was in the middle of a story!" Joseph complained.

"Yes, please." Douglas pushed his cup forward.

"Mary?" She shook her head and then began to clear away.

"Strength's as much a knack as anything," Lester declared. "There was a fella I knew in Liverpool—they were all terrified of him—big fat sod—sorry—beggar—type of man who could eat one more potato than a pig, you know, great big belly hanging over a leather belt, but hard as concrete—well, for all that, there was a little fly-weight, Johnny Calford, he was Northern Champion—he just clipped him—right on the point of the jaw—his fist can't have travelled more than six inches—and this gorilla was down. Timing, that's what's half the battle." He duffed his own chin, lightly. "Just clipped him like that. Bang!"

"When we had the pub," said Joseph, "just a bit after the war—no, later, never mind when, we seemed to get a run of little drunken fly-weight and light-weight boxers down from Scotland, mainly from Glasgow. And bantam-weights—I bet you'll never see a bantam-weight in England in your day—I hope you don't anyway—they're for starvation times—I've seen two or three come in one year—two or three—these little fellas—some of them top of the bill as well—white-faced little fellas. And do you know what I think ruined them? The wasting! The wasting! All that grub they weren't allowed to eat. That ruined them. Poor little buggers. They'd all been famous once and we knew their names—we were proud to shake their hands—but there they were—on the sharp road down hill. Wasting! That's my theory!"

"What was the other fella like after your battle, then?" Douglas asked Lester, whose eye he had avoided until now.

"Oh! He says he fell down some stairs," Joseph chuckled. "At Carlisle Station. Didn't you, Lester? He thinks we're all daft, you know." Joseph looked around the room roguishly and Douglas felt a stab of warmth for his father.

Lester kept his mouth tight shut and let it pass.

"I was just thinking," Harry began, searching for a way to bring the conversation round to old John once more.

"Never," said Douglas, toasting Harry with his tea-cup. Then he clicked his tongue in annoyance with himself. The silly nervous joke had shut Harry up.

"Your *big* Christmas present's on the bed in the spare room," Betty said, to give John the chance to leave the table and the room. "We didn't send it when we knew you were coming."

"Can I go and see it?" The boy addressed himself not to Betty but to his mother.

"Of course." Mary got out her words quickly: she realized she had been trying to display her right to be the person in authority over the boy and blushed as she caught Betty's troubled reaction. "You know your grandma always gets you such lovely presents."

"We don't want to spoil him, though." Betty was anxious not to push herself before the mother. "We've enough to answer for, spoiling Douglas."

"It's just that I was wondering," Harry took advantage of the slight pause, "I was wondering what the arrangements were for, er—'grandfather'—tonight. I mean, just wondering what —what the arrangements were."

"He likes to be on his own," Joseph declared emphatically. "He's independent-minded. I'll try to get up after midnight and so will Douglas. We got up there together these last two years—didn't we?" This coincidence struck Joseph as positive proof of the strength of family feeling. "Aye. All three of us—three generations there—four with little John here—he can come next year—three generations bringing in the New Year very quietly, so as not to disturb his neighbours. I don't know why we had to be quiet. Most of them are deaf in those flats. But he insisted on that, didn't he?"

"I don't remember," said Douglas. "I don't know whether I'll come into Thurston this year. I'm tired." He looked at Mary: there was no reaction. "We both are."

"You're always tired," his mother retorted. "I don't know why you bring it on yourself. Why do you clash yourself?" she asked, slicing to the centre of her worries—but then she turned away—not wanting to unbalance the company.

"You'll be coming down to The Crown for a drink though, won't you?" Joseph asked, cajolingly. He liked Douglas to turn up in his local.

"I don't know. If we come, we might drop in at the Rugby Club. Mary isn't too keen."

She forbore to protest against this shifting across to her of the responsibility for unpopular decisions. They had made all manner of local promises on their previous visit, but the most

42

constant was that they would turn up to the Rugby Club New Year's Eve Dance. Douglas, she knew only too well, was genuinely tied by such promises: it was almost neurotic, she thought, this compulsion to keep faith with his past. Obligations to a few old schoolfriends could take precedence, as threatened to happen this evening, over the very future of their marriage. Insofar as she understood this, she despised it.

"No," she affirmed, helping him out. "Douglas has just come back from America. I've been busy these last few days —we've driven three hundred miles in hellish traffic. It doesn't seem unreasonable to say we might not want to go to the Rugby Club."

"They're expecting you," Harry said.

"We *might* turn up," Douglas replied. When had he last actually seen Alan Jackson? Three years, four years ago? The face was so plain in his mind now, looming there, steadily in focus.

"I don't suppose any sleep'll be lost either way," said Lester, "whether you turn up or not."

"John can still stay here," Betty tried to find a form of words which would express her meaning precisely. "So that you have the—option, is it? Option!"

"I've got no bloody option," Joseph said. "If I'm not in The Crown by eight-thirty sharp, there'll be three fellas there'll want to know the reason why." He looked around, triumphantly, glorying in the fierceness of his bond to the "three fellas" in The Crown.

As soon as the women had cleared away and left the room, John, who had waited for this moment impatiently, popped through the door dressed in his new present—boots, hat and the gun which, in his imagination, slaughtered the lot of them. He was inspected and approved—but not without both Joseph and Lester commenting on the comparative paucity of Christmas presents in their youth. Douglas had always done well.

Lester now felt bullish. The fear had subsided; he wanted to boast of his fight but the earlier lie prevented it. Yet he was full of himself. Nobody was going to grind him down. He would go back up to London and take them all on! *Luck*. That was all he needed. And he was due some. Overdue. John, abandoned in

43

his expensive rig-out, squatted Indian fashion on the carpet in front of the electric-log fire and pretended to be intensely intrigued in the workings of his gun.

Lester suddenly lifted himself on his arms, swung himself out of his seat, knelt on the carpet and gripped the cumbersome armchair by one of its short, thick legs. He tensed himself and then lifted it, held it steady, paused—John was fascinated by the vein which quivered in the middle of his forehead, Harry noted approvingly the whippet leanness of the man's muscles—and then stood up, the big armchair at arm's length. Full of strain, he reversed the process neatly but quickly. A thin line of blood came from the cut at the side of his mouth: he licked it off.

"And that's a heavy chair," said Joseph, who had always been a fan of Lester's physical prowess. "There's many a man twice your weight couldn't budge that."

"It's to do with balance as much as anything else, isn't it?" Douglas asked, amused at the way in which this trick had absorbed him as much as the other three. "And there's a knack for clearing it off the ground initially, isn't there?"

"*You* do it," replied Lester, who dearly wanted Douglas to fail.

Douglas tried, heaved, joked, tumbled over, kicked his legs in the air, assumed the pose of an All-In Wrestler and chased John around the room as he diminished the occasion from Lester's point of view and made the real achievement seem nothing but the crude accomplishment of lumpen sinew.

When this was done, Harry, who had never tried it on such a large chair before, took off his jacket and came to take his turn. He considered it carefully and then, in one swift movement, lifted it, hoisted it, himself stood up and held it out before him as if it were no more than a torch. Lester grimaced and slapped him on the shoulder.

"I'll have you on my side," he said, "any day."

As Mary and Betty washed up in the kitchen, they talked about how similar the three young men looked. It was against the odds that they should. It was even a little "creepy" (Mary's word) that Harry should be so like the other two. But all were very dark haired, light eyed—hard blue in the case of Douglas and Lester, a soft blue-grey in Harry's case. They were about the same height—just under six feet—Lester the shortest but the strongest looking; Douglas, soft-featured, soft about the jawline, contrasting strikingly with Lester's tough profile; Harry disguising his considerable physical power in a manner of diffidence.

"One's kind, the other's not a bit and Douglas is half and half," said Betty. "He can be violent."

"Harry's good, Lester—worries me—" Mary stopped. Was the book called the Good, the Bad and the Beautiful or the Good, the Bad and the Ugly? And who was what? That line of speculation would only upset Betty. She suppressed it.

"Douglas is all head, Lester's a labourer at heart and Harry's nicely balanced," Betty continued, rinsing the plates swiftly, enjoying this game.

Mary thought of a rather brutal comparison on sex but she instantly repressed it: Betty did not like the language of the recently liberated women. Mary had to concentrate. Soon she would be in her own cottage and be able to relax: she badly needed some moments to herself: so much was unresolved.

"The three brass monkeys," said Mary, turning to smile at her mother-in-law, who looked worried, she thought, and a little lost.

"The Three Stooges!" Betty laughed. "They're certainly *that*."

"The Three Blind Mice!"

"The Three Men In A Boat!"

"The Three Musketeers is how Douglas would like to see them," Mary guessed shrewdly.

"They never had much to do with each other as boys," Betty said. "It's a miracle to get them together really. You would think they would have so much in common. But apart from rather looking alike—there is nothing much. Not really. And they could go from one year's end to another without seeing each other, without really missing each other. Except, of course, Harry always likes to see Douglas. But he's a bit—over—what is it? Not 'put-out'—"

"Overawed?"

"That sort of thing—by him."

45

"Douglas always speaks very highly of Harry."

"In London? Yes. I'm inclined to think he likes this place and everybody in it far better when he's away from it."

She regretted the tartness in that remark, but did not apologize for it. She was feeling a little put out by the speed with which her son and daughter-in-law were passing through her house. Everybody was so harassed these days. Where had all the time gone? The time for talking and just sitting about. The time she had once had to spend with friends and relations. Nowadays you had to make appointments to see each other and when you did meet you were hemmed in by other appointments. Too many appointments, so much happening, nothing caught; so much activity, no repose. She did not like it and at times it seemed a waste of time to spend so much energy on pretence.

When they went back into the lounge, John pulled the trigger of his gun and the bang caused Mary to clap her hands to her ears with an involuntary gesture and call out, "For Christ's sake! *Stop* that bloody noise!"

The boy stopped, the gun drooped sadly before him. To his school blazer and short trousers had been added a large stetson and plastic calf-boots which were sprinkled with silver paint like the gun and the hat. Mary's outburst embarrassed everyone.

"I have a terrible headache," she lied, despising herself more for this evasion. Why not say she was in a state of tension and could not take even the playful shock of her son with a toy gun? They had talked of separation—for Christ's sake—*separation!*—herself and her husband, so blandly quizzical there. Parting for life! How could he just tuck it away?

"You can add to it," said Joseph, coming to the rescue and tapping the stetson. "There's the pants and the jacket you can get, and there's a lassoo and—what else was there, Mother?"

"Everything you can think of," Betty replied. She saw how the boy's present had been spoiled for him. Somebody should rush over and comfort him. He needed it. *She* could not do it with the mother here. And then, in the way he had which would always take her breath away, Douglas reached out, gently lifted his son onto his knee and, without any fuss, began to examine the gun. Soon the room rattled again with the unpleasant banging of the imitation weapon.

They left as ungraciously as they had arrived. Lester to his own house and a watchful night about the town while he took stock. Harry to the flat he had insisted on finding for himself, despite Betty's declaration that he would be "always welcome" to live with them. It had been a difficult decision for Harry to take but he was sure now that it was better all round. And finally, in a flurry of embarrassment, half-promises, some regrets and some impatience, Douglas and Mary, who clipped herself into the safety belt even for the short trip up to the cottage in the hills. Joseph followed them out after a few minutes and went to his hallowed drinking ground.

Betty felt so tired: "As if I'd fed the five thousand," she said to herself. It was all worry, she thought, and it should not be like that. It should be calmer, pleasanter than that—after all, they were part of each other, they were part of the same family. They were all well enough off. Times had improved out of all recognition. So why so tense? Maybe, she thought, hoovering the room as John sat in the bath playing with the American whale, maybe she asked too much. Maybe life was just like this now. Surely not, though. Surely those people she saw in the street or heard in shops or saw with their families—they were happy, they felt helped and loved by each other—did they not? This desolation could not be everywhere the same, could it? She hoped not: she longed to find a hub of life in the family. She ought to speak out.

Come on—she beat down these miserable reflections. It was just her mood, it would pass, life was a bit complicated at the moment. Douglas and Mary, she had seen directly, were not hitting it off at all. Douglas was always extra-polite to her in public when things were bad. Sometimes she could not make out her son.

She knocked off the Hoover and put it away. She would lay out glasses and cups and saucers later, in case anyone dropped in after midnight to bring in the New Year. Then she realized that there was no sound coming from the bathroom.

She went in. The boy was sitting upright, goose-fleshed, the cheap whale in his hands, broken, refusing to respond to his

47

attempts to mend it. His expression was so unhappy she felt her heart lurch in sympathy. He looked so neglected. And she had been so self-pitying! How could she give in like that? He looked up and shivered fiercely. There was plenty to be done, she thought, starting here and now.

"It wasn't my fault," he said, "I just wound it up."

"I don't know anything about those things either."

"I daren't take it apart in the bath, in case the water gets in."

"Give it to me. You can fiddle with it while we watch a bit of television. Your grandfather's bound to know somebody who can fix it."

"Will he?"

"Oh yes." She was beside him now, soaping the big yellow sponge, about to wash his back. "He knows all sorts of people, your grandfather." She looked at the toy: cheap, she thought, and far too young for him; a gift with no thought in it.

"Daddy brought it from America."

"Did he? That was nice of him." She rubbed him vigorously to warm him up. "It shows he was thinking about you."

"He was in Hollywood."

"Was he? Where all the film stars live. When I was about your age—just a little bit older—all of the girls wanted to end up in Hollywood. We used to daydream about it."

"I think Daddy wants to live there." The boy paused: Betty felt a tremble in him which was not to do with the cold, nor yet the effect of her sponging. She knelt beside him and put her arm around his shoulders. Though she assumed full knowledge of her grandson by right of family, Betty sometimes found herself confronted by a well-mannered stranger. Not now, though: his sadness brought them together.

"If he goes," John sobbed at last, "he'll take me with him, won't he? Won't he?"

48

# 2
# Resolutions

The story had to be resolved. Perhaps it was the tiredness and the recent dramatic changes of location which had upset his sense of proportion. Or, more simply, there was an urgency to make a shape of something which was an instinct as deep as greed and fear. Whatever it was, as soon as they reached the cottage, Douglas carried the suitcases to the door, excused himself unconvincingly and inadequately, and went up the path onto the fells to be alone with his thoughts, by now obsessive, on the death of this friend. He had to put them in order.

It was a picture-book midwinter night, the sort of landscape which appears impossible or artificial only to those who do not know the country. The moon was up, clear, crisp, luminous. The stars glittered in their thousands, the Milky Way an easily discernible gauze, the Plough, the Twins, the Pole Star— simple to believe that these were God's spy-holes in the stretched black canopy of heaven. In the moonlight the snow-ridged hills stood clear as Christmas cards and the loudest sound was the scrunch of bracken beneath his ruined city shoes. When he stopped to listen, he might catch the scurry of a sheep, the rustle of a fox, a hare's light lollop. The silence caught his heart and, for the first time in weeks, he felt a breath of ease.

For a few moments he looked along the coastline, picking out the towns and villages he had cycled to, circling empty Sunday streets for girlfriends who had no idea he was within ten miles, racing away to swim all day; there, the pits where his grandfather had worked ran out under the sea. Born, bred, familiar smells, names, places, memories, history, sounds, shapes, air. He felt earthed.

Why had Alan gone into the woods and perished; allowed himself to die?

When he had known Alan Jackson, at school, the boy had travelled in from the country to the local Grammar School and, though he was a year younger than Douglas, a friendship had been set up from the beginning. This might have been to do with Douglas' missionary desire, at that time, to help those who appeared to most need it; it could also have been to do with the fact that Alan was generally thought to be the best scholar the school had taken in for years and Douglas wanted to keep an eye on the front-runner—but those reasons would be to deny the force of Alan's part in the affair. He, after all, had returned the friendship. Nor would it do to underrate his own action. Almost alone in the school he had sought out Alan and truly cared for him: talked, spent time, been interested, felt affection. It was less selfish and possibly more accurate to call it simply—a friendship.

Alan was exceptionally shy, exceptionally withdrawn, from the first, somehow, trapped inside himself. He was unnaturally neat, extraordinarily conscientious, altogether modest, a scholar to the ends of his long, white fingers. The dead languages which caused so much trouble to everyone else opened up to him without effort; mathematics, physics, chemistry—all the "tough" subjects were calmly understood. He was no good at all at sport but, because of his authority and his calmness, no one teased him over this: soon some fabricated agreement relieved everyone of his entirely useless pursuit of rugby balls, cricket balls or tennis balls. The teachers got him out of it, despite his embarrassed protests that he enjoyed games even though he was no good. They assumed he was merely being helpful in putting up what must be a token struggle. They rejoiced in his singularity, which they treated as eccentricity, forever referring to it with affection and driving the boy to blazing flushes of embarrassment and ignored disclaimers. Although he spoke slowly and chose his words after obvious consideration, he held on tenaciously to a broad Cumbrian accent which wavered not at all throughout his schooldays. No more did his hairstyle, no more did his routine. His background was poor, rural and entirely unprepared for such an intellectual oddity as he was: yet he strove fiercely to keep loyal to it. He was not handsome, but he was not bad-looking; his face was large, rather gaunt, but not grim. He was broadly built but carried little fat. Above all he appeared self-contained and seemed to need no one, although Douglas, perhaps alone of the boys, sensed that this appearance was false. Alan wanted affectionate attention and careful friendship, like everyone ever born.

There was, though, about him, occasionally, a smile of great inner delight, or it could change and appear to be a terrible detached and puzzled sadness. Douglas had noticed this. Even now, willing himself to assemble his thoughts on this man, he could summon up the memory of that smile. It seemed to say "what a place this world is!" and hesitate between joy and despair, between a question and an answer. Douglas was mesmerized by what he now thought of as the profundity of Alan's awareness. For there was no doubting that his sensitivity matched his intelligence; he knew how the world worked. Perhaps Douglas' attraction to him was the perennial pull between the philosopher and the clown. While Alan spun his own web, forever ravelling and unravelling in his mind the meanings and vanities of the life he saw, Douglas would be strutting out his hour, now boldly, now hesitantly, now anxiously full of questions, now ridiculously over-stuffed with answers. Douglas saw Alan as one who ruminated scrupulously over life, and though his own questionings were so erratic as to make all comparison vain, he felt again as he had felt then—deeply attached to the quiet, isolated figure.

But how would he tell the story? All he knew about Alan's background was that it was poor—then a bearable and decent post-war poverty which would now be classified as destitution. He had been brought up in an abandoned hamlet—once a row of miners' terraced cottages—beside the woods he had died in. There had always been illness in the family—the mother. He saw the thoughtful and obedient boy helping silently about the small, illness-stricken house. He had never spoken of it. No one from school visited his house, ever. But his mother's illness became "known". His father had worked on the council, as a caretaker or cleaner in the offices; the job which Alan himself had gone into, a year after that unexpected failure at the school.

For, having walked through one examination after another, Alan had suddenly failed in the final examination—the pre-University tests—but failed in such a spectacular, such a disastrous manner that all sorts of reasons had been introduced to explain the lapse. His father had died a few months before the examination but surely *that* would not have such a drastic effect? Alan had simply left school, taken on this job, which he could have easily taken on at fifteen, without any of his qualifications, and faded into the town as a young, lonely eccentric who "hardly spoke", "bothered nobody", "very quiet", "goes for terrible long walks", "keeps to himself", "no friends"—sometimes went off for a few days alone—"simply disappeared". His mother died soon afterwards. He moved into a terraced cottage on the outskirts of Thurston.

Where had he gone on his days off? What had he thought about on those long walks? Douglas thought he might have to invent cruelty in the childhood—not physical battery, but the battening effect of humble service both to an invalid and to someone who did not understand. All the childhoods that leap from one class to another share the same pains. Here, though, was someone who had refused to leap. Looked but walked away. Now, Douglas saw that as an enormous strength. Perhaps there could be a double life somewhere; perhaps this unworldly abstinence could be counter-balanced by spasms of excess or, worst of all, failed attempts at excess. Alan had aged while Douglas was on the rampage he called his life in London and abroad and lately he remembered seeing him across the street—the same neat Fifties belted raincoat, he could have sworn, now oily with dirt, the same tidily tucked-in school scarf, the expression more fixed but, when he turned to Douglas' honking "hello!", still that same rare, lovely, profound smile. What was in that expression? He teased out his memory of it. Fear? Resolution? Clarity? Understanding?

Why had he failed the exam? That would have to be invented. Anxiety of continuing and being a burden to his mother. The obvious wanting to "help at home". But more, perhaps—a sudden disillusionment with the work? Exhaustion from the battle he must have had (who had not?) with the flesh—as far as anyone knew, a battle fought alone. Or had he arrived at a sudden crisis of knowledge, as some very intelligent youths do? One teacher said that Alan knew too much to put it down at the swift, plausible length which had become second nature to Douglas; he said he was writing something of his own and did not swot for the exams; he said he had learned all they could teach him and someone reported they had once heard Alan say: "Nobody knows the answer to anything. That's all there is to it. Nobody knows a thing really."

That stuck in Douglas' mind. For he was certain, the more he thought about it, that he had been in touch, in slight contact, with a "rare spirit", with someone who "saw into the heart of things". All the more desolate, then, that life had taken him on such a parabola: from a home in the woods, through his many gifts to scholarship, to a settlement for his father's occupation and then back to those childhood woods on a quest—for what? Certainly not for continued living. He had been ignorant of all survival techniques, it appeared: his shelter was the crudest hole in the ground inside a large holly bush. He had moved about, Harry had said, they could tell that—and Douglas strained to imagine the search and the desperation in the man's mind as he had blundered alone through those insubstantial woods. What did he find? What had been concluded?

It might have been the stress of the last few days, but Douglas discovered that he was crying and under his breath he heard himself murmuring "the poor man", "poor Alan", "poor man". What a waste and a loss! What a hateful enemy death was! Yet at times, he recollected, lately, he had thought it would not be such an enemy to him.

So, so. He had worked something out, roughly thought it out. He would like to write it to make it appear as a memoir—that could be his lifeline back to writing the stuff he could respect himself for. He must let it rest longer in his mind and then work on it, find a shape, but now at least he knew its weight in his mind. Using Alan? Yes. That would have to be faced too. "The Death Of A Friend", he could call it. Sentimental, melodramatic—yes. That was the starting point. He would try to reclaim him.

Released now from the peculiar thrall in which he had been held by will or by need, he came down, shivering violently, from the mountainside and jogged along to stave off the cold. Down indeed—to a wife with whom his life was unresolved, to problems filial and paternal, to difficulties financial and emotional, facing a year in which there was no certain prospect of a job. Yet, through some blessing, feeling emboldened and somehow cleansed and optimistic, after the tryst kept alone with the memory of a dead friend.

## (2)

He tripped over his own suitcase, which was where he had left it—on the doorstep—and, as he picked it up, he knew that war had been declared yet again.

Mary was kneeling, as if in prayer, before the fire in the downstairs room of the small cottage. She must have heard him coming in but did not for a moment interrupt her reverential huffing and puffing into the bottom of the grate, as she strove to stir up some life in the dampish twigs.

Douglas bit on his tongue and headed for the stairs with his suitcase, taking hers also, by way of appeasing her (but she could not see as she did not turn to him). "I'll take yours too then," he said, unable to do good by stealth. Upstairs there was the "big" bedroom and the box-room John used—one and a half up and down it was, enough for their occasional needs, with the outbuildings standing ready to be restored and inhabited later (if the cash flowed in)—promises of future settlement. It was in a remote hamlet, about eight miles south of Thurston, neighboured by a few farms. A small, stone-built, seven-teenth-century cottage—firm-driven into the hillside for warmth; no views. He unpacked rapidly, kicked his empty case under the bed and came down to find Mary sitting on a small stool, poker in her hand, rapt in the puny flickerings of flames which tottered about the coals like a child taking its first steps.

"Drink?" he asked, still on the crest of his sudden optimism. "Oh blessed drink! Ice-breaker, match-maker, embarrass-ment-diverter, acquaintanceship-sealer, pact of friends, arm's length of enemies, godmother of parties, goddess of social intercourse, consolation of solitude—and much else; someone ought to write a book about it."

"We have none," Mary replied, not without satisfaction, he noted; and yet he was easy on her.

"America," he announced, glad to have the chance to surprise her. He held up his large duty-free cartons. "A long way to go for your scotch, I agree, but beggars can't be choosers. Half and half?"

She nodded. He poured two stiff ones, topped hers up with water and then came to sit near her on the comfortable old sofa which, like the rest of the furniture, they had purchased from the local auction. "Cheers." Again she merely nodded.

"It's marvellous outside." He heard his enthusiastic tone: it sounded emptily hearty; and yet he could not be more sincere—it *was* marvellous outside. Why, then, did it seem phony? Mary thought it was phony too. She sniffed. He was sorry she did not believe he meant it.

"Cheers," she said, and took a large drink, cutting off his attempt at conversation.

"There's a letter of Malcolm Lowry's to a young man who wants to write a book but complains that he can't because for one thing he doesn't know anything about nature. Lowry replied that *not* knowing was enough of a subject. I liked the answer. I thought I knew what he meant. I've just been out 'not-knowing' about the stars."

"Could you pass an ashtray?" He did so. There was another pause. So it was this variant: O.K. After a few moments, she said—

"You could have asked me if I'd wanted a walk."

"Did you?"

"Yes."

"I wanted to be on my own," Douglas said.

"When are you anything else?"

"Can't you understand that?"

"You didn't answer my question."

She had not looked at him, even taking her scotch and the ashtray in an outstretched hand, at right-angles to her gaze, which continued, intent, on the fire struggling to be born. Douglas let the silence gather about them. There was still enough resilience and optimism in him to relish the quietness so enwrapped about the thick-walled building.

Mary was red-haired; deeply, lusciously, Forties-Holly-wood-dreamy-red-haired. It waved and tumbled about her face and over her firm, square shoulders in abundance. It was like a dowry, something to be remarked on, worthy of a psalm of David. Whichever way she wore it, she suited it, and the wealth of it would often move Douglas to bless his unaccountable luck, even now, almost a dozen years into a scarred marriage. For with the richness of the hair went a character just as rich, which their marriage-war might have impoverished irreparably. He did not know. Nowadays they spoke over a no man's land of hurt.

Her face was open and intelligent with eyes not quite hazel, a nose that ended in a little, sharp, defiant tip and a large, calm mouth which fell away slightly at each end, not sadly but sensuously. Her figure was good, waist still slim, bust firm, stomach flat. And the hands quite ordinary. Yet, when he met her, she had been on the brink of a career as a pianist. Her first concert at the Wigmore Hall had been well received. She was poised for triumph. The marriage had robbed her of it. They had been very deeply in love at the beginning, and then again, two or three times, but the periods between had been cold, often bitter and once before (as now) malevolent and destructive.

"There are no faces in the fire," she said. "The three of us"—her sisters and herself—"used to sit for hours at the fire. Wherever we went we had a fire—even in South Africa."

Her father had been an officer in the R.A.F., stayed on after World War Two and trailed his family half way round the globe and back again. Douglas had once been convinced that this had given Mary a privileged, middle-class life which he had used against her in times of argument. Even then, though, he would concede that it had made her the woman he wanted to marry. Now the gibes were irrelevant.

Douglas wished that he had not given up smoking. Even though he had stopped for five years now, he still wanted one on most days. He could, this moment, see a packet of *Disque Bleu*, the soft, rather slippery packaging, the malleable cigarette with the black spiky tobacco looking as if it had been packed raw—what was the actual taste like? He had not a clear enough recollection. He smiled to himself. In order to describe it properly, he would have to smoke again.

Mary smoked steadily.

The fire had caught now. She put on a couple of logs, wedged them firmly exactly where she wanted them. Douglas watched the flames miss her hand.

Outside the stillness, snow, hills there long before man and most likely there long after him, the sea a few miles off, a few farms surviving on the hillsides, and, down in the towns, the process and procedures of entertainment well under way.

Lester on his way to a pub to meet some old pals who would protect him and take him round the town as their mascot, thinking him a millionaire and believing his answers to their questions about pop stars and sporting personalities. Harry meeting up with Aileen, Lester's serious-minded sister, who had so successfully "taken herself in hand" and got away from the influence of her mother, to London, then to a training college, and now she was a lecturer in economics and on the list of Labour candidates. She would spend the evening with Harry, whom she liked more than any other man she had met, even though his politics were primitive! Joseph deep in a serious school of dominoes. Betty and John watching a "galaxy of international talent" preparing to see off the Old Year on the television—the boy flushed now, a little feverish, she feared, but at least cheerful with his bottle of pop and a packet of crisps, sitting in his pyjamas and his cowboy boots, still nursing that cheap whale. The man whose name he had taken, old John, asleep, his infirm legs clumsily splayed out on the fender before him, the fire dying. Had he, too, the grudging but still genuine faith that on this particular calendar night, as custom ordered that one year be gone and another take its place, it was a true moment for change? Was the habit of New Year Resolutions a cry for free will? In the bleak midwinter, stocks low, land dead, nature withdrawn, was it then, when everything seemed against a man, that most of all he had to stand up and say "no—I *will* do this, I *will* do that, despite the fact that life

57

looks unimpressionable"? Or were resolutions no more than a handful of dust flung in the face of fate?

"What are you thinking about?" Again it was Douglas who had to break the silence. Mary stared into the fire, almost hidden by her hair.

"Us," she replied, eventually, dully.

"What about us?"

"Yes. What about us?"

"This is a bit like serving lobs at Wimbledon."

"Want some coffee?"

"Have some more scotch."

"O.K." She held out her glass. He waited. She got the message and turned to look at him. Her expression was so hurt and beaten that he wanted to gather her in his arms and nurse her; but it was too far gone for that. "What were you thinking about when you were on your own?" she asked.

"This and that." He poured out a large, splashy measure. She could hold her drink.

"What?"

"Well. Money for one thing." He lied easily. The story of Alan Jackson had to be kept secret, or it would lose its potency in his mind. He sipped slowly at the scotch: taken six thousand miles; returned six thousand miles; still tasted the same as ever: looney. "I can't understand why I'm in such a twist about it. I've never been deprived of it, I've always had enough for my needs. It's this freelance caper. I've been brainwashed against it. Why the hell am I in such a comically painful panic about it now?"

"You went up a mountain and thought about money?" Her scorn for what he thought were his valid anxieties about earning a living was something which irritated him greatly: which she did not understand. "I don't believe you thought about that. You're a poor liar, Douglas, sometimes."

"Why should I lie?"

"Because you want to keep to yourself what you are really thinking: therefore whatever you tell me is untrue."

"You should be in New Scotland Yard."

"Life with a moral criminal makes you act like a policeman."

"Heavy."

58

"You're still high." Mary lit another cigarette. "You're still on that plane, or in Los Angeles or in London—you've been in neutral for the last hour or two—only talking because you can't bear silence."

"Who can?"

"Who *is* she?"

"Who?"

"Never mind." Visibly, Mary pulled herself together and turned to her husband without rancour. "So why don't we work out the bare minimum we need to live on and go on from there?"

"Who is who? Whom?" He paused. "O.K."

"Do you want to live in London or in the country?" she began.

"On the one hand," he did the "Fiddler On The Roof" act, "metropolitan getting and spending: on the other hand, rural sitting and stewing: and vice versa: on the other hand, city—superficialities: on the other hand, country—pedantries: and vice versa: urban flash, rural blankness: ennui and accidie." He registered her boredom and stopped. "There is no other hand. They are the same."

"Is that what you really think?"

"We have good friends in London and I have old friends here. Yet you like this cottage probably more than I do—I suppose I'm a bit worried about being cut off from the metropolitan plug, from the odd jobs for freelancers down there . . ."

"Frightened of having as much time to write as you'd like to."

"Below the belt."

"What is the bare minimum we need to live on?" she went on.

"Well. We have to sell the cottage anyway." Douglas was relieved to be able to announce this in a suitable context. He had held back for weeks. She took his news calmly. "We borrowed seven thousand five hundred from the bank, we have to pay back a hundred pounds a month, plus fourteen per cent interest—it's too much. We'll have to put this on the market, hope that prices are holding up and we can get what we gave."

"I see." She paused. "That's settled then." She loved the cottage very much. Her childhood travels had made her long for roots and this was her place in England.

"Virtually. Unless you can change your job and find a comparable post up here—which is highly unlikely with teaching in the state it's in, and I can set myself up with an advance and maybe—*maybe*—a regular review space to keep us jogging along—again highly unlikely with publishing and newspapers staggering along the brink: we can't run two slum properties at either end of the country."

The cottage had been classified as "unfit for human habitation" by the council when they had applied for a grant to improve it. In London their maisonette was in a very down-at-heel street, thought of as a slum by Douglas' mother. Mary's parents insisted it was "quite pleasant".

"O.K.," she said, "London." She took a pencil. "I'll note it down."

"Mortgage and insurance—say seventy-five—say eighty pounds a month: say a thousand a year."

"Yes."

"Rates—three hundred; electricity—what? two hundred and fifty; gas heating—two hundred and fifty; telephone—madness now—three hundred; running of car—five hundred and fifty, say. Food?"

"Allow up to a thousand. That'll include wear and tear inside the house."

"What else? Well, I'm going to cash in all those small Sixties insurances—that should be about four thousand—to reduce the overdraft. I'll take out a straight Drop Dead Insurance—a large sum for you and John should I Drop Dead—no endowment. Say two hundred and fifty. Pension scheme—well, I want to put seven-fifty into that if I can—next to sinking in a swamp, it's old age penury that gives me the biggest creeps. What else? Booze, your fags, clothes, books, out and about—say five hundred. Accountant—two hundred and fifty. What are we up to? Plus ten per cent contingency."

He need not have asked. He had done the sum many times over, during the past few months. He had a list of plans. This was Negative Cut-Back Stage One, based on selling the cottage.

Negative Cut-Back Stage Two involved selling the London place and moving into a flat. Negative Cut-Back Stage Three—which depended on a successful and calm continuation of the marriage—was to sell the London place, come back to the cottage and batten down the hatches. Negative Cut-Back Stage Four was to get rid of all he had, rent a hovel in the hills and live rather like a land-locked Robinson Crusoe for a while. All four were on the cards at the moment. There was a Total Negative Switch-Off, which was to disappear and leave Mary with some loot and peace.

"Five thousand plus ten per cent equals five thousand, five hundred."

Even though he knew the sum, Douglas whistled in appreciation.

"Amazing, isn't it? Call it six thousand. Plus provision for tax. For us two and a child living in what any petty bourgeois Victorian would have described as squalor. On the other hand, living in a way in which my grandfather would have thought of as princely—central heating, good food, travel, fags, booze, etcetera. Let's see—he earned fifteen pounds a quarter on his first job. At that rate it would take him—about a hundred years to earn what we need—minimum—for a year."

"How will we get your basic minimum if I stop teaching?"

"Why should you do that?"

"I want another child."

"Not that again." He paused. "Sorry. But—not *now*, Mary, not when we're trying to re-group for going out to a hail-fellow night with lots of half known old half-friends—it's too hard." She accepted his decision to go down to Thurston. Argument seemed utterly pointless.

"I just think you ought to know I'm going off the pill."

"Oh hell!"

Mary smiled. It was a friendly, open smile. She had said all she wanted to say.

Douglas read it as a sarcastic reaction.

"Why do you always make me feel like horse manure?" he asked.

"Perhaps you are." She giggled.

"O.K. So I am."

"That's another trick."

"Would it satisfy you if I slowly castrated myself, bought a briar pipe, went for walks with a rucksack and did the competitions in the 'New Statesman'?"

"That's another trick." Again she laughed.

"She laughed!" He paused. He knew she was laughing at him, but pretended he made her laugh. "Take note, notetakers—she laughed."

"I'm serious," she said abruptly. "I want another child."

She stood up and stretched herself fully: a vague memory of the morning crossed Douglas' mind, but he could not catch it. He watched her appreciatively.

"Mine?" he asked, surprising himself by the question. Why had he thought to ask that?

"Yes." She took her time before repeating the word, unemphatically. "Yes; even after all—yes—I'd still want it to be ours—if we're sticking together as a family."

"If not mine—somebody else's?"

"If you push me, Douglas, yes."

"Anyone in mind?" His throat was dry; his stomach suddenly dissolving.

She paused for long enough and he knew the answers: her pause inoculated him against too severe a reaction.

"Yes, Douglas." She spoke gravely, standing now looking down on him sprawled in his chair. She was white faced and serious, somehow pitying, like the madonna on a stained glass window in his childhood church. She had often reminded him of Her—especially—sacrilegiously—when she had been strewn naked in bed in low light, dawn light, dusk, white, white skin, spread red hair, the expression of pity mingled with piety, after they had made love.

"I see." He was brisk, to get it over with. "Do I know the lucky donor?"

"I'll not answer that."

"Putting all our friends on the list of suspects. Clever move, Inspector."

"I'll answer anything else."

"Well?" He would not ask her if she had been "unfaithful" or "betrayed him". The phrases were—to his credit—stoppered by his realization of their hypocrisy. But he longed to know.

"No. He wanted to. Very much. And so did I. Perhaps equally as much. It was so nice to be wanted and loved for a change, without all this unhappiness and distrust coming between."

"So why didn't you?" Douglas hoped he sounded merely curious: the panic was held down hard.

"Don't you know?"

"I want you to tell me."

"Reassurance? Again? Again?"

Her scorn thudded into him. He did not acknowledge her taunt.

"I won't be unfaithful to you until our marriage has 'broken down'. I couldn't be."

"Thanks for that," he said. His sense of relief surprised him. "I mean it. Thank you."

"Though why what's sauce for the gander shouldn't be sauce for the goose, I do not know."

"You have no need to say that."

"You mean I have insufficient evidence?"

"Perhaps—"

"You did have an affair, you know. You did admit it." She blushed at the memory. "I was in love with you. When you are in love with someone you know when they betray you. Without any doubt—ever. I had two alternatives. Either I could accept you were 'on the town'—which was demeaning and trivial—or I could imagine I was going mad and not the person I thought I was. I could have one explanation which wounded me terribly but left me sane and the others— *yours*, repeatedly lied about—which supposedly left me whole but feeling as if I were going out of my mind. I'll not put you through that."

When he did not reply, she took out of her pocket the piece of paper the American woman had given him on the plane. He looked at it and waited.

"While you were sleeping in the car on the way up I stopped for petrol," she said. "I hadn't enough change—as usual; you never allow enough for these trips—and so I went through your

63

pockets looking for a couple of pounds. This felt like a note so I pulled it out." She handed it back to him. "Sorry."

He took it, glanced at it again, screwed it up and threw it into the fire. He had kept it out of an old feeling of adventuring. But there was nothing to be said.

"It's an easy name and address to memorize," Mary said. Douglas nodded.

"Now, I don't mind if you've been screwing in L.A.—'abroad is different', that's what you say, isn't it? Let's say it is—but what I want to know, and what I hope we can work out soon, is whether you love me enough for us to stay together. Because one of the things—you're *so* typical, Douglas—"

"You and your bloody amateur psychology!"

"One of the characteristics of men like you is that you become so guilty that you take it out on your wives. You can't either be a true bastard or a true husband. So while you have a 'good time', I have to have a 'rotten time' to prove that your 'good time' is tough on you as well. Or rather, there has to be a victim and, as it isn't going to be the scarlet woman, it's either going to be Douglas or it has to be me. Well, I'm announcing the end of that role from today. I am not willing to carry the can, take the dirt, be the nursing-home or the analyst's couch or the whipping boy or whatever other object you need me to be so that you can keep your balance and your sanity. I am no longer your *thing*, Douglas."

"Can I say something?"

"Let me finish."

"I didn't—you know—Miss St John's Wood—I just met her on the plane."

"Oh, forget it."

"It's true."

"You don't read shorthand, do you? Of course not! Like all the other practical and sensible things you don't do. Well, underneath her address, Miss U.S.A. had scrawled quite a pornographic little come-on."

"*Had* she?" Douglas—inexplicably, and, he knew, reprehensibly—was delighted. "*What?*"

"You're not wriggling out of this, Douglas. I'm going to

finish. Oh, what the hell." Mary leaned on her chair as if suddenly faint. Douglas got up, came to put his arms around her. She shook her head, violently, and, offended, he stepped back.

"We can talk this out tomorrow, can't we?" He was tired. It was not the time for this.

"Why not now?"

"Well, for one thing I'm exhausted, I think, I must be, musn't I? All that non-sleep, jet lag, booze etcetera? And for another—we'd better be on our way down to the Rugby Club for the jig."

"Must we?"

"We have promised."

"Promised whom?"

"Friends."

"Your friends. I don't mean that to sound spiteful—but they are. Sometimes I don't know why you knock yourself out so much to keep things going. You're often embarrassed; you know you're a target; you're forever being hauled away to talk to people you never knew; you drink too much to get over your nerves. You end up as the caricature of yourself that you most detest. And yet you go on with it. Why is that?"

"'I do not know. I cannot say. I have not had. My — today.' The question now is, are we going or not? It's after nine—if we don't get down there before ten we won't get a seat and we needn't go."

"When you're sober, you're so terrified of showing off that you say nothing at all about the life you lead in London. When you're drunk, you seem so worried about not living up to their fantasies that you hint at things which never happened—you don't *quite* lie—it twists you up completely and yet you rush down to it as if you were going to be suckled in mother's milk. I don't understand it."

"Neither do I." Douglas could add to the list of discomforts and inadequacies. "I like those people, though," he said. "I screw it up because we always meet up in a hectic context—it's a party or a dance or some sort of celebration—and so I'm way behind on the quiet bits, on the gossip that continues to keep

65

them together as friends. But I'm prepared to take the bashing I get because I like them."

"You romanticize them."

"No, I don't. It's just that when I look at them—there's what?—about a dozen fellows my age—schoolteachers, accountants, that sort of thing; one or two small shopkeepers —most—the vast majority—with, apparently, stable marriages, apparently a secure domestic life, satisfying jobs. They seem integrated. They have time for hobbies and sports. They put a lot into the community. That club for a start: and the sports teachers take the kids to Away matches and big games in Edinburgh or London, some of the others lay on Christmas treats for pensioners—that sort of thing—or they're on the council or in the Civic Trust. And besides, they've stuck together, they have the friendship of knowing each other inside out. The old pattern has changed. Once upon a time, the story went, provincial boy—or girl—left for the big lights at least partly because of the lure of a better social life and for metropolitan plunder. But over the last twenty years the social life of the younger lot has arguably been better outside the big cities than inside: just as many car-jaunts, parties, nights out, trips, clubs, dinners—and houses which are better, same generally with schools, hospitals, all amenities. Wages much the same. And information centralized through the newspapers, radio and television, so that except for the chance to pop up to the West End theatre—and how many in London can afford *that*?—they are better off. It's *we*, the pirates, those who struck out—for the first time, perhaps, we're the losers. We should have sat tight. Probably I do romanticize them, but only a little. It's more envy, I think. I've got out and got on—so it seems and so *they* say—but, in fact, I've missed out on what's been ten or fifteen years' solid achievement and companionship and good times. They're always telling stories about each other's misadventures here, there and everywhere—we never tell stories like that in London. The reason I say so little here—to them—is that I have so little of real interest to retail. Then the reason I say too much is because I want to pay back what I feel has been given. They cancel each other out."

66

"So you're neither one thing nor the other. Again."

"As usual. Yes." Douglas hesitated and then came to a decision. "Why don't we sit here and get gently drunk and be nice to each other in front of the fire of this snug little cottage we're going to have to get rid of? Eh? Quietly. Yes? It's ironic, isn't it, that my grandfather had to start out his married life in a cottage such as this, which he would regard as about the bottom of the pile, and now his so-called affluent grandson can't cope with a similar place. The pattern isn't *quite* that neat, but there's something in it. We could stay—we could spend a long night making love—that would be a change, wouldn't it? Could we summon up the desire now? We could . . . But somehow I'm geared to go down to that noisy, crowded club, crashing with rock music, to shout platitudes at strangers and then traipse around the town after midnight desperately keeping up a custom of First Footing whose origin nobody in the entire district could be sure of. Destinations—Headache, Frustration and probably Drunkenness." He finished his whisky. "I'm sorry," he said, "we have to go."

Mary sat down and held out her glass.

"Just a small one. Then I'll get changed." She smiled. "The women are always so smart. Never mind. We used to have the excuse of being broke and couldn't-care-less. Now we're supposed to be better off, my lack of even an attempt at a glamorous outfit looks a little odd. Enough." He stopped the flow of whisky and poured in water. "Right to the top. Thanks. Some of them are wearing dresses costing sixty or seventy pounds or more."

"Just nerves," he said. "Cheers."

"Cheers." She was relaxed now. "You could be right," she said, taking the lead. "It could be that up here you would lead a steadier life. There would be fewer temptations. That would help. Opportunity's half the trouble."

"Come on, Mary."

"You're always on about your family—well, look at them. Your grandfather: old John's a man—he stuck to what he was given. Joseph annoys you at times—but only because he flusters you by taking your pretensions seriously—he's kept some sort of shape to his life. Harry, of course—and even poor old Lester in his shipwrecked fashion. But you—you're all over the place."

"Yes. I am." Douglas dropped all games, all pretences and spoke as truthfully as he could. "And that's my way, Mary. Sorry. That's it. To you it looks like a mess and to me it looks like a mess—but I'm not going to run for cover into other models, past or present. I want to keep in touch up here because I love my family and friends—not because I have any silly yearning for a golden past, or any wide-eyed admiration for them as types. They're my family and friends, that's all; in a place I also love, that's all; and I want to keep up with them because my life's here as well as all over the place, as you so rightly say. But when I envy the men at the Rugby Club, I don't want to *be* like them—or rather, only when I'm *weak* do I want to be like them. I admire my grandfather and my father—but their lives are not mine. My grandfather was given a spade, a pick or a gun—labourer, miner, soldier—low wages, bare living; large families encouraged, little education, expectation ground down. I don't pretend that is what I have. My father got a little more, but too late in his life. His childhood was just as circumscribed as his father's and so he drifts in the straits of possibilities he never had the opportunity to learn to navigate."

He paused for a moment, then: "I think I've got choices. I can find ways to be more free and more fulfilled. Some of these are illusory. Some already appear to be no more than alternative methods of self-destruction. But what I have the chance to do is to try to weigh up the balance of a number of things and come to my own conclusions about them. If this includes taking chances with personal loyalties as well as a career—then so be it. I am in a mess, yes, up to my eyeballs! I'm bred to lust after security and yet I'd think myself a coward if I did not try to be totally freelance and attempt to ride on the back of the world's whims. I'm trained to all the routines and virtues of domestic fidelity and yet up come the questions—what is it worth? What is its strength? There's a decent, even a very good education been given and yet the temptation to act out of stupidity and even to act in conscious knowledge of doing myself harm is sometimes too tantalizing to resist. The very idea of resisting temptation has been one of the most powerful strictures in my social

68

training—and yet why? What *is* wrong? All the—to you—silly, immature, self-indulgent, spoilt and blindly selfish acts of wilfulness are *not* part of a plan or a pattern—I wouldn't claim that—but they are to do with the way I live in my time now—which is a mess in a mess. My business, I think, is to live through it, and I'd be even more of a failure, I think, if I built a little Ark and sailed out of it! I don't know how to build the Ark and I don't want one anyway. So there you are and here I am."

Mary sipped, she hesitated, and then, speaking softly, she said slowly: "And yet, after all that, I still don't know whether you're behaving like a child or whether there really is something in what you're doing." She puzzled to be fair to this man she had once loved so much and still felt responsible to. "Because, besides being reckless, you have got guts—you take risks; besides being self-deluding, you try to be honest; you're spoilt but you're also serious. You try to think life through for yourself. You're brave in that. I don't know, Douglas, what you're worth. I just don't know."

"Neither do I."

"We'd better set out for the Rugby Club dance," she said, gravely. "I'm a little drunk."

"Do you want to go?"

"No."

"Neither do I."

"I'll wear my black dress. I can hang some of that cheap Arab junk on it you brought back from Israel. That looks quite sexy, doesn't it?"

"It does."

She stood up. So did he. They put down their glasses and embraced tightly, keenly, lovingly it would seem. Their hands caressed each other. They rocked slightly on their heels.

"I mean it about the pill," she whispered. "I want another child."

"So it's my responsibility."

"It is."

"Kid or bust?"

"That's about it."

"I'll have to work it out."

69

"Take your time." She kissed his ear and then bent her lips to that tender part of his throat; he looked down onto the glossy deep red hair and buried his face in it to draw in the scent and the comfort. His hands were on her breasts, her hips were locked tightly against his—and yet, in this poised moment of pleasure some demon ignited him with despair: for his disloyalties and failings, for his weaknesses and cowardice—the litany rose again but there was no appeal, no "Good Lord Deliver Us". Mary pulled back, tugged off his jacket, looked him full in the face and grinned—as she used to.

"Don't panic," she said. "It just finished a couple of days ago." She tugged at his shirt. "Have this one on the house."

(3)

And so the New Year came in.

Roving reporters took television audiences to Scotland for "the real, the authentic Hogmanay", where tipsy Celts and grinning Picts waved at the cameras on which the Northern sleet fell steadily. From there the armchair celebrants were whisked about the planet, images bouncing off the satellites which circled the earth remorselessly, and everywhere people were cavorting and cheering, either participating in a huge confidence trick they were playing on themselves or truly caught, for the moment, in the notion that there was a witching hour, a turning point, a pause for change.

In Thurston the church bells rang out, the pubs emptied out their rooms and people swarmed up the street to the church square as if they were hurrying to the summons of a mediaeval war. A gigantic circle was formed around the Christmas tree and smaller circles set themselves up like mere planets around this huge cheerful group, which somehow hit on a common note and chanted in faltering unison the hearty words of Robert Burns.

"Should Auld Acquaintance be forgot
And never brought to mind
Should Auld Acquaintance be forgot
For the sake of Auld Lang Syne."

Most mumbled, not knowing whether it was "should" or "would" or even "let", but no one stumbled on that great emotive trio "Auld Lang Syne". As the chorus was repeated, the circle advanced to its centre like a slow-motion rose crumpling; back again to the perimeter and then in once more, with the men happy to barge and be barged, the women saying goodbye to ladderless tights and nylons, those kids let up for the event caught up in the totally untypical circumstance of hundreds of adults prepared to be knocked around, toes trodden on, drizzled on, hustled about and embraced by strangers whose password was no more than "A Happy New Year!"

The bells rang, "A Happy New Year!" Men and boys went around shaking hands all about them, searching for relatives, making do with acquaintances, diving in to kiss attractive women, snatching the willing hands of men they had nodded to for years but never addressed—for some minutes there was a happy bedlam and Douglas, who relished these few minutes more than he cared to say, missed it.

He tried to fit in the Rugby Club's own "Auld Lang Syne" and then belt down to the church. But the greetings and mutual good wishes at the club had taken much longer than he had anticipated—spoiled, too, by the nag in his mind of that date he had made for himself with the event at the church. And so they came too late. The church square was by now empty save for two or three drunks and two young policemen. Douglas walked over to the Christmas tree and tried to imagine the scene of half an hour ago. He had taken in a large load of drink during the evening, failed to remember four or five people whom he was sure he had thereby offended, discovered himself dancing too closely to a pretty woman he'd never met before, had nothing to say while the rich banter on the last rugby tour had built up between the half dozen leaders of the pack—and generally swung between self-disgust and bare acceptance of his conduct. (A cooler, sterner voice told him, rightly, that nobody bothered much what he did.) Mary was well liked and followed her habitual routine, which was to begin talking to the person next to her and be quite content to stay there all evening.

The two policemen decided that the odd couple gazing at the Christmas tree were not about to tear it to the ground, and set off on their "low profile" walk through the town, glad of the regulation boots to keep out the slush.

71

"Grandad," Douglas announced, "on our way."

Mary had drunk sparingly at the club and drove carefully. As they went up to the old man's flat, they passed groups coming out of houses, going into houses, linked arm in arm, totting up the number of places they went First Footing. In the course of the evening, Douglas and Mary had received more than a dozen invitations—"any time till about five o'clock". There would be a cupboard full of drink, pyramids of sandwiches, platters overcrowded with cakes and cold meats of all sorts. Douglas—unable to say no—had equivocated—guaranteeing, he knew, that this would cause some offence—but what could you do when faced with a point-blank invitation which was the social equivalent of a hold up? If you said no—then even greater offence would be caused. If you said yes, you were committed. You had to equivocate. But he was such a bad equivocator; even in his equivocations he was not firm.

But he had his routine. First his grandfather—so that the old fellow could get off to bed. Then his mother. Then his oldest friend, who could not come to the Rugby dance because of baby-sitting complications. Then a couple of other good friends. By that time it was, generally, almost dawn. In the car, he sang:

> "When that I was and a little tiny boy,
> With a heigh-ho, the wind and the rain,
> A foolish thing was but a toy,
> For the rain it raineth every day;
> With a heigh-ho, the wind and the rain,
> The rain it raineth every day.

Too true. Toooo true. The rain it never stoppeth." He turned to Mary, who was peering through the drizzle-smudged windscreen. He was now well and truly drunk—the fresh air around the Christmas tree had finished him off. "I know we're here. I am looking for Grandad's bottle of scotch, purchased in Los Angeles. Got it!"

The flat was in complete darkness. Indeed, in all the block there were only two very dim lights—which might have been nightlights. Mary cut off Douglas' attempt to barge in and see if

72

his grandfather was awake. They argued, Mary quietly and determinedly, Douglas loudly. She won. They left and the carton of scotch was propped against the door with Douglas' scrawl saying "A Happy New Year" and then "love" which was badly crossed out. "I forgot myself," he explained to Mary. "I can't start saying 'love' to my grandfather. It would never do." He printed his name in wayward letters which trekked around the seal and placed it carefully by a small parcel and then they went to round out the morning's celebrations about the houses of the town.

Old John had heard every word. He could not quite distinguish the voice—it could have been Joseph, it could have been another of his sons—but he guessed it would be Douglas, who had made a thing out of coming up First Footing on New Year's morning. It was difficult for him to concentrate on anything outside his own head; it throbbed with fear. He had woken up by the dead fire—been awakened by the cold—and, seeing the time, made shift to sort himself out for the night, knowing there would be visitors. He had stood up, and collapsed, cutting his head, as he fell, on the back of a chair. It was not a bad cut but it bled a lot. John had tried again to stand, resentful and furious at being laid low: but he could not. In his frustration, as he lay there, the blood warm on his cold skin, he had felt tears come once again to his eyes, but he had forced them back. He resolved he would not cry again as he had done in the afternoon. He was determined not to repeat that weakness. Whatever else happened—and clearly, for he saw it all—there would be a swift decline into senile infancy—there would be incontinence and bedsores, there would be forgetfulness and the stealing hopelessness of irreversible decline—but whatever else happened he would not cry.

Feeling a fool, though he had no reason on earth to feel so, but feeling a fool, he crawled to the sink as—he remembered—exactly as he had been taught to crawl in the First World War. He gripped the side of it tightly and began to haul himself up. The sink came away from the wall. He let go and rolled aside, looking up at the cheap fitment which jutted out from the wall now, like the prow of a ship. He waited for the water to pour out, but the pipes had not been damaged.

73

Lying there, on his back, staring at the white ceiling, crippled, bleeding and very old, he heard the church bells peal out twelve and knew he would have to hurry if he was to avoid being seen.

He crawled over to the door and locked it. Using the door handle as an aid, he reached up and knocked off the light. Then he scuffled himself through to his bedroom, undressed, pulled himself into the bed and only then realized that he had done nothing about the cut on his forehead. On the bedside table there was a glass of water: he wetted his fingers in it and dabbed the cut, which felt quite nasty to his fingertips. He kept doing this until he felt the wound grow cold. The spilt blood coagulated on his cheek.

His first visitor was Mrs. Fell from the flat next door: she knocked once politely, a second time timidly and then left her gift, a chocolate cake which she had baked that afternoon, beside the door and shuffled back to her own flat.

Then Douglas and his wife came. John could not remember her name. There were so many new names. He heard the car start up and leave and wondered how many others in these old people's flats were as wide awake as he, how many suddenly overtaken by life, quite bewildered that they should be at the end of it when they could so easily reach back to the beginnings and see themselves young and fresh and strong, how many knowing they were waiting, as he was waiting.

## (4)

Harry and Aileen had been to one or two pubs, then, of course, to the Rugby Club, where Aileen had talked to Douglas, whom she liked and trusted (despite his compulsive tendency to run himself down)—and they had left in time to get to the church for the big circle. Lester had been at the church, looking as if he had been in a fight—but he had sworn not and his friends had backed him up with virtuous indignation. Aileen was not too happy about these town friends of Lester's: they egged him on, she thought, and brought out his worst side. She preferred the few friends he still had in the country, those he had met when he

74

used to be a fell runner—farm labourers or mechanics at small garages—men, did she but know it, who were greatly envied by Lester himself—in his "down" times, such as this. For, though they would never believe it, these men were better off than him—certainly at the present time. And in his rare moments of insight Lester would guess they would always be so. More importantly, though, they lived in the country, which Lester knew about and genuinely loved. Much more than Douglas or Harry, he was a country boy; he had poached and been shooting, built camps, dammed up rivers, snared rabbits, tackled rock faces—he was never happier than when he was in the country—it was a tribute to the power of the metropolitan poison he so greedily sucked in that the fantasies he chased so clumsily and ineptly should stand in the way of the real, acknowledged pleasures and rewards he had chosen to abandon. He was not morose, though, Aileen was relieved to see: he had met up with some men: "big smart fellas," he confided, "where the money is, 'Gentlemen Farmer' types!" They were up from the Midlands with a pack of beagles and after chatting with him they had invited him to join them in their sport on the fells behind Skiddaw the following morning. "My luck," he announced, "is in again."

She kissed him and wished him a "Happy New Year" with her usual sisterly fervour. She found her father, George, pleasantly piddled; and her mother on the arm of her latest fancy man. Harry had gone around pumping hands as if clearing a flood off the decks. Then he took her to Betty's, where he always went immediately after the church square "do"—and Aileen had been glad of the chance to sit quietly for a while. Joseph had whirled in with two or three friends and half a dozen strangers, decimated the sandwiches, attacked the drink, turned the place upside down looking for a bottle-opener—and left on his own route around the town. Aileen and Betty had talked town gossip.

In the car, she leaned her head on Harry's shoulder and felt deeply comfortable. He took care, she noticed, as much as he could, to ensure that her head was not jarred nor jolted. She loved his care for her and for others. It was altogether marvellous, she thought, how sure she felt about Harry and how innocent he still was of her set intentions. She knew nobody as unassuming and as inviolably good. In his reliability, his modesty and his fidelity, she had basked for about three years now, knowing that the unspoken, unofficial arrangement they had would be more binding to him than all the rings, certificates and vows in the world to anyone else. Aileen had learned to value what was sure. Her own early life had almost been ruined by neglect from irresponsible parents. She had taken refuge in food and silence. Even today, she could be surprised at how she had managed to escape from that tired, soporific, sullen, fat, passive body and lazy mind. She was proud of the way in which she had pulled herself together, but still aware of how near a thing it had been. Only the intervention of a sympathetic schoolteacher had pulled her through. One consequence was that she was wary of everyone but Harry. Only her own efforts mattered; other people would surely do her some damage. Except Harry. This fearful self-dependence had made it hard for her initially but then, when she had got interested in her work at the college, it had been the best possible ally. She had worked alone, set out and stuck to her own standards, was now secure in her job and about to take on a new career, she hoped, in politics. But first she wanted to get married. She would tell Harry that evening. New Year's Day would be the right time to set it all in motion.

They went up to see old John. The thought of him had nagged Harry all evening. He saw that the lights were off and bit his lip in annoyance.

"We've hung about down there too much," he said. "He must have packed in and gone to bed."

"We could knock," Aileen said. "People expect that tonight."

"No. If he's put the lights out he'll want to be on his own. I hope this car hasn't woken him up."

"You can come up in the morning."

"I will, yes. But I hope somebody was with him tonight. I've just realized. Maybe nobody was."

"Why is it important?"

He told her, glad to be able to tell someone.

"I'll come up with you tomorrow," she said. "We might have

76

to get him into a hospital and you'll never be able to persuade him yourself."

"Of course, he could be all right," Harry said. "It could just have been a turn."

"We'll see."

"I'll take him his present."

Harry took the crate of Guinness from the back of the car. Old John appreciated whisky, but it was a bottle of stout a day that "kept him going", he said. Harry put it down beside the whisky and the cake and laid a bottle-opener on top.

Then he left and took Aileen back to his flat where they talked until he found he was about to be married and they went to bed about the same time as Joseph finally reached his father's flat. He banged on the door several times and then sat on the crate, worn out with his evening's pilgrimage, and opened a bottle of Guinness to settle his stomach. As always when alone and almost drunk, he thought about how he would have liked his retirement to be. A certain comfort—not much, peace of mind, books to read, long, interesting conversations, above all, security. Instead, what they had saved, which had seemed so huge to their mid-War minds, was just a drop in a pool. Without his part-time job as school-caretaker (which was a grand title for sweeping up the classrooms in the Comprehensive every evening) and Betty's few pounds from the lunch-time work she did in the bar of the King's Head, they would be unable to manage. Money, he concluded, had become senseless: and, with the deliberation of the very tired, he took out a five pound note, folded it up and tucked it inside the whisky carton before replacing the empty bottle in its slot and setting off for his bed.

Even later, grey with weariness, Mary and Douglas reached their cottage. He had slunk, drunk, from house to house, occasionally lurching into coherence—intense, grandiloquent, or confidential—always brief. Mary had kept going and not pressed him to give up. On the way back he had fallen deeply asleep after declaring: "Do you know that Tennyson was inspired to write about Excalibur on the shore of Bassenthwaite—two miles from us—what a thought! That hard shaft shooting up from that flat lake! Why are shords so symbolic? Sorry. Shords are. So . . . I learnt that in Hollywood!

Tennyson. Hollywood!" In his sleep he muttered broken sentences. Mary stayed in the car and smoked a final cigarette, looking out to the grey which was slowly rising against the darkness. She had given in again and she would give in again, but she had also made up her mind. If Douglas did not want a family and if he was not prepared to be stable enough to enable her to devote more time to John and to any others she might have—then she would, indeed, leave him.

He was slumped on her shoulder. His hair was dirty: it stank. He breathed like an old man and was white with exhaustion and drink. Somehow he reckoned that the world would take care of him and let him dry out, return to normality, go on as before. There was nothing about him now, as she looked down on the ageing face, which touched her, let alone moved her to love. Even his helplessness wearied her: it was such an indulgence. Yes. She would have to make the decisions. She threw the cigarette out of the window and nudged his head with her shoulder quite brutally. "We're here," she said. "Get out." It was still dark. The First Day.

(5)

Old John had not slept at all. Time stretched so far when you did not sleep. The night had gone on for so long.

His legs, useless to him now, ached and burned, while the rest of him was cold, despite the blankets. He had heard the comings and goings and almost called out to Joseph, who would have understood—but by that time his mind was set. He knew that they would take him to a home or a hospital and he did not want it done in the middle of the night with all the fuss. He would wait.

There was a feeling of vigil about the watch he kept over himself and yet the waiting lacked a point of arrival. For what was he going towards? He would not see another New Year, that was certain. He might just make the summer, though he doubted it. Maybe the spring: he would like to see one last spring. But what would he see from a hospital bed? He would like to see the new lambs—most of all the lambs—and the leaves and the flowers, yes, those too. His first wife, who had

78

died so long ago, and his second, who had gone five years before—both had been keen on flowers. He mixed their faces up now; an expression here on a face there; and the children, *their* children, friends, Mrs. Fell with her kind cakes. He would like a drive around the places he had been hired—to see the fields he ploughed and dug and worried over. Just to see them again. That was all.

For what else was there? As the terrible long night went on so very slowly, the old man tried to ask and answer the question which was now so urgent. What had it all been *for*, this life? Would there be another life, another chance, another birth? He thought not. No. But, even so, it could not be quite meaningless, could it? What had it been for? He clenched his teeth to stop his tears as the humiliation of incontinence overcame him and he wet the bed. At last there was a bit of grey outside. They would break the door down—no—they would get the spare key from the Warden. It would be good if he could close his eyes, now, now, this moment, knowing it was over. But that was not allowed. Another car went by. He heard some children playing on their bicycles, ringing the trilling bells. They would find him soon.

# 3
# "London Bridge"

The church clock struck six. He could hear it when the wind
was in the north-east. It was odd, somehow, in London, to
hear so clearly the toll of a church clock; especially such a one as
this, which was tinny, unresonant, villagey, like an alpine bell.
He had been awake since about four—as usual whenever he had
too much to drink. The pattern never varied. A brief, slugged
unconsciousness, a startled awakening, the whirling head, the
pint-of-milk-and-three-Paracetemols cure and then the difficult
decision: back to bed or try to read? Bed won. He had learned to
stop fussing about alcoholic insomnia: he lay on his back,
settled himself comfortably, and rummaged around in a mind
now made companionable by the drugs.

Mary slept deeply. It was still dark outside but he could "see"
her clearly. She slept face down, legs splayed, arms hoisted up
onto the pillows, hair obscuring her face. He reached out his
hand and let it trail gently down her back until it reached the
rise of the buttocks. She stirred; he did not persist. Despite his
inebriated lust, he did not want to disturb her.

They had been back from Cumbria for three months and she
was not yet pregnant. Sometimes he tried, sometimes he did
not. Mary was still not quite sure whether his behaviour was
based on fine calculations or excusable obstinacy. So far she
gave him the benefit of the doubt, choosing to ignore his
unspoken but clearly felt resistance to this demand of hers. For
she had got him to agree to it, but only through a manoeuvre
quite close to blackmail: for if he did not, she said, then she
would indeed think of seeking to have a child by someone else.
She knew how violently jealous and possessive he was.

Douglas would not explain his reluctance. For if he was
thinking of breaking the most serious bond in his life—his

marriage—how could he ever think of tying them both together with more flesh? It was cowardly to hesitate but perhaps also he was giving the marriage a last chance. Chance was the word—for they *did* make love: maybe, before leaving, he was throwing out a last challenge to the luck which, in his pagan state of mind, seemed to have so much power.

His lack of contentment disconcerted him. At the very least it felt like selfish ingratitude. As a boy he had never imagined that he would lead such an outwardly pleasant, easy and entertaining life. His discontent made his existence appear indulgent, as well as negligible. Yet there it was, squatting like a toad in the middle of his mind and immovable, it seemed. No appeal to Third World poverty, to Calcuttas of the body and spirit, to Gulags of the mind and conscience, to lost Empires, domestic injustices—none of this could goad his self-soaked mind to stir into that bracing activity traditionally guaranteed to dissolve selfishness and destroy this boring misery. Hedonism had ended in the cul-de-sac of responsibility. Ambition was suspect. And mere accumulation vulgar. And he had blown family life, hadn't he? He had broken a trust which, like a broken egg, could never be mended; or, like a sacrificial cock, could only be killed the once. Perhaps life was not the answer: perhaps it would be better to read. Just to settle for a bed-sitter and a clutch of library tickets and read all the best books written. Leave it at that. Let what happen come. Life would crowd in fast enough: it always did. Or he could go to the U.S.A.— West Coast—pretending amnesia, and start again as a literary hobo. Why not? Infantile fantasies were the stuff of real change and revolution. Or settle down to Write The Big Play. Or work for the Labour Party. Or go into the church (which he would have done if he could have believed in God): or jump off Brighton Pier: or Blackpool Tower: or wherever was convenient. Non-existence seemed sweet and drink was the nearest substitute.

How the hell had he got into that state?

The alarm rang. He leaned across Mary and banged it shut. "I'll get up first," he announced, and the glow of virtue rose up to be quelled by the renewed pressure of the hangover.

He made the breakfast—cornflakes and scrambled eggs on toast—and saw John and Mary set off for school together. John had a cold and looked pinched, orphan-like, Douglas thought, guiltily. Mary was almost silent in the mornings; the two of them, mother and son, went off to school as if embarking on a penitential pilgrimage. So much for family life.

Douglas worked at the story.

The mail brought him an invitation from the Arts Council to go on a writers' tour of Cornwall and Devon for one week, with three other writers, for a hundred and twenty pounds plus travel expenses: he accepted. A tax account, which he stuck with the others and resolved to sort out soon, when he answered the pile of correspondence. An invitation to a lecture in the House of Commons, Committee Room Eleven, on "Censorship in Contemporary Society" by Richard Hoggart. A couple of circulars and a picture postcard, for John, from Betty, which read, "Thought you'd like this. We're glad you like your school now. Love and kisses. Grandma. XXXXXXX."

The phone rang but he had made a rule not to answer it while he was writing. Another rule allowed him to ring out whenever he wanted to.

As usual when he wrote, he would think either that it was the most satisfying and enjoyably difficult thing he ever did, or that it was utterly useless and completely unreal, sitting there scratching his ink out on narrow lined paper.

For about three hours he worked as hard as he could on something which would probably not make him a penny. He was quite happy. The invented world kept out the real world and here he ruled, a harmless tyrant.

Then he answered some letters and let others rot away in the pile—the difficult ones, hoping that somehow they would change nature, like dead cut grass ending up as live manure. Occasionally that did happen. A couple of phone calls, a desultory trot around the Canadian Air Force Exercises course (twenty push-ups—*quite* enough, and, each time his nose touched the floor, it was rubbed in the badly frayed carpet, like a symbol of his lack of husbandry), cheque book, credit cards, keys, book to read in emergency, out onto the street, making for the Underground. No coat, no scarf, no gloves, walking fast in the cold; as usual buoyed up to be diving into London—free to loot the capital.

As he waited for the tube, on the empty platform—it was a comfortable time of day to travel—he read the introduction by Gide to James Hogg's "The Confessions of a Justified Sinner". Gide had clearly been enraptured by the book's concern with good and evil. Douglas had picked up the book after he had re-read "The Immoralist".

Gide quoted from "The Doctrine of All Religions" (1704) on the heresy known as Antinomianism—founded in 1538. "Antinomians, so denominated for rejecting the law, as a thing of no use under Gospel dispensation. They say that good works do not further, nor evil works hinder salvation: that the child of God cannot sin, that God never chastiseth him, that murder, drunkenness, etc., are sins in the wicked but not in him."

The silver train shook the red tiled walls as it bolted out of its tunnel. The guard waited while a fat woman tugged at the sweets machine and finally extracted her bar of chocolate.

Into Soho at forty-five miles an hour, a day's freelancing before him. First, lunch with Mike Wainwright of the B.B.C. He looked forward to that. He read another page or two of Gide. "The child of God cannot sin!" Think on that!

(2)

There was something about the look of Mike Wainwright which said he had come through. He had. The look represented the reality.

He was in his early fifties, squarely built, neither stout nor slim but firmly muscled, light on his feet, physically poised and secure. That security had been earned and yet needed attention, you felt, for there was both evidence of past strain on his wary face, and a feeling of frailty, as if a sensitive set of features had been superimposed on a tough base, or vice versa. For there was a flickering interplay of alertness and achieved calm, of vulnerability and tranquillity. He looked experienced and yet still open to experience, as if he had learned hard lessons the hard way but, despite that, was not afraid to be open to what came. He had the look of a wise fighter, whose mind and life had raked over too much, but managed to gather together some fragments to shore up an independent personality, which existed in its own right. For that, most of all, was what Wainwright gave off: the smack of being independent, self-sufficient, self-resolved—not the self-satisfied and islanded complacency of the very rich or very powerful, whose poise depends on their distance from the rest and the maintenance of that distance by fair means or foul, by loot or by crook. Nor was it the anarchistic arrogance of the man who does not give a sod for the world, secure in the knowledge that the world does not give a sod for him—in short, the mere reckless pose of the brazen self-destructor, who can always claim a passing regard because of the chord of pointlessness he touches in us all. Wainwright had earned his independence, you felt, had been tested and not found wanting, had fallen and picked himself up again, accommodated weaknesses and wounds and carried on, selflessly. For he was, to a few like Douglas, a touchstone, incorruptible, a man to whom the word "integrity" could be applied without a twinge of embarrassment or a grain of pomposity.

He had caught the last two years of the War and seen a bit of action. If you don't get shot, he said, and you think you're on the right side and the whole business *means* something, then war for an eighteen year old is all they once said about it. There is the unblushing talk of courage, endurance, even heroism. And eighteen was a time when most men unselfconsciously wanted to be brave, to show courage in Hemingway's sense and prove themselves. War could soon seem very natural.

Mike had been on hand when the concentration camps had been "liberated" and such notions had been blown away like euphoric frost. That sight, he thought, though it was only to his wife he had admitted it, had been so devastating and yet so strange: for at first he had felt only detached natural human pity at those skeletal men. And then the mass graves were discovered and at first there was a kind of wonder at it all, as if his world were being turned upside down in very slow motion. Finally the settlement had come, the meaning of it had hit him. In 1945, aged twenty, the day the War was over, Michael Jeffrey Wainwright from South London out of the West Country,

Raleigh's country, playing football to celebrate victory, suddenly trotted off the pitch, went behind the huts they had taken over from the Germans and found himself crying helplessly but with no feeling of relief: for there was a great weariness and burden suddenly on him: a vision of the hell of the world fixed in his mind.

There followed a time of listlessness which he thought might becalm him for ever. He went to university and drifted: he had no real heart for games, although he had once enjoyed playing rugby and cricket; he was interested in his work—Modern History—but not interested enough to satisfy himself— tutorials with a man a few years older than himself dwindled into gossip about the War, lectures were soon cut, reading digressed into vacant daydreamings or private discoveries such as Camus or T. S. Eliot's "Waste Land" and "Prufrock", which shot into his system like insulin into a diabetic. He drank quietly and consistently. He was chaste. His parents had died during the War and his vacations were spent around the Mediterranean, wandering among the remainders of other lost civilizations. He failed to go back after his second year and left on a whim for America.

He read extensively, feeding on modern literature, hunting through it for certainties and clues. Like tens of thousands of others, he criss-crossed the continent, looking for a lodging place. The tiny inheritance from his parents soon gave out. He got whatever work he could, lived rough, went up to Canada where he was asked to run a lumber yard and "get on the ladder to be a millionaire", went to Mexico, where he lived for six months with a young neurotic German sculptress who finally abandoned him for an insurance salesman from Chicago. Wainwright ended up in Greenwich Village, where a short ironic account of some of these adventures introduced him to one of the small magazines of the day. In that predominantly immigrant Jewish intellectual community, where ideas and their expression were declared the most important matter in life, he flourished. He wrote little, but what he wrote was respected and encouraged. His interest in films began, caught flame and rapidly developed into the compulsive passion he had been seeking. He made his first documentary in Canada

—returning to the lumber camp in which he had worked and making a fine piece of work on the men who had been teased and drawn out into that wilderness. On the promise of a possible feature film, he returned to England.

The film was "well received" but made no money. About two years later, a second film was even better received and made less. On the back of the good notices, however, he was whisked off to Hollywood, where he spent eighteen months trying to do a film he wanted to do. He failed and walked out of his contract. Libel suits cleaned him out of the modest amount of money he had. Back in England, he set up a film too quickly and failed to make it to his own satisfaction. It did quite well at the box-office and he was bankable, in a modest way. But the five or six years had churned up a reasonably balanced marriage, left a small daughter stranded with an entrenched mother who drank far too much. Wainwright, after the divorce, devoted himself to setting the two of them up in a decent house, well appointed, with regular monthly cheques in the bank. For himself he took a small, plain service flat, just north of Soho. That was where he still lived. He had never remarried.

Throughout the Sixties and Seventies he had freelanced. His basic work was making documentaries, chiefly for television. He did some journalism. There had been one published collection of semi-autobiographical essays, which had not done particularly well. At present he was setting up two new series for the B.B.C. He liked Douglas and had arranged to meet him in Bianchi's for lunch.

(3)

Elena brought them a second carafe of red. The first floor of this little Italian restaurant was packed, as usual, while downstairs, though the food came from the same kitchen, the tables were comparatively undisturbed. It was Elena's welcome, an elegant Italian mamma who swooped like a swallow—and a consistent and loyal link with the literary/film/television/theatre younger crowd which kept the upstairs full. At times it was like a club. That helped. And the prices were reasonable.

Douglas had nodded to the half a dozen people he

86

knew—from vaguely to quite well, a tricky but well practised scale of nods—and been amused to watch the transparent barometer of feelings on the face of one young trendy critic in particular—a very clever chap, recently down from Oxford, much given to scorn, garlanded with recondite epithets and contempt, which he implicitly justified by comparisons with the All Time (Dead) Greats, beside whom all contemporaries were as midgets, etcetera etcetera. In fact he was following the usual and safely worn trail set by many young men in a hurry to capitalize on the energy garnered during three years in a university. The rules were simple—hit out at prominent figures, thereby getting yourself talked about, thereby getting some of the spotlight on yourself, thereby becoming a "name", thereby acquiring a market value (on a market which, naturally, you despised). Said young person—quite a cheerful, shy, decent fellow, under the twin terrors of failure and not being in fashion which currently had him by the throat—had given a brisk no-nonsense nod in response to Douglas' brisk no-nonsense nod but then, seeing that Douglas was with Wainwright, he had missed no opportunity to bow and wink and leer knowingly throughout the meal. It was so blatant that it was comical: a self-abasement Douglas had never come across in his youth, or anywhere at all. It was the sort of craven bum-boot-licking he had been told to expect but rarely encountered in Big Corporations. It was most odd. The explanation was simple. Wainwright could introduce him to the beginnings of a television career (which, naturally, he despised). He knew Douglas slightly from one or two literary cocktail parties (which he despised) and, sure enough, over he came after his unfattening veal—dragging his rumpled and lovely girlfriend—to struggle through a few banalities and at once assume and, as he thought, initiate a relationship with Wainwright. Finally, with much, much nodding, he left. "He'll do well," Douglas said. "But why does he want to do well in that way?"

"We do need a hand at the start," Wainwright said. He had registered Douglas' reaction to the young man and thought it too harsh. "Or most of us."

"Agreed."

"You didn't."

"I was lucky," Douglas said, fittingly averting any opportunity for a compliment. He hated them.

"I believe you." Wainwright took out a cigarette. "What are you doing?"

"Trying to finish some work."

"Do you still have the same system?"

"Which one was that?"

Wainwright laughed.

"You used to go and get some 'loot'—your phrase—and then simply wrote until you had used it up."

"That was one of the better systems," Douglas said, "but it's changed lately." He looked around: the place was almost empty: he still felt the guilty privilege of sitting about while others were working—yet that was the prime benefit of his "freedom", wasn't it? "How did *you* keep your nerve?" he asked. "As a freelance?"

"Desperation's a big help," Wainwright said, "or success."

"I pass on both," Douglas said. "At present."

"What are you doing now?"

"Looking for work."

"Any ideas?"

"One or two. One worthy but not necessarily dull."

Douglas outlined his idea for a series of programmes in which writers would take a region of the U.K. and produce a script which would work through from the geology to the present self-awareness of the place. He had prepared a document based on Yorkshire. Cumbria would have been too obvious. Yorkshire included great industry as well as a tradition of sport, public life, the arts, and that self-conscious "Yorkshireness" which often filled indifferent outsiders with feelings of bored desperation. This document had been sent to Mike a few days previously and he had read it. Nevertheless he let Douglas make the case: slightly resenting this, Douglas semi-deliberately made a mess of it. There was a self-destructiveness in him on such occasions which was out of his control. He stopped talking.

"It was a better idea on paper," Wainwright said.

"Most ideas are."

"Not all. Sometimes... You don't like singing for your supper, do you?"

88

"No."

"But that's the freelance life."

"Not necessarily. You can duck a lot of it. You don't do as well. That's all."

"You do it to avoid being bossed about?"

"Partly. Yes. A good part. Silly really."

"Why?"

"Well," Douglas was beginning to be muzzy: the plonk felt as if it were seeping corrosively across the runnels of his bare brain. "Well, unless you're lucky or a genius you work for *someone*. The attraction of writing is that you work for yourself. But—here's the catch—'yourself' can be a lousy boss. Still, we're free, aren't we? That's the point, isn't it? We've done with 'perfect service'."

"Do you think this freedom is something you have to have?"

"Not really. It's probably just another face of selfishness. Though what isn't?"

"Do you think much about it?" Wainwright asked.

"Why?"

"It would seem to me that your lot, even those of you who started out as provincial puritans in that good old British tradition of earnestness—plain living and high thinking—most of you simply don't concern yourselves now with what used to be called 'fundamental issues'—indeed such a formulation would make you flinch. I thought the approach nowadays was cynical, pessimistic, elliptical and somehow sapped of the moral energy that keeps those considerations alive."

"I don't know. I don't think it's an age *of* anything much. Perhaps what they say is true: the atom bomb and the concentration camps between them make a pair of inescapable pincers. We've got the stuff to blow us all to smithereens and we've got the proof we're evil enough to try it. So why bother?"

"You bother." More wine was poured.

"But I don't know why I bother to bother. And I don't bother much. Maybe it's just for something to do."

"I don't think so. But you *do* need work?"

"A fix?" He paused and sobered up in that part of his mind which needed to see sense. "Yes. Work could see me through whatever it is I'm in. I'm not complaining, you know." Douglas added this anxiously. He wanted Wainwright to be absolutely clear. "I'm not begging for work. I'm not on my uppers." He was. He took a large drink and pronounced, "I still find it incredible, sometimes, you know, to be six or seven miles high in an aeroplane with a plate of food and a glass of Beaujolais. And now—just the same—a working day—what is it?— about three o'clock—and here we are—I am babbling on in this pleasant place, swigging booze, just being here. There's some sort of fluke in it. Got to be. Millions starving, millions slaving away, millions dying, millions in factories, in sheds, in pain, in noise, in filth, in terror, in depression—what have I done that I should be living the life of Reilly? Nothing at all is the answer. It's enough to drive a man to drink." He poured himself the rest of the carafe. "Nothing!" he repeated. "Nothing at all!"

"Cheers!" said Wainwright.

"No wonder the rich and mighty worship the past—their old houses and ancestors and connections and clubs and schools and collected clutter of ages of looting and buying—the past is the only thing that possibly sustains them in this privilege with any validity whatsoever. That's why the self-made men are always such a threat. They say, 'We deserve what we've got because we've got it by our own endeavours and we owe the world nothing.' They inhabit their own moral universe. In a way they are our chiefs and heroes, but as most of us want to nobble chiefs and trip up heroes in the greater cause of making sure nobody gets too much power. We don't like them much. We prefer the luck of the past or the luck of the draw. That's real life. It's some ridiculous quirk of fortune that has me here with the time and leisure and education and drink and food and interests which would be the envy of an eighteenth-century nobleman and a grandfather who mourns for a past when eight brothers slept toe-to-tail on a mattress on a damp cottage floor which can still be found in any rural community from Pakistan to Mexico and back again. And there will be retribution. Got to be. Unless, that is, we redeem our privilege by courage. Unless we stand up and are counted—Oh God! Sorry."

"Why?"

"Boring."

"I didn't find it so."

"That's because you're a pal and I'm half drunk."

"No. I was interested. There was nothing new—"

"Thanks."

"But I was interested. Is being boring a cardinal sin?"

"Yes. *The* cardinal civilized sin."

"Your regional notion," Wainwright said, "is very worthy."

"Worthy *and* uncontroversial *and* dull," Douglas corrected him. "Carefully composed for the market."

Wainwright grinned. "I like that."

"But not the idea."

"Not much."

"I thought that was the idea."

"What?"

"Not to like something much. Liking something much might introduce that gypsy strain of passion or commitment which the B.B.C.—'on the one hand—on the other hand be our motto and we have as many hands as any goddess in Bali'—stands to stamp on. If you get my drift. On the other hand. It is *quite* a decent idea you know and if we get the right writers—say that again—and we do *have* good writers who actually *live* in regions and know a lot about them and would do this sort of thing, I'm convinced, out of a nice sense of commitment—it could work very well."

"I agree."

"Well then?"

"It'll have to take its place in a queue."

"How long?"

"About a year."

"Sod it."

"Relying on it?"

"I've just this second realized that I was. Coffee?" It was ordered.

"What'll you do?" Wainwright asked. "Anything on the stocks?"

"Nothing that would make money. Ah well." He drank the scalding coffee in two or three gulps and felt better. "I've been avoiding a crunch by an inch here and there for years. Like Jerry in those Tom and Jerry films, you know, where he walks

91

through one potential disaster after another, missing them by a whisker. Now it's here."

"And how do you feel?"

"Quite calm," Douglas said. "Have to change that. Give me an hour for it to sink in."

"You'd banked too much on it."

"Yes and no. The more important fact is that I've no other iron in the fire at the moment. No play on the hoof—I'm too involved in this story. No other television. Not a tickle from feature films, of course. One or two reviewing possibilities—yes. That could, perhaps, be worked up. It's as if I'd sorted it all out so that it would *have* to depend on one throw of the dice."

"'Regionalism'?"

"I agree. Not exactly Dostoevskian daring. And you see—it didn't come up. Well. There we are. Your lunch? Mine? Ours? Or Theirs?"

"Ours," Wainwright said.

It cost them nine pounds fifty each.

They went down the steep and narrow stairs and into a bright spring Soho day. "I'm going to Parliament," Douglas said. "Friend from back home—oop North—making his maiden speech."

"I'll walk along with you."

They went through the packed, village-narrow streets of Soho. Sex shops, food shops, strip clubs, and the remorseless crowd of voyeurs, visitors and villains: through Gerrard Street, Chinatown now, though once, Douglas remembered, used by Dickens to house that wonderful lawyer in "Great Expectations"—strolled down through Leicester Square, now become a "pedestrian precinct" and consequently a cul-de-sac for loafers and alcoholics, wriggled around the National Portrait Gallery and entered Trafalgar Square in a blaze of sunshine, fountains playing, tourists chasing the hundreds of fat pigeons, motor vehicles circling three deep, Big Ben dominating the middle distance and Nelson—

"What would he make of us?"

"He'd have given us all up years ago," Wainwright said.

92

"Who would be put up on a phallic plinth now?"

"Footballer? Pop star? *Intelligent* pop star—who writes his own stuff: Dylan, Lennon, McCartney."

"Raven?" Douglas asked.

"Most of all."

"What about him?"

"For a programme?" Mike was clearly interested.

"Yes." Douglas caught the chance.

"I thought he was uncontactable." They were now walking down Whitehall: on their right a pornographic farce was playing to a packed house on this perfect spring afternoon—Oh to be in England—while on their left the massy mausoleum of ministerial offices administered away, enscripting Britain into a legislative maze apparently as complicated as that which was spun out from the Escorial when the Spanish Empire declined and fell: farther down, on the right, two soldiers in scarlet and white with plumes in their hats confronted an inordinately large gathering of amateur photographers as they stood guard —over what? A last full stop for the Empire. And out of all the imperial past came—the Pop Star.

Merlin Raven. Life like a fairy story. Brought up in an orphanage in Widnes: "everybody" in the U.K. and the U.S.A. knew the songs about Widnes: ran away to sea. Jumped ship in Panama—bummed around America like a late beat—and that journey too was eventually turned into songs. Taken up by an austere poet in New England who educated him, loved him and, when Raven left with a woman, broke down into drink and remorse. Then Raven came to Liverpool, formed a group, let loose his songs and became one of the biggest Superstars in the Business. "Thus Spake The Raven", his first L.P., sold nine million copies and the others almost matched that. His wealth was estimated between ten and thirty million pounds. His name was associated now with poets, now with minor royalty, now with the drug-bug clique, now with a woman, now with a man: but, despite the publicity, he managed to retain an elusive quality. The associations which were said to be certain often turned out to be nothing but rumour; those who claimed friendship were discovered to have no more knowledge than a passing acquaintance; the glamorous jet cum arts cum smart set he was

93

alleged to inhabit rarely saw him. And so an alternative legend grew up, alongside the plodding mass-media descriptions. In this, Merlin was a strange loner; someone who could walk out and put on a false beard and hitch a lift coast to coast; a man who sought out pals from the past and spent days with them just around the place, the pub, the streets, the cafés; someone who wrote and rewrote his songs and was working on a play or a script or a book . . . There had been a massive charity concert in Newcastle. Tens of thousands of fans had come to the football ground to hear him. Fights had broken out. Two teenage girls were stabbed to death. Raven had disappeared.

"Two years ago, wasn't it?" Douglas said. "Then—there was talk of a Greek island of course: and the Coast—of course. He hasn't done anything—released anything—since that concert. Lester knew him."

Wainwright knew about Lester.

"He claims he met him and even managed him for a while in Liverpool. Then lost him. Of course."

"Would he know where Raven is?"

"Are you really interested?"

"Yes."

"Another documentary on another pop star?"

"Raven's spoken to no one since the early days."

"When he spoke to everyone."

"He's interesting. He goes his own way."

They had reached the bottom of Whitehall and turned left to face Westminster Bridge. The day glittered more and more brightly: the row of tacky souvenir shops seemed cheerful: the Gothic pile where legislators sat and stood and ate and drank and talked and shouted and often made sense, that again seemed cheerful enough, as if it had been given a polish by the sun; one or two policemen stood about rather like Gilbert and Sullivan characters, aimlessly waiting to be prompted into song; the steady traffic was reassuring in its evidence of movement, even of industry.

"I enjoyed that lunch," Douglas said.

"Do a film on Raven," Wainwright said.

"Why?"

"He's worth it. You need the work. The film could be good."

"Regionalism, Mike: regionalism. The coming and going thing. Back to the Seven Kingdoms. Bring on the churls."

"Next year."

"I'll see."

"What are you thinking about?" Wainwright asked him and there was, in the unexpectedness of the question—unexpected, that is, from someone he knew so well and with whom he had been talking for two to three hours—something that forced Douglas to focus on the answer. But first he stalled for time.

"Why do you ask?"

"I've had the impression that your mind has been fixed on something else all the time we've been talking. It was as if you'd turned on an automatic pilot: the words came out, but you weren't there."

Douglas considered this carefully, not so much in order to counter it or answer it but because he scented that there was a much more important question or statement which this query was masking.

"Anything wrong?"

"Oh, that." Douglas laughed. "You worry too much, Mike. Everything's wrong and nothing is. The usual."

"Mary?"

"Fine."

"Drink."

"Under control."

"Writing?"

"Is this my ten-year test?"

"Don't you need one?"

"Why?"

"You're in a mess, aren't you? You can't focus on anything. You've talked to me endlessly without once seeming to me to understand there were two people there. Now you're headed off—for what? I can guess. Why? I can't guess that. You're sliding away somehow, Douglas: nothing matters enough to you. I'm worried."

"Save it for a worthier cause."

"Are you still fooling around?"

"I've never talked about any of that, Mike. Why do you ask?"

95

"Because I care about you. When I first knew you, you had a lot of optimism and balls: you didn't say so, but you were going to do your best, attempt great things, take on the world, make a mark: you had all that innocence and wide-eyed power that fools take for foolish naïveté. Now look at you."

"Yes."

Wainwright paused: and then did not resume. Douglas felt the sting on his cheeks of alcohol coming out to meet the sun. It was time to go.

They had walked onto Westminster Bridge and leaned against the parapet. Behind them Westminster Pier and the river boats, already taking trippers down past the city and the Tower and the awesomely derelict wasteland of warehouses to the spacious symmetries of Greenwich: before them Millbank Tower, glittering greenly in the sun, and the domestic skyline following the river to the vast parks and commons around the west of London.

"When I first came to London I got up at dawn just to be on this bridge at the time of Wordsworth's poem," Douglas said. He smiled ruefully: the whole telling was in some way suspect, he thought, smacking of the Innocent Abroad or the traditional Provincial Up For The Day To The Big City: yet what he said was true. "Just to be here when he was. 'Earth has not anything to show more fair'—I recited it. 'Dull would he be of soul who could pass by'. I stood—smack in the middle looking towards St Paul's. 'Ships, Domes, Towers, Temples'—did I get the order wrong there? Why should you know? And I recited it." He paused and then looked keenly at Wainwright, met, as often, by the calm force of the older man's interested and experienced look, aware that he was being shepherded and resenting having to acknowledge it. "And I remember—very clearly—that I felt brimful of pleasure—all sorts of pleasures—I cannot imagine what that sort of happiness is like any more. 'Open to the earth and to the sky'. You see, I have to be half-drunk, prepared to embarrass myself and be with some-body like you—no—*specifically* you, to use those lines or refer to that occasion. Anyway." Douglas made a last effort to make sense of it for himself and to somehow include it in the exchange he had been having with Mike. "The point is that I am certain

96

that there will be no more times like that and that was a very good time."

"You'll talk yourself into something you'll regret," Wainwright said. "Age. Responsibility. Tiredness. Limitations. Drink. Guilt. Slows you down."

Douglas wanted to reach out and grasp Wainwright by the hand, he wanted to tell him, not that he agreed with him, but that there was something he was thankful for: but that instinct was checked by an apprehension which he could not articulate. And so the moment passed by and the two men turned to look down the river, like two sailors looking out to sea from a boat.

"There's a story I'm working on," Douglas said. "I think that matters. I was at it all morning. I won't be able to do any more today but it goes on in my head and while we've been talking I've been making notes about certain words that are wrong, particular sentences I want to re-write. I suppose that's been ticking away. I hope it has."

"Call me," Wainwright said. "Look after yourself."

The men nodded to each other. Wainwright left. As he walked away, Douglas as it were realized him as a physical presence for the first time. What Wainwright had said was true: while they had been talking he had not "noticed" him: taken no care of what his friend was wearing or how he looked. It was true. He was sinking inside this metropolis. He felt a sudden lurch of gratitude towards Wainwright for caring so much: he wanted to run after him. But . . .

So. To what was left of the day. (a) Listen to his friend be sturdy and admirable in Parliament. Then (b) go to see a film producer, a cockney who had gone to Hollywood and reputedly made a fortune, but still managed to owe money to several of those who had trustingly worked with him in the old days when there was idealism and "the great adventure of making a British Movie". Douglas was owed £2,500 and was going to attempt to beard him: he had heard he was back in London, installed, inevitably, in the Dorchester. Then (c) he would go and see Hilda. This would be melancholy. All the excitement, indeed the furore of the affair was over, but they still needed to see each other regularly, perhaps for some sort of reassurance or perhaps because they still had some hope—or perhaps out of habit. For

97

whatever reason, he would go there and be under strain: be polite, think of Mary, feel guilty as a choirboy stealing altar wine, fumble around and then, perhaps, miraculously, discover a true feeling set alight or rekindled. Then (d) he would creep home and lie and lie again.

As he went along the railings to the Houses of Parliament, he described himself and tried to work out a story line on his future.

A rather drunk, rather untidy, no-longer-young man, unwilling to face up to Great Issues, unable to devote himself to Profound Issues, distrusting both: unbelievably luckily married and slowly screwing that up, despite a clear preference for monogamy; likewise poisoning other drops of good fortune which had come his way. And someone sucked into a weary acceptance of all this, or determined to test the strength/weakness of his position, unable to summon up the moral energy to rectify these faults, or unwilling. Unwilling or unable, often, to accept them as faults, although they were disabling. But nothing was anybody's fault any longer, was it? He went down the cold corridor of busts and into the lobby of Parliament. "The child of God cannot sin." Right? And if God were dead then the very concept of sin was destroyed. Either way it was nobody's fault any more.

Inside the Gothic pile the democratic process continued: and Jack, Douglas' friend, a not-so-young man who had given up hundreds of nights to work for his party and to help and as he saw it educate and politicize people, a man who had left a safe job with a pension and gone through a rather dirty bye-election campaign, someone who was truly pained at the lack of time he could devote to his family but had decided, after a lot of thought and a lot of discussion with his wife, to do what he thought right and help the community, got to his feet, glanced nervously at his proud parents in the gallery, nodded at Douglas, who came in at that precise moment, as if on cue, and began his maiden speech.

(4)

And all the day, the story of Alan throbbed inside his skull. On the streets of London he found himself slipping into the patch

98

of woodland in which the man had gone to his end—willingly? Hopelessly? Or—as Douglas believed—in order to find some order, some satisfaction in life, some connection with his beginnings, a shape, and release the pain and drag of the past. The gauzy oil fumes of the city gave way to the sweaty tang of sodden leaves. The buildings would dissolve and he would see the disordered ranks of beech and spruce and pine. The noise would cease and he would hear—most of all—the remorseless sound of the man's feet trudging through the undergrowth, moving, seeking, ill, and yet, in Douglas' story, perhaps within sight of an illumination which might, might just, be some compensation for the compacted miseries of a life meaninglessly blocked, uselessly unheeded, brutally unused. For, in Douglas' story and in Douglas' memory of the man, there had been a pure love of scholarship in him and a clear, easy, unstrained talent which had been sunk in the psychological and social confusions and limitations which came upon him as an adolescent. Waste, waste. Yet, careful: no propaganda. Just the man, the story, the words, the weather, scraps of knowledge rising from old text-books, warming his mind, lines from Virgil, theorems, a sudden scroll of dates from English history, quotations from the Bible. And not a mile away was the road, buses, cars, the bustle, the business, the real world. Real.

Douglas was now in the grip of this man. However exaggerated that might seem, the fact was that the man drew him on. He dreamt of him. His story was the most consistent thing in Douglas' present life. Of course, marriage, earning a living and so on—these—in their crucial phases—were more important: but, as far as his thoughts went, they centred now far away from London, in that lonely strip of woodland, with a young man walking to his death.

# 4
# Three Women

It had taken her more than a month. That is, a month of active searching. Before then, she had waited and hoped. She had taken herself to pubs which she and Lester had used and once or twice she had been to the Marquee in Wardour Street in Soho, when there were groups in which she thought Lester might have an interest. She had never encountered him.

Emma knew so little about Lester's daily routine. He had come into her life out of this city, out of the provinces, out of a class and background as strange to her as hers was to him. They had made contact a few times and then he had gone away, back into the anonymous metropolis, perfectly camouflaged by the crowd. He was not the sort of man to be in a telephone directory or to have a regular job or even to have regular haunts for long. He had once had a pad in Queensway. She remembered him saying that—"pad" sounded grand. Emma had never been allowed to visit him there. But that was where she began her search, hopefully walking about the area after work, after dark, peering in restaurants, slowly dragging her feet past the acres of grand town houses now converted into flats or bed-sitters. Where once the Imperial English rich had reigned, a cosmopolitan pot-pourri teemed in all-mod-cons warrens. The colonialists had been colonialized. Occasionally she went into a pub, well protected by her pregnancy. As she grew bolder, or more desperate, she began to ask around. Again, her pregnancy induced civility.

It had changed her. Curiously, in the four months in which she had carried the child, she had lost weight. The wodges of puppy fat which had outstayed their time had almost entirely disappeared. She was still firmly built but those pouches of fleshly self-indulgence were also gone, replaced by a purposeful ripeness, an attractive fullness of body. Even the life-long double chin was vanishing, and, with her hair drawn back neatly in the Emily Brontë style affected by many of her artistic contemporaries, her face had a shapeliness never before revealed. Even more curiously, she felt healthier; lighter on her feet, less lethargic, stronger. She drank less. She walked to and from the job she had found. She was a receptionist in a newly opened Information Centre, which served part of the City of London. It had been set up at considerable public expense and in considerable style. Very few people used it and the staff spent a lot of time inventing ways to become essential to the community which, they all admitted, did not really exist. Emma, who found she could regain her poise in such a do-gooder outfit, observed it all with a certain amusement and sat comfortably in her swivel leather armchair behind a teak-topped reception desk, catching up with her reading. Her back was supported by a plump purple cushion bought her by the staff to celebrate (and/or commiserate with) her "condition". She read the classics.

That was the feature of her new life. She had reverted towards the type of person her parents had always expected her to be. She was neat—the room in Kentish Town was now barrack-room bright; she was conscientious—in her visits to the doctor, her care over dosages, her attention to the job which, though easy, indeed nearly a sinecure, was yet proof of a disdain for the lack of responsibility in her earlier life. She read more, and inside her mind she was calm and determined. For the first time in her life she had a single definite goal which she was going to attain.

All this was duly noted by her friends from the theatrical world, that gang of hangers-on, of whom she had been one. It was a desperately cheerful flotsam which had sustained itself throughout endless work-droughts with stalls in antique markets, interior decorating, odd-jobbing, waiting on, not unlike the unemployed baggage train of an unextended mediaeval army, scouring the place for sustenance, longing for an engagement. She became known as "the vicar's daughter". A fine irony, they all thought. Irony was a word they relished: most things in their theatrical half-lives were "ironic".

A sweet earnestness replaced the defensive jokiness which had been her habitual expression. When caught reading a classic she would hear herself explain, "I'm thick, I have to catch up. Anyway, George Eliot's *good*." When friends stepped into her stunningly tidy flat, she would say, "It's not because I'm a fetishist or anything. It just makes it all less boring if you know where things are." When complimented on how well she looked, she would reply "Pregnancy's good for you. Like Guinness." And they would all laugh.

But these achievements, and the future she felt within her, were little compared with the love she had for Lester. She was now absolutely certain of that and nothing would budge her. The constancy of this affection was the foundation of her life. She respected herself through this love. It was extraordinarily (though not unusually) humble. She did not expect Lester to feel the same way about her.

She had no hope of marriage and little hope of living together for more than the odd few days here and there. She could see clearly Lester's shortcomings and, in one part of her, even deplore his faults. None of this had the slightest effect on what was now settled and resolved in her mind as her constant love. She was even, in one way, proud that she did not want this feeling analysed and that it resisted explanation: she wanted it to be a grand passion—something which existed "in itself"—the phrases came back to her from the romantic novels she had raced through under the sheets in the dormitory of her mean boarding school—"beyond reason", "came from where she would never know", "a love that would never die", "a love born to live forever". And indeed, it was all true.

Slowly across the metropolis she moved towards him. There was little panic—and then only momentary— for she felt certain that she would see him to tell him what had to be said. Only for one fortnight was she thrown, and that was when she returned from an evening in Queensway to a message from the old lady downstairs that "Your young man's been and gone. Didn't want a cup of tea. Didn't say when he'd be back." A few questions confirmed that it had been Lester. She stayed in for the next dozen nights, to be there, in case. But he did not turn up again.

She met someone she recognized as an acquaintance of Lester's, although at first the man denied all knowledge of him. Emma's vicarage look was again a help, though: the man thought she was some sort of social worker and passed on the possible location. It was a drinking club. She found a café just across the road and watched it as she sipped very milky coffee and occasionally risked glances at her novel—"The Mill On The Floss". A novel accompanied her at all times now, like a bible. Still, though, she did not see Lester and it was another acquaintance who gave her another address—just east of Soho—she could walk to it from her office, which she did, that afternoon, taking off a half-day.

It was a strip club. Hard core, specialist, nasty. To get to it you first went into a pornographic bookshop and either intimated your inclination to the manager or, if he thought you "safe", were approached by him and led through to the back where a couple of dozen wooden chairs, in rows of four, faced a minute stage. Curtainless, undecorated, bleak, the whole room was as camouflaged and conspiratorial as a clandestine chapel.

Emma finished her second tour of the shelves in the main shop, wincing a little at the hectoring, full-frontal display of bared breasts, bushy vaginas, rubbed nipples, splayed thighs, limp cocks, gaudy undies, whips, masks, other expensive sexual aids and ejaculative exclamations. All wrapped up in cellophane. Not to be dirtied by hand that would not pay the price.

The man, who prided himself on being good at "not-looking"—he had to be: many of his nervous customers probably suspected (rightly, as it happened) that he was a criminal, a pimp and a rough-house merchant—now turned his gaze on her and picked his teeth carefully with a match. He, too, thought she must be a social worker. You had to be careful. The police could be paid off: these do-gooders could be trouble.

"You writin' a book?"

His voice, sudden and loud in the empty shop, startled her. She had expected Lester to be working in the shop. She did not know of the existence of the strip club through the door marked Emergency Exit.

"What sort of book?"

"I thought you looked that type."

He took out the matchstick and tried his gruesome "come on" smile.

"No, I'm not."

"Sometimes you can tell. What people do. From the way, you know, they, you know ..." The smile finished the sentence. Emma felt constrained to return it. As soon as she did so, his expression changed.

"So what do you want, lady?"

"I was just looking around."

"No you wasn't."

Clearly, she had been. On the other hand, he was right. Emma would have buckled under in the face of such a dilemma only a few months before. Now, however, the resolution seemed clear.

"I'm looking for Lester Tallentire."

"Are you?"

He waited. She could be looking for Lester for a hundred and one reasons, a hundred of which would be unacceptable to Lester. The man moved the match from his left hand to his right and gouged it into his molars. Above him, a blue plastic sign went on and off, advertising a rubber penis.

"I'm a friend of his."

"I see."

"Does he—work here?"

"You're a friend of his. You should know where he works, lady, you know what I mean?"

"We've got out of touch."

"I see."

"How can I convince you?"

"What of, lady?"

"I could wait, I suppose, just wait here until he came."

"You can't hang about without buying anything."

"Is it illegal?"

"You can't do it, that's all."

"I see." Unintentionally Emma echoed his tone and smiled. Which made things worse.

"You'll have to go, lady." He stood up. He was very big.

"Please tell me where he is. He won't mind, I promise you."

"You'll have to go, lady." He moved towards her, deliberately menacing. She felt a clutch of alarm in her stomach and instantly, fearing for the child, retreated.

"That's a good girl," he said.

He watched her go out. He came to the door and he supervised her as she walked along the street. A couple of men went into the shop and only then did he leave her be.

She walked up and down, keeping her distance, for about twenty minutes. During that time nine men went into the shop. None came out. Just before five o'clock, Lester arrived—from the other end of the street. She shouted. He turned to her. She was sure he recognized her. She waved and began to run. He went into the shop.

It was empty but for the man. Only now there was rock music coming from another room.

"He said he'd see you after, you know what I mean."

Now that he knew what was what, the man had lost interest. It was an effort for him to look up from the Greyhound edition of the "Evening Standard".

"Where is he?"

"Working."

"Working?"

"S'what I said, lady. Working. Now then—hop it—don't crowd the place out."

The music stopped and she heard a few thoughtful handclaps—as at a village cricket match.

"How long will he be?"

The man looked up, and with cruel insight jabbed as hard as he could into this relationship which was obscure to him.

"Depends how long it takes, don't it? You oughta know that. Scram."

Outside she leaned against the wall and breathed slowly, counting to ten, while she inhaled, holding it and then exhaling just as slowly.

Eventually the men popped out, one by one, like parachutists taking their turn to jump, and each one moved away smartly, shoulders back, brisk and even military in bearing. Lester came out with a couple of girls. One of them left him, the other took Lester's arm and wrapped it around her own. She was rather under-nourished, disturbingly white faced and wore a chestnut wig which had slid slightly to the left. Emma took the initiative when she saw that Lester was about to slip from embarrassment into surliness.

"Hello, Lester." To the girl she said, "Hello." Unexpectedly, the girl smiled warmly and nodded. "We generally get a cup of tea at Alf's," the girl said, "and a sandwich. To build us up." She giggled. "I like that dress."

It was a sweet gesture. Emma's dress was a painfully plain folksey brown smock, picked up in a superior Oxfam shop.

"Thank you."

Although the sun was hot, the girl shivered and clutched Lester's arm even more tightly. "C'mon then, darlin'. Tea and a sandwich."

Lester nodded.

They went to Alf's, a small sandwich bar on the edge of Soho. It was as narrow as a railway compartment and about as long as a bus. Big Maltese Alf filled half the space behind his counter, which was piled high with sandwiches, biscuits and fruit cake. All wrapped in cellophane—like the dirty magazines, Emma thought. The girl ordered and tactfully left Lester and Emma alone for a few minutes, insisting that she would "bring it over". Emma could see that Lester felt humiliated and her pity momentarily overwhelmed her. She reached out and squeezed his hand. He withdrew it, sharply, and looked at her antagonistically.

"So what do you want?"

"Nothing."

"You've been following me around for weeks."

"Yes."

"So?"

He leaned back to give himself poise. But his aggression was false. Emma saw that he was miserably down on his luck and all she could do would make it worse. Alf was methodically stacking the sandwiches on the plate. There was no point in trying to win Lester back or do anything but deliver her message. But she could not resist an attempt to restore old ties through gossip.

"I was beginning to think you'd gone back to the Midlands—with those rich beaglers—do you call then beaglers? —the huntsmen you took up with in Cumbria over the New

Year—you told me about them. They were very rich, you said. One of them wanted to set you up in your own business . . ."

"He turned out to be a bastard. Like everybody else." Lester lit a cigarette and the action made his face appear gaunt. She knew how successfully he had so far managed to dodge his way through even the most desperate circumstances. He would never tell her what had driven him to this, she thought—but, as if he read her mind—and as proof to Emma for lonely weeks afterwards that there really *was* "something special" between Lester and herself—he said, abruptly, "He fucked me up rotten. I have a lot of debts. I pay them off by the week. It's cash they want."

She nodded and with an effort resisted the recurrent desire to reach out and comfort this forlorn and hapless man she loved so much.

The girl was now glancing over to them—the tray being laid by Alf was almost complete. Emma took a deep breath. She had to keep her voice neutral: she remembered that just in time.

"I just want you to know this, Lester. It is—the baby— yours. You see, there wasn't anybody else after you. After we did it. Or in the months before. I only pretended I'd had lots of men. I hadn't. After you I didn't want anybody else. No. Please. I want you to know. And I'm happy. Everything's fine. I'm having it. I'm living in the same flat. And you'll always be welcome there. Always." She paused and made the final effort, which was to subdue her tears.

"Tea up," the girl said. "I got corned beef and tomato."

Emma felt weak and shaken. She took the thick white mug of tea between her hands and warmed herself. Her throat grew constricted at the thought of a sandwich and it lay across the small white cardboard plate, its wrapping undisturbed, gaping at the mouth with ripe red tomato.

The girl was pleasant and chatty. Either she was used to gossiping away the times or she sensed the difficulties between Emma and Lester and talked in order to help: either way, Emma was grateful. She wanted to ask the girl's name but that moment had passed. Lester, she thought, was merely glum.

She was wrong about that, as she discovered when she made

her excuses and left. For he followed her, promptly. They walked together in silence a little way down the Charing Cross Road, already lit with street lights. At the gap between the two buildings of Foyle's, he took her arm and led her towards the archway into Greek Street. He stopped after a few yards and while she waited for him to speak she looked at the windows full of books. New novels: none of which she had read.

"So it's mine," he said, over her shoulder. She saw his reflection in the window, among the glossy books.

"Yes, it is, Lester."

"I'm supposed to have another one or two around the place, you know." This pathetic boast only served to stir her sympathy the more.

"You told me. But you said you couldn't be sure." She turned to face him.

"You can never be sure."

"This time you can." Emma was afraid to say any more: he stood there so tensely: like a hare just before it gallops away. Thin and fit as a hare, too, she thought: too thin though.

"I might ..." He paused and took in her loving glance: he dropped the lie. "I'm no good for you."

"I think you are."

"Not me. Not my sort. I couldn't settle down. I couldn't put up with all that—not me."

"Are you sure?"

"You know me."

"I don't. Not enough. I think you might like to settle down."

"What sort of job? In a factory like the peasants back home?"

"You said you'd enjoyed it in Cumbria at Christmas."

"Only because I knew I was getting out in a week. It's desperate up there."

"Are you happy?" Her confidence was now building up rapidly. Lester shook his head: not in answer but in disapproval. She had trespassed on the area he held to be inviolate: his feelings. He took out a wallet and handed her three five-pound notes.

"I'm a bit short or I'd give you a bit more."

"You needn't ... I ... thank you."

108

Her gratitude came just in time and helped him rediscover something, an echo, of his old swagger.

"I might drop in from time to time. Don't count on it."

"O.K." She would not cry, she said to herself, very firmly. She would not lose him that easily.

"Take care," he said, lightly. He looked around as if he wanted to make sure he was not being followed and left her.

She watched him to the corner—too short a distance for her want to see him as long as she could. She felt the three five-pound notes in her hand and squeezed them in her palm. She would put them towards a cot for the child.

## (2)

For John's sake, Mary tried hard not to appear to be afraid, but her apprehension was transmitted to the boy despite herself and he held her hand very tightly.

She had been there often enough before. No one had ever molested her. There had been nothing but kindness shown to the attractive white woman who brought her little boy to the illiteracy classes.

The Inner London Education Authority had introduced night-classes for those who could neither read nor write. Those fell broadly into two groups: the middle-aged immigrants who had first arrived in London after school-leaving age and never received an education in English, and the teenagers who had slid through the school system without picking up any proper knowledge of the language. There were about a dozen in Mary's class, the oldest a Jamaican—Fairbright Anderson was his name—in his late fifties, who reminded Mary of the Uncle Tom in her childhood illustrated version of that book; the youngest, a flash Barbadian, Alan—"El-Al" he called himself—of sixteen, who wore a butcher-boy cap and wanted to get "really into it, now, Miss, this education bit". Between them were two Indians, three Pakistanis, two Moroccans, a Nigerian and two other Jamaicans, one of whom was a telephone operator. He had conned his way into the job and "remembered" the connection between name and number on his board by a network of tricks and bluffs which he was delighted to explain to anyone who wanted to listen. Unfortunately the firm was expanding and his nerve was giving way. Mary, whom he regarded with a doggy affection which embarrassed her, had a particularly difficult time with him, as it was impossible at first to break him of the habit of finding a way to memorize the words without actually being able to read the letters or spell it out. His system was so highly developed that it was uncanny at times. It had taken her all the first term to make him realize what he was doing: now, towards the end of the second term, he was beginning to put the letters together, one by one, and, most important of all, Mary thought, he was starting to think that it was a smart thing to do.

There was great satisfaction for Mary in this voluntary work.

John, too, seemed to gain a lot from it. She had taken him along once or twice at first simply because there was no way to solve the baby-sitting problem. Douglas had been in—as he had promised—for the first few weeks and then he had been away filming. Reluctantly she had taken John with her—but he had enjoyed it instantly. Instead of feeling patronized, as Mary had feared, the group were delighted to see her son and (she suspected) they liked her more because she trusted them enough to bring in her child. The marvellous thing, though, from Mary's point of view, was that John was a help. He would sit quietly beside one of the class and talk away, drawing the letters, bringing his own recent learning to bear, often more effective than Mary herself. Soon they would compete to have him sitting beside them. And, accordingly, he bloomed. Mary brought him every time now. She was frightened that she was losing touch with her son, frightened that the strain between Douglas and herself would damage the boy, over-anxious about John's silences and capacity for isolating himself, troubled by the conflicting loyalties of her own life, her husband and her son. To see him happily employed was a great comfort.

She was not a timid woman and yet as they walked along these decomposing west London streets, she was as apprehensive as a scared child in a dark wood. She had taken her washing to the launderette, asked the woman to see it through for her and then, because the night was bright and cold and clear, she had decided to walk to the school in which the night-class was held.

She kept a steady pace so as not to encourage her panic. On one side were the houses: on the other, a corrugated iron fence which protected the railway. The fence bore scores of posters—every one ripped or defaced.

Mary looked down at John's small white face. (Why did it look so under-nourished?) Was this concrete, brick and litter all that she could give to her son? What effect was it having on him, she worried, as he walked under pale lighting, the world tinged with orange. What would he know about life, about the cycle of nature, about things that grew and unfolded, bloomed, gave fruit, stayed awhile and then died to be reborn? In her good moments she thought that the cosmopolitan zest of London life was a fair substitute; in her realistic moments she thought that—well, life will become, increasingly, city life and so he might as well get used to it; but at times like this all she wanted to do was to follow her deepest instincts and run away.

John's hand tightened on her own and he looked up, carefully. He said nothing. She wished he had not grown to be so firmly in control of himself and his emotions. She glanced back and noted again that a couple of men were still following them; about sixty or seventy yards back, dim under the weak street lighting, but steadily walking along this lonely road—behind them. It was final proof, she thought later, of her tiredness and tension that her heart instantly did a sickening somersault. She almost stumbled and when a man came unsteadily out of a side street and bumped into John, she snatched the boy to her as if he were in danger of being kidnapped. She broke into a run and then stopped, counted to ten, walked on. Looked back. The two men were still there.

Walking faster now, she turned into her badly lit side street and faced a totally empty vista. Half-demolished houses to the left; half-completed flats to the right: the only bright spot a big notice which read DANGER: GUARD DOGS.

She thought of asking John to glance back, but his set face dissuaded her. He had caught her fear and all his effort was bent to controlling it.

Her throat was strained with nervousness but she decided

III

that she must not run. The men drew nearer, walking more quickly than ever; John edged closer to her. But she stood her ground.

They came up.

They glanced at her, deliberately, and then moved even more rapidly and broke into a race for the pub, laughing and jostling each other. One of them shouted, "Cock a doodle do!"

Mary was shaking.

"The school's that way." John pointed it out, urgently. A lit-up refuge.

She clutched him to her, tightly, for a moment and then went in.

(3)

As he lay asleep beside her, Hilda stilled her restlessness by going over in her mind what had just happened between them. Sex was like unwrapping a secret present, she thought, knowing there would be pleasure, knowing it would be unlike anything else.

Even to herself she was shy of recollecting the details and yet she wanted to go over each moment, to be able to luxuriate in them in the voluptuous knowledge that Douglas was beside her. She was completely in love with him, as she had never been with anyone else—this she had told him solemnly and earnestly —but she could not put into words the "rightness" she felt about Douglas.

Hilda lived alone in a small basement flat in South London. She was, to a month, the same age as Mary. Douglas recognized much about her background and admired the way in which she had worked her way out of it without repudiating it. Her family had been very large, very poor and at war with each other. Deprivation, a thin gruel of affection, illness, broken schooling, neglect, a world of indifference: she had landed in the labour market aged fifteen, withdrawn, upset, unwell, barely educated and, as a result of yet another painful and abrupt parental move around the Midlands, isolated. Yet within her, not buried quite and always flickering, however feebly, was a self-generated sense of the fun of life. You could see it in the sly peeps of

112

amusement with which she regarded the pompous and the bullying and the bureaucratic—many of those who ruled over her early working life in cold offices, sandwiches in the drawer.

Slowly she had built a life for herself. Gone to night-school and then taken a correspondence course, taken herself abroad, gone to museums, caught onto learning at its fringes and held on tight.

This had taken up her twenties. By the end of them she had re-created herself. She had got an interesting job at the British Film Institute, where she could do research as well as earn her keep by her designated job, which was still that of an "assistant"—or a superior typist. The energy she had put into constructing a life for herself had left little over for the manipulation of a career.

In her emotional life she had been unlucky. Her looks were fine rather than obvious—the blonde hair, the pale grey eyes, the shy walk. There had been one real love affair and she had spoiled it by asking too much from it. All the excuses were good ones: she was too young, she was extraordinarily nervous about committing herself, he was too young, he was unsure, he was not interested in music or books or paintings, as she increasingly was. She had mourned him for three years: pride had stopped her going back to him although she had wanted to do so several times. When she heard, eventually, that he had married, she felt sick to her stomach. Since then there had been a number of boyfriends but only one affair.

Hilda was not promiscuous. But nor was she puritanical. What she believed in was not sex or success or serenity or money or even marriage—but Love. What she wanted was a single great love which could be served by her and could be the nucleus of her life. It was her misfortune to fall in love with Douglas. It was made intolerable by the fact that he had fallen in love with her. Yet now, she knew, he wanted to get out of it.

Any time she wanted she could remember the stages of this love and, in the bed, curtains open, bright late-winter moonlight whitening his skin, she traced her fingers up and down his spine and, to comfort herself, recalled what had passed between them.

At first very little—for a long time—for almost two years.

Douglas had been in and out of the film offices proposing or completing various projects. They had exchanged some words, some glances, nothing more. Once, after an office party into which he had strayed, half-drunk and by accident, with someone with whom he was having a bitter row, he had made a clumsy pass at her. The rebuff had been accepted instantly. He had telephoned to apologize the next morning.

Then she recalled, taking it carefully out of her mind, opening it slowly, the time when they had declared themselves. In a small café, where they had gone for a cup of tea, after he had done a long day's editing and she had typed up the transcripts. They had caught each other's look. He had taken her hand, held it, and it was as if her life, all she had, went from her body into his and then returned, accompanied by his love. She also remembered, although it always gave her pain—but she was strict with herself—his first words after that silent communion.

"It's no good," he said: but he did not let go of her hand.

"I agree," she had replied, hearing this voice so familiar to her speaking brightly, even chirpily, above the numbing force and pull of her feelings. "It's hopeless," she had added, and yet she had to smile.

"Hopeless."

"So let's go no further," he said. He too was smiling. But they were not joking.

"My point exactly," she said.

Still he held her hand. They beamed at each other.

"Stupid, isn't it?"

"Very stupid. Very stupid indeed." She paused and took away her hand. "But one of the things I will not do is to have anything to do with a married man. I've seen my friends get too hurt that way."

"And I've seen my friends screw up their lives."

"Maybe our friends know each other," she said.

"So. No-go?"

"That rhymed."

"Speak Chinese fruentlee."

"I knew you were clever."

"You're lovely."

Again she felt herself wanting to rest in him, to give herself—all the clichés, all the truisms, all the truth. She felt that she had found whom she had been looking for. That the journey from overcrowded, over-hurtful, rejected and anonymous life had been aimed at this—unknown until now, but now revealed. And he was unobtainable. "You're lovely," he repeated.

"You musn't say that," she said, grimly. She pretended to busy herself. "You musn't say that."

For more than a year they had left it so. He saw her only occasionally, and then never alone—in the office, in the pub for a quick drink, once at a party. His life went on: hers too. But when they did meet, they knew that a life was waiting for them if they chose to take it.

It was strange. There was no doubt in the minds of either of them. They did not even flirt. What kept them together was as invisible as air. It was, Hilda thought, looking back on it, one of the most perfect times in her life. There was a loving security in it which she had never known before and the knowledge of it would overwhelm her with gratitude, happiness and hope: which she spiked as hard as she could.

She had a boyfriend whose intentions were serious, whose attachment was close, whose affection was genuine. They slept together. What began to happen, though, was that she would imagine he was Douglas. She did not will this on; to the contrary, when it happened she did all she could to beat it away. It was unfair on her lover, unfair on herself and unfair, in its assumptions, on Douglas. Yet it would not be beaten away. She tried to drive it off by the exercise of that willpower which had enabled her to do so much, make so many efforts—but it would not be driven off. She stopped seeing the man for a time. Then resumed: it was worse than ever. She broke off the relationship, to the astonishment of her friends, who had anticipated an engagement or at least an announcement of intent, and to the surprise of the man, who had suddenly lost what he had thought he was sure of, without any explanation which made sense.

Then Hilda was isolated, alone once more as she had so often been. Alone once again in mundane surroundings, in a mundane way. Nothing, she thought, was special about her at all. She did not mind that—but at times she questioned why it had been such a hard struggle for her to achieve the normality so many of her present friends had effortlessly inherited. She rented the tiny flat; the furniture had been in when she arrived and she had added only a few ornaments—any spare money going on books and records. Just living her life took every pound she earned: there were no savings, there was no back-stop, there was no hidden treasure, there would be no inherit-ance. Rather, there would be an increasing responsibility and liability for ageing parents. She did not want much out of the ordinary. A husband, two or three children, adequate pro-vision—she could make do without luxuries, without any frills. She wanted a proper family life with someone she loved. But she loved a man who was committed to another woman.

On an impulse she had eventually sought out Douglas, found him, and said it was about time they got together.

"You know what that means," he said.

"I'll find out."

"You know it can't work."

"Let me be the judge of that. Not just you."

"Tomorrow?"

"Yes."

Both of them, she remembered with an onrush of sweet nostalgia, had been nervous, guilty and at a loss for words. They had gone out to a restaurant in the West End.

"Aren't you afraid of being seen?" she asked, protective and anxious for him.

"I'm not going to skulk about. There'll be enough deceit without that."

The restaurant was overcrowded, over-noisy and they were so placed that any conversation had to be shouted out. After-wards they had walked back to her flat, so reluctantly that, for a while, each had thought of bolting. But they had gone in, then hovered about each other while a cup of coffee was made. A quarter-full whisky bottle was found, music put on: each move was heavily punctuated by silence.

And then, in a cathartic onslaught of self-pity and self-indulgence, but also of confiding honesty, Douglas had told her about the death of his daughter a few years before. Its effect on Mary, on John and on himself.

"And after the first year or two when all the effort went into just keeping us going, when I saw, or thought I saw, that things were at least, at least functioning again—I went berserk. I drank like someone who wanted to poison himself. I would end up drunk in strange beds, alone or not, impotent or not, but betraying Mary. There was something—I'm not proud of it, I'm not trying to excuse it—but something terrible—like a lust for sensation—to have everything—drink, sex—and a licence to roam around the city like someone unfettered. I couldn't get enough of it. All was excused—despite my claim to be without excuses—by the—by her death. Disgraceful. But I must tell you about that. And all the time there were two things—no—more. Firstly, I would try to square this behaviour by trying to fool myself that it was 'all experience', that writers—not just writers—people—anybody with guts—needed to go to the limit. I took seriously—bloody fool that I was!—the idea that unless you were straining yourself and testing yourself and on the edge of destroying yourself, you were not, in a full sense, alive. I fell for that fallacy and acted on it. Of course, all I did was to hurt myself and those I lived with. Then there was the deceit, the lies which became another drug, the inability to stop and rest and build. Finally, the self-loathing, which even began to turn towards the convenient exit of self destruction. And so in the three or four years when I should have been consoling my wife and comforting young John and consolidating my marriage and my work—I blew it. And here you are."

They had made love and it had been as extraordinary then as it always was. Hilda had slept with very few men and rarely found much satisfaction: she had sometimes found excitement; mostly she had to be content with the fact that the act was at least being done; and sometimes it had been terrible.

Douglas was strong, he was sometimes violent, but although she saw him above her, drawing his hands up her legs, stroking her shoulders, kissing her breasts, her belly, her thighs and then clutching her tightly, almost desperately until she felt that she would—she could not put it into words. Not even when he came into her and she, light, ready, felt the thrust going deep—he would stop, sometimes, and stay inside her and touch her until she came, or kiss her gently or, as if in kindness, slowly move her about him so that she moaned out and he whispered her name. It was no good. For it went on, longer than she had known or thought possible, and she would be lifted, turned, thrown, penetrated like a sheath to the hilt and then rocked as in a cradle, while she licked his skin and behind her closed eyes lived in a time outside the time spent. And he would bring her ready before he came—this, too, this wonderful coincidence worked for him—until she was ready, and then he came and she, spread beneath him, felt the cascade and was entirely his.

But what had now become of it?

To ask that question brought Hilda up against a fear which she dared not face. Douglas asked and answered it almost every time they met, forever prevailing on her to expect little, to rely on nothing and to trust him not at all—until she cried out against the injustice and inhumanity of this.

"You say that you want it to be just as it is," Douglas answered her, "and yet you act as if I am entirely at your disposal."

"What do you expect me to do? I love you. You say that you love me."

"I do."

"Well then. I can't just sit and wait. I would like to, but I can't. I want to see you," she said plainly. "What would you think of me if I didn't?"

"But look, Hilda, I have a wife, a son, a family, which I am not going to split up for anyone."

"I know that. You're always telling me that. It doesn't alter the fact that I love you. And you say you love me."

"But I can't give you what you want."

"Nobody else has. You give me more than anybody else. I just want to see you more, that's all."

They made rules. And broke them. They made plans. And broke them. The time they had together was eaten up with regret for the time they did not have together. Lately, they had come to the point of agreeing that each meeting would be as if it were a "one-off". There would be no promises and no recriminations. The affair would have no future.

This filled Hilda with panic. She needed security, she realized, for dear life.

"I'm not complaining," she said. "I'm not blaming you. I'm not blaming me, either. But I just keep saying to myself—why has it got to be so hard? Why couldn't I have met you years ago? I know it's stupid. I know all that. I feel silly saying it, but if I can't say what's on my mind to you—who can I say it to? I love you, that's all."

"And I love you."

But there was a remorselessness in Douglas which led him to reiterate incessantly the uselessness of relying on their love or allowing it to attract any expectations at all. Until, in the end, Hilda had burst into tears and Douglas had to apologize. Yet, within a couple of days, he was once more on that theme.

"What's happening is that I see you more and more, I make excuses, 'practise deceit' as they say, tell lies and perjure myself—and the more I see you the more I want to see you and yet the weight of wrongness just gets heavier. Because I'm never where I should be. When I'm with you I think I should be with Mary: when I'm with Mary I want to be with you. I don't know which of you I'm betraying. Neither of you is happy. Each has every right to think I'm a shit. But that gets me nowhere, because I admit I'm a shit."

"What you're saying is Eternal Mistress or it's over."

"Am I?"

"Yes."

"Oh Christ!"

To both of them it slid between dream and nightmare. For there were times unlike any other: they smuggled themselves away to the coast and walked along the cliffs one day and the next on the downs: the connecting night spent making love greedily. There would be times of calm, of "blessed ordinariness" when they would just read or listen to a record, have a cup of tea, refrain from making love, let it go. They had good moments. But a flick of mood could send them down.

"She wants a child? *I* want a child. I feel that I have as much right to have your child as she has. I understand why you won't leave her—but I still feel rejected. I feel it means you can't *really* love me, but I try very hard to understand. I know you feel

119

loyal. I know that John mustn't be hurt any more. I think he's being hurt far worse by things being as they are, but I've been through all that, you know all that and you've made your decision. But you can't stop me wanting what I want and trying to get it. You *say* you love me. Well then."

"It's possible to love more than one person," he said.

"I don't think so."

"Why not? I love you, I love John, I love Mary, I love my mother, I love two or three of my friends."

"That's different and you know it's different and it's not the point."

"It *is* the point. If only it weren't."

"Not the way I mean it."

"You could call your love, then, just possessive."

"You can call it what you like, it's what I'm stuck with and so are you, or you wouldn't be in such a mess."

"You're a working class heroine, that's your problem. The man said."

"What you are is not polite to say."

"You're a love."

"I don't feel like one."

"You feel nice to me."

"Hands off."

"Private property?"

"Certainly."

It would dwindle into *babillage*, or ride to a climax of tears or loud exits soon repented.

Now he slept. They had enjoyed an unusually long evening. Despite her best intentions, Hilda clocked up the hours spent together and tonight it came to eight. He had arrived just after seven. The producer he had wanted to see had not been there. It was now just past three in the morning. They had gone out to a restaurant—choosing with care, as they always did, to find a place which had what they wanted—"separate tables that really *are* separate" (Douglas)—"plenty of people so you can trust it" (Hilda)—"somewhere new" (Douglas)—"somewhere nice" (Hilda)—"somewhere unexpected" (Douglas)—"somewhere I've just read about" (Hilda)—and they would use this choice to play the unimportant games and enjoy the unimportant arguments which were so soothing and normal. Douglas had insisted on music and they had gone to a place in St. Martin's Lane where a band popped up at ten o'clock. Then they had come back to her place and he had fallen asleep as soon as they had finished making love. She knew she was being selfish in not waking him but she had so little of his time that she ignored that. Besides, the agreement was that you were responsible for what you did, you were fully responsible for your life and dependence was out. Douglas had been fierce about that.

Yet she was a good woman and the thought that she might be getting him into a real difficulty could not be stilled, even by using his own arguments against himself. A great deal of her misery and the twisting moods in her affair was to do with the contradiction between what she thought she ought to be doing and what in fact she was doing. Her conscience pressed against her and there was no avoiding it. None. She was cheating another woman, she knew that, all her declarations were contaminated by that, all her love was shadowed by that and yet all her life was there to be given to the man who brought her to that. She was a willing accomplice. She gave herself no rest. She was doing wrong. There was no way out of it. Her only defence was that she could do no other.

She paused a moment and then kissed him awake. It was almost three thirty. He embraced her as gently as she could have imagined and came inside her so sweetly, she moaned for joy. Afterwards he made no comment about the time, but left, calmly, already inventing his lies, letting it be a good night for her. Stole out like a thief. Waited for a night taxi in the wide streets. The city was a shell now—ready to be taken over. Lights still on in some shop windows. No leaves on the few trees, no animals, the smell of petrol, empty.

The taxi went along the Embankment and swung around an empty Westminster: he saw that the bridge was deserted as it had been those many years ago. What a neat diagram he could draw if he obeyed the impulse to take the taxi to where he had once stood: then, young, he had been innocent, optimistic, full of good feeling, wanting to be useful, to do something worthwhile. Thinking warmly about the world, willing to help put it to rights, and sober. Now—half-cut, tired, corrupted in marriage, aimless, self-centred. Yet such self-criticism began to smack of inverted boasting, he thought—"Look at me! Look how *awful* I am!" It was better than that. His voyage of discovery was destined to be in this windless and mindlocked sea.

The taxi roared to a stop outside his house and the engine kept up its reverberating din, seemingly for hours, while Douglas discovered he did not have enough cash to pay for it. Mary was awake: she handed him her purse and he went downstairs aware that half the street was now disturbed by his late arrival. Paid off, the taxi driver then insisted on doing a difficult and very noisy three-point turn in the narrow street. When he left, the silence was palpable.

## (4)

Mary had put on the kettle for coffee. Douglas went into the living room and switched on the electric heater. The place was chilly. As if he were decorating a set, he closed the curtains, put on the two table lights, knocked off the main light, tidied up the newspapers and puffed up the cushions on the sofa before sitting down and squashing them again. Mary came in with two mugs of Nescafé.

She was in her new dressing gown. She had given him no hint of the name of the donor and, despite his lapses, Douglas still felt secure about her fidelity. He relied on it.

They sipped the steaming coffee carefully. She smoked. Douglas felt a *frisson* of anticipation, almost as if he wanted the worst to happen. Despite himself, he had to admit this, there was a way in which he was looking forward to the quarrel, so far gone was he in his carelessness about such securities as he had. To Hilda he was far more thoughtful, because of the essential fragility of her position. Just as he was prepared to devote enormous care and time and energy to a story which would make him little if any money and bring him little if any success or fame, rather than take up the security of Wainwright's offer of a film. In his own way, he was set on some sort of important test or on a path of self-destruction: it was impossible for him to decipher which.

In the silence, Mary's presence grew stronger and it was as if his eyes were clearing and focusing on her for the first time for ages. She looked strained, older, sadder—no wonder. There was still the loveliness, the translucent patient intelligence, the honesty to what she believed in, but the lustre was going: her hair was even lank. She seemed so infinitely superior to him. Douglas felt himself morally outclassed and was both impressed and resentful.

Mary saw a man she had once loved, now out of reach. Clearly exhausted, white-faced, anxious, apprehensive—but also, and this hurt her much more—set in a wild, exhilarated obstinacy which blocked her out. For she could see that she was not to be admitted to the debate which was ravaging him. The enthusiasm and gaiety she had loved was now no more than a coarse look of boldness; the giving, the way he used to tell her about what he had read, who he had seen, what he thought about anything under the sun—that had dried up. She could accept that time and habit had performed their usual corrosive work. She could accept that love died. She could accept his sense of failure and respect his hopelessness. But she could no longer respect herself unless she confronted him and made him face himself in her mirror vision of him.

It was five o'clock. She lit a second cigarette.

"I suppose I'd better tell you," Douglas said, eventually.

"Yes. I suppose so."

There was a stiffness about them which was weary: outside it was dark and chill, the hour most vulnerable, the hour for unexpected attack. There was no traffic, a dead metropolitan stillness. And on both their faces, in both their bodies, there was a weight of pain which signalled the admission of defeat, the final realization that an end of a line had been reached: unhappiness.

"I don't know how to begin really." Douglas considered: considered the lies he had told over the past four years, the way he had evaded truth while attempting to hold onto the skirts of some approximation to integrity—which meant not much more than maintaining a balance—somehow not offending against the marriage too much, within a system which allowed it to be violated: or rather which *he* allowed could be violated. The moral superiority and inviolability of a faithful marriage was a

123

standard against which everything else was measured. Douglas accepted that: it was the nearest he now had to a religious dogma. Therefore for some years now his life had been a failure, or a succession of failures, and his reaction had been that of a self-acknowledged sinner. Something of the stiffness of a long overdue confession also tinged his attitude now.

"Do I know her?" Mary asked, looking away, always looking away now.

"No."

"That's something."

"Not much. Still. It's serious."

"I know that. I wish you'd told me when it started."

"So do I."

"Why didn't you?"

"I suppose ..." Douglas hesitated: the only thing that mattered now was to tell the truth as faithfully as he possibly could. "Either I was frightened of the row and ducked out: or I wanted to have my cake and eat it: or I wasn't sure enough of her and wanted to let it ride out and see what happened."

"Choose any card." Mary laughed. There was plenty of misery behind her and before her: at this moment she felt a certain relief. "You should have told me. It was cruel and degrading not to."

"I know. But—it would have been like breaking faith, like destroying something."

"You made it far worse by not telling. You destroyed far more."

"We've survived."

"No." Mary felt a sudden lurch of tears and before she could stop it she was crying. Douglas watched her from across the room: he made as if to go across and comfort her but she waved him away. She controlled herself. "We haven't survived. We've changed so that we didn't split up. But it's all a sham. You don't love me, you tell me lies, you can't bear to spend time with John, you drink far too much, you play around with all this freelance business: you're nowhere near the man I married. And what do I do? Fret about you and about John: try to concentrate on teaching which seems to get harder every term: smoke far too much: mark homework, watch an hour's telly, go to bed generally well before you and never touch the piano—never. We use London so little we might as well live in Cornwall—*I* use London so little, that is. You seem to have licensed yourself to rove around like a pirate. What's she like?"

"Do you really . . .?"

"What is she like?"

"About your age."

"That seems a waste."

"She has a decent job, a rotten background and very little else."

"Ah! You can patronize her, can you? You'll enjoy that. And educate her? Did you ever . . . Did you ever—sleep with her and then come back and sleep with me?"

"No." He hesitated and repeated, "No."

"Does she want you to leave me and marry her?"

"Yes."

"Why don't you?"

"I didn't. That's all."

"You mean you needn't. Presumably she's there every time you want her and I'm stuck here. All you get is a bad conscience and all that makes you is bad-tempered to me and John. In fact, because you haven't told me and I'm here all the time like a fool, waiting for you, cooking you meals, washing your clothes, doing the shopping, trying to give our son a hope in life—because I'm here you behave as if I knew—because in a real sense I *did* know—and so you treat me with contempt for apparently accepting your behaviour."

"Well." Douglas was dry-throated. He was cold. And he could see that this was not a passing quarrel: there was in both of them a set purpose to see it through to the end. Whatever that might turn out to be. "If you *knew*—and I accept that—why *did* you put up with it?"

"Because I loved you." Mary looked at him, dry-eyed now. "Or that's what I kept telling myself. I'm not sure now. Not at all."

"I can't blame you."

"You once said you wouldn't mind if I went off and had an affair. Do you remember?"

"I've said a lot of stupid things."

"Why did you say that?"

"Maybe—I wanted us to be more even. After all, couples have mutually agreed to have affairs before now."

"But you hadn't admitted anything then. Did you hope I would do all the work—even that?"

"Yes." Douglas said. "I suppose so."

"And didn't you care?"

"I didn't know where I was."

"That's no excuse. Nor is Anne." Their dead daughter. "You gave up."

"No. I gave in. To something that was more honest than anything gained by holding out. I was trying to be honest."

"And this—woman. Was that honest as well?"

"Yes. It was."

"How many others?"

"For Christ's sake! What is this?"

"So there were others. You needn't answer. But this one—this—woman—why do you protect her so much?"

"Oh for God's sake, Mary. She exists. As a matter of truth I get no more—never mind."

". . . out of her than you get out of me. Poor her. Can't be much fun being a neglected mistress."

"You want a showdown, don't you?"

"I think I do." Mary stubbed out her cigarette and lit up instantly. She felt a lurch and a swoop of physical dizziness. But the decision was made: it had been moulded over years and months and it appeared in her mind—*set*. "Yes. I do."

"I'll make some more coffee," Douglas said. "Would you like a cup?"

"Yes. Thanks."

While he was out of the room, Mary tried to think once again, yet again, of what she had rehearsed so many times. But all she found was the memory of that curious afternoon when Mike Wainwright had brought her the dressing gown. He had met her some months before and, for a reason she still could not fully explain, Mary had found herself telling him about her unhappiness with Douglas. Mike was Douglas' friend, of course: he was also older and therefore a safe repository of confidences, but it was the quality of his sympathy which drew her on. They had begun to meet regularly, chastely, but increasingly confidentially. It was such a relief. There was repose in Mike's interest: there was also, as honesty soon forced her to acknowledge, affection and possible love. But, miraculously, it was neither forced nor strained. When she went to Cumbria for the Christmas period and made her statement to Douglas about having another child, she kept clear of Mike for two or three months afterwards—not from fear of sex—for, even up until now, there had been none, nor any but the most demure tight-lipped kisses—but in order to show to herself how serious she was. Mike did not insist but they had bumped into each other one Saturday afternoon when she was shopping in Oxford Street, trying to find a reasonably good, reasonably priced new raincoat for John, who was with Douglas, on a rare outing, at a football match. Mike had been prepared to pass on but she liked him so much and he, as importantly, gave her the feeling of being liked, likeable, even loveable. With Douglas now she felt a burden, a nag, a spent partner, a drudge dedicated to the maintenance of an obsolete marriage machine. Mike's niceness opened her up like a Chinese paper flower in a bowl of water. They talked. She relaxed. Time passed. She realized suddenly that she had only a few minutes to buy the coat. They rushed into the nearest department store and, while she sorted out her purchase, Mike, uncharacteristically, she thought at first, until she reconsidered it, turned up with this dashing dressing gown. Later she understood. It was a tribute to that particular moment, to the fun of being together, to a certain relapse, for both of them, into a welcome frivolity. She adored it and tucked her legs carefully under its full skirt. It was cold in the room. Douglas brought back two mugs of hot coffee.

"So what do we do?" he asked.

Mary felt the mug almost unbearably hot and her body seemed to grow suddenly colder: he had accepted it. He wanted a separation. He had not fought her at all. She steadied herself. "Well. We should—live apart."

"O.K. I'll move out."

She wanted to ask him where. Where? Where. But it seemed unjust. He was only doing as she asked and making it easy for her, leaving her the place. He could not be harried. "Where to?" she asked, dry-throated.

"Not with her, if that's what you're thinking. I'll get a bedsitter or a flat. Doesn't matter. I'll go up to the cottage for a few days and leave an ad. in the paper. O.K?"

"I think we should keep the cottage," Mary said, helped by having something concrete to discuss, "and sell this place. With the money we got we could just about pay off the cottage and have enough to rent a flat each. I think you need the cottage: and John does: I love it as well."

"Whereas we won't need this desirable maisonette now. Good thinking. Prices are on the up again. It could work out well. Agreed. What else?"

"I thought we'd talk about it."

"It's done. It's been talked about. We've had it in our minds for months and years. All the arguments have happened in bits and pieces here and there. But let's call it a separation."

"Why?" The start of hope in her body and her voice surprised her. "What else would we call it?" she added more sedately.

"A split up. A bust. But, let's wait a bit. For John's sake, if you like. It could work out less messily than we fear. You never can tell."

"What do you think?"

"Not much at the moment, Mary."

The sound of her own name so tenderly spoken stung her to immediate and profound nostalgia.

"What happened?" she asked.

"I don't know." Douglas hesitated. He had no more to say but she deserved more than his bare honesty. "It slid away when we weren't looking. It *was* a lot to do with Anne, whatever you say. And I behaved very badly. There's little forgiveness for that, not really, not when you hurt those you've loved. Then there's all this scrappy, half-arsed way I earn a living and the pressure that puts on you. You deserve a lot better. An older guy, maybe, someone who appreciates how marvellous you are. I can't any more. I can't see you any more—not as you are. You're hidden under a mass of deceits and disguises: it's like a fairy tale where the princess is turned into a monster. The way we've behaved has turned you into someone else in my eyes. You deserve to be seen for what you are and lead the life you *can* lead—decent, ordered, calm, happy—not this. So I don't know. Except that I think that you are right: a separation is what we're ready for. What happened was that I wasn't up to it."

"No, not that. I think you've tried. You've hurt yourself too much not to be respected. I don't think you're a shit, or greedy; and you're not weak—however hard you claim to be—you're the most determined man I've ever met. But you are determined not to make your mind up. You're a romantic, Douglas, I think, without a romantic ideal to serve. 'Love' is the nearest, and one of the reasons you ran out on me was because, inevitably, we ran out of first love. You're adrift, Douglas, but you're trying to find a course and a place. I respect that."

"So what are we doing agreeing to separate?" He paused: so did Mary. But even that reaching out, that touching, could not change what was settled. She did not reply.

"And you know," he said, "two things. While we've been talking. In my head alongside all this—and other things—two things ticking away. One—what a lovely dressing gown. Two—I want to get back to that story I'm writing because I fear it's no good. I think it isn't working."

"Oh Douglas. I'm sorry. But maybe . . ." she stopped. Polite comfort was useless.

"So I'm going up to get on with it," he said. "Take it by surprise. It doesn't expect an attack from me now in my state of mind and at this hour. Perhaps I can get it right. Can I go?"

"Yes."

"Thank you."

He stood up. He was very stiff, very tired and weary—and yet he had had a fresh thought on the story, a notion of where to trim up the development of the man's character, an idea which could restore it. He wanted to be with it.

"I'll leave this evening," he said. "After John's in bed." He paused. "Good idea to sell this place. I'll still keep up the payments to the domestic account, of course." He grinned. "If I've got the loot." Still he could not leave. It seemed that an occasion of such moment demanded more of a "mot", a statement, an acknowledgement of its gravity, a respect for its importance. "Sorry," he said, and went out.

Mary sat on for a while: the night was done. She felt the cold seep into her. Eventually she heard John's alarm clock go off and she stirred herself to begin to prepare breakfast for the three of them.

The argument had been decided long ago. In the careless rebuffs at night, perhaps, or the lack of caress and contact through the day. The lies had rotted the structure—yes—but both were capable of understanding deceits of the flesh. It was their love that had died. The fact and truth and unacceptable banality of that was something they had hid from for years. And both of them, for different reasons, wanted love. A marriage of convenience was, sadly, not enough. So there was this sorrow between them now, a sorrow which, paradoxically, bound them closely. There was this loss, this love, gone; and nothing to do but mourn.

# 5
# Lester's Luck

He came back from Brixton market on the bus, the two carrier bags crammed full, one on each knee, squatting on his lap. When he got off, just before Stockwell Station, he had to hump the two weights—for such they had become—onto a low wall and give himself a rest. Although nobody in the wide blank streets was watching him, Lester took out a cigarette and made a fuss of lighting it in order to disguise his weakness. Spring was under way but the South London sky was still grey, the pavements like a true reflection of the spirits of those hurrying pedestrians who ducked their heads into the wind and left no prints from their thin shoes on the scruffy concrete floor of the city. Lester could not trust the plastic handles of the carrier bags and so he was forced to carry them before him, cradled in his arms, belly height, pregnant with provisions. By the time he reached her flat, having had to walk up to the eighth floor as the lift only worked between the tenth and the twentieth, he was wet with sweat and trembling from the strain.

Fiona was in a worse state. "It's only flu," she had kept saying. Both of them shared a contempt for illness, which was not generally accepted to be "real". But their refusal to yield had only made them tired and finally they had given in to it, lying in Fiona's narrow three-quarter bed in the small flat she had shared with an old friend, Janice, who had taken her in as an act of charity and accepted Lester with the greatest regret and bad grace. Lester returned the loathing. Janice, who worked in a pub, was one of those women who do not seem to be in step with themselves. Her body was large, voluptuous, altogether desirable. And yet, sitting on top of it, like a boyish, startled addition, was a small, cropped head, a face frozen in eager-to-please innocence, an expression totally devoid of

131

sensuality, a look which seemed unaware of the forces so generously assembled below the neck. But she was shrewish and shrewd. Lester described her as a "cock-teaser" and thought no more about her.

To his surprise and gratification, he was wrapped up in Fiona. The starved-looking, cheerful, stringy-haired blonde whom Emma had seen him with had become an object of affection. He was even proud of his capacity for such a feeling. He felt protective towards her. He had even done the bloody shopping. Now he set about opening the tins, cutting the bread, "putting a meal together," as he described it, "got to build you up."

It was the mutual illness which had done it. He had talked to her as they had lain there, sweating, aching, agitated by the noises from the other flats, abandoned by the fastidious Janice, who had left them "to stew in their own juice", as she had said, charmingly. She was due back that evening. They passed the time in talking about their childhoods—something which Lester had done as rarely as Fiona. They were alike in their pride in their toughness, in the mixture of hurt and anger which had taken them from their families—hers in Deptford, dockland, his in Thurston, near farmland. It was the same story. The coincidences seemed to Lester like a stroke of fortune. To his astonishment, he heard himself telling Fiona that his mother was a "tart. I mean, she didn't walk up and down the street swinging a big black handbag—but she was after men—'fancy men' they called them up there then—and they would buy her clothes and rings—she used to tell me they were diamonds—she looked very good—she was a lovely looking woman—that's what they said anyway—a bit like you—not as, you know, good, but—still . . ." Fiona's mother had been "on the game no messin'. They used to wait outside the dock gates those days and have whoever had the price of it. She wasn't ashamed of it or nothin'. 'I'm off down the gates, darlin',' she would say to me and my brother and we'd be left with Gran, who would just curse away all the bleedin' time, except when my mum was there—then of course she daren't. My mum would just hit her. She hit us an' all. She could draw blood with the flat of her hand."

132

As the enfeebling flu dragged through them, they whispered and confessed the painful events of their lives—without self-pity, often with an access of scorn and viciousness—but for both of them, and particularly for Lester, it was a rare form of release and communion. Lester had detested his amiable, frightened father and still preferred to believe (which was the truth, in fact, though never admitted) that he was someone else's son. His serious sister Aileen had annoyed him because of her fatness and plainness: now she annoyed him because of her cleverness. He had relied on Joseph for a while but nowadays he felt totally displaced by successful Douglas and conscientious Harry. He missed Joseph's confidence in him. Betty had never forgiven him for stealing money from them—even though it had been years ago and even though he had repaid every penny. He would have benefited from her support, but now she could only seem to give it, and he could tell the difference. She had given him up. As for everybody else—well, in Lester's view and experience the world was made up of a few winners and a lot of losers, generally identified as the few who were lucky and the mass who weren't. Most people, he thought, were bastards or would be, given the chance: those who were not were usually cowards. The lucky ones ran the show, made the loot, got the girls, snapped up the big jobs, grabbed the headlines and had the fun. The only place to be was on top, in Lester's philosophy. To say anything else—as Aileen did and Harry and Douglas did when they had argued about it—was rubbish. And luck was the ticket to the top.

Every point that Lester made in his confession was capped by Fiona. Her hurts were deeper, her hatreds more intense. He still had a residual attachment to his background. She would have bombed Deptford, had she been able—especially the "sodding flat" in which her "sodding husband" lived with their two "rotten kids". But talk of her children would bring her to tears and she would sob, exhaustedly, while Lester comforted her, crooning meaningless phrases, "it'll be all right," and "we'll work it out," and "there, there," which had always made him curl up with contempt when he had seen them in films or books. In the two days of the worst period of the flu, he came as near to falling in love with her as he had done with anyone.

133

Perhaps he did love her: certainly it was "different", he told himself, and he had never fooled himself about this sort of thing. Her misery, her unhappy life, even the viciousness and the foul language all appeared to Lester to be endearing.

Now he sat on the edge of the bed and cut up her food for her. Then he lit her cigarette. He did not think of tidying up—their invalid state had rapidly brought the small flat to squalor. Fiona did not seem to notice this. Up until now Lester had automatically dismissed as a slut any woman who could not keep her place neat and tidy. All this was forgiven Fiona. She looked gaunt, unmade up, no mascara, no false eyelashes, no eyebrow pencil to contrast with the blanched blondeness which wanted constant attention; her hair needed to be dyed at the roots; her skin was bad; like Lester, she stank: and he looked at her as if she were Cleopatra. Took away the tray; washed up. Came back with a strong cup of tea. Wanted to make plans.

"The thing is to get a place of our own with a bit of class. How can you impress anybody in this dump? A council flat!" Fiona lay back and stared at the ceiling, trailing her cigarette to and from her mouth. Now that she was through the worst of the flu she was making her own calculations—but Lester did not notice. "I know I owe a bit of bread around the place, but we can do better than this," he went on. What he did not want to discuss was the prospect of their returning to work: he could no longer go on with the sex shows, not feeling about her the way he did now. He had hinted this to her and thought that from her attitude he could glean a similar conclusion on her part. "I've got this friend: he'll do anything for me." Lester was referring to Emma. "I thought I'd go and see him this afternoon—catch him when he comes in from work—he's the sort who knows where you can get these stylish little places cheap. He's good at that." He paused. It was most strange that he should be taking the trouble to lie to a woman. When he thought about it, he was confirmed in his hunch: if she was worth lying for, then she was worth a lot. "You'll be all right, won't you, if I leave you for a couple of hours?"

"Yes. Did you get those fags?"

Lester took them out of his pocket with the aplomb of a

conjuror shooting an ace from his sleeve. "Janice'll be in tonight," he said, not wanting her to feel lonely. "I might have to root around a bit."

"Janice'll throw up when she sees this place."

"She'll have something else to clean up then, won't she?"

Like a loving husband, he leaned forward, pecked her cheek and then leaned back, looking at her as if he were admiring his handiwork. He had not told her of the full strength of his feelings: nothing so direct. Not his style. And he wanted to get this one right. But, in his own mind, he had no doubt.

From Stockwell, the Northern Line took him directly to Kentish Town.

Emma had gone.

"I know she was trying to get in touch with you," the landlady said. She had most grudgingly admitted Lester into the hall, but barred him from going farther. Emma's room was still empty. The landlady was pleased to see him flounder; she had never liked him. "You needn't look up those stairs," she said, "the room's empty."

"How much a week is it?" Lester asked.

"Who for?"

"I might be interested myself."

He smiled. It was meant to be a reassuring, even a seductive smile, but the older woman was not impressed. Illness and time spent caring for Fiona had made him unaccustomedly careless about his own appearance: his clothes were rumpled, his white open-necked shirt grubby, his shoes split and unpolished. The landlady considered the state of a person's shoes as the key to his character. And his face was white and thin, bringing out an untrustworthy, aggressive expression which his smile only emphasized.

"It's already put aside for somebody," she said firmly. Lester guessed she might be lying.

"I could do a squat in it," he said. "That's what all the students tell you to do now. What if I just went up and did a squat?"

"You wouldn't do that." Squatters were her greatest fear: they had replaced burglars, for at least after robbery you could claim insurance. With squatters, all you got was filth, loss of income, abuse and, somehow, unfairly, a bad conscience. Her daily shopping outings were made uneasy through fear of squatters.

"I think I will. I'll squat this very minute." Lester made for the stairs and feebly the old lady put out an arm to prevent his progress.

"I've a letter for you," she said. "Emma left a letter."

"You're just saying that to bribe me, aren't you?"

"No. Really. You are Mr. Tallentire, aren't you?"

"The same man."

"I'll get it. Wait here." Her anxiety was comical to Lester's eyes. She had found a way to prevent him from going up the stairs—but in order to carry through her tactic—for thus he saw it, convinced she was off to telephone the police—she would have to leave him alone—rampant among her flatlets.

"I'll come with you," he said, lightly, at first relieving and then intensifying her fear. "I'll step inside with you." Still he wanted no trouble—but the desire to torment her was irresistible. Her terror of him goaded him on: did she think of him as a murderer or a thief? She behaved like it. He would teach her a little lesson—*and* keep an eye on her. "I want to keep an eye on you," he said. "I know your tricks."

"Tricks?" It occurred to her now to phone the police. If they got here fast enough before he got his friends and furniture along they might be able to stop any squat. After all, it *was* her property, left to her by her husband, a builder, who had died in early middle-age of a coronary. "What tricks?"

"It's written all over your face, ma. Now then. This letter. Pronto."

She had no alternative but to retreat into her own flat and Lester had no alternative but to follow her. Both of them went past the telephone as if studiously avoiding a massive DANGER sign. To his surprise, the letter was in his hand within seconds.

"You haven't steamed it open and read it?"

"Of course not!" She was truly outraged. "Certainly not! And I'd be much obliged if you would leave now."

"I thought you said something about a cup of tea."

"I did not."

"No? Was it sherry? I see some sherry there. I'll have a glass, yes, thank you." He made for her small, rarely used drinks cabinet.

She felt quite giddy now: before her rose up the prospect of intrusion, squatting, and worse—the man looked bad enough for anything. In her confusion she said what was uppermost in her mind. "If you don't leave I shall call the police or start screaming and someone's bound to hear."

"I'll be back," Lester said, savagely. "You listen out for me. Some time in the middle of one of these nights. You'll hear very little sound but I'll be back. I know this house up and down and inside out. I'll be back."

Her face was miserable with panic. He looked at her for a few deliberate and cruelly silent seconds and then left, closing her door and the front door very quietly.

Sometimes he was not in control of himself. The violence of his feelings towards that harmless woman had been terrible. He walked slowly to calm himself down, looking out for a café in which to read the letter. What got into him at times like that? He put it out of his mind. He had to pull something out of the hat for Fiona. He had to impress her. He had to show her who he really was.

Dear Lester,

If you read this it means I'm not here, so I'm sorry about that. Things started to get rather difficult and my mother came and insisted on taking me back with her, which I am too feeble at the moment to resist. Unfortunately it looks as if I'd be sensible to stay up there until after the birth, which means I have to give up this room here which is a nuisance. However, I'll write to you care of *this* address and I'm sure Mrs. P. will hold the letters for you. Or you could write to me! I'm at THE RECTORY, WARMINGFORDHAM, SUFFOLK. I enclose a letter from Douglas. He gave it to one of my friends who'd told him about us ages ago, an actor, anyway the gossip came in useful because here's the letter! It would be *super* if you

137

wrote and gave me an address! Don't worry about anything at all. Good luck and all my love.

Yours ever,

Emma XXX

P.S. I've bought a second-hand cot with your money: at a
local sale. It's *lovely*! Many thanks. E.

Dear Lester,

I hope this reaches you. A man called MIKE
WAINWRIGHT, a B.B.C. producer, has been trying and
failing to get in touch with me. He's interested in doing a
big documentary on MERLIN RAVEN. I seem to recall
that you were his manager once, back in Liverpool? No
one else can get near Raven—they know where he lives
etc. but, as usual, he's surrounded by protectors who
probably don't know the alphabet. Mike Wainwright's a
very distinguished producer and even Raven would be a
fool not to consider any offer from him. It might do you a
bit of good if you were the connection—but you know
what these things are—they could use you and lose you.
Your risk. Wainwright's number is 742–1373, extensions
6768 and 6350. Up to you.

Hope all's well. Good to see you in the New Year. Glad
Aileen and Harry are getting hitched. About time. See
you.

Douglas.

As luck would have it, Lester did know where Raven lived
when he was in London. He had been connected with him,
authentically though briefly. And in some obscure but definite
reckoning he sensed that Raven would see him, if only to cancel
out any slight shadow of a debt from the past. He would go
directly to Raven, he thought: then he could bargain better with
this Wainwright number.

(2)

"I'm the butler," the man said, exaggerating an accent already
feminine.

138

Lester was drained of all strength by the force of the envy which clubbed him. He went into a massive room, a black glass window covering an entire wall, through which the London lights appeared as dainty and carefully composed as hundreds and thousands on a cake. Everywhere, Lester saw Wealth: in the chunky leather furniture, the thick glass tables, the ankle deep carpets, the unbelievably expensive Hi-Fi equipment, the paintings on the walls—real paintings—and above all the crowds of flowers—all white—which blossomed on every surface, thrusting out of the most expensive vases. Raven's collection of Art Nouveau was extensive and valuable; most of it was in his heavily guarded manor house in the country, but the few pieces here cried out "style" to Lester. He wanted all of it; he would have done anything human to get all of it; as he stood at the door he was like a poor starved hound who'd run all day without water and would die for want of a drink.

Merlin put a finger to his lips, pointed to the turntable and waved Lester in. Lester managed to sit uncomfortably on a chair which had cost £1,350 for its comfort. Merlin smiled at him and then looked up to concentrate on the music. Lester was grateful for the chance to regroup his plans: he had so often lost out by wanting things too much and too impatiently. How often he himself must have come near all this, he thought! And he had missed it, missed it—he could have broken out in a tantrum of self-pity and frustration. This was his last chance: bound to be: at this level. He would never have had the nerve to come and see Raven if the B.B.C. thing hadn't come up. He had to make it work. He had to make the best of it. He had to get it right this time. He had to pull himself together.

He would have had trouble recognizing Raven. To Lester, whose physical condition meant so much to him, Merlin was portly. The lean, whispering lad of the Sixties had not bloomed but ballooned in his retirement and the loose oriental-styled clothes only added to the impression of a grossly over-fed young man—like one of those young noblemen in ancient cultures who was selected for slaughter and spoiled for life, or a young Buddha. Lester was reassured by this. He waited and fought to expel his nerves. He did not recognize the music, which sounded to him to be classical, modern and difficult: more, he considered, to be endured than enjoyed. The sort of stuff which, in Lester's opinion, the intellectuals listened to in order to prove that they did not like what everybody else liked. Lester was totally convinced that the basis of elitist taste lay in a determination to be exclusive: he bore no grudges about this. When he became rich he too might fill in the time by pretending to like the sort of music that Merlin was now absorbed by. But no one could tell him it was any fun. Lester resolved to refuse any offer of a drink: one more stiff one—and they were always stiff in this world—would finish him.

The music stopped. Merlin paused and then, at the third go, he levered himself out of the white satin covered four-seater sofa and came over, hand outstretched, a smile on his face, more open and friendly than Lester had ever seen him in his life or on the screen. Lester jumped up, tense as a spring, and they shook hands firmly and heartily like Americans. "Good to see you," repeated twice. "How do I look?" Merlin asked, still gripping Lester's hand. Lester hesitated. "Don't tell me. You'll lie. Your touch has given me the truth. Body language can't lie. But I'm getting better. When I'm eleven stone I'll put up all the mirrors again"—he pointed at three large unoccupied panels of the walls—"Adams—never mind. Sod it! It's *dark*!" He stumbled across the room and closed the curtains—green velvet. "Windows become mirrors at night," said Merlin gravely, "have you noticed?" Lester was about to agree but Merlin had begun to talk once again, while Lester's deferential response rattled up his throat and collapsed on his tongue. "I wouldn't have seen you," Merlin said, walking the length of the curtains like someone crossing a stage, appearing to ignore his guest, "but it's time to get back. What happened to us all, Lester? Where did we make the wrong decisions? And why? Nobody asks *why* today. Everybody's too clever to ask why. Well, I can afford it. I'm asking now. Why do we live like pigs? Tell me that. Did the Sixties almost destroy us?"

Lester was bewildered but, more importantly, he was overwhelmed by the warmth of the contact coming from Merlin. For Merlin had been notorious for his "cool": he had said so little that those intellectuals who did not think him inarticulate compared him with Pinter and Beckett. His songs were praised for their economy and imitated by a generation of elliptical lyricists and lock-jawed songsters and his track record as a public figure was most unusually and impressively discreet—free of the clutter of interviews which ententacled his contemporaries. That was power. Two interviews only—to the best pop journalists—heavily controlled by Raven. Everyone respected his silence. For the old scrubbers like Lester, he was a prince, unapproachable. Now, however, there seemed to be no stopping him. Lester risked a reply although he did not know what the hell Merlin was getting at.

"Well, Merlin, I think ..."

"Geoff! *Geoff*! Geoff Fletcher for Christ's sake! *Geoff*! That's why I let you in. I wanted to talk to somebody who knows *Geoff Fletcher*! *Geoff*! Merlin Raven is dead as the Phoenix. Merlin Raven was invented by an agent—a man I do not like. It's *Geoff*! Geoff Fletcher from 31, Harrington Road, Birkenhead. Do you drink? Do you want one?" That Birkenhead address had been his for his first six months only. His parents had been killed in a train crash: he had been moved into the Home immediately afterwards.

"Yea. Yea. Yes. Geoff. Please. Anything'll do."

Merlin put his Moroccan slippered foot on a bell which was dug into the smooth white carpet like a belly button.

"It'll have to be soft," he said. "I'm running a dry house at the moment. Gotta lose some of this *fat*. *Fat*! Disgusting. Why are fat men disgusting, Lester? I'll tell you. Because it's walking waste. I'm a mobile manure heap and that's polite! What do you think of this room?"

Lester looked around: it was Hollywood, it was fairyland, it was class, it was power and women and kicking everybody in the teeth who had hurt him, it was where he would have brought them all—to show them, to make them grovel. He worshipped it.

"Shit!" Merlin said. "Isn't it? Waste! Over-expensive chic sold to us by ponces who would strip a pickpocket."

The butler came in, immaculate in a freshly laundered and well tailored denim suit. Conversation stopped. He handed a large chunky glass of fresh orange juice to Lester, his eyes lowered, and a little Slimline tonic to Merlin. Then, noiselessly, he withdrew. Lester guessed he was about twenty-one.

"Do you know about Primals?"

Lester thought that Merlin must be referring to a new drug and in order to keep the flow going, to ensure the continuity of this great flood of words which bathed him in reassurance, he lied and nodded.

"Course you bloody well don't, Lester." Merlin drank off the tonic and made a face. "Cheers! What do you want?"

He heard himself praying inside his head, he could hear his own voice pleading in a whisper, "Oh God, help me, help me, help me God. Oh please. *Please.*"

"There's this man called Wainwright," he whispered. "Mike Wainwright." The muscles were kneading his Adam's apple fiercely. He kept on.

"Know him. Go on. Don't be nervous."

"And Douglas—Douglas Tallentire—he's my cousin." Implicating Douglas was a blind inspiration.

"Your cousin! Saw a play he wrote. Go on."

"They've approached me with a proposition—a deal—not quite a deal—an idea—not worked out yet—it all depends on how you want to play it—"

"It always does. Yes?"

"You're in charge. Ha! So. Whatever you want really." Lester stopped. He had lied again and not thought it out.

"Whatever I want really where?" Merlin continued to pace about like a heavy neurotic in a significant thriller. His ruthless diet was almost driving him insane.

"This film. They want you to make—with them—they'll make it—you needn't do anything." Lester was clueless. All he knew now was that this man must not be bothered, must be approached obliquely, must be given everything he wanted always.

Merlin stopped and, with cruelty, stared at his visitor. Lester was quite clearly buggered. He looked awful, dressed cheaply and sounded beaten. He had never been bright but failure had impaired his nerve, which had always been good. Under Merlin's stare, Lester actually, physically, shivered and then smiled, as if in apology.

Then a song, one of those short, exact and poignant narratives which no one else could write, began to form in Merlin's mind: it felt right: it felt certain. It was long since he had experienced that true register. The last few years had spawned nothing but meandering tapes on philosophical themes and significant subjects—deep thought: often, shallow music. Merlin had been shrewd enough not to release any of it. The record company, whose executives neither understood nor liked the material, had paid an Arabian sum to prevent anyone else ever turning those dirges into discs. But, it was a very long time since Merlin had heard that little click somewhere deep inside his brain: that instant comprehension which told him—"it's there, it's real, use it. Click. In one. It's a song."

"You bring me luck," Merlin said. "Wait here."

He went through into his studio and swiftly wrote down about ten lines. At his white grand piano, using two fingers, he picked out a melody and put it on tape. "Good!" he whispered, eyes closed, hearing it all, overwhelmed with relief and pleasure. "Yes. That's it. Yes." The whole operation took about seven minutes and exhilarated him as nothing had done for months. The song would become a great hit and earn him more than a million dollars in the first year and about forty-five thousand dollars a year for the foreseeable future.

When Merlin returned, Lester was still standing, too nervous to sit, too intimidated to walk about.

"We'll go and eat," Merlin said. "I'm allowed one meal a day. Boiled fish, fresh veg. and fruit. We can talk there. Then we can maybe find a couple of women. You still like women?"

His old friend nodded. He did not dare trust himself to speak because he was near to tears. Just to be seen out with Merlin Raven in one of the "hot" spots—and Raven made a spot hot—would up his chances a hundred—two hundred—five hundred per cent! He really was in luck.

"I like women too," Merlin declared, seriously. "They're something else."

It was four o'clock in the morning, the dead hour, time of surprise attacks, low body temperature and intractable anxieties, the fullest stretch of the rack for insomniacs, the time when policemen stole a nap, the old witching hour; and Lester was utterly drunk and so full of happiness and love for his fellows, so brimmed up with what he would tell Fiona that, as he swayed in the gutter waiting for a taxi, it was a wonder he did not spill over onto the orange pavement which rocked gently way down at his feet.

Merlin had ordered champagne which, his doctors said, did not make you fat.

Stirred by the delicious food—he had been encouraged by Merlin to choose the most costly dishes (Merlin delighted in seeing Lester stuff himself with over-rich, over-sauced food)—Lester had begun to talk about poaching. He was led to this subject by Merlin, who had recounted with disdainful gusto his own failed attempts to "live off the land": to Merlin all this was now "phony, just another cul-de-sac, just another abortion—that's no answer—there's nothing in it. Crappy cabbages and bloody chapped hands—what does that prove?" Some phrase of his had set off Lester, though, and, for about an hour, he talked in a way in which Merlin had never heard before, nor in the least expected. Moonlit nights about the fells, gamekeepers, wardens, tickling trout, snaring rabbits, country anecdotes came out easily and naturally and Merlin shed his patronizing contempt for the man. He saw someone as lost as he was, barred from his past by a self-made debris which was impenetrable. He promised to meet Douglas and Wainwright and talk over the film "seriously".

At the well known club in the well known street where, at weekends, photographers prowled about like stray cats about the restaurant dustbins, Merlin continued to order champagne and set about picking up two women. It was so simple it was no fun at all. Lester was curious about this new development in Merlin's emotional life, but too tired and still too subserviently cautious to say anything. They returned to the penthouse flat and took their partners to separate bedrooms. Lester did it because he was too scared to break his luck by refusing. But he did not want to and felt that he was betraying Fiona: and again he was surprised that such a feeling should be able to surface through the sores and scabs of his burnt-out feelings, and again he was rather proud of himself for having such a capacity for loyalty.

When he and his partner went through to the big room, Merlin was already there, sulking, gazing at his image in the black window, now bared once more. Lester took his leave and tapped his top pocket to show that he still had the private number given him in the restaurant. Merlin scarcely noticed him. Lester's partner was pleased to see him go. She preened herself for the attentions of the superstar who continued to stare, gloomily, deep into his dark reflection, unsatisfied and building up to a characteristic explosion of irrational and violent anger which would soon scatter the hapless girls down onto the empty street and half wreck the room.

Finally a taxi came and soon Lester was bouncing over the Thames, heading for Stockwell, with the news for Fiona, still unable to believe his luck.

(4)

"She isn't here."

"Don't be bloody daft." Lester buffeted the door with his shoulder, putting no force into the action, a token assault.

"She went off just after I came. She said to tell you she's gone back to her old man and she don't want you to cause no bother."

"She's in there." Again, Lester dumped his shoulder against the door.

"Would I be sayin' this to you if she was standin' beside me, would I?"

"Why'd she go?" He could not repress the question even though he knew it exposed him.

"I never interfere."

"What did she say to you?"

"I've told you."

"She must've said more than that. You'll have talked. She must have had something else to say. Or a note."

145

"She didn't leave no note." Janice laughed and the cosy little tinkle of sound flew tauntingly through the thin door and into the bare corridor, lit only by a night light. The laugh made Janice real to Lester and he saw that silly little head—always so spruce and neat and well cared for—on top of the large, trussed-up body. "Fiona wouldn't leave you no note."

"So you know more about her than I do, do you?" Lester's voice rose: until now he had spoken in a strong whisper.

"I should do. I've known her longer. She's never changed. She never will."

"What do you mean by that?"

Again the burden of the answer came in that cosy tinkle of laughter—phony, Lester thought. She needed a King Kong screw, this stupid bird, to knock her out of that bloody laugh!

"There's no need to raise your voice."

"Let me in. I want to sleep."

"You must be jokin', darlin'." Safe and sound, Janice was in a pink quilted dressing gown which swept from its El Greco high collar at her pointed ears to a Cardinal's robe effect at her hidden, pink-slippered feet. She was enjoying this. The flat was finally hers once more—she would never share again, she vowed—and she had never liked Lester. Her Saloon Bar voice was designed to put him firmly in his place—as someone over whom she had complete control.

"I'll leave in the morning. Let me in. I just want to sleep."

"You'll never get in here, my son, oh no."

"I'll break this bloody door down." This time, he bumped against it more determinedly.

"Don't you swear at me. And leave that door alone or I'll scream this building down. And I mean it."

Lester stopped.

"I'll kill her."

"Charming."

Lester punched the door violently. This bumptious bar-room chat of hers was all wrong! He was in love with Fiona! Janice had no respect for his feelings. Janice was a cow with the head of a page-boy.

146

"I'll kill her," he repeated, feeling in that sentence a warm surge of affection for Fiona which threatened to bring him to tears.

"Listen, mate. You don't deserve this—but stay away from her, firstly because her husband's a bigger bastard than even you are and second because her brothers are back. If I know them they'll be looking for you now. In fact," Janice continued, with inspired intuition, "I wouldn't be seen around this place for a very long time, maybe never, if I was you."

He looked at the brown door: he looked up and down the murky corridor.

"Just give me my suitcase and I'll go."

"I'm not opening this door to you, Lester, not tonight nor no night."

"What about my things?"

"I'll leave them down with the warden. He has an office. Nobody'll pinch what you've got."

"Don't be bloody stupid. Just shove my suitcase out. Why the fuck should I want to touch the likes of you?"

"Don't you swear at me, mate. *She* took the suitcase. Yours'll be in a carrier bag. Now you'd better go—I want to sleep."

"I'll get you, Janice."

"You just try."

"I'll catch you. Don't look over your shoulder. Slut."

"Listen, Lester." There was not a suggestion of panic in Janice's voice, only the sternness which comes from someone who is determined that there be no mistaking her meaning. "If you touch me—I am very friendly with people who would break your legs and arms without stopping for a breath. So take your threats somewhere else. You've got enough problems with Fiona's lot, I'd say. You won't frighten me. Piss off!"

He felt very tired. Fiona was gone. "You're not worth the skin you live in," he said and kicked the door loudly. The sound boomed about the corridor. He had the satisfaction of hearing her draw away from the door. "Cock-teaser," he said. "I'll be back."

The lift was still broken; the stairs were unlit. He walked down carefully, conscious of the struggle between alcohol and temper. Not being able to explode into violent action made him

147

feel strange. When he got out onto the street and the damp coolness of the hour before dawn hit him through his meagre clothes, he swayed and staggered for a few steps before thrusting his hands into his pockets and somehow, thus balanced, set off for the West End.

A double-decker bus, empty, lit up, moving fast, appeared from nowhere and careered away like something in a ghost story. Along the small, shop-lined and terraced empty streets of South London, there was only the occasional reminder of life: a woman, wrapped up heavily, trudging about her business, a young man with a briefcase walking briskly, one or two dogs, the occasional car.

Lester wanted there to be some grand climactic feeling within him: he wanted to be full of despair or revenge. He felt badly hurt: he would have beaten up Fiona if he could have got hold of her. But Janice's warning hand had neutralized the second course. He trekked through the empty South London streets, convinced that the one chance of a real love which might have led to "shacking up together" and even to marriage, if she had wanted it, had gone.

He would not be so soft again; that was it. Kaput. Forever.

He missed the convenience of Emma now. There was nowhere else he could turn except Douglas. Out of respect for Mary, he waited until seven before he rang. By this time he was in Westminster, seeing before him, across the road from the telephone box, the Houses of Parliament, faintly pink in the early clear sunlight. Traffic was beginning to build up and he pressed his free hand to his free ear. He did not realize how cold he was until he came into the little box and then began to shake quite violently.

"He has another number now," Mary said, reluctantly. "Is it urgent?"

"Yes. Oh yea. It's to do with the B.B.C.—a film—all that—the man—Wainwright—said I have to talk to Douglas."

She gave him the number. He dialled but there was no reply. He headed for Charing Cross and some hot tea. He would keep trying.

He stood at the kerb while a juggernaut went past. Its load was scores of tree trunks, bare and neat, parked row on row.

Lester wondered where they had come from. He'd wanted to work in the forests, once. Maybe he would have been happy. Who knows?

The thought of the hot tea surged through his mind and, simultaneously, he thought of Fiona, in bed as she had been the previous morning, asleep, spread-eagled like a child. The memory hurt him and his eyes stung with self-pity. He had loved her, but there was no way to get her back now. He had to make it first. To take this chance. And then find her again, when he was loaded. Yes. He would do that. Women went with the money. He respected her too much to go and beg and at the moment he had no other option. But it would change. Then he would seek her out. That was what you did. Came back stronger.

He trailed stiffly across the road, watched by two policemen who had been patrolling the Embankment for vagrants throughout the night. Another customer in the offing, some time in the near future, they agreed: they could always tell.

# 6
# The End of the Day

Old John's death, just after Easter, had been so long anticipated
that Joseph was surprised at his grief. It seemed indecent that a
man in his sixties should seek out quiet places to cry. In public,
to reassert himself, he was even more hearty than usual and one
or two people thought him a little lacking in respect. Betty took
it more evenly and it was she who attended to all the funeral
arrangements. John had said that he wanted to be "buried not
burnt": the plot was there beside the grave of his second wife,
Joseph's stepmother. More than three hundred people came to
the funeral.

Betty was shocked by how ill Douglas looked, but she said
nothing directly: not only ill, she decided, but miserably
unhappy and at odds with himself. Mary, he said, could not
afford to take the time off, otherwise she would have come with
him. He had come up on the morning train and intended to
return in the evening, but the weight of the family dissuaded
him. It would have seemed too abrupt. He stayed on. There was
nothing to draw him back.

The funeral tea was pleasant. Three of Joseph's sisters were
there and his youngest brother: they exchanged stories about
their dead father and soon they were laughing at revised ver-
sions of their childhood. All of them had in some measure
feared him: his daughters had resented his domineering and his
harshness but they had adored him too and their stories were
about his monstrous deeds and their perpetual survival. To
them he had indeed been a lord. Now that he was gone, their
memories turned towards the capturing of anecdotes and incidents which absolved and redeemed him.

The tea was in the Royal Oak: small tables placed together,
making a flat-bottomed U about the room; heavy starched

tablecloths; friends hired as waitresses moving across the open area with giant pots of tea and plates of cakes. It could have been an Old Persons' Outing, Douglas thought, or a break in a genteel bingo session.

He was sickeningly self-absorbed. "The spiral," he said to himself, "has come a full circle." He loathed his self-absorption and that increased it, which intensified the loathing.

They saw a man on the brink of early middle-age. They saw someone who had been offered opportunities and grasped them. They saw freedom, success, an interesting life, wealth and yet still "one of their own".

He saw old people in their best clothes: faces from past centuries—lines, strain, weather, inadequate nutrition. He saw the end of a life's struggle for common comforts clothed in chain-store affluence. It was more than most of them had dared dream—but there was an overwhelming feeling that they had come too late. They had seen their children and grandchildren grow up to a world largely without the privations and basic pressures which had been their disabling lot. He saw them left out of the feast they had funded.

They wanted him to talk, to dazzle them, to drop names and claim glamorous acquaintanceship. Had he done so, they would have been critical but delighted. He did not and they felt as if they had been found wanting.

He wanted to say, "Excuse this jaded tiredness." He wanted to be what they wanted him to be. It was not much to ask, or to give, for an hour or two. Was this the best he could do? Sit like a stooge and think his own thoughts? Why could he not bring back trophies worth winning?

But they did not question him at all. In the futility of his self-pity, he had begun to weep and the worn-out tears of exhaustion went down his cheeks as he thought of Mary, betrayed, alone now; Hilda, betrayed, alone now; John, betrayed, alone now; the story finally finished and himself weary from the effort of it. He had come to identify completely with the man who had sought death and blundered to it in those thin, wet Northern woods. An uncanny identification. It was as if he could now hear the very pitch and tone of the soughing despair in the man's head. He was drained by it. And there was

151

the nag of Lester's plea that he make this film on Raven for Wainwright and his own need to make a living for all of them.

It was as if, as a boy, he had taken on a great pack and set out on a pilgrim's progress to find out about Learning, and then about Literature, and then about His Own Capacities and then about The Real World—and here he was, with nothing to shore up self-respect, nothing to salt intellectual curiosity, nothing to excite energy, worn to a wafer of himself by the contradictions which a certain consistency of attitude had brought about. For where you loved you followed, did you not? And yet to follow two women seemed only to split him from heart to conscience and make him either perverse or impotent. And to choose to be as free from dependencies as possible ought to bring its own reward, ought it not? Yet he hung onto his odd jobs as dependently as a beggar around the kitchen doors of Grand Hotels. To write what you felt most deeply, that was to be true to your art and to your self—surely? And yet the sad elegy he had just finished—was that any more than a sentimental gesture? And what was it worth? Why was it so tiring?

"Here." His mother pressed a small handkerchief into his fingers. It was edged with lace and bore her initials woven in blue thread. "Take this."

She looked away, but not before he had seen the respect in her glance. Joseph, too, regarded him with admiring compassion. Harry, he saw, was nodding at him, vigorous with sympathy.

Douglas realized that they thought he was crying over the dead old man. His display of deep feeling had moved them all. The party broke up and people went away to catch buses, share cars, or walk through the empty early evening town to talk about the funeral in private. In his lifetime, John had held them all together.

Douglas' tears had been a fine and proper tribute, they thought.

(2)

"But it'll have to be a church," he said.

"Why?"

"It always is. Nearly always. Up here it is anyway."

"I don't believe in all that guff."

"I do."

"I am *not* getting married in St Mary's and that's final."

Harry smiled and Aileen, thinking she had won, threw a cushion across at him. They were in his flat, Harry rather drunk, still wearing his black tie, glad of the chance to have his mind taken off the funeral, which had moved him so much that he had been forced to fight very hard not to show his feelings and upset the others—who had more right to grief than he would ever have. He caught the cushion easily and spun it back gently so that it cuffed her hair.

"We're getting married in St Mary's Church, banns, choir, and all the trimmings," he said, "and *that's* final."

"But I'm pregnant."

"It doesn't show."

"I'm an atheist."

"You only have to answer a few simple questions."

"It's expensive."

"I'll pay."

"You're on the dole."

"I've my savings."

"*Not* on a wedding in church! For Christ's sake, Harry—what are you talking about?"

She regretted the edge which had come into her voice but his insistence struck her as absurd. She had discovered herself to be pregnant and had been surprised at how happy it made her. Harry, naturally, she thought (proudly), had been pleased and instantly begun the arrangements. She had thought that his idea of a church wedding was no more than a tease and taken no notice at first. It was much more important to give attention to the problem of Harry's job. He had been made redundant.

"Harry," she said, trying hard, but unsuccessfully, to keep the lecturing tone out of her voice, "let's stop being silly about this. You are unemployed. The way things are you could be unemployed for some weeks. Even if you get a job, it will most likely be a temporary job and you'll have to wait until God knows when before you get a job you want. We're about to have a child. I shall have to give up my lectureship and come back

153

here, which means that *I'll* be unemployed too. Besides which, I'll have to be at home for the first year or two—I have plans but they don't stand much chance—with one thing and another, darling, it is *not* the time to get married in an expensive and anachronistic ecclesiastical setting."

"It doesn't cost all that much," Harry said. "The dresses are what the money goes on and you can buy a new dress for yourself and be married in that."

"A maternity gown?"

"There's no need to joke."

"I am *not* marching up and down that aisle with half of Thurston coming to gawp."

"It might rain. Nobody would come then."

"That's hardly the point."

"What *is* the point, Aileen?"

She paused, but by now she had dug her heels in and the intransigence blunted her sensitivity. She was not aware of the new tone in Harry's voice, the unusual nervousness of his hands, the look in his eyes which pleaded with her to let him be.

"The point is that you should live by what you believe. I'm not religious—everybody knows that. I refused to go to church from the day I joined the Young Socialists, and I'd feel and look a fool if you made me go against what I stand for. I know you're a Christian and I respect that but you have to respect my point of view as well."

"I do."

"In that case—the Registry Office."

"No."

"Please, Harry."

"I didn't want to say this." He paused. "You see—it wouldn't be for you—getting married in church—it would be for Betty—for 'mother'. Douglas ran off and got married in Paris or somewhere abroad—somewhere—she never saw it. You know how much she loves weddings and how she's always wanted to be in the middle of one. Well. Here we are. This is her chance."

Aileen shook her head and tugged out a cigarette. Every time she smoked now, Harry remembered that advertisement which declared: "SMOKING CAN HARM YOUR CHILD" and showed a pregnant mother puffing a fag to its tar-soaked and cancerous tip. But he had said nothing: she could work it out for herself and if he tried to influence her—he would only make it worse.

"For Betty?" she asked.

"Yes."

She paused. "O.K."

He had won! The weight of Harry's relief indicated how strongly he had meant to hold onto his position over the wedding. Betty needed to be looked after, he felt, and there was little enough he could do: but this small thing was possible.

"No need to grin like a fat cat," she said and held out her hands to him. When he took them, she snatched at him and he allowed himself to be tugged down onto the floor where she lay on a heap of highly patterned cushions.

"I've got some news," he said. "I didn't want to say it earlier—I don't know—it would have struck the wrong note." He hurried on without giving her the chance to ask what he meant by that—her favourite conversational trip-wire. "I've got a job down at the factory. It's clerking in the loading area—about the same money as I got before."

"Not exactly professional work—or a career spangled with glittering prospects."

"I like it down there. There's plenty of the lads play for one or other of the teams. They're a decent bunch of blokes. I think I'll enjoy it."

"I'm sorry."

"No need to be sorry. I'm not."

"I didn't mean sorry for you. I'm sorry I was a bitch—all that 'not exactly professional' bit." She frowned. "It shows how infected by the bourgeoisie you can get—and how snobbish. Silly. Sorry." She kissed him on the cheek, noted the patronizing nature of such a peck, and putting her arms around him, kissed him strongly and long on the mouth. "The trouble with you is that you're so very nice, so very, very nice, and I've forgotten how to deal with people who are very honest and very nice."

"Frank Edwards works in the same shed." Harry hesitated. "We'll be able to discuss tactics."

"For the next game," she said, solemnly.

"For the next match, yes."

"You. Are. A. Lovely. Clot." The words were separated by kisses planted from his forehead down to his throat. She began to undo the buttons of his shirt. He responded immediately by loosening her clothes.

"You're not really interested in *my* plans, are you?" she asked.

"Of course I am. Put your arms up." She did as he asked and he drew off her dress.

"I'm going to try to stand for Labour in this constituency at the bye-election."

Harry continued kissing and undressing her without the slightest loss of pace or rhythm.

"It's safe Tory," he said.

"Nothing's safe nowadays."

"Tights," he said, "are an abomination."

"You could have impregnated a future Member of Parliament."

"Let me put out the light." He walked across the room naked: Aileen loved his body, its leanness and toughness and whiteness. She kept this to herself, though, for it embarrassed him to hear it.

"I meant it. I'm going to try for the nomination."

"It's handy, you being pregnant, one way, isn't it?" He turned off the light and the electric fire grinned its two scarlet bars of fire at them.

"That's nice," she said. "Harry. Harry? O.K. But I'll *not* wear white. Ssshhh. Don't say anything. Don't say anything at all."

Although he did not hurt her, he made love fiercely. All that was never said, all that would not go into words, went into actions and Aileen held on for dear life as he lifted her, turned and swung her, so easily moving her. As she began to come to him he hoisted himself onto his arms and rammed down into her again and again until her body shuddered and ached to be satisfied.

Harry shook his head and the hair, damp with sweat, tumbled over the white face she saw above her, his eyes tight shut as if in pain. "No," he said, and repeated as he had done on the last two nights, "NO! No! No! No! No!", the rhythm that of his body: the word a savage exclamation. For, since John's death, Harry had "seen" him when he was making love to Aileen. As now, as the pressure and the swoon grew stronger, there he was, the old man he had loved so much, blue eyes laughing, his face eager for life.

(3)

The truth of it all had hit Betty like a fist in the face. Douglas and Mary had parted. That was why he evaded her questions. That was why he glanced away when she asked for the usual detailed statement about John. That was why he looked so neglected. He had gone out drinking with Joseph and she waited impatiently, determined to say something which would bring out the truth and yet afraid to say anything that would make things worse or hurt him. He had looked so ill, she thought: Mary should not have let him get into that state.

To occupy herself she polished the brass as she watched television. She now had a large collection of these small brass ornaments, which hung in rows down the walls until the living room was a little like a gift shop. Cleaning them was only described as a chore for the purpose of conversation; in fact she found the activity satisfying and soothing. She worked away, sat on the edge of her seat in the same attitude of attentiveness and unease as that of her rarely worn glasses, which rested at the very edge of her nose. It was after eleven, they would surely be back soon—even though Joseph always used to tell visitors "they shut the door prompt at ten thirty in Thurston pubs —and them inside have to stay there for another two hours at least!" He was boyishly proud of things like that: out-of-hours drinking, the occasional extravagant tale of gambling—when the town presented itself as a place of Stories and Characters and Plots Comical and Tragical, then he was happy. The mundane doings of the place bored him increasingly. Douglas was drinking too much—Joseph had told her that the last time they had seen Douglas—when he had come up for two or three nights to the cottage "to see a potential purchaser"—so he had said. She had believed him then, of course: now she suspected he had come to think matters over.

The thought that her son's marriage might be over terrified her. She knew that it happened more frequently nowadays—yet the fears and the taboos remained. She knew that there was an increase in the divorce rate, she accepted that it was sometimes better for those who did not get on to part, rather than prolong what might be an agony—there was nothing but tolerance in Betty for anyone in pain. But Douglas was her son. His loss would be hers; his failure hers; the hurt he inflicted would be her responsibility in part; and there was the child. She had a feeling of sacred protectiveness about the child. He must be spared as much as possible. That would be the starting point. After that, what would be, would be. This conclusion appeased her a little.

Joseph did not come back until almost two o'clock. He was alone and tired and drunk.

"Douglas wanted to go up to the cottage to be on his own to think things over," he announced, taking care to pronounce each word clearly, taking care also to answer the question which she would most want answered and, by this act, defuse the anger which would surely be his welcome. "Sometimes you have to be alone," he added and suddenly dropped into a chair. "I'm tired," he announced.

"I'm not surprised."

"Any chance of a cup of tea?"

"You'll need more than tea to sort you out." She got up to make it and left him alone.

Joseph thought of taking off his coat and then decided against it. He would have to get undressed for bed soon enough and he could do the whole lot in one go. Besides, he was cold. He looked around the neat and pretty little room without interest: surroundings had never meant much to him. The harmony and cosiness so assiduously worked out by Betty, the polishing and painting, the re-arranging, the patient purchasing of matching curtains, carpets, cushions and the compulsive re-arranging of the ornaments which gave her a definite sense of peace—all this influenced and affected him not one iota. He would have been equally at home in a barrack room.

> "Pack up your troubles in your old kit-bag
> And smile, smile, smile."

He sang softly although there were no neighbours through the walls. A detached house, even though a bungalow. His own estate. Yet it gave him no feeling of achievement at all. "We're alike, Douglas and me," he said to himself, "can't settle, can't be contented." There was contentment in that observation. He wanted his son and himself to be alike and the pleasure of the evening had been in their mutual confidences.

> "You are my sunshine, my only sunshine,
> You make me hap-py, when skies are grey."

"Drunk and singing on the night of your father's funeral," Betty said scornfully as she brought in the tea.

"Yesterday." Joseph looked at his watch. "If you want to be nasty, be accurate." He hummed on a little, while the tea cooled on the small table beside him. Then he stopped and waited for her to ask him some questions.

"Well, I'm off to bed," she said.

"Don't you want to know what I've been doing?"

"I can smell what you've been doing."

"That's not very nice."

"Have you finished your tea? I'll take it through."

"I thought you'd want a talk. I haven't finished, no." He poured another cup, not slopping, and took up a wholemeal biscuit.

"I must say that Douglas could have *said* he wasn't staying. I made up the bed."

"We got talking," Joseph said, darkly, the biscuit blocking his mouth.

"He could have said. Still. There we are."

Again the silence started to roll up and Joseph could not sustain it. He swallowed the biscuit, washed it down with his cup and sat back comfortably, his rather small white hands crossed on the lap of his burly black overcoat in an attitude of piety.

"He and Mary have—they're having a Trial Separation," Joseph announced.

"I'd guessed something like that. Fools!"

"How did you guess?" The hands fluttered up in agitation. "What else did he say?"

"We talked a lot."

"Very well."

Betty got up, went across to Joseph, took the tray and set off for the kitchen.

"Where are you going?"

"Bed."

"Don't you want to listen?"

"I'm not going to drag it out of you, Joseph. What you have to say means a lot to me and either you say it now or I'll wait until the morning when you're sober."

"I'm not drunk."

"That's as may be."

"I'm upset, that's all. It's been a hell of a day for me, Betty. Nobody thinks I feel anything—just because I stay cheerful. But that old man meant a lot to me. And I meant a lot to him. It was always me he turned to to sort him out. He loved me, so he did, and that went for me too. And now with all this Douglas carry-on—I'm upset as well, you know. You only have to drag it out because I don't like talking about it."

Betty's self-righteousness slipped away. She saw this fuddled man, in his sixties, dumpy, exhausted, drunk, unable to define his grief, unable to control his reaction to Douglas' confidences. She understood how much it must have meant to him to have passed this evening with his son; and she thanked Douglas for that. Aware that she could not satisfy Joseph's needs, she could still see and be grateful when another could.

"We're both very tired," she said. "Perhaps it would be better to talk in the morning."

"I'll never get round to it in the morning," he said. "Anyway. There isn't much to add once you've got over the initial shock.

Sit down, though, love. I feel that you're a policeman standing there."

She could not resist popping the tray through to the kitchen so as to keep the living room tidy; nor could she resist taking up another brass and re-opening the Duraglit as Joseph unbent to describe the evening.

He went over it in detail: how they had gone up to the flats to take a drink to John's old friends, how they had called in to see a schoolfriend of Douglas', how they had landed up in The Crown after popping in the Kildare and the Lion and Lamb. He told her what Douglas had said about his work. "He's going to stick to this writing now come what may. *Come-what-may*. I admire him for that." He explained, with awe, how Douglas was stony broke and needed to sell the maisonette in London. With total recall he went through Douglas' idea for Regional Portraits: he had been absorbed in the unaccustomed confidence and caught by the detail; usually Douglas said so little and that so general that it was not worth remembering. Here, though, he had taken on the burden of their conversation and used the television idea as a way to communicate with his father. He had wanted to show the respect that was due to him on such a day, and he regretted how often he had neglected to "honour his father", how soon the filial had slid to the friendly and the friendly to the unfriendly.

For by seeing his father as a "pal"—the contemporary way—he had attempted a new relationship in his adulthood which had no guarantees of success. Pals, friends, happened by accident or mutual concerns: his connection with his father was an accident only in the cosmic sense and their mutual concerns were profound but without that surface of shared life which bred gossip and easy reference. And so it would have been sounder to have remained the dutiful son. Indeed, as Douglas delivered his life to his father in the way of a prodigal, he felt unanticipated benefits flowing from the sureness of that state. The old order worked. Both of them noticed that and relaxed. Yet both knew it would most likely be no permanent thing: Douglas had moved too far out of Joseph's range of experience. It was the father who was often the learner now. The younger who had broken new ground and the old taboos over jobs and money and risks. No old order could remain if the balance which supported the structure went out of kilter; but when it worked it gave rich sustenance.

"Then he told me all about it." Joseph finally arrived at what Betty wanted to hear. He was as shy to talk as he had been embarrassed to listen. It was strange, he reflected, an adult lifetime passed with this woman before him and yet there were still large parts of the life between them which were smothered in a mutual shyness and bled by diffidence. Still a mass of subjects which were simply not discussed because they had found no way to discuss them without embarrassing each other. Perhaps this armour was necessary for a long-term intimate life. However, it left Joseph stranded, now that he had to tell his wife about their son.

"Well?"

"I don't think it's finished, like, between them, not a bit of it. I said to him—'I like Mary. Your mother and me like Mary.' I wanted to say that."

"What's happened?" Although Betty was almost screaming to know, she realized that patience was the only course.

"Well, the thing is," Joseph sucked hurriedly on his cigarette, "he's—gone off—gone off and got himself a flat—rented."

"On his own?"

"What do you mean?"

"On his own?"

"Why shouldn't he be on his own?"

"Come on, Joseph. There's another woman involved in all this."

"Is there?"

"It's written all over your face."

Joseph could not deny it. But her insight caught him short. He had wanted to protect Betty and Douglas by retaining and concealing this information. It demeaned both of them, for he knew she would take the betrayal personally.

"What's written all over my face?"

His manoeuvre was so feeble that she did not even acknowledge it but sat, intent and alert now, tense with expectation, waiting for the truth.

"He isn't living with *her*. He assured me of that. Not that I asked. But I believe him. He's on his own. That's the top and bottom of it, Betty. He's on his own."

"He always hated that."

"He's gone up to that cottage on his own."

"That surprises me as well." She paused. "What did he say about her? Don't say 'about who?'"

"Not very much, really." Joseph relaxed into the truth. "She's not a silly young girl. That much I do know. And he's genuinely fond of her. I could see that. Mind you, you see, he's still very fond of Mary—as a matter of fact I've never heard him speak about her so much. It's hard to make out."

"Is *she* married?"

"No."

"Does he want to marry her?"

"He doesn't know. He doesn't know what he wants."

"He should by now."

"There are times when you don't," Joseph said, and although his manner was overlaid by a patina of ponderous mystery-making, there was, in his tone, a conviction that impressed her.

"At least you should know what you should do." Betty wanted to tease this out.

"You should. Yes. But it doesn't always happen like that."

"He has a wife and a little boy to keep and a family to build up. That's plain enough. It is for most people."

"Maybe so. Maybe not."

"What do you mean by that?"

"A lot of people pretend, Betty. You know that and so do I. A lot of people are quite happy just jogging along pretending. But there are those who aren't. There are those who think pretending isn't good enough."

"Douglas said that. I can hear his voice saying it."

"No. Or—maybe he did, yes. But if I am quoting from him then I'm quoting in agreement."

"Pretending what? You have to get on with it. That's all."

"Not necessarily. There's no reason why things shouldn't change. If people want them to, that's their business."

163

"If he's run off with another woman that's his wife's business!"

"He hasn't run off with anybody."

"Did he say why?"

"He doesn't really know."

"After all his education he can only come up with 'he doesn't really know'! I could tell him. Anybody could."

"I think he's a very unhappy man," Joseph said, carefully. He had considered the matter all evening and this was his overriding comment on it. "Very unhappy indeed."

"That's no excuse."

"Maybe not."

"You sound as if you're on his side."

"I understand him, that's all. We understand each other. After all, we ought to—father and son." He stopped. But Betty was too distressed to answer him. She had flung replies and questions at him with no real purpose, for she had guessed the true state of affairs and was badly disturbed. Joseph could see that she was near tears: he could not remember when last she had cried. When? So many years ago. He felt a surge of love for her, a pulse of spontaneous protective affection which came like a voice from the past. He wanted to reach out and take her hand—when was the last time he had reassured her? She had scorned it for so long. In that one moment he stepped back across the wilderness of habit and boredom which had been the character of so much of the second half of their life together. But he could not reach out his hand: the gesture was too sentimental and would have been rebuffed. Instead, he talked on.

"I can see that he wants to make something of his life on his own terms. He's lucky to get the chance, I know, but he wants to do things his own way and not just do them because everybody else's always done them like that. I don't approve of what he's doing—but I can see how he gets himself where he is. He wants to think things through—that's why he didn't want to come back here—no offence to you—he loves you—he always has—but he just wants to be on his own. It's a different world he's in, Betty, it's a different way of seeing the whole thing."

"What's different about where he is now?" Joseph's speech had given her time to check her tears and will herself to staunch

164

the flow of unhappiness. "He's stuck up in the hills in a little cottage—exactly the same sort of place his grandfather was stuck in at his age. Exactly the same sort of place his grandfather was *born* in, for goodness sake—and just waiting to be hired—from what I can learn—just the same as old John used to go out to the hirings to get hired. What's the difference in that? None at all. And there's no difference in family. A wife and a child are what you have to stick by if you take them on at all and there's no way out of that."

"He takes things very hard," Joseph said, "very seriously."

"Mary would say he wasn't taking this seriously enough."

"It's all a question of how you look at it."

"No, Joseph. There are some things that are wrong and you can look at them until you're blue in the face but they'll still be wrong."

"Well, there we are."

He was tired now. He wanted to be alone now with his own thoughts of John, he wanted to remember him, he needed to think of him.

"It was Annie," Betty said, speaking of Douglas' daughter, sadly, and now there was no holding the tears. She bent forward until her head was in her lap and wept aloud. Joseph came beside her and stood, one hand gently rubbing her shoulders, unable to do more to help. "He blames himself," Betty said, "because he was gallivanting around in America when the little lass was so ill—he blames himself—which he shouldn't—it's silly—it's altogether bad—but he does—and since she died he's changed—you can see it—there's—he looks desperate. But he shouldn't."

She looked up at Joseph, who was determined not to cry. Annie had been such a lovely child, Douglas' first, their adored grandchild—such a sweet creature—to be taken from life at the age of eight by the antique Victorian affliction of double-pneumonia seemed too cruel and futile to contemplate. And indeed all thought of it wearied Joseph as nothing else did. "But he should have got over it." Betty sat up now and forced herself to behave. "You can't use the past as an excuse," she said. "You have no right."

165

About three weeks later, Joseph was in the cemetery at the end of a Saturday afternoon, squaring up the grave. There was little to do but he had wanted an excuse to spend some time there: to have said he had gone there alone to meditate on his father would have been as unacceptable to him as it would have been to his friends. Yet all of them would have understood that this was sometimes necessary: they too would have found a mundane excuse and hidden the deeper motive.

It was just before dusk. The cemetery was to the west of the town, firmly on the Solway Plain. Standing there, he could see the fells, Skiddaw guarding the northern entrance, now smoothly outlined, the delicate grey sky just beginning to absorb the longer reddening rays from the sun, which had been clear and solitary most of the day in the cold blue early spring sky. Beyond those fells was where his father had been hired: before them was where he had been born: to the west was where he had worked in the mines. As Joseph smoked and looked about him he could take in most of the geographical world of his father.

He had expected to have great thoughts. He had hoped to draw conclusions about life and death. Perhaps he had even hoped to recapture the keening which had swept through him the few days after the funeral and been suppressed, as usual, in his doggily jocular manner. But all he felt was a kind of everyday tranquillity. Nothing grand or profound. Nothing to take back to his own world and re-illuminate his own life. Just a plain peacefulness.

From where he stood he could see the big War Memorial to World War One—covered with so many names, two of them his own. John had gone through that and received only a slight wound in the leg. The Memorial to World War Two—less impressive, with fewer names, but again, Tallentire inscribed on it—reminded him that he, too, had been through a war—and burst an eardrum. Spread about him were the graves of friends, strangers, known and unknown, but townsfolk all, once alive in the sprawl of brick and stone now glowing in the evening sunset, once walking along the streets among the sand-stone buildings which sucked in this late light as if it had been sent only to furbish the façades of this town, once as warm as the sun's rays—now six feet under, decomposing, penned into a small space by a grey wall which was green with lichens. Joseph nipped the cigarette and put the butt end into his pocket, for tidiness.

Well, there it was. He gathered up his implements. "John Tallentire"—beneath that small, neat mound. Nearby, the first green ears of snowdrops could be seen among the grass. How did they know, so deep in the ground, that they could grow, that the sun would be waiting?

Joseph's eyes smarted as he stood for a last moment there. It was difficult to leave. The sky was now lurid with the dash of the sinking sun—as if flares of life were being sent out as reminders, displays of colour and wonder—proof of the sun's power, as if it too did not want to go. About the cemetery one or two other people walked away. There was the thud of a spade. Joseph's face felt cold. What could he say? He wanted to say something. Foolish, stupid, call it what he would to himself, he wanted to say something over his father's grave. Well then. He was near to tears now. "So long, old lad," he said.

It was over. The man was dead. Joseph turned away and walked quickly home.

# PART TWO

# I
# Setting Out

## (1)

He woke up in the middle of the night and, on a sudden impulse, dressed and came downstairs into the tiny cottage kitchen. It was still very dark outside and, despite the promise of early spring, cold. Douglas made himself a cup of Nescafé, chewed through a couple of apples, and then set out.

Walking soon had its usual effect. When he was agitated, it could soothe him; when he was depressed it could pick him up; when he felt that a decision had to be clarified or a course of action resolved upon, the steady rhythm would provide the best accompaniment he had yet discovered. As now, it earthed him.

Despite the lack of light, he was sure of his course. Down from the cottage and the fells to the village and then west along the main valley road to the plain by the woods.

It was wonderfully quiet. His mind seemed to crunch against the silence as surely as his feet pressed on the surface of the lane. It was as if he swam in the quietness, tumbled and swirled and floated in it. Yet, in London, the metropolitan din was a measure of its vitality and he liked to be in the middle of that equally. He would be spending even more time there now: he had signed over the cottage to Mary and John.

There had been no need for that, but he wanted to make the gesture. They had sold the place in London for a good sum and Mary had immediately moved into the nearby garden flat she had found. Douglas had helped her with the furniture, but she had wanted no help with the arranging of it. That was to be her business. Douglas, who had inevitably felt both awkward and a little noble at joining in so heartily with the removal, had soon discovered his awkwardness superfluous and his nobility un-acknowledged. Mary was brisk to the point of rudeness and clearly glad to see the back of him once the heavy stuff had been heaved into the appropriate rooms. On reflection, he had been relieved at her command over herself.

He put the residue of the money into an account in her name. This made him feel good and released him from weekly payments, should he wish it—and Mary was quite prepared to meet him on that point—but he had made a deal with himself that he would pay her the amount of the relevant maintenance allowed each week. That would keep him plugged in. He needed it.

His own ugly, bare little bedsitter, with nothing of his own in it save a few clothes and the start of a new accumulation of paperbacks, gave him an irresponsible sense of liberation. To be such a metropolitan nomad was the life which had been waiting for him, he thought. And the first few weeks had been guiltily exhilarating.

It was a cell. Those monkish qualities in Douglas which had reinforced his impulse to be a writer felt a great relief in the two-barred electric fire, white walls, utility furniture, cheap crockery, gas stove, uneasy chairs (two). All that time he had wasted with other people when there was this solitude attending him, here, in the middle of the city. Alone, anonymous, working away at re-writing the story, setting up a freelance shop as a reviewer–broadcaster: still no more than tinkering with the Raven deal.

He began reading with an avidity he thought he had lost forever. He got up early, went for a run around a nearby bleak park and then put in four or five hours at the table which served admirably as a desk. The rest of the day was his. His only tie was to check with Mary, sometimes to meet John from school (they had soon, and with surprising accord, fallen into the "weekend dad" routine of most divorced/separated couples), otherwise to rove at will.

Douglas had never belonged to any group or clique and so he had never developed or cultivated that regular pattern of pubs/restaurants/parties which keep such gangs in touch. Once he had earned enough for Mary and himself, he could be whatever he wanted all over the town.

At first he had found it difficult to believe the licence he had given himself. He would be in a new pub east of the city, or in a strange club off Kensington High Street, or find himself at a party in Wandsworth and feel—on all occasions—that he was trespassing, that he had broken bounds, ought to be the other side of that particular part of life. Then he had begun to discover that if you were on your own and unburdened by ambition, then the world was indeed an oyster for your grit. He had taken the risk of self-ridicule and gone to various exhibitions, once again revisited the Wallace Collection, the John Soane's Museum, become an instant film-buff and, above all, dropped in on all those places—however unimportant, bars, cafés, acquaintances' flats—and all those people, he had not had time for before. It was as if he had come into the promised land, for he was living off his own wits, still supporting those he owed support to, and willing and able to range all about the place.

Those few weeks, like many comparatively short periods in any lifetime which collect disproportionate significance from their intensity, seemed now to Douglas like a great blessing. But the treat could not go on. He was too committed now, in his life, to feelings of responsibility for his parents, for Mary and for John, and to feelings of responsibility over what he himself should be able to attempt, in the society in which he found himself. He could not drop out or even fly out. He was in this society and if he could not find a role to have faith in, or a faith to have a role in, then he must take from the past what served and invent something for himself to see it all through.

He had his inherited responsibility as firmly strapped to his conscience as Christian's knapsack to his back. He would go back to Mary and John. He would tell Hilda all of this and leave her. He would settle himself firmly in work and provide for all to whom it was owed. But first he would spend a long morning in that wood to collect some final details of description which he thought his story lacked. The walk had resolved everything.

(2)

It was so cold underfoot and so miserable. He had not emphasized that enough. It had begun to drizzle quite heavily and his feet were sodden. It was not surprising that the man had not survived here. The truly surprising thing was how people in the past had managed. Pre-everything except fire—and that must have been tricky in this climate—how had Iron Age man hung on? Plenty of game, yes; plenty of meat, yes. Few people—few to bother about—yes. But the misery of the elements and the boredom—or were they fully stretched merely in surviving?—that made his mind dizzy.

Or it could have been lack of food. He had traipsed about the woods for about four hours now and he was tired. He was also depressed at his lack of knowledge: he had been able to name only half a dozen of the common types of tree and the undergrowth was "just ferns". Ignorance, it was true, could be a goad: though, generally, it merely goaded you to frustration. But he had taken stock. He would re-write those parts of the story which, he had thought on the last re-reading, needed strengthening. There were some useful points to be made. And the primary point—which he had never doubted—that someone could cut himself off entirely from the contemporary world in such a small wood—was well taken. He had neither met nor seen a soul.

He had not brought a compass but he had studied the map before he set off. He reckoned he should be near the Aspatria end of the woods and should reach that town if he kept walking in the general direction he had first taken.

It was cold. Here, at the very spot, he had been unable to feel any emotion at all about the man he had written about so concentratedly over the past three or four months. Often when he was writing, he would break off and think about that lonely figure, a figure whose invented life went further and further away from the few facts known to Douglas of the real life—but he would think about him and feel sorrow, pity and sadness. Yet here, in the place itself, he could evoke nothing. Nothing of the clumsy, stumbling young man returned to his childhood paradise; nothing of the thoughts he had thought for him or of him; he did not exist in the wood.

By the time he reached Aspatria he was ravenous and he made for the fish and chip shop. It was boarded up. Douglas had been hungry in the wood and hungry on the walk into the small town: now, faced with no prospect of the nostalgic feast he had promised himself, he felt starving.

He looked up and down the street. Midday. Empty. Two cars parked. Most shops closed. No traffic at present mobile. Aspatria, born as an ancient Saxon village, perhaps from a Roman fort, and fattened on coal mines, now unworked, seemed dead. Another observation: he was the only human being on the street: and it was a long street: cruel neighbours in Thurston and other small competitive towns would talk of Aspatria as a one-street town. Cars, regulation closing hours, fridges, women working and schools had swept the centre clean of people.

There had been a restaurant, he remembered, near the cinema. There was one crucial afternoon tea—spam fritters and chips, if he remembered correctly—which he had endured for the sake of unrequited love: or, more accurately, a few reluctant kisses and half-swivelled legs on the back row and, after that, a brisk goodnight. He walked up the street in search of it.

Aspatria had been his first adolescent adventure. These things were clearly marked out. As a boy you could go to socials, church dances, A.Y.P.A parties, Scouts and Guides Christmas Revels, all this and more was in your grasp, but on every occasion the event would be supervised and subtly or not so subtly dominated by Adults. At about twelve you were too old for that. Alas, you were still too young to go off to the village dances, which would not effectively start until the pubs closed, or to Carlisle, the great city, where packs of city boys roamed like starved wolves and girls of fathomless sophistication and experience turned up at every dance hall on a Saturday night. Long trousers and more cash, height and *savoir faire* than a twelve year old possessed were essential for that leap into the big time. Aspatria filled the gap. This for three reasons. Firstly, it was not Thurston and therefore away from home and therefore an adventure, with all the dangers that implied: for it was well known that Aspatria boyos would massacre any Thurston boyo on sight (eight miles might be the distance between the towns: each side claimed that whole epochs of culture divided them). Secondly, the picture house had a coffee bar attached to it. This, in the mid-Fifties, was so racy as to be considered indecent. Methodists hurried past it with their heads averted. School-teachers singled it out for moral disapproval in their R.I. lessons. Parents built texts on it, outlining the perils and degeneration which would come to you after that first terrible step of sniffing around the picture house café in Aspatria, drinking the wicked Espresso, ordering the loose milk shakes, playing the wicked Jukebox. For there was a Jukebox. The first in the district. Sat there like Queen Elizabeth the First. A whole generation was proud of it. A whole generation lined itself up behind the Jukebox, willing to be profligate with scarce sixpences, careless of complaint, defiant of the dreadful stories of the evil consequences which came from associating with Jukeboxes—the inner city crime in America, the racketeering in Soho, the White Slave Trade in North Africa, the Drug Trade in Hong Kong and Prostitution and Assault the world over—all seemed to be accompanied by the Jukebox, which brought out the sermons of the Salvationists and the scorn of the W.I., the Rotary Club, the Church Wardens and the condemnation of all Schoolteachers. It was irresistible. And, because of this, it made Aspatria picture house café the most attractive place for miles around. And, thirdly, there were the girls. Aspatria girls were different, Douglas had reckoned and he reckoned it still. The school he had gone to had drawn pupils from an area embracing three towns of roughly the same size: Silloth, a port and seaside town; his own, light industry and a market town; and Aspatria, still connected with coal, although the miners in the Fifties had to be bussed west to dig for it, rather than finding it in their own backyards. Maybe it was something of that kick of life which is found in most mining communities—or maybe it was just the difference itself—a slight but noticeably different accent, different jokes, a tougher line on misfortune, a nimble flirtatiousness—whatever it was, Aspatria girls were different and Douglas fell in love with about four of them between his twelfth and fourteenth year. There were one or two intermissions for Thurston girls, a village girl and even, anticipating the Big Time, a brief and uncomfortable liaison with a Carlisle girl (the Carlisle theme was to come later in its fullness) but Aspatria dominated that time of his life and the girls had dominated most of his thoughts.

The whole thing had happened on two levels. At school—furtive glances (generally unreturned); awkward notes (generally returned); alternate boasts and denials. Very unsatisfactory. Then came Saturday, and after the rugby in the morning, the work about the house and the rugby watched in the afternoon, would come the preparations before clambering aboard the five-twenty-five bus. Hair, rinsed with cold water, flicked over with Brylcreem, then knocked into shape with a secret and infallible mixture of vaseline and solid brilliantine, which made it obey orders like a Horse Guard on parade. The style would be as near to Elvis Presley as he could get away with, i.e. as his mother would allow. Then off in the bus, to the café, to the pictures, if lucky with a girl, then the wary mooch around the alien town, finally homing in on the fish and chip shop and the nine o'clock bus back. Or—if gold had been struck and the heavens opened—the nine-forty. Replete and, occasionally, rewarded.

It was on that bus and in that mood he would meet and talk to Alan, who would have pursued his own solitary and, Douglas even then suspected, quietly amused path amid the Saturday saturnalia of his hot-skinned contemporaries.

The restaurant had gone. Completely. There was a hole in the street: he could see down towards the new Rugby Club and over the fields into the open country, all of which so thinly cloaked coal.

He went into the nearest pub, hoping for the best—and found it. A clean, well heated place, hot sausages, freshly cut sandwiches, decent bitter, an unpushy landlord, a comfortable chair and a table to himself. There was even a paper he could borrow from the bar: the "Telegraph". He read it with an aggressive pleasure and enjoyed the half hour greatly. He had made a settlement, he thought, and come to a necessary compromise. The rest of his life would be devoted to the attempt to make the compromise work. He could not have all that he wanted, but he could avoid all that he feared and feared he deserved. Now that he had "come through" in some way, he felt yet again the stack of luck and privilege which bolstered him up on any reasonable comparison with most of the rest . . . but, be that as it may, he had his own garden to cultivate as best he could.

The prospect, now that he thought about it, exhilarated him. He went out to catch a bus.

"You won't know me," the man said confidently, relaxed, amused.

"Of course I do," and Douglas, who saw before him a man his own age, size and shape, now dressed in a black donkey jacket and rough cords stuffed into wellingtons, instantly flicked back more than twenty years to this same person in a school blazer, short trousers and crumpled grey socks, looking every bit as confident and amused, as they had sized each other up for a fight. Joe—! Joe —! His mind scattered and fled before that surname—damn! Damn! Joe—.

"It wasn't a bad fight," Joe said. Douglas grinned at the inevitable coincidence of memory.

"Who won?"

"They stopped it," Joe said, "but I would say you were well on the way to a hammering."

"Most likely." Then Douglas jibbed at the inverted patronizing quality in his acquiescence. "It wouldn't have been a hammering, though. I was never hammered. Usually, in fact, I won."

"You were fly, I'll give you that." Joe smiled. His look was steady and pleasant. "Still are, by the look of things. You've done well."

"Oh, I don't know. What are you up to?"

"I labour for my brother. He's set up as a builder. I was at the factory. Good money but—boredom. You won't know about that in your job. It's the killer. So I walked out and ended up carrying hods, mixing cement, a bit of a brickie, a bit of a joiner, slating a speciality. Half the money, but there's some satisfaction in it. Married?"

"Yes. You?"

"Yes. Kids?"

"One. You?"

"Three. Well, that's settled." Joe looked around the small bus station. "Were you waiting for somebody?"

"No. A bus."

"Where's the car?"

"I walked here."

"From that spot I've heard you have—up in the fells?"

"Yes."

"Must be nice and quiet for you there, eh, away from it all?"

"Yes."

"I'm going near enough there to deliver some sand. I was picking up the van. You could have a lift."

"Thanks. Thanks."

They walked in step along the pavement. Joe had been one of the cleverest boys in Douglas' form at school. Immediately after O Levels—Douglas remembered that Joe had taken and passed in nine subjects—he had left to work in a garage: then he had gone into Lancashire and they had lost touch. They had played rugby together at the school—Joe was first class, played for England Schoolboys, then he had turned professional for a local Rugby League side, suffered a bad fracture of his leg and been out of the game before he was out of his teens. There was still, though, that physical confidence, the balance, belonging to all fine sportsmen. Douglas had always been a little in awe of him. Joe was someone who could pick up a tennis racquet, never having tried the game before, put in a respectable performance within half an hour and an hour later be stretching his opponent quite consistently. Any ballgame. It was a gift, people said, and in every generation two or three boys in the district came up with this talent, which was always most admired by hardworking sloggers like Douglas, who loved the game and appreciated every success and failure of a player like Joe. They walked silently for a while.

"Still got as much to say for yourself, I see," Joe said, turning to grin at him.

"Still can't shut up, yes."

"I used to be a bit worried about talking to you," Joe went on. "We would ask you a question—about homework or something—and you'd go back a hundred years to start your answer."

"You didn't need to ask many questions."

"Oh, you could always beat me at that stuff. I couldn't get interested in it. You couldn't get enough."

"Do you see many of the others?"

"A few. Quite a few's stayed around here. Those that haven't tend to drift back—like you—I don't know whether it's for local colour or roots—neither, I expect. Just to see the families."

"That'll be it."

"Norman's out at Workington—he's in Customs and Excise: I still see him down at the Rugby Club on a Saturday. He's a selector now!"

"He was good."

"He could play a bit. John worked with me down at the factory—he's still down there. A lot of them are. That new part took on a lot of those you'll know—on the scientific side, in the labs and such—Dawson and Eric, Raymond—lads like that. I worked in the old bit." Joe stopped, quite suddenly, and turned to Douglas, almost aggressively. "Do you know what I did? For nigh on three years?"

He did a brief mime, as if in a charade. There was nothing to it. He bowed or bent deeply from the waist, pulled at something with his right hand, adjusted something, stepped back, looked at his handiwork and made a lifting gesture.

"That was it," he said. "Sum total." He paused. "It nearly drove me mad. We had to have a regular wage so I stuck it—we'd managed to get hold of a little terraced cottage in the town—you'll see it in a minute—but it was in a shocking condition and I needed time to do it up. That was what kept me going."

Douglas had nothing to say. They walked on.

"There's a lot of fellas going quietly mad, I think," Joe said, resuming his cheerfulness. "Looking at those machines, performing some task the Japanese give to robots. You can see it on their faces at work—and they're on the lookout for anything to get out of it. Half the strikes are just a way of getting variety into the work, I'm sure of that. Anything. That's where *you* score."

"Yes."

"Good luck to you. Here we are."

Behind Joe's house was a neat small builder's yard. The van was already loaded. They drove directly to Douglas' cottage, chatting fairly easily about the district and people in it. When they arrived there, Douglas politely invited Joe inside for a drink.

"Oh, I could make this place sing." Joe's enthusiasm was unfeigned and it released him from any guardedness he may have felt. "If you stripped the boarding off that ceiling you'd find cross-beams. I did a cottage similar to this recently. Early seventeenth century, isn't it? And you should get a decent door for there. Those windows were just shoved in: you should get them taken out and the original size of window put back. Could I have a look upstairs?"

He went through the house, alive to every detail of it. Douglas trailed behind him, a little put out, as if a good friend of his had instantly been won over and claimed by a total stranger.

"That damp needs seeing to," Joe pointed out as they came down the stairs. "Mind you, it won't fall down and if you keep heat on it won't get wet. But you should run a damp course through there." He finished his drink and smiled at Douglas. "I don't suppose you'd know how to do that, would you?"

"No. 'Fraid not."

"Nor make a door, strip a ceiling, put in a decent set of windows and that fireplace, throw a concrete casing around that bathroom and so on."

"Sorry. No good at it."

"You would be if you tried."

"I don't think so. It once took me three years of woodwork lessons to make a key-rack. A bit of wood with four nails in."

"There you go." He finished his drink. "I'll be on my way."

"Right. Thanks again for the lift."

"No trouble." He looked around once more. "If I could live in a spot like this—you've done well for yourself, Douglas, with this and the work you do in London."

"Been lucky."

"Luck's earned. So long."

He left, briskly, and Douglas was relieved and pleased to feel that he had encountered and begun to know again someone who might, in the long run, turn out to be a friend.

It reinforced his resolution to go back to Mary and start again: tried and traditional ways were the best way through his confusion.

181

# 2

# Women Alone

## (1)

Superficially, Mary was in very good shape. Better shape, some of her friends told her, than she had been during the last year or so with Douglas. They told her she looked smarter, slimmer, altogether better "got together". And it was true, although another opinion could have concluded that she was not slimmer but thinner and not smarter but newly anxious about the effect of her appearance on others. She rattled through her work with an extra degree of efficiency, as if determined to prove that she was improved by the loss of a husband—and her senior colleagues noticed this and were moved to compliment her on it. One or two extra-curricular jobs soon found their way onto her timetable. With John she made very great efforts and the boy appeared to benefit from the considerations and attentions. He was encouraged to bring home friends to stay at the weekend; he was taken to the pictures regularly and encouraged in all his schoolwork as never before. And again, it seemed that things were better, for the two of them got on well, things went smoothly, there was none of the exasperating, uncertain, ill-tempered, unsettling presence and absence of a husband/father to disturb and disrupt the steady machine of a day's organization. Night brought her up against herself and each day was half spent re-grouping and half spent fortifying herself against what was to come. She could employ all her waking moments—but full consciousness, like the day itself, went only so far. There was night: there was the sub-conscious. Then her organization fell away and she was naked, alone and frightened.

It was the fear which took her most by surprise. There was the solitude of the flesh, and after many years that took getting used to, but there was a certain relief in it too and a stubborn pride in holding out on one's own, an obstinate and to some extent a sustaining conviction in the proof that she could exist alone. To that extent, the day's activities and the next day's plans reassured her. It was this fear, this uncontrollable terror which lurched into her head instead of sleep, as if it had been waiting in some cave of her mind, growing hungry on the neglect of the day, growing even more powerful through the attempts to ignore or starve it, by means of organization; growing, growing in its inscrutable ambition, which seemed to be to drive her mad. For it seized on her like a physical being: something very like actual teeth seemed to grip her brain and chew and cramp it: spasms and sweat broke out, as if some real animal were in the room, prowling about the bed, giving off a powerful odour, ready to turn on her and savage her. And there seemed to be no way of coping with it. She would be forced to sit up, switch on the bedside light and reluctantly look at the alarm clock, to discover it was no more that twenty past two or ten to four. She would swallow another pill, read another chapter. Try again.

By day she had all the comfort in the world, for the world, as usual in those circumstances, had, perhaps wisely, fallen back on the ritual behaviour of a contemporary tolerant society. That is to say, all blame attached to the man: all sympathy was extended to the woman and child: all sniping went in the direction of the mistress. Even though Douglas had not left Mary for Hilda, the reaction strayed not one iota from that norm.

Douglas kept to his word about his comings and goings, far more scrupulously than he had ever done as a husband: he was polite when they met, he was concerned for her, never lost his temper, took an interest in what she was doing, financially did everything he could without fuss, demanded nothing, stuck to the rules she made, made it as easy as he could for her, was, in truth, a friend and comforter. But often, after he had been there for half an hour or so, she could have screamed. Or she could have begged him to scream. He was like the night: he tore at what was essential in her. And she behaved badly to him, tried to spike his docile overtures, unfix his careful plans, disrupt his new laid plots with John: she tried to get him out of her life.

The fear, she decided, came from two movements: the first

was a movement away from a marriage, a passion, a love, a friendship, a husband, a family life, which had consumed her for more than fifteen years. There was an undeniable retreat from this. Something inexorable had decided that this would no longer be the way she lived. Against that was the force of regret and, within the regret, no real notion at all of what a new life would be or would lead to. Therefore there was a double fear: that something was being lost which had been proven and precious, despite its drawbacks and flaws and inadequacies: and that something would have to be found which was as yet untested and unimaginable and therefore bereft of the power of habit or the strength of adventure. This brought her little comfort. The night plundered her resources.

Mike had been a great support and yet Mary felt that she had to turn him away, before there developed a complication which would further confuse and exhaust her.

He had behaved impeccably. Once a week, Mary would go out with him to a nearby restaurant for a late supper, while John was guarded by the late-teenage daughter of a neighbour. Over the meal, she would chat about her work or listen to Mike talking about his work: there would always follow a discussion of some aspect of Douglas' character or achievement. Mike would be unwaveringly appreciative of what the younger man had done. Mary would want some specific example, put carefully in context, of the weight and worth of a piece of work, a programme, some writing, an article. It was as if they were discussing a friend who had fallen away or run into serious trouble, not of his own making. The odd thing was that, between them, no blame was ever fixed on Douglas. At some point, Mary would abruptly switch away from the subject of Douglas and there would be the awkward conclusion to the evening. For the questions—why was he asking her out? And why did she accept?—would loom up between them, unspoken but surely demanding some answer soon.

As the weeks passed, Mary in some way realized that she was moving by instinct and that she had to trust it. Her zest for the day, which had inspired her to plan it like an eager military cadet and carry it through with corresponding enthusiasm, began to wane as more and more of her life was thrown into the internal struggle which seemed forever to be demanding more recruits, as if indeed a Great War were being fought within her between entrenched and embattled forces, which called deeper and deeper for powers to sustain a struggle whose only certain end was exhaustion. So the first period passed: the time of vim and renewal, the flush of new resolution, the crisp attack of fresh endeavour, all petered away and she was left with her resources stretched merely to cover the despair which now occupied not only the night, but rose to the surface of the day and threatened to break out in public, and disrupt and sear her waking life.

What she wanted above everything else was what she also feared—to be totally alone, without acquaintances or friends, or even John, somehow to creep into a state of emotional hibernation, curl up tight over the pain which bit and gnawed at her and perhaps nurse it through, help it pass. Luckily there was a school holiday near and she paced herself towards that as a man stranded in a desert might fix his mark on a distant oasis: and like him she knew that what she would arrive at might be no more than a mirage.

Quite suddenly, simple matters appeared totally impossible. Getting breakfast was, one morning, a profoundly weary task which was performed only by dredging up scarce resources of will-power; it was as if she had been struck by an instantly disabling virus and indeed Mary did think, throughout the day, that she had "caught something". That phrase found an immediate response with her colleagues, who insisted she go home after lunch and see the doctor, who diagnosed depression.

The word itself clubbed her down. She had read about it, indeed much of the literature and drama of her contemporaries was steeped in it. It seemed to be the new Enemy, as much of a plague in its way as cancer, something that would not let go its grip of you once it had battened itself on your mind. She was given pills and advised to come again to the surgery in a fortnight if things got no better. She had a horror of these pills and yet she took them, forcing them down with large glasses of water, feeling that just by taking them she was putting herself on a road which could only draw her towards what she did not wish to be. For, as she took the pills, it was as if, she thought, she was saying farewell to independence of mind and of action, to that belief in her own capacity for living her life, her own strength of decision, her own initiative and control. Depression, Depression, Depression—the doctor's word tolled in her mind and intensified the pressures.

She had forced herself to go back to school the next day and she was glad of it, for the effort and perhaps the effect of the new pills enabled her to have the first deep sleep she had enjoyed for weeks. Yet that was the briefest of respites. Soon she was again in this claustrophobic pit of herself, battling faceless enemies who were wearing her down.

That week her meal with Mike had broken the pattern. For a while she had been monosyllabic, not rude but simply glad to be able to slump into the depths she felt without the fear of offending who she was with, or of setting off a sequence of despair which she would do anything to stave off when she was alone. Mike's strength protected her and let her be as she felt. It was after the meal was done and they had stayed an unaccustomedly long time in the place, so that it was almost empty and freer as a place in which to exchange confidences, that she began to cry. The tears were silent. At first she did not know they were there, simply felt them come down her cheeks. Mike reached out his hand. She took it. It was the first time there had been such a declaration and chaste, simple, modest as it was, Mary felt a surge of gratitude which led directly to danger. She had been talking about putting up some shelves in the kitchen when the tears had started, attempting at that stage to reclaim something from the evening for Mike, whose patience, she was sure, had been unfairly overloaded by her parched companionship. Now once again she took refuge in continuing the description of this mundane job, which had succeeded in reducing her to impotence: plaster on the floor, screws aslant, a fingernail broken and the intractable shelves still stacked against the wall, useless. Mike offered to come around on the Sunday afternoon when she was alone—John would be with Douglas—and put them up. She agreed.

He had not been to the flat. She had been fiercely protective of her new territory and even Douglas was not encouraged to stay for much longer than a decent minimum of time. She wanted to be with Douglas, she longed to be with him sometimes and would walk about the silent telephone like some animal smelling familiar prey, fighting off the ache to ring him up and quenching the pain which came from his failing to ring her up. But the flat, she had decided—and again this was a decision which came to her "ready made", from instinct rather than any reasoning, the flat had to be uninhabited by any man; it had to be free of everyone but John and herself. Without any explanation being offered or necessary, Mike had understood this and consequently the invitation was accepted with a full awareness of the possible implications.

The job was done quickly and well. He was a handyman who enjoyed such straightforward work and could turn his hand to anything, including, as Mary knew from the times she and Douglas had gone to his place for supper in the old days, cooking quite complicated meals.

It felt good to have a man in the house again. There was no doubt about that. Loneliness and liberation were not enough.

She made some tea and took it into the living room. One of the minor attractions of the place was that there was a small functional fireplace and, although it was late spring according to the calendar, there was enough coolness about the weather to make a coal fire a welcome sight.

Mike looked pleased with himself and more relaxed than he had done for ages. It would not be hard, she thought, to fall in love with him. His face was wise and strong: his manner was gentle but sure. He was everything she had hoped Douglas might become. And he too, she knew without his telling, could find her good. They sipped tea as if it were cognac, nursed it down, thoughtfully.

"That cupboard in the hall needs fixing," he said. "And the window above the sink needs attention. I tried to open it for some air. It sticks."

"I've noticed."

"They can be a nuisance unless you catch them early."

"Like everything else."

"Yes."

Mike hesitated, then he took two steps back.

"That is, I could fix them if you needed me to."

187

"I know."

The same intake of breath, the same dryness in the throat—she had not experienced this since Douglas had fallen for her and declared himself, all those years ago: and here it was again. She had been fancied and "propositioned" in those years—in the staff-room at school in the late afternoon, towards the end of the week, towards the end of term. But never had any overture struck home. Not once. Her fidelity had been absolute. Even the one or two pleasant friendships with men, which had sometimes been her lifeline to sanity during Douglas' bout of hurt rampaging, had been conducted with strictly platonic formality on all occasions. But now—for one reason or another—either her defences were unaware or her entire emotional life had changed or she was willing a course of revenge or merely seeking the sympathy which is sometimes essential in order to live—whatever it was, there was that stop in the flow, that pause, that uncanny recognition that a moment was here presented which could be grasped; which needed only a nod, the slightest nod, to let it through.

Before she could speak, Mary had to swallow in order to ease her throat.

"I think," she whispered, and could not speak more loudly, "I think it would be better if you did not come round again."

Mike let the implication strike into him and he repressed the surge of protest and argument and persuasion which sprang up inside him to defend his interest and win the prize he now realized was so much desired. It was at this instant that he knew how much he loved her, but also he saw before him a woman fighting for a life she could not yet see or imagine, yet determined to fight by herself. It would be possible, perhaps, to wear her down and force himself on her: it would even be possible to take her in hand and drive her to the course he wanted because, at a time such as this, a benevolent tyranny can seem a blessed release. But Mike appreciated the effort she was putting into her fight. He loved her, if that were possible, all the more because of that. And he could see how hard she was holding on, how easily she could yield, how important it was—in some mysterious way understood by neither of them—that she should not yet yield to him. At least he could give her that.

He finished his tea.

"I can mend that cupboard in ten minutes now," he said and went out to the hall.

Mary let her head slump forward, as if she were a marionette and a vital string had just been cut. Mike was a good man. Maybe she could love him.

She has had a very great shock, Mcke thought, as he unscrewed the cupboard doors. His picture of her now was complete. He saw her as brave, pure in heart, dogged, loyal, a fine ally for Douglas, willing to help him even to the point of sacrificing herself. But now the sacrifice had been made, she took the consequences hard. She took them seriously. Inside that room, literally a few feet away from him, was a woman he loved now, would always love and could cherish for the rest of his life: both of them, he knew, would be nourished by it. On all sides there would be healing. Yet because she had whispered "no", he would make no move.

(2)

They were in Hilda's flat. It was a comfortable place, Douglas thought, and he felt quite guiltlessly at home in it. Its very smallness and the earnestness of the mind which had assembled that, largely paperback, library, those often-played classical records, made him feel loving and protective to the person who had built it up. She had held to a measure of independence, a standard of intellectual satisfaction, and the cultivation of a mind which had been discarded by the school system in early adolescence. In its way, Douglas saw Hilda's achievement romantically, especially when he was in her flat, for she had made it so uncompromisingly hers. It suited him. It could have been designed by him—the emphasis on comfort and on neatness, on books and records, one or two small paintings, a few drawings and prints and, like tropical fish in an English pond, sudden splashes of gilt extravagance, small indicators of baroque impulses, capable of infinite inventiveness.

It was late. They had eaten at Hilda's place. Although Douglas had brought along a bottle of wine, he had taken no more than two glasses and Hilda had sipped at one. She had

189

sensed something of his purpose even before his arrival and the abstemious formality of his behaviour had confirmed her suspicions. But the meal had passed cheerfully enough.

Cheerfulness, in fact, was the totally unanticipated obstacle. He had come to tell Hilda that he was going back to Mary and could not see her again. Yet no sooner had he crossed the threshold than he felt relaxed and comfortable. The meal had been chatty and agreeable, altogether neutralizing the atmosphere of drama which Douglas had carried about him all that day.

Finally, after they had washed up and he had made coffee, they sat down in front of the small electric fire which managed to make the place look cosy, and he had plunged in. It was then that her doggedness had shown itself.

"But if you say you love me," she repeated, "then I can't see what all the fuss is about. I could see it while you were with Mary and John; I understood that. It hurt me a lot but I could see that you were in a marriage and you felt a responsibility to it and you were frightened to get out of it because of what might happen. But you have got out of it. And according to you—and I've got nothing else to go by—things haven't fallen apart. According to you, when you go and take John out he seems happier than he used to. And Mary—you say—looks better and says that she feels better than she has done for years. So, although you might have been right to be frightened, they've both survived without you. They've even done well. And you say you love me." She paused and waited for confirmation.

"I do."

"So." She stared in front of her, eyebrows almost meeting as she plunged on, concentrating so hard that she was oblivious of Douglas' appreciative appraisal. He saw her long legs thrust forward, hips sunk in the seat, breasts firm and supple under a tight old sweater. He remembered the times they had slept together and knew how hard it was going to be. "Why don't you live with me?"

"I can't," he said, instantly.

"You won't."

He hesitated. But she was right. "I won't."

"Well then," she spoke slowly now, concentrating on her

line, "you seem to be forcing me to believe that you've been a hypocrite." He did not reply. She looked at him, openly: there was no use denying it. Now there was no urge to smile. Between them a sudden clarity appeared: as if, until that time, the air itself had been misty. "Well," she asked, quietly, with no accusation or irritation in her voice, "is that it? Were you lying all of that time?"

If he said "yes", it would be over. And he wanted it to be over. But he could not say "yes". To have done so would have been to have denied everything else he had said and done with Hilda. Yet this was a way. He had decided to leave Hilda and return to Mary: this, in a sense, was the easiest way—to admit or pretend that he had been a liar, a hypocrite, a fake, and at least then leave Hilda with the sustaining strength of anger, a grievance, something to help her push herself into a world without him. If he really loved her, perhaps he ought to say "yes": then at least it would be a clean and final cut, it would give her a chance. But the word stuck in his gullet.

"You see," Hilda said, softly, tenderly, "you can't lie, can you? We can't lie to each other, can we? You want to say 'yes' because it would make it easier for both of us at this present moment—but when it comes down to it—you can't do it, can you?"

Again he did not answer.

"So," she went on, deliberately, "we should live together. Either you move in here or I can move in with you or, better still, we find a new place where John can come and stay for a weekend."

He had to speak.

"That is, if you love me," she said.

"It isn't as easy as that."

"I know it isn't. I've understood that for several years. I've told *you* that, when you wanted to leave Mary and John. But now you have left them. What else can I do but want what I've always wanted. Somewhere to live with you: and a family—an ordinary family, just a family that sits around a fire and listens to the radio or the gramophone on winter evenings and plays cards and plans summer holidays and takes the bus to the Tower of London on Saturdays. That's what I want. And that's what you

want, I think. Not this floating about the world, thinking
you've got all the opportunities going—which you haven't; or
thinking that you're well off—when in fact you're broke and
rapidly approaching the age where you cease to be employable.
You want an ordinary decent life, with a job that seems worthwhile and a family you can rely on, and then, if you have
anything to write—it'll find a way out, but whether it does or
not doesn't really matter as much as you and me being together.
That's what I thought it was all about."

"I had all that with Mary," Douglas said, "in fairness. The
family, the job. All that."

"Because you *wanted* it. That's my point. The fact that it
didn't work with her doesn't mean that it isn't what you want.
You came to me, most likely, because it *is* what you want. I've
got nothing else to give you. Except that I know that it *would*
work and we *would* be happy. I'm sure of that."

"How can you be?"

"Because I love you and I know you love me and because I
know that we want the same things, really. It's like you said, we
seem to think alike, we react in the same way, we have the same
sort of—oh, embarrassment when people show off or act insen-
sitively. You know all that. I don't need to tell you."

"Everything's so clear-cut to you."

"Because it *is* clear-cut, that's why."

Douglas laughed aloud and Hilda, released by the laughter,
relaxed and joined in.

"But I *have* to go back to Mary," he said, abruptly. It was as if
the laugh had cleared his mind.

"Only if you want to. You've left her now. She'll never be
able to forget that. If you go back it'll just be to part again."

"Not necessarily."

"Why did you leave her, then? You've made every excuse not
to for years, although it's been perfectly clear that neither of you
were getting anything out of it. And now you've finally found
the courage to do it you want to run back?"

"I'm not sure it *was* courage that made me leave her."

"Yes it was. Everything about you, the place you've come
from, all your ideas about loyalty, all the worry about not
hurting people—all that meant that you were *made* to be the

sort of husband who puts up with what he's got to preserve the peace or because he thinks it's the best he'll ever get."

"Perhaps it is."

"Only if you want it to be. You can stay where you are—lots of people do that and they say it's for the sake of the children or for their career or whatever excuse it is. My parents did that and as a consequence we were all nearly driven as crazy as they drove each other. No. You can change your life if you want to. You have changed it. That's why I haven't pressed you until now. I knew what a big thing it was for you. I knew what an effort it was. But now you have to think about us."

"I think I should go back to Mary. There we are. That's what I think." He looked at her and then looked away. Finally.

In the silence Douglas felt as if Hilda suddenly fled from him—from having been close, intimate, a part of him. Suddenly she was gone, running, wanting to put as much distance between them as possible. After a long pause, she said, weakly and bravely, "You'd better go then. No. Don't say anything at all. Just go now. If you have to, you have to."

It was as if he were moving in slow motion through a heavy atmosphere. He both acted and saw himself act: saw himself get up and reach for his jacket, put it on, find his book, scan the room, seek out Hilda's eyes—unsuccessfully—hesitate while looking at the utterly dejected figure beside the electric fire, all so slowly, so portentously.

"Goodbye then," he said.

He waited for a reply but she made no sound nor any move until he was gone and she had heard his footsteps die away. Then, weary and in pain, she got up and went over to the bed. There was such a pain in her side and such pressure about her heart. She lay on the bed, her knees drawn up to her chin, trying to ease the pain.

Douglas had rejected her. She had thought, at first, that he had needed no more than some stern confirmation of what they would do. So she had rehearsed again the arguments which had become stale and unnecessary. It was only when he had said "there we are" . . . and looked at her and then looked away, that she had realized the truth of the matter. He would *not* live with her. She could not understand it. She loved him.

And he loved her, he knew that now: as he walked slowly through London he was in no doubt that Hilda was a woman he loved. But there was a force which prevented him from following that through. Perhaps for the wrong reasons and certainly belatedly there was, he felt, a right thing to do and he would do it. She had been so gallant there at the end, he thought, making no appeal, using no blackmail of tone or phrase, simply letting him be free. She had plumbed his need and made it easy for him. She had known what he wanted. She knew him better than anyone he had met. He walked very slowly, pausing now and then.

Hilda was cold, but did not want to move for fear she would break up. She had wept but even that had brought no relief. Love could kill. Men were cruel. Life was meaningless. She, for reasons beyond her, was destined to live it alone. What was she going to do? What would her life be now, without him, what was there to live for?

The city was so empty. In how many houses were couples going through the same doubts and partings and self-imparted distress? *What* was it, this conflict? What did it serve, that to achieve one right you denied another? There must be a better way, he thought.

Hilda began to shiver, a little at first and then violently. She made no attempt to stop it.

(3)

At first she had been nervous of being in the church on her own. Even though she had attended it as a child, gone to Sunday School in the front pews, passed through the period of teenage piety in the back pews of the south aisle, been married there and attended other marriages and funerals there; even though Douglas had been baptized there and she had gone to see him confirmed, to hear him read the lesson in the service of the Nine Carols, to hear him sing—the church had a place in her life like a remote friend encountered and re-encountered along the way—yet at first she had felt nervous of being in the place alone. She had taken on the job of cleaning it. For this she was paid three pounds a week. The money, said the vicar, was the best he

194

could manage and was not important: Betty agreed. She had had enough of the lunch-times in the pub.

She had got the job accidentally. Mrs Anderson—or rather Jennie Beattie, as she had been at school—had taken care of the church for years. She was one of a large family of strong church people who had managed, unruffled, to remain strong church people through all the ebbs and upheavals of the third quarter of the twentieth century. Jennie had been at school with Betty, in the same class: and although they had never been particularly friendly, they had always been pleasant to each other. They had seen each other two or three times a week around the town, nodded, perhaps exchanged a bit of gossip about family or moaned about the weather and through that apparently slight contact a friendship had been built up, the strength of which surprised Betty: for when she heard that Jennie had been taken to hospital with suspected cancer, she felt miserable and went to see her as soon as visitors were permitted to go.

Betty was shocked to see her. Jennie had always been so calm and steady. Now she cried self-pityingly: she blamed her husband for not noticing earlier that she was ill; she blamed the work she had had to do; she complained that her children had visited her only once and were not as upset as she had expected. She spoke darkly about "not expecting it to turn out like this after the life she had led". Betty listened and nodded and was moved by the woman's distress and, when Jennie began to worry about the state of the church, Betty saw and seized the opportunity to be useful. She would clean it, she said, until Jennie was better. She would stand in for her. That was one thing Jennie need not worry about.

A few weeks after that decision had been taken and implemented, Jennie died. The funeral packed out the church. Everyone had a good word for her.

Betty was asked to continue in the job and she agreed, despite Joseph's angry objections to the large amount of work in "that cold old barn of a spot"—his concern for her health was genuine and she was touched by it, although his growing pre-occupation with ailments and illnesses rather depressed her. Nor was he satisfied with the three pounds a week, but he did not make an issue of that, believing, like Betty, that, in certain circumstances, money was of no importance. Indeed he muttered that "she might as well do it for nothing and let them give it to charity" and Betty considered that, but rejected it as being too grand a gesture.

The nervousness passed as she became used to the echoes in the place and the size of it. She became used to being alone in such an unaccustomedly large area, while doing something hitherto firmly associated with extremely small areas—dusting, polishing, hoovering, cleaning. She had always enjoyed seeing places well cared for, whether it was the council house of a friend or one of the stately homes of England she had gone to on an outing. She loved things to be right for their place and in the right place and cared for, and she did not object at all to the work involved in caring for them. There was something about the complicated arrangements of objects in a room which satisfied her profoundly. Having had to struggle to create a feeling of family and having, as she now thought, failed, she still longed for domestic contentment and found that rooms themselves, certain rooms, indicated that in a way in which nothing else did. The choice of chairs, of colours, of tables, curtains, carpeting, wallpaper, photographs or paintings—the arrangement itself gave her a feeling of contentment. And very soon she began to experience and be nourished by a similar contentment in cleaning the church.

She admitted it to no one, but she began to enjoy those solitary hours in the church. It was a pleasant place, a Victorian reproduction of a Georgian church, a light and airy church with a grand organ, a gallery, a finely decorated ceiling, but—once she had got used to it—still small enough to feel cosy in. The work there seemed to steady her considerably. She slept better. She felt calmer. There was balm for that emptiness which had threatened to grow and pull her down. There was so much there.

The altar still filled her with awe. Mentally she tip-toed to it, her duster careful to disturb nothing. Passing in front of the cross confused her. As a child she had been told that whenever you were directly in front of the cross you should bow to it. The cross represented the Holy Trinity, God the Father, God the Son and God the Holy Ghost, and all earthly forces should bow down before them. This imposition had been sternly laid on her generation and now she found that it had been branded into her mind. There was no help for it. Whenever she passed by the cross, though the church was empty and she was there to clean even the cross itself, she paused and executed some sort of a bow. Yet, oddly, having tugged the cross forward and started to clean it, she just cleaned away and polished it almost like any other thing. Once back, however, in its true position in the middle of the altar under the large east window—much of which, alas, had been blocked out by an idealistic vicar in the early Fifties, who preferred the effect of a walled-up window to what had once intrigued and delighted Betty, Victorian stained-glass scenes of Christ with little children—once the cross had resumed its place, it reassumed its authority and she would bow again.

Mostly she would organize herself so that she did not have to be directly in front of it.

The church became a familiar place, the pulpit, the vestry, the font, the Lady Chapel, the choir stalls, each window with its broad sill and its stained-glass Bible-story became places, individual, particular, and all of them places in which Betty felt a different sort of emotion. For working here, doing the steady, easy cleaning, unhurried, at her own pace, released her comfortably into thoughts and speculations which nourished her. She would come out of the church feeling strengthened and consoled. Whereas when she came out of a church service she generally felt tense and a little agitated.

It had been a problem of some delicacy—whether or not to attend a service. Neither she nor Joseph had been regular church-goers since their teens. Nowadays it was the Carol Service, Easter Sunday and perhaps the Harvest Festival, to see the decorations. Betty did not fancy what would have seemed to her a rather complaisant plunge into instant piety.

On the other hand, it would have been talked about had she not gone to church and Betty would do almost anything to avoid being the subject of the slightest gossip. Cleaning the church meant that one belonged to it.

Eventually she decided to go to the Sunday morning service—what used to be called Sunday Matins, before the arrival

of all that Series I and Series II business and the up-to-date
Bible which never rang in her mind except to remind her that
something essential was missing. No matter. The important
thing was to go on the Sunday and so she did.

Curiously, bonuses followed from that decision. It gave a
stem to her Sunday. She would prepare the vegetables and put
on the roast before she left and come back ready for the brisk
final touches without that dragging feeling of just Hanging
Around for The Sunday Dinner. Moreover, it gave Joseph the
chance to sort himself out in peace and quiet, after what was
usually a rather fuddling Saturday night. His sabbatical surliness had evaporated by the time she returned—and her piety
put him at a further disadvantage. Sundays were to some extent
relieved of what had imperceptibly become a deadening
pressure of the boredom that so often characterizes dutiful
intense cohabitation.

Joseph would even offer to get out the car and take them for a
drive to the Lakes or the coast.

In a short time, Betty was a pillar of the Anglican community.
The church itself, it was hinted—no disrespect whatsoever to
Jennie—but the church itself had never been so clean. It
gleamed. All that was supposed to glitter glittered, all that
benefited from real polishing shone with real polish, the flowers
were daintily and deftly arranged, the hymn books were neatly
stacked, as were the hassocks. The carpets were flawless each
Sunday and this was noticed and remarked on. The other
stalwarts accepted her. Jimmie, who had served the church,
boy and man, for about fifty years, as choirboy, server, and now
verger, as Father Christmas, boilerman, odd-job man and constant help—Jimmie, who lived alone "and very comfortably
thank you very much. *I* take no harm, I'm telling you" and who
was completely absorbed in the detail, history, society and daily
life of the church, on which subject he was a humble but quite
remorseless authority—Jimmie took his time about it, was not
afraid to run a finger over a pew back in search of dust, scrutinized Betty (who had known him and liked him all her life, joked
with him, and was largely unaware of how threatening her
thoroughness could seem to his christianlike possessiveness)
and finally capitulated. The Sunday School teacher had always

liked Betty and that was no problem and the choirmaster and organist appreciated the sparkle on the organ's woodwork. Fairly soon, then, people she had known slightly for most of her life became much more important to her and she found a community there, a centre for her life outside the bungalow. And she realized this and vowed to herself to hold onto it for as long as she possibly could.

(4)

It got better and better. As the pregnancy went on, Emma felt stronger by the day. She could never remember feeling so buoyant, so fit, so clearly in tune with herself. Emma's body had, for most of her life, been a husk she was always ready to be ashamed of. From childhood she had absorbed the notion —rarely made explicit but, indisputably, there—that fatness was not only unattractive and unhealthy, it was also rather common. Vulgar people were fat. Landladies on Donald McGill seaside postcards; wives of the labourers in the village; women who trudged around the shops on Saturday morning in the nearby town—Emma's parents had unknowingly passed on a hearty but effective snobbery. For fatness—so went the implication—was to do with ignorance and self-indulgence, the two conditions—or vices—which the then confident middle classes of England attributed to the working classes more in pity than anger. Of course there was the occasional middle-class fat woman who was again either (gently) ridiculed or firmly pronounced "stout", "well made", "a good figure of a woman" *or* "jolly" *or*—finally—"troubled with her glands".

But such certainties were past—or they had gone underground temporarily, it was impossible to tell—as the working classes took on middle-class habits and proletarian militancy. Such fairly innocent snobbery withered away and that, too, benefited Emma, whose life had been made near-hellish at times because society had decided, in one of its tyrannical decrees, that it was comical and unfashionable to be fat. Dresses were not made for her, nor were clothes shops places of pleasure but little penal settlements to which she banished herself from time to time to endure the punishment of trying on what would

199

not fit and hearing the sympathetic or politely mocking (it made no odds which) voice of the salesgirl, trying to pretend that she did not bulge out of the dress like a big parcel tied up with too little string. And Fat meant short of breath and rotten at games and excluded from the gang that took the risks and had the most fun. And Fat meant being left out when friends clicked with boys and finding excuses to save them embarrassment over the inevitable neglect: and Fat meant resigning yourself to lesser satisfactions, lesser goals, lesser expectations, lesser possibilities, even though the needs and desires and ambitions roared away inside you as fiercely as in anyone else. Sometimes there would be a fat girl who would manage to funnel this force into action and she would breeze across Emma's line of vision—only to make her feel more isolated and threaten her with being in the worst condition of all—sorry for herself: because then there would be undeniable evidence that the remedy was at hand if the will and purpose were discovered. Emma's will and purpose disappeared down a series of abortive diets, abrupt spasms of exercise and plain starvation, all of which always ended in hopeless bags of chocolates. There was no way out for her, it seemed: she had to live under this strange but powerful social curse which declared that fat women must suffer.

Then Lester turned up and banged into her without a single word about her fatness. And wanted to have her—she could tell without question, for it was unlike anything that had happened before. No kindness in it, no feeling of third best, no averted eyes and comments, no friendly reassurance and patronizing compliments—just the urgent act performed with various degrees of brisk brutality. She loved him for that.

Now the child was about to be born, and—as it were—when she least needed it, the fatness melted away. She looked like a slim young woman who was normally and even gracefully pregnant. The grace came from this unaccountable sensation of being tremendously lucky. She was lonely, she wanted Lester to be near her, she had to work quite hard to live equably with her parents, whose intentions were never less than good but, inevitably, from time to time, chafing. All this, however, faded away at the prospect of having her own baby. Her own child. She would bring the child into life, she would love the child, there would be someone lovingly bound to her and dependent on her and, despite her educated awareness of the travails and distress of unmarried motherhood, Emma wanted to clap her hands with pleasure at her own good fortune. It would be the finest thing she had done or could possibly ever do, she thought, and she was lucky to have it.

The days passed pleasantly in the vicarage. She helped her mother in the garden and, when she grew tired, she came in and read. She did not travel far from the house—there was no one she particularly wanted to see, save Lester. She wrote him many letters and posted only one or two of her briefer, breezier ones. As the time came near, though, a matter of days now, she thought that she should give him the chance to be at the birth. She had read in the paper that Douglas was going to do a film with Merlin Raven for the B.B.C. and she sent the letter to Douglas with a note asking him to forward it urgently.

Dear Lester,

I thought I'd write and tell you how things were going. Well, in a word. I'm well and, according to the ancient doctor who examines me as if I were a specimen on a slab, the about-to-be-born-baby is well, too. So you needn't worry. And don't think that this letter is blackmail or a nagging word. It isn't. Everything has been done that could be done and I have been very well looked after. No complaints! I *would* like you to be here, though. Naturally. I know that you have a lot to do but if you could make it or if you want to know where it's all happening (!) I'll be in the Maternity Ward, Ipswich General Hospital, Ipswich. From about Saturday next (the 14th), the doctor seems to think. Or you could write here of course—parents will always forward.

So. What are you up to? I read your stars regularly in all the magazines I can lay my hands on and you seem to be due for "success, excitement and unexpected rewards". I believe everything they say! Mine are quite good too.

I think about that place in Kentish Town quite a lot. I wish I'd been able to see you before I left. I know it wasn't your style but it might have been (temporarily) useful to you to have taken it over for a few months. It was very cheap and I would have liked the idea that you were there. The landlady was a bit of a grump, though.

Everything's fine here. My parents have been ace and, of course, would be delighted to meet you. They're a bit stiff and poshish, but I think that you'd like them well enough. I've told them that the baby was my fault or rather, my—what I wanted—which is correct, in a way, even though I didn't plan the accident! And that you have a busy life and there's no reason *at all* why you should be involved at all unless *you want to be*. So you are totally free. (As if you didn't know! You're the freest man I've ever met!)

And they understand all this because it makes sense and, most of all, because I'm in such good spirits. I have my downs, of course—who doesn't? And I *would* like to see you—but I'm not going to whine. What keeps me going—in fact what keeps me happy—is the thought of your baby inside me and me ready to look after it. I'm *sure* you think that's horribly sentimental and sloppy. Well—people tend to *get* horribly sentimental just before childbirth, I'm told.

There's lots I could write but I guess you hate long letters. Probably haven't even read as far as this.

I think about you a lot and love you very much. Good luck, God bless.

Love, Emma. XX

(5)

Mary had already put off two meetings with Douglas. He had phoned her the evening after his last encounter with Hilda, asking if he could come round, but she had pleaded exhaustion, which was true. They had made a date for the following night but she had asked him to confirm it and, when he rang, she again put him off. She sensed that something significant, something demanding was being prepared and she wanted to be ready for it.

She had the clear knowledge that she must tread very carefully. She had never thought that her head and her feelings could be so jangled, so liable to a sensation of break up, so hair-triggered and full of fear. Beset with a kaleidoscope of unpredictable and often new and panic-provoking feelings, she was passing through storms of the mind which left her bewildered and worn out. There were times, for example, when she would be able to think of Douglas as nothing more or less than a monster. She would recount to herself the list of his suspected infidelities; she would go over the times he had come back drunk; she would even allow herself to think back on the death of their daughter and turn *that* against him. She swung from trivial objections to Douglas, to the most profound disgust for him, and from a feeling of utter dejection at his retreat from her to some elated glimmerings of freedom.

When he did come round, finally, she was as ready as she could make herself. The flat was spotlessly tidy. John was still up, in his pyjamas and dressing gown. Douglas had not been prepared for this but appeared to welcome it, genuinely, and they played draughts for a while. It was unusual for Douglas to devote so much time in the house to John. His normal methods of executing his duty to his son and (to be fair) enjoying the boy's company, were to take him out—to a match, a film, a museum or into the park for a kick-around. Mary, while pretending to read, watched Douglas cynically: so it took a break-up and, who knew?, possibly also a breakdown, for her simple picture of family life to come true!

After John had gone to bed, Mary made some coffee. She refused Douglas' offer to make it. She did not want him pottering about the place as if he naturally belonged there. It was increasingly important to her that this flat was hers and John's, and everyone else who came to it came as guests.

They sat a little awkwardly, sipping the "real" coffee. Douglas with a small scotch; Mary was not drinking. She wanted to be as calm and controlled as possible.

The silence built up. The flat was in a quiet crescent and there was no noise from traffic. The weather had begun to turn and, although there was a cool edge to the air, there was no need for a fire, Mary had thought. She was even more careful now about every item. But she wished she had not economized on this: the longer they sat, the colder she grew. And then she thought she understood the reason for Douglas' constricted silence. She flushed with fear, shame and embarrassment.

"You want a divorce," she said. "That's why it's so formal. Isn't it?"

"No. It isn't that at all."

"Yes it is. Don't lie, Douglas."

"Oh for God's sake, Mary. I'm not lying."

"I can always tell. All the times you used to come back and say you'd met one or other of your friends and gone back to their place for a drink after the pubs had closed—do you think I'm stupid? Of course I know when you're lying! You can't help lying. You're compulsive. Do you know what it's like being lied to? And knowing you're being lied to? And accepting it because *not* to accept it would cause disruptions? You become an accomplice. I became an accomplished accomplice! Without my help, your lies would have been shown up for the tacky little cheats they were, because the funny thing is—I used to think it was the redeeming thing—that you're a rotten liar. But, because I made it so easy for you to lie, you took advantage. You take advantage of everything. I've made it easy for you to split. Oh, you've been very good about money and when I read about other poor women or hear about them I am truly grateful for that, although it's still tight—but, apart from that, it *has* been easy for you. But I can't handle a divorce at the moment. It's humiliating, you know. However much sympathy I get—and most of our friends agree that you're a prize bastard: in fact I seem to spend half my time defending you to them. But I can't—I'm not strong enough for a divorce! Not yet!"

She stopped. Lit a cigarette. She was shaking.

During her outburst, Douglas had experienced distaste, apprehension, sympathy, shame, admiration at some of her insights, but, finally, hopelessness.

"I did not come here to ask for a divorce." Say it, he urged himself, say it! "In fact," Say it! "I came to say I thought we ought to get together again." He smiled ruefully. "And that's the truth," he added.

"Just like that?"

"Yes."

"Get together? Tonight?"

"You'd have to think about it, wouldn't you?" Douglas was perturbed by his adverse reaction towards the suggestion that he stay the night. He had not thought he would be given that option so soon. He had imagined that Mary's pride would enjoin her to hold him off for some days while she thought over his proposition. Now he discovered that he retreated from the idea.

Mary seized on his hesitation, acutely sensitive to the anxiety in his mood.

"You don't want to stay tonight, do you? Do you?"

"That isn't the point."

"That isn't an answer."

Douglas took a deep breath. No. He had to go on. Nothing else made sense.

"If you would stop ranting on and scoring debating points we might get somewhere," he said, roughly. "Ever since I've walked in you've behaved like a cross between a Christian martyr and a prison governor. Besides telling me what I think all the bloody time. Now calm down. We're not talking about jumping into bed. We're talking about a life and a marriage."

"Nice one, Douglas." She puffed nervously at her cigarette. Both of them were aware that she had winkled out his evasions.

"So where does that get us?" he asked.

"Where do you want to go?"

"Don't be smart."

"I'll be whatever I want."

"Sorry."

"That's another of your favourite tricks. 'Sorry.'"

"Meaning?"

"I don't have to spell it out."

"You've got me pretty well taped, Mary. You seem to have made good use of the time—I'm Shit Number One."

After a pause, Mary began to cry. Douglas, who had been sitting opposite her, went across and took her in his arms to comfort her. For a while they sat together like that.

"You see," she said, as if picking up from a point they had reached in another conversation on another day, "I want you to come back, of course I do. I miss you terribly. But, Douglas, something's happened since you left. I still don't know what it is. But so much has collapsed and changed inside me—I'm not putting it very well: I don't want to be dramatic—it's just that it feels like that. So much has changed. I feel that in a way I'm becoming a different person. And although it scares me—I can't go back. If you come to live with me, I'd go back to what I was. I don't want that. I want to change. I'd become so horribly dependent on you for everything. I know I had a job some of the time but outside that—and even that in a way—our life—*my* life—was *your* life. I feel it now. I feel as if something has been peeled off me—something as important as a skin has been peeled off me. And it scares me so much I don't know whether I can come through. I don't know whether I can even breathe the next breath, sometimes. It's indescribably awful. And I long for you to be here—but I know that I've got to be on my own. I've got to. It's a way of becoming—I don't know—myself, I suppose—how pathetic—growing up, maybe—but I want to do it. Your mother wrote, saying she would welcome John for the holidays. He's going there to stay—he'll like that. I'm going to stay with an old girlfriend—she has a cottage in Sussex. There's a little chalet affair I can have for myself. I want to be on my own, Douglas. If you want to help me, leave me alone. That's the best you can do now. Everything else is exhausted. Somehow it's all over. Now I have to start again."

(6)

Douglas read the letter immediately.

My darling,
    I know that you would prefer it if we had no contact at all but I have to write to say one thing. It's very hard to say. You know that I love you. I still think and believe that you love me. But I have grown tired of the waiting and this final decision of yours has left me without any hope. You must have known that when you made it and when you told me.
    I feel you must know this. I don't respect you for what you have done. I don't think it's noble of you to return to

your wife and leave me. I don't admire you for it and I don't think you've done the right thing. From what you've said and from what I can put together I think that your marriage is over. Going back will only be putting off the eventual split up. But the reason I don't respect you isn't because I think you're mistaken—it's because you seem to me to have betrayed the most important thing you were supposed to stand for.

Please don't try to see me or contact me again in any way. *Please*. It is going to be very hard for me and I'll need a lot of work to survive. I *can't* take sympathy, talk, *anything at all* from you. *Please* leave me totally alone.

I love you.

Hilda

# 3
# A Portrait of Merlin Raven

"O.K. O.K. Understood." While Lester spoke into the telephone, he looked directly at Douglas across the mixing desk, as
if he were on stage playing to an audience of one. His voice was
unaccustomedly quiet, controlled and almost as business-like as
he wanted it to sound. That was the new style for pop-
managers: not only cool but professional, boardroom cool, and
deep piled rich, international fixer confident. They had become
copycats of high finance and the low profile big deal operators
on the Market. Douglas refrained from smiling. "Understood," Lester kept saying, earnestly, every so often. And
occasionally he would add, "No hassle" or, "You name it." He
was being talked to by Merlin, who had the dictatorially eccentric habit of using the telephone precisely as if it were a person in
his room; a person whom he treated rather badly. For he would
put the phone down and get himself a cigarette, fix a drink, even
wander off to another room—but his correspondent had to stay
there, on guard, at the ready, unfazed. And the phone had not
to be put down by anyone but Merlin. He had been known to
keep the game up for an hour. Lester had cottoned on to this,
fortunately, when he had been in Merlin's place and seen him in
action receiving a call from the chief press man of the biggest
recording company in the world. At one stage on that occasion,
Merlin had gone for a shave. Lester had helpfully picked up the
phone to explain this only to be met with a controlled, quiet,
mid-Atlantic pinstripe voice saying "Understood. O.K. O.K.
Understood."

The purpose of the present call was simple. Merlin was
already eight and a half hours late for the first day's filming.
Douglas had called the crew for one o'clock in order to set and
light for a two thirty start. The crew had now been on overtime
for four hours and costs were starting to soar. Douglas was

working out how he would handle it when—if—Raven turned up. He was furious at being mucked about. The two thirty start had been guaranteed. Here they were in the enormous recording studio, lights rigged, microphones ready, camera positions marked out—and he had to absorb not only his own frustration but the frustration and visibly ebbing interest of two cameramen and their assistants, two sound recordists and their assistants, three lighting men, a P.A. and a researcher. They had all been on jobs involving Prime Ministers, Presidents, opera stars, ballet stars, scientists, high news-value names— and they were not very amused at being stood up by a guy whom half of them (at least) thought of as no more than the "best of that cruddy bunch of lucky little sods who can turn out the songs that get into the Top Twenty".

Douglas, who was directing the documentary as well as writing it, knew that it was important to retain the crew's interest, especially when you were dealing with individuals who could easily feel the weight of collective opinion and would inevitably react badly to the sort of disapproval now building up. So Douglas had to watch the crew carefully, staunching with a joke or a laconic rebuttal any serious sign of that snowballing discontent which could ruin the atmosphere while yet allowing, even encouraging, the sort of groaning and complaining which was therapeutic. The main thing was to keep Merlin Raven's reputation as intact as possible. This Douglas did, quite shamelessly, by two methods. Firstly by letting drop the amount of money which Raven had acquired for certain records—here he was helped by the studio's own sound crew, who had turned up to provide the technicians for an authentic studio mix. They had worked with Merlin in his great days and let drop statistics which commanded very considerable respect: a four million dollar advance for an L.P. which finally grossed nine million; a two million dollar yearly retainer from the record company with no strings attached; the full use of these studios at any time of the day or night—orchestras, other groups, whomsoever, to be displaced if necessary—discreetly, but definitely. When Merlin wanted to turn up and make a tape then the studio had to be available and so had his preferred crew. The cost of that impressed everyone, too.

Secondly, Douglas found ways to remind them how rare this occasion was: that there had been nothing on Raven for years: that there had never been a substantial interview: that he had promised them a New York concert at which they could film exclusive footage: that there was already massive American, German and Japanese interest, even before a foot had been shot: that they were, in short, on something very special which would be very big. And he had to disguise the fact that his own resentment was mounting by the minute. Who the hell did Merlin Raven think he was? (He was, of course, somebody who could keep an entire crew waiting for a week if he chose to.)

The fact that after ten o'clock the overtime began to climb into astral regions also helped, Douglas realized: and he used that too. On the other hand: he was fed up.

"Understood. O.K. O.K. No sweat. Understood," Lester said.

"Ask him when he's coming," Douglas said, very loudly. "We've had a hurried tea break and some lousy sandwiches for supper so as not to desert our post. I want to take the crew out for a bowl of spaghetti if they're going to work through the night. There's a place around the corner. Salvatore's. He can join us if he wants. We're breaking for an hour."

"Understood. O.K. O.K."

"Let's go!" Douglas bellowed, quite suddenly angry. "I'm famished."

Lester cupped his hand over the telephone.

"He might be coming along any minute," he said.

"We'll be at Salvatore's," Douglas repeated. "We'll keep a chair for him."

"Douglas. You're taking a risk, Douglas." Lester's veneer cracked. "What the hell am I supposed to say to him?"

"Salvatore's."

"You could have blown it."

"Nature calls. Food. Let's go."

He bundled the crew out and left Lester stranded with the recording crew, who looked enviously at the liberated television team.

"Understood," said Lester, making a great effort. "O.K. Er—Merlin—er—they've . . . they had to—union—the union says they have to break for an hour. No. The TV lot. Not *our* lot. Good? Oh yes. Understood. O.K. O.K."

Lester replaced the phone and smiled bleakly.

"He'll be here in two minutes," he announced. "He wants to start mixing right away. While they're not here."

"Understood," the mixer said. "O.K.?" To the others.

"O.K.," they chorused: and laughed at Lester's disconsolate expression.

"You'll get used to it, Lester."

"Don't worry, kid. Understood?"

"Understood."

Lester grinned back at them all, swore a little and went down to the machines for a coffee. He found their taunting hard to take but he had to put a bold face on it. They had discerned that his connection with Merlin was a whimsical one. They themselves, engineers, musicians, an accountant, a P.R. man, knew their worth, could always find work elsewhere in the pop business, especially after working for Merlin in this new emergent phase which was already causing a big stir in the music game and the industry. They were secure in a way which had always eluded Lester.

Yet, ironically, it was his personality which had been the catalyst to all the present activity. For Merlin had "taken to" Lester and, since that first night, he had begun to write those seemingly simple songs which were hummed by millions and treasured by minorities and worth a fortune. Some combination of the time and the man had proved perfect. Merlin had snapped out of the long tunnel of self-indulgence, self-doubt, self-absorption—and Lester was the man who had given him the final heave out of the hole. With a fine sense of judgement, though, Merlin sensed that Lester's value would be limited—and so although he was unashamedly piratical and open in looting Lester's affections—professing friendship, throwing his arms around him, hugging him, taking him out for meals, asking him (particularly) to talk about the past, his adventures, the countryside—yet he made it clear to others that Lester was not really essential. With regard to pay, for example: Lester now worked full-time for Merlin and, although the job would have been hard to describe at a Labour Exchange, it demanded all of such talents and energy as he had, and the hours were elastic to breaking point. For this, he was handed fifty pounds a week, in crisp fivers, by the haughty pretty-boy accountant who managed Merlin's money. No insurance was paid, of course, nor were there any conditions of employment—no cover at all. But fifty lousy pounds! Lester only survived because Merlin let him sleep in a bedroom in his flat—some nights.

Lester held on for two binding reasons: there was no better alternative available and he still believed that somehow he would manipulate this connection to his own unbounded glory and advantage. He would not let go this time. Already he thought he could see that his reputation was being restored around the place. A nod here, a wink there, and now and then the big hello from fellows wouldn't give him the time of day a couple of months back. Oh yes. Raven was power, no question. But how to turn it, that was the problem: how to make the first killing, do the big one, get on the trail to where it mattered.

He saw the chance in this film of Douglas', even though the idea of working with Douglas was a pain. Difficult as it was for him to admit to himself, he had been surprised and impressed by his cousin's ability. At times, indeed, he was in danger of being as overawed by Douglas as he was by Merlin. Douglas' grasp of the entire operation—the ideas in it, the structure, the final shape, the cost, the details of shooting and editing, the laws of copyright, the rights of the different unions, impressed him: most of all, though, it was the fact that Douglas was in charge which surprised him. He had always thought of Douglas as physically a bit tentative, something of a mother's boy, uncommunicative about what he did, secretive even, not to be taken for a man—and yet there he was totally dominating the lot of them. And still with the same (to Lester) unconvincing manner: that was the peculiar thing. No shouting or ordering or bulling or bullying: an occasional rapped out decision, true, but very occasional.

Yet the camera crew respected him and listened to him. The crew in the studio had soon been in much the same relationship. Merlin, who had met Douglas for a long lunch in order to clinch the deal (contracts for which were not yet signed, though a

sufficient measure of agreement had been reached to enable the
B.B.C. to go ahead), had declared himself "quite impressed".
Yet Lester kept remembering Douglas, hesitant with his father,
self-deprecating before Harry, hang-dog about his wife, grubbing about for gossip on Thurston from himself, altogether a
pushover. This image persisted in Lester's mind, despite the
evidence before his eyes, and he was banking on its essential
truth; for, in the end, Douglas had only agreed to make the film
because Lester had virtually blackmailed him into it—using as
his threat the truth: that if he, Lester, did not get a job out of
this, then he was finished for good. Merlin was his lifeline. And
Lester knew that Douglas had been shifted, finally, by this
appeal to family solidarity: the man Wainwright had confirmed
it, telling Lester that without his persuasion there would have
been no project, which was why Lester made an extra twenty-
five pounds a week from the B.B.C. as a "consultant". Douglas
had insisted that Lester get a screen credit to that effect. So
Lester's reasoning was that having moved Douglas once and
shifted him into something which served his own purpose, he
could do it again. He had a plan.

When Douglas and the crew finally came back it was almost
midnight. They had been gone for an hour and a half. They
came into the control box, a noisy crew, well-fed and watered,
ready to quit or bust a gut for a couple of hours to get the
material.

They had ignored the red light. Merlin was recording. They
quietened down.

The desk which organized the music coming up from the
studio was like something out of the space programme in Hous-
ton. There were literally scores of levers, switches, buttons,
lights, plugs and keys ready to mix a multitude of tracks. Even
the simple songs being recorded by Merlin now were being laid
out on sixteen tracks. At the moment (although his group—a
couple of guitarists, a keyboard player and a drummer—were
in the studio to help him) all that was being taken was his voice.

Like everyone else, Douglas was soon charmed by that voice.
It was charm which was at the centre of Merlin's attraction, he
thought. Charm in the older, most profound sense, of spell-
binding, disarming, the siren voice, the pipes of the Pied Piper,

the soothing lute, all the charm of psalms and simple songs read about in epic histories. Merlin had that for this age. He caught it in those clever, stylish, often *faux-naïf* metropolitan tales, one of which now wound about the studio like an ancient traditional air, though it had been written only a couple of days before. He was good, Douglas thought. Bloody good.

The take ended. There was a pause. The mixer pressed down the talk-back button which allowed him to speak directly to the studio.

"That was fine by me," he said. "Fine."

Merlin's voice came back out of the studio cave, rather irritable, even carping, the tone of a man engrossed in attempting to perfect something and unable, in the final stages, to find anyone to help him in that last assessment before the thing was done.

"I thought the first eight bars were a bit too soft." He thunked the strings of the acoustic guitar he used and did a witty parody of himself. "Too much like that. Needs to be harder. What do you think?"

"We could do it again."

"We've done it twenty-seven times! Is this a record, I ask myself? Did anybody else hear it? Is anybody up there receiving me?" He paused. "Was that Douglas and his mob who came in? What did they think?"

"They came in half way through."

"I thought no bugger was supposed to be allowed in half way through."

"They just came in."

"What's the use of having a red light?" Merlin hesitated. "Let's hear it back," he said, sharply.

Douglas went across to the sound engineer.

"Could I use the talk-back?" he asked.

The engineer was a little anxious after his joust with Merlin.

"He wants to hear it back," he said and pressed the button which whirled back the tape.

"This won't take a minute," Douglas said and leaned forward to press the button. "Merlin, this is Douglas—hello." It was faintly ridiculous talking into the spindly little microphone which jutted out of the control panel like a loose end. Below them, in the studio which could easily house a full classical orchestra, four youngish guys in jeans—the waiting band—swigged beer out of cans and lit up while the fifth, Merlin, entered into that long and involved system of his own, that dicing and playing ritual which was never a routine but necessary, almost as if he put himself in a trance, listening for any hint or sign which would switch him in a happier direction and give his work that final, "distinguishing" charge.

That was why he demanded to work with the same engineers, even if they had to be flown over from L.A. That was why he had used the same studio for every one of his major records. That was why a hundred and one small acts of superstition and professionalism had built up into a pattern of work which only he was allowed to be fully aware of. Merlin could always find a tune and construct a song and find words and they would work. To improve, though, to make tune, accompaniment, lyrics and performance better, needed a mixture of persistence—which he had—and this acute sense of being in the perfect mood for that particular song so that it sounded just "right". So that it could never again be done as well. It was as if he were in part a satellite returning from orbit, nudging for the absolutely correct point of re-entry. And, until he got that feeling, he was willing to keep looking for it, whatever the cost to anyone else.

"Hello, Douglas," Merlin said, with just the lightest touch of jokiness—the touch that put him above Douglas in the authority stakes in the power game they were playing. "Have a good nosh at Salvatore's?"

"Pretty good."

"It's a nice place for spaghetti. If you like spaghetti. Did you have spaghetti?"

"Merlin. It's late. We've been here about twelve hours now. The crew's tired. Some of them have a long way to travel and families waiting and so on. We've already screwed up tomorrow morning's shooting because we're so late we've run into the ten hour rule. So the question is this. We can stay and film now. For, say, two hours. Or we can go and do it again some other time. Up to you."

The words, Douglas calculated, were reasonable. So were the statements. The tone was not. Despite his admiration for

Merlin and despite his awareness that to walk off the story tonight would be to walk off it altogether, Douglas could not exclude his own annoyance at being buggered about that bit too much. Lester glared at him for presuming to call the shots.

"We're in the middle of a song," the engineer said, warningly.

Merlin took his time about replying.

"Tell you what. I'll listen to it back. Do it once more. Then we can film. How about that?"

Douglas hesitated. He knew that Merlin was quite capable of stringing them along in this manner for the rest of the night. He did not believe in his promises. He took counter-action. "I'll ask my crew." He turned to them and deliberately left the microphone open so that Merlin would "accidentally" overhear them. "Well?"

"I think we should call it a day," one of the cameramen said. He had been itching for home since seven p.m.

"I liked that song," his assistant announced. "I love that song. I think it's one of his best. I could sit and listen to it all night."

"Five minutes," said the sparks. "Give him five minutes. Then I go, I'm pissed off."

"O.K.," Douglas said and turned to the mike. "I think once you get into the record there'll be no stopping you. Fair enough. If you're going to stop you might as well stop now."

Merlin smiled. He would welcome the break. There had been two good hours and he wanted to clear his head before having a final session on the song. An interview with Douglas and larking about the studio doing a bit of filming would be just right.

"Lester!" Merlin shouted. "Go out and get us all some fish and chips, will ya? We're starving down here." Then, as an afterthought. "Right, Douglas: let's get going, man. 'The B.B.C. Int-er-view. Ho Ho!'"

(2)

"It's good," Mike said, taking care to make his words carry the weight he intended. He put the typescript of "Death Of A

216

Friend" back on his desk. They were in his office at the B.B.C. "It might be very good."

"It's too short." Douglas felt a little like a pupil receiving comments on an essay. But he had wanted Mike to read it. "For the publishers. '35,000 words are hopeless.' Unquote. I'm supposed to write another of the same length and they'll 'make a book of it'. Or·a paper boat. So: 'Birth of An Enemy'?"

"That's a pity." Mike found it increasingly difficult, these days, to talk to Douglas about anything other than the work they had in common. "But it'll come out some day."

"Perhaps." Douglas paused for a moment. "It's the best thing I've written."

"By far."

"So. New York's on."

"Yes. The budget was agreed when I told them what it was for. They reckon that if we can get world television rights, they'll be able to sell the programme in enough places to make it worth their while. Exclusive footage of Raven's first concert for—how many years? And New York will be good for the other bit."

"The life-style stuff?" Douglas nodded. "I'm bored with all that. We've got an interview: we'll get the music—that'll do me. That's what it consists of, doesn't it?"

"Of course. And the interview was good."

"Could have been better. There's something so elusive about him that you don't see the sidestep until he's passed you by. And he *will* speak in those colloquial clichés which you have to re-interpret if you're to get the full meaning—which he intends you to get *but* he wants *the fans* to know that he's still the laddo and they mustn't be left out. He's got a double radar system: one going out to pick up the shape and size of the audience: the other is to scan his own reactions for songs. He's very clever. And when you de-code him, he's still clever."

"That comes out."

"Not enough. Why the wallpaper in New York?"

"I think it's important," Mike said. "I know you don't, but I do. He talks well—good: we hope he'll play and sing well—even better. But there *has* to be something of his

217

'life-style'—as you disparagingly call it. You've never been prepared to give enough value to scenes like those."

"Velvet-clad young rock-poet wandering alone through Central Park, hand in hand with a B.B.C. crew?"

"You may laugh."

"Oh no. Laugh's the last thing I do when I see 'life-style' stuff. Throw up, more like it."

"Douglas. You and I think that this man does what he does very well indeed, better than anybody alive and as good as most dead. Maybe it's an easy trade or art—maybe. But he excels. On top of that, literally millions of people, millions, think of him as a pal, a guru, a prophet, a poet, a rebel, a rocker, an idol—whatever ideal of fantasy they have is projected onto this one man. Now we'll see him sing and play—all well and good. We'll see him answer questions—fine. But we'll get nowhere near the business hassle which he's so good at. Those charts you say you'll have which will show his companies and businesses —O.K., but from what Lester says he's obsessional about money and possessions and material power—those charts get nowhere near it! And what about the sexual ambiguities which have always surrounded him? And the connections with—High Society? A few newspaper clippings? Tepid. At least this, let's see him in a suite in the Plaza Hotel or the Pierre, paying out four hundred and fifty dollars a day and being flunkied by liveried Americans. Let's see him walk through the crush bar barriers to somewhere like Studio 54 and hear le Tout New York grovelling, as le Tout that sort of New York always will at a Success. Let's see some of those magnums of champagne he sips—and many people will get far more from that than they will from the interview. You find that hard to swallow or understand, Douglas, but it's true."

"What will they see?"

"There are people who read into pictures—wallpaper as you call it—far more than you do. You're a word man. Fine. So am I. Up to a point. But words are only part of communication. Often a small and unsophisticated part compared with what we can see, the other sounds we can hear, what we can deduce from carefully edited images. *More* can be got from that. All the things that you have, frankly, failed to deliver in your film so far, can be reclaimed in the 'life-style stuff'. If he *is* the ruthless bastard I suspect from Lester's very guarded comments, then you'll catch that—if you're a good enough director and aim in the right direction. *And* the sex: it'll come out, in a disco, in a restaurant, in an unaware moment—I know he has fewer unguarded moments than most but it *will* come out and a good director would know when and where to look for that and lead to it. And there's all the rest—the social ramifications, for instance: what happened to England that a young man who got on no longer felt it necessary to ape aristocratic manners or attitudes? Up until now, the social ladder has been pretty clear for all to see and each step has counted. Who cares now? Feminists would go mad, but the fact is that a number of women still care. Do men? Do young businessmen or drama-tists or television producers or whatever want to talk like or live like aristos? And, if they do, do they take it at all seriously? Here we have one of the richest, certainly the most famous, clearly among the most intelligent men of his generation, who has decided to build up his own life-style, taking a bit here, a bit there, beholden to no system yet all of a piece. How do you show that? It could be fascinating."

"O.K. New York." Douglas grinned. "Maybe American wallpaper will be better."

"You're not a film maker," Mike said, happily.

"Nope. I make programmes. A deep, dark and significant difference. But I'll try to capture the magic of Merlin on the magic of celluloid. You certainly earn your wages, Mike."

"So do you." Mike's return of the compliment disturbed him. This was not his way. It was a strain not to tell Douglas of his interest in Mary, but she had asked him not to. It was less than total openness in friendship and Mike did not like it.

"What is this?" Douglas said. "Ping-pong flattery?"

"Worrying. Let's go for a drink."

"To the B.B.C. Centre Bar?"

"There's nothing else within miles."

"When I retire, I'll take a pub outside the gate and make a mint from the likes of us."

"It's not so bad if you abandon all hope before you enter."

It was not so very bad. The problem was that it was neither

fish, fowl nor good red herring: or rather, neither pub, club nor glorified snack bar but an uncunning mixture of all three which made it rather like a trough, a place where you came to guzzle and no more. But the people were nice.

"That's the best thing about this place," Mike said, as they took their drinks over to a vacant stretch of crimson leatherette, "the people. Cheers!" They sipped in unison. "Of course, it's such agreeable work, it's likely to attract agreeable people."

"And the rest," Douglas said.

"The Rest are everywhere."

"When I first came here—it was much smaller then—it almost looked like a bar then—I used to be delighted to see that sort of thing"—Douglas pointed to three ladies in full Elizabethan costume having half of lager each—"or that sort of thing"—he indicated five men smeared in green jelly, long, lank, green ringlets drooping about their Gorgonzola faces—"or all of the Famous Face business"—Famous Faces dipped in favourite drinks. "And the odd thing is," Douglas went on, "that although the feeling of delight wore off after a year or two, it's come back. It's like getting feeling back in your fingers after they've been frozen." He drank hastily to mask the openness of the confession. "Same again?"

Mike finished his drink and considered what course to take, while Douglas went up to the long service bar for two more drinks. There must have been scores of people in this bar in an analogous position—or with experience of his present dilemma. These producers and directors, presenters, designers, cameramen, actors, actresses, researchers, production assistants, all inhabited a world just that bit more bashed below the marriage belt than most. In an age of steadily increasing divorce, separation and declared infidelity, this curious mix of public service, drama, show-business, sport, thought and art, was more used to and more tolerant of marital failings than most. Yet Mike felt as prudish as a Sunday School teacher and for this he both blamed and admired Douglas.

Over the past few weeks, as they had worked closely together and Mike had learnt again to appreciate the thoroughness of Douglas' grasp of what he was doing and the determination to do it, he had again come across the man's solitariness. It revealed itself, paradoxically, only when you got to know him well. Douglas was apparently affable and easy-going to work with, although he was liable to strong action and reaction if anyone fell down on their job. He had friends—either from way back in Cumbria or from his first year or two in London, in his early twenties. He saw them regularly and they were steady: he was liked and trusted, as indeed he was by Mike himself. But there were certain questions which would not go away. Why did he appear to be so hapless about a career which with even the slightest guidance would have been at the very least well secured, full of interest and primed with the possibilities of interesting promotion within the broad acres of this grand institution? Why did he refuse to do any of the hack writing jobs taken up by contemporaries whom he declared, truthfully, he admired? Why, though his political ideas were clear and stoutly adhered to, had he not taken advantage of the cliquish polarization which would have worked so well in his favour over the last fifteen years? Why, perversely, did he turn up with a substantial and excellent piece of writing which was, in the present market conditions, virtually unpublishable?

More important than that, Mike felt, there was a moral nerve in Douglas which it was easy to hit. The trouble was that it was not always in the same place. Yet, curiously, for someone of undoubted worldly experience, Douglas gave the impression of being disapproving when dirty stories were told or deep-throat personal gossip was being bartered or even (though he himself would swear his head off on occasions) when four-letter words flew about the place. And that was symptomatic of a general vein in his character which, unusually for the times, Mike thought, still saw most things in sternly moral terms, despite his own manifest failings. There was still a sense of sin in Douglas and, worse, Mike thought, a hopeless hope of redemption. That isolated him.

"Cheers."

"Cheers."

"Let's drink to the moving wallpaper in New York."

"Good."

"Now, this regional business." Douglas pulled out of his bust briefcase a neatly typed half dozen sheets, which he handed over to Mike. "That's the re-think with the budget, the schedule, the structure, who I think should be in it and why, further sources and references to a couple of books and articles you might read. It's unusual, I know. Not a single man's wander *à la* K. Clark, D. Attenborough, J. Miller and all—but it's an important idea and, if it's done well, it could always be sold as a series of linked documentaries—which wouldn't scare anyone. I still think it's important." He took out another sheet. "Here's an idea for a small studio series on—well, you'll see. It's a B.B.C. 2 idea. Late night. Fun."

"Anything else?" Mike asked.

"Not at this moment."

"Why don't you sign up full time? Come onto the staff. You'll only have to work one-tenth as hard then."

"Too much else to do." Douglas paused. He was quite willing to make a confidant of Mike, but at the moment something held him back. He could not analyse it. "I'm keeping up that review spot for the World Service and there's another useful reviewing job coming up on the 'Guardian'. Fortnightly. And E.M.I. scripts have asked me to do some reading for them, plus I'm starting something else of my own. You may smile, but I need the money, with two establishments—even though mine is a ground floor garret—and the spur of honourably needed loot is, I discover, a great and revitalizing kick into honest endeavour."

"Stopped drinking?"

"Certainly not. But cut down."

"Why?"

"Hangover loses an hour a morning. Can't afford it."

"Fair enough. But you said you were going to Cumbria again after New York—something about an election, what was that?"

"My cousin's standing as Labour candidate in a bye-election. She doesn't have a hope in hell. It's one of the safest Tory seats in the U.K."

"She?"

"Lester's sister. Very unalike."

"There's a Cumbrian Mafia."

"I'm working on it. And she's pregnant. That'll help. She married my foster-brother."

"You really have an umbilical cord as thick as a rope, don't you?"

"Round my throat? Umbilical? No. People I like and know. I could cut it off and start again, say on the West Coast."

"You sound like Huckleberry Finn."

"Yes. But doesn't this—one life only business—not hit *you*?"

"Of course. It hits everybody," Mike said, matter-of-factly.

"It's extraordinary. To face that you are animate now and soon will be inanimate: no more breathing or seeing or tasting or anything. Just an end. It is overwhelming."

"Is that why you have become a workaholic?"

"Yes."

Once again Douglas would have found some relief in talking to Mike about Mary. He talked to no one at all about her and the pressure to do so threatened to spill over into this innocent conversation. But he respected his deeper instinct, which was to say nothing. There was a pause.

"What's the attraction of a bye-election?"

"It gives you a chance to ask a lot of people a lot of interesting questions." Mike nodded and Douglas went on. "That's the basic attraction of all interviewing. You get to ask the questions you would like to ask but feel too awkward to ask on any occasion but a formal interview which, after all, has been convened for the very purpose of asking such questions."

"You enjoy it. That's the point. And that makes it work."

"That too," Douglas said. Then, although he sensed that this was a move whose fullest significance he did not understand, he went on: "You and Mary get on well, don't you?"

"I always like to think so."

"You know that—you've worked all that out. Yes? We're living apart."

"I knew that."

"Well." Douglas hesitated. He detested people who brought others into their personal quarrels. On the other hand, he saw no way round this pressing anxiety he had. "The New York trip could take over a fortnight if we have all the trouble we expect. I don't like to think of her being—not so much alone—she wants that—but—without anyone to turn to." Mike was about to speak. Douglas held up a hand to silence him. "No, don't feel obliged. Just think about it. A phone call or two or maybe, I don't know, a meal out sometime. I wouldn't want to drag you into anything or compromise you. But there we are. O.K. Thanks for the wallpaper pep-talk. So long."

Douglas got up and went off immediately, leaving Mike with the convenient excuse that he had simply not had the time to tell Douglas what he believed he should have told Douglas. But he was fully aware that it was no more than a convenient excuse.

The bar was emptying as the offices and studios called back the living. The three Elizabethan ladies had long finished their lager: the Green Men had shuffled away, clutching crisps: Famous Faces, flushed salmon pink now, glanced at watches and agreed it was later than they had thought, just knock it back. The bodies which fed the machines which shot pictures into twenty-five million households trooped and traipsed and tripped back into the business of getting the show on the air.

Mike ordered himself a double scotch, added another for safety, collected half of bitter as a chaser, and, with a new packet of cigarettes, sought out a corner seat to think through, with the intention of arriving at a conclusion he would act on, the dilemma which now faced him. For he was in love with Mary and knew that they could enjoy a happy and decent life together: and he suspected now, for no reason that he could lay his finger on, that she just might have him. If he got it right.

(3)

New York, to Lester, was the playground of the Western World. The skyscrapers at the foot of Manhattan were symbols of power and riches more potent than Tutankhamun's Tomb, Buckingham Palace, St Peter's and the Stock Exchange crushed into one. The concrete canyoned streets excited him, the swashbuckling black Brummels brought the cordite of competitiveness to his nostrils, the raunchiness of the women seemed to him so much more "real" than the either tease-me-please or you-can-have-anything-for-a-price of London. He liked the loud-voiced men in the restaurants, the Brooklyn jawed and jewelled and vowelled and mawed mammas who

224

served coffee and wisecracks in the coffee lounges. He saw 42nd Street as his kind of jungle and cruised around Harlem in a cab, eyes half-closed, weighing up the shots. In the Italian quarter he could be the tough brother in "The Godfather"; around the docks he was Brando in "On The Waterfront"; on Park Avenue and Fifth Avenue he was surprised to discover he remembered odd phrases from songs and thought he could walk into a musical any minute. When the police cars wow-wowed he was Kojak. New York was a movie and he was the whole production.

He had never had it so good. That was a phrase he had picked up somewhere and found very little occasion for. Now he could use it every day and mean it every day. He had never ever had it so bloody good!

To be in New York was enough. To be in New York when somebody else was paying—in this case a closely argued split between Raven's accountant and the B.B.C.'s contract department—was very cool, very cool indeed. To be in New York with a film crew and the open sesame that gave, not to mention the conversation starter for those evenings full of well exercised New York talent—that was very neat. But to be in New York with Merlin Raven was just something else.

New York went hysterical about the concert. Madison Square Garden was sold out within three hours of the box office opening and coast-to-coast breakfast show news bulletins carried live interviews with the plucky lucky fans who had begun to camp around the building the week before. A fierce trade in black market tickets developed, when it was murmured that among the guests for this single performance would be Frank Sinatra, Princess Margaret (who was flying up from the Caribbean), Rudolf Nureyev (who was flying in from Caracas), the wife of the President of the United States, Liza Minnelli, Francis Ford Coppola, and Muhammed Ali; Diana Ross broke an important clause in a Las Vegas contract to get there; Hal Prince re-scheduled the London rehearsals of a new opera at Covent Garden to fly back; Jackie Onassis announced that she could not make it and then changed her mind and threw the box office into a hundred per cent panic; John Lennon said yes, he would go; Paul McCartney said he'd heard most of the tunes but it was time he brought Linda to New York for a bit and he would most likely have a look in; the head of the record company hired Studio 54 for the post-concert party, fell out with its proprietor because he was manhandled at the door by the mob of youths hired to keep people out, and switched to Regine's; Nigel Dempster leaked all this gleefully; David Hockney did the poster; Edward Gorey designed the programmes; David Frost, Dempster said, had volunteered to be M.C. and was reported to be "most disappointed" when his offer was turned down.

And the only film crew allowed inside the entire place was Douglas' B.B.C. outfit. Four cameras with four old B.B.C. sweats as cameramen, four sound men and six flustered "sparks": all linked to Douglas by headphones. He directed it like an Outside Broadcast. The American TV stations were so angry that they threatened to take final and fatal action against the Garden, against Raven, against the B.B.C. and against Douglas—but he had worked out his deals carefully, spent boring and unhappy hours with the relevant and the irrelevant unions, and his contracts were watertight. The American TV stations had to take news footage at the door and no more. They burned up the lines to London for an American sale and the B.B.C. was almost alarmed to discover that it had a very hot property in its hands. Hands were rubbed. Heads were put together. Heads of Department met on the sixth floor. Nods as good as winks were exchanged and returned to sender. B.B.C. executives spoke knowingly about "Pop" and "Amazing" and "Jackie Onassis" and ". . . of the United States, old boy—*and*, would you believe it—Canada! Oh—I see," "And we *have* it all, old boy. Wainwright. Mike. *Very* bright chap. Good chap. Mike Wainwright. Producer."

The programme became a two-and-a-half-hour special, to be transmitted at peak time on Christmas Eve. Mike found his grubby, cubby-hole office suddenly become the Kings Cross of the B.B.C. with interested executive traffic and schedulers, contract men and reporters pounding through it all day. He borrowed an empty office on another floor (Religion) and was undisturbed, except by the phone calls to and from New York. For the pressures on the production had become very big and he was worried that Douglas might have no energy left to do the actual filming.

Then he saw the first four days' rushes and ceased to worry. Douglas had never directed anything better. What was more, he had adopted an interviewing style which up until now he had steadily abjured: that is to say, he asked questions as the crew was setting up, as Raven was doing other things, amid the confusion he generally so deplored. His usual method was to collect evidence, sift it, research the man or the matter as thoroughly as possible, work out a line, get the best possible conditions for thoughtful and sustained conversation and then drive it through. All this had been done in the studio that night and Mike had been delighted with the result. But it was nothing compared with this stuff.

Mike telexed Douglas to tell him as much and advise him that the budget had been increased, as had the air-time, and he could stay on another week if he needed to.

But it was when he saw the rushes of the concert that Mike knew they had a serious winner: a programme that would not only entertain and enlighten and stand for what it believed in, but something that would print itself on people's minds and leave traces found long after in all sorts of asides and recollections and impressions of the time. For Merlin was sensational.

His style was quiet, undemonstrative, intense and totally compelling. He had taken fastidious care with the band and the music balance, in that vast acreage, was almost perfect, certainly far, far better than any other similar bands had achieved there. He sang some of his old hits but, again, he had taken trouble over them: they were rearranged, sometimes subtly re-worded—which delighted the fans who knew them by heart and gave a useful stimulus to the critics who saw "development", "self-parody", "progression", "re-working" and even "re-thinking". And he sang some of the numbers which had been triggered by his meeting Lester. These, it was agreed in the serious music press, were quite simply some of the best popular songs written. They had the wit and freshness of the early songs, the unerring intelligence which hit a contemporary attitude or anecdote so accurately that it seemed to speak for a whole generation, and the intervening time had enriched the words and music. The music press had not been as interested since the early Dylan, the mid-Beatles or since Raven's own first few L.P.s. And the audience was with him all the way.

It was a nice balance. The audience was just on the edge of that berserk applause which would have wrecked the finer enjoyment of the concert. But Merlin did not let them out of his grip. That was the revelation to Douglas. Merlin's authority. He came onto the stage when the band was well into the first number and took up his song instantly, thus quenching the roar which had fired up at the sight of him. Indeed he came on so very abruptly and was playing and singing so soon that there was an element of wizardry in it. When the number ended he bowed, brusquely, turned to the band, waved, they began to play again and once more he was in harness, the lead horse, his voice racing across the famous American Garden, compelling attention.

Douglas was impressed.

The finale was spectacular. Merlin had made no concessions to show-business or to the prevailing fashion for lights, shapes, film, stills, blow-ups, eidophors and circus effects. He was a man alone, his band half unseen behind him, that was all. When the concert ended he left as sharply as he had entered. It was the audience which provided the spectacle. At first scores and then hundreds and then thousands of small points of light appeared all over the vast gloom of the indoor Garden: matches were lit, some had brought candles, lighters were fired, there were those with small lanterns and those with torches and soon the entire place was full of lights, held steadily aloft while feet drummed on the floor and a long baying cry went out. "More!" "More!" "More!" "More!"—not hysterical, not pleading, but demanding that this time of satisfaction be repeated, this revelation be played again. It was indisputably religious in its mood and in its display, Douglas thought. But what followed from that he did not know.

Merlin did not reappear.

After an hour, the crowd left the building and Douglas, having helped the crew wrap, went backstage, allowed through the massive security ring after some difficulty, despite his twenty-two carat pass. Merlin had gone to his dressing room and seen only a couple of critics, one at a time. Douglas let it be known he was there. All he wanted to do was to say "thanks", excuse himself from the party afterwards and confirm a last filming date later in the week. He fully expected not to be seen and had braced himself not to consider this to be a rebuff. The backstage scene smacked of hoods, Hell's Angels, drugs, drink, fast money, fast sex, the skid row of the instantly over-rich, over-licensed, over-exposed and over-privileged. He was surprised at how very little he cared for them all. For they were, or were often portrayed to be, the true types of the Seventies, the character of the times, at best full of hedonistic audacity and licentious aplomb: at worst full of shit. But, in either guise, this lot, this gaggle of over-dressed young men and women, were at some peak in a society which had lost sight of most peaks. It was they and their kind which dominated the new exclusive discos, the new restaurants, the flash events—world title fights, glamorous first nights, charity fairs—and though the media massage might represent very little in real terms, the whole point was that the real terms were either permanently or temporarily at a discount. "Who" (i.e. which intelligent bright young person) cared about the High Society represented in London and the Shires by the fag end of the Hickey Brigade and, in America, by the Wasp wasted pioneering Prots and their plutocratic side-riders? Some. True. But not "the people", not that moving intelligence within a society so cleverly cottoned onto by the best gossip columnists and scandal feature writers. This clustered, sparkling, shrill, champagne swigging, coke sniffing, clothes conscious, figure conscious, only semi-word conscious gaggle of youth, youth authentic, youth spurious, and youth lost but clung onto, were as people from Mars to Douglas. He had been around and about them one way and another, without really belonging, but naturally intrigued, for some years. Now, backstage at Madison Square Garden, he thought—yes, they should have their due, they are acting out that fantasy-dream-led-life which in different civilizations had been led by princes and priests and soldiers and even scholars once or twice—but the deepest feeling it aroused in Douglas now was not loathing or contempt, but tiredness. He could see no point in keeping up with it all. And more than that, it gave a kick to a puritan conscience which had been challenged and made to retreat in London—and, Douglas had thought, for sound reasons. But not so beaten as to be able to look on this compact of idle wealth, abusive liberty, narcissistic mannerisms and self-indulgent hauteur without feeling distinct twinges of disapproval at such waste, which was so ignorant of so many needs. Still, it was uncomfortable, to say the least, to moralize when you were a guest in the middle of the feast.

He waited, then, hoping for the refusal polite, and happy to think of an evening alone. He gave his messenger ten minutes. That seemed fair. He stood against a wall and watched. Need he be a guest? Why did he always think of himself as that? Even now it was no more than the other side of the coin from being the servant. And the one definite lesson he had taken from a family which did not pretend or presume to pass on "lessons from family tradition" to their offspring, was that to be an independent man, independent in as many ways as possible, was the best goal. Yet, since Douglas' hoist out of the working class, privileged through Oxford and laundered through the B.B.C. and the London middle-classless media, he had in many ways become a guest. The guest of a society which paid good money for the trained talents of an approved good education: very welcome, provided he played the established games and carried on the established traditions. A captive guest.

It was about time to quit, he thought, as the satin-clad messenger beckoned him towards Merlin's dressing room. Yes, he would quit all that. The decision came quite coolly, even coldly, but there was something in it which Douglas recognized as final. He would quit the deference.

They finally lunged through the mob, only just escaping serious injury from the security guards.

Merlin was in a chair, composed, not sprawled, a glass of champagne in his hand, the rest of the bottle in an ice bucket beside him.

"Come in," he said to Douglas. And, equally amiably, to Douglas' guide he said, "Get out, will you?"

"Drink?"

"Thanks," Douglas said. "I'll get my own."

Merlin watched him carefully and, returning the look, Douglas saw how exhausted the man was. And he realized that Merlin wanted a talk, wanted a pal, wanted something normal and friendly to balance the stupendous weight of adulation, satisfaction and triumph which he had just provoked. Yet Douglas did not want to be drawn in. There was something finally alone about Merlin which found a direct echo in himself. Douglas knew that however gently and genuinely Merlin had reached out now, it would be the preliminary to an attempt to destroy in order to control.

He poured himself some champagne.

There was the homosexual aspect. This had been successfully played down by Merlin and ignored by Douglas but he was as aware of it now as he had ever been. Merlin brought a distinctive sexual charge to every single relationship, Douglas assumed: there was no hiding it and not much attempt to blunt the discomfort of others. Part of Merlin's character was that he could, as it were, switch the mix of his personality whenever he wanted to, ensuring always that he got his own way.

"I don't fancy you, you know," Merlin said.

"Thank God for that. Cheers."

"Have you ever had—a bit of the other?"

"No."

"Been tempted?"

"No."

"Been interested?"

"Certainly."

"I'd've called you a liar if you'd said your straight-arsed 'No' to that one. What interested you?"

"The people, of course."

"Not the action."

"That strikes me as unnecessary, painful or, in its way, just the same as ours. Not the action."

"What about the people?"

"Simply that I know and like some people who are homosexuals and, as part of my interest in them, I am interested in their homosexuality. I am curious. And you, Merlin, are flirting. More champagne?"

"Help yourself."

"You were very good in that concert," Douglas said as he

231

topped up Merlin's glass and filled his own. "Very. I was prepared to be impressed, I suppose: or rather I was prepared to be unimpressed. I was impressed and amazed. You're some sort of balladier for our times. Good luck to you."

"'Balladier for our times'," Merlin sipped at the champagne. "Christ!"

"I'll think of a better title before the night. But that's what you *are*. *Not* a poet, though you're like a poet in some respects; not a full composer, though you can write better tunes than almost anyone; you're like some Villon—footnote follows —that's who you are."

"Was I flirting?"

"You know you are doing everything you do."

"Bothers me sometimes. I think I should be able to let go. When I did—it was just—down and out. Hell. So."

"I won't bother you. I came to say thanks. Confirm we'll do the last studio session on Thursday. And—I'll be off."

"On the town?" .'

"I don't know."

"There's my party to go to." Merlin held out his glass for more champagne, a knowingly infantile gesture which Douglas ignored. Merlin poured his own. "Finished. Shall we spin a coin to see who opens the next bottle? Or would you, please?"

"Sure."

Douglas went over to the fridge. It was rather misleading to call the place a dressing room. Merlin's instructions had been carried out to the letter. The place was decorated and fitted out very like the lounge in his London penthouse.

"Are you going to your party?" Douglas asked.

"Of course not."

"What'll *you* do?"

"Watch some TV." Merlin grinned happily. "Then I'll go cruising down 42nd Street, see what bum I can find. Something rough."

"Lester told me you were on girls."

"Sometimes. But they're not dangerous enough. The only risk is clap. Who cares? Or maybe I'll go into Harlem."

"Alone."

"I'd be chicken otherwise. You could come along. Or,"

232

Merlin paused, "I'll pass out here and be discovered intact in the morning by my gooks outside who, believe me, will neither knock nor at all disturb me until I say so."

"Careful," Douglas warned.

"I had some sex right after the show. In the corridor. But I'm restless again. Anyway, no relationship can be interesting without its quotient of sex."

"You could be right. But consummation is different."

"Lester's a silly prick!" Merlin said, viciously. "His time is up."

"Why?"

"Why?" Merlin mimicked him and got up to wander around the room, leaving Douglas beached.

Douglas finished off his champagne as Merlin pressed a button which flicked on the large colour television set. He went from channel to channel until he found a news bulletin. His concert was the number two story, following a report of a key speech by President Carter on the current almighty oil crisis, but beating news of shootings in the Middle East, riots in Pakistan, bombings in Ulster and incipient storms off Florida.

"Don't you think," Merlin said, timing his remark to coincide with the exact moment when Douglas was leaving his seat to leave the room, "when you see people's faces on television, talking about world affairs or economics, whatever it is ... don't you think—how can they be so wrapped up in it? What about the birds and the bees and the sun and that? We'll all be dead and gone in no time. How can they all get so hooked on what they say? Look at that gook talking about his housing programme! O.K.—let's build houses. I'm not knocking him. But you look in their faces to see if there's anything else in their lives, you know? Some mischief maybe or some dirty little secret or some clean big secret but you see nothing. I can't understand it. The people I like are people who've got that kind of business going on inside them even when they're saving the universe. You can tell it by their eyes—and they're always just about to smile as if they were having trouble keeping in a very good joke."

Douglas had indeed thought that and come to a similar conclusion: so similar that he was disconcerted. He did not

233

make any display of agreement, fearing to seem merely flattering. But it was uncanny.

"I wasn't trying to pick you up, you know," Merlin said.

"I realize that."

"I play these games." He flicked the television from channel to channel with sulky restlessness. "What the fuck do you *do* after a concert like that? You've heard of 'mind blown'? Of course you have, yes. Well, it's like that. My mind is blown. There seems no skull-case. There are a billion bits of brain drifting around somewhere like the whole galactic system after the Big Bang. Do you realize what it's *like* out there? If I said 'Do you love me?' they would yell 'We love you!' If I said 'Shit' they would send it back. And if I said 'Down with America' they would cheer. And *'Sieg Heil'*?"

"No. They might cheer but that's no more than cheering. They were there to shout and make an event of it. That was all. You have some influence, no power, little authority."

"What're you doing tonight?"

"Well." Douglas was on his feet now. "When I'm in New York or wherever abroad—Abroad being Different—after a day's work like this I always think I ought to hit the town, find a lady, get drunk, have adventures, end up ripping and roaring somewhere, leading the life I somehow think I'm supposed to be leading. What I want to do is what I usually do—have a couple of Buds in a quiet bar and go to bed. That's what I'll do."

"I'm going to take in a movie," Merlin said. "There's that 'Nosferatu' remake by Herzog. Surprise you?"

"No."

"Then I'm off up the East Side with the classy Jackie Onassis crowd. They wanted me to go to supper but I can't eat now. A movie, then the uptown party. Been there?"

"Uptown?"

"Yes. Uptown rich, very very: butler, classical this, period that, Mr Secretary of State, Ambassador, your famous violinist and conductor and sometimes writer and actress—all that High Society—still goes on, still very tasty. Know it?"

"No."

"Want to?"

234

"Honestly—no."

"Fool." Merlin grinned and punched Douglas very lightly on the shoulder. "I like you, Douglas. You're full of shit but I like you. You're not ambitious enough, that's your problem. You don't want enough hard enough. But I like talking with you. I'd like to talk to you a lot. You know a lot, you've made an effort to try to think about this and that. But it wouldn't work. I've got to have the edge and you don't want that. Correct?"

"O.K." Merlin sipped some champagne as he began to undress. "Lester tells me you've left your old lady but, as he puts it, haven't got the balls to shack up with the Scarlet Woman. That right?"

"Just about."

"Don't get gloomy, Douglas." Merlin was naked. He looked at Douglas and then held out his hand. "I need a stinking long bubble bath." He held Douglas' hand hard. "I've liked working with you. And what I read of yours I liked. It was O.K."

"Take care."

Merlin suddenly threw back his head, beat his chest and let out a violent Tarzan yodel. He stopped abruptly.

"So long," he said, and turned away. "Kiss my arse?"

(4)

Douglas decided to give him another half hour and be ruthless about it. The bar was crowded, even at 2.00 a.m., and the thud from the disco music upstairs, like nails going into the coffin of rock music, he thought, was pounding through his head without respecting any barriers of skull, thought or talk. Talk was minimal. He had settled down in the corner of the singles bar which Lester had denominated, and was fretting under the strain of being book-less, pal-less, partner-less and drinkful. The barman was the only safe person to talk to and he was a disco freak, clucking the beat between his teeth as he bellowed a parrot reply to your order.

It was a fashionable place up on the East Side, First Avenue, near Maxwell's Plum: once, some years back, one of the hottest

235

spots in New York. Trust Lester, Douglas thought, to be
behind the new fashions. And to choose a singles bar. And to be
late.

Douglas had soon arrived back at his hotel after his talk with
Merlin. He had walked through the streets, unmugged, unap-
proached, from the Garden to the modest, even austere little
hotel into which the B.B.C. shepherded those contributors lucky
enough to cross the Atlantic on its "business". It had no bar, no
restaurant, no coffee shop and served no breakfast. It appealed to
Douglas' sense of thrift and anonymity. Despite having the
characteristics of a block of service flatlets, it seemed to him to
allow him to have more of a character than he felt was ever
permitted him in such grand hotels as the Plaza or such charac-
terful places as the Algonquin. At this place, you were on your
own. The B.B.C. crew liked it because it was cheap and they
could claim expenses on everything else. It was also central, just
two blocks away from the Avenue of the Americas in the mid-
Fifties. Douglas had enjoyed walking out into the Americas for
his breakfast, searching out a coffee shop in that spectacular
canyon of skyscrapers, feeling the exhilaration of newness and
glass and height and structural cleanliness which either intoxi-
cates or incites all European visitors to the Big Apple.

He had planned to bath, change, eat quietly nearby—there
was a Japanese restaurant he fancied—and then flick through the
late night/early morning television on the way to sleep.

Lester's note had said, "See you at Ben Gunn's at about 1 –
1.30 a.m. It is urgent we talk together tonight because I have to
go to L.A. tomorrow. So come. Lester."

So there he was. Against all his clearest wishes and desires,
propped in the corner of a trendy bar which was decked out in
foliage so dense as to make a Kew Gardens conservatory seem
like the barren Egdon Heath, drinking Jack Daniels with Buds
as chasers, avoiding the possibilities for pick-ups and trying to
find ways to fend off the computed thump of the disco discs
over his head.

Yet he was only pretending. He was tired, that was true, and
irritated with his doggedness about family loyalties, and on the
way to being drunk. He drank too much, he would remind
himself, in the gaps between drinks: he ought to cut down—a

resolution for the next New Year. He wondered why he was just sitting there doing nothing—was not the world his grit and he the happy oyster?—but things were coming into focus, he thought. Even as he thought it, he mentally crossed fingers and physically touched the wooden bar before him: which reminded him that he needed another drink.

He had tried to work out where the crew had gone to but then he remembered that a strip-crawl had been on the agenda. They were going to move as a herd and motor through the dirtiest bars, clubs, movies and whatever came up they could find. Excellent sport for the fourteen married men. It was as well Douglas was not with them. They would come back with enough stories for a six-month.

Douglas tried to focus on the notion that things were coming into focus. It was difficult. All around him, energetic—still, at this time of night—young Americans, at the last stop before bed, were being American. He was fascinated by them. Their difference from the English. The whys and hows of the difference. His intent look was misinterpreted a couple of times and remarkably attractive girls (what were *they* doing here?) came and asked for a light. And left soon after he had given it. He was not impolite. It was just that the deadening thump of the dead men's disco beat somehow slashed the tendons of his larynx. Smiles, however sympathetic, were not enough.

Anyway, pick-ups were out. More important, the idea that he ought to be interested in pick-ups—because that was what life consisted in if you were abroad, alone, free and virile—was out too. A great leap forward. Work was in. The previous few months had given a coherence to his life which he had forgotten about. Work was the village, the extended family, the source of all fruitfully complicated intercourse, it was stronger than marriage or friendship. He needed it. This film on Raven would set him up in work for a year or two. He would stick to it. He might even have a career.

As for the rest—Mary and Hilda—he had the hope that if he continued to try to get everything right, a solution might offer itself there too.

When Lester arrived, he gave Douglas the distinct impression that he felt he ought to be announced by the Queen's

Own Buglers. He had been to the party, sniffed coke, sunk champagne, chatted with superstars, slapped celebrities on the back, patronized other singers' managers, condescended to one or two old acquaintances, told lies to a beautiful Manhattan woman publisher, who was even now waiting for him in her expensive duplex willing to "do anything". Lester was King Kong for the New York night.

Douglas liked to see him like that. But, even so, he could not get the words out of his head. The disco beat had finished it off.

They found an empty bar a few blocks down and Lester persuaded the owner to let them drink there for a few minutes. His method was simple. He offered to pay two or three times the price of the drinks. The owner said. "English? English. You're all crazy. I had a guy in here yesterday wanted to challenge somebody to drink a bottle of vodka in one. You know? Crazy English. No—stay over there. I'll clean up around you. Drinks are house prices—no more. When I need to swab that corner—you go. Correct?"

Lester gave Douglas a wink. For a moment, Douglas was moved by it. For the wink said—what a life, eh, for two Thurston kids who wore clogs to primary school and kicked sparks off the pavement! What a life for two guys who came into late teenage thinking three pounds a week was a good start on ambition's ladder and two weeks' holiday a year a bit of an extravagance! What a journey from two halves of mild to this, from Carlisle County Ballroom to Studio 54, from provincial obscurity to Raven, from way back nowhere to up-front somebody! What a life, it said, that look, and spoke to Douglas' fondest memories of Lester, whom he had feared and loved and admired as a boy, being alternately impressed and daunted by Lester's physical powers, his trouble making, his great attempt to become an athlete, his petty crime, his pop *demi-monde* reported success. That amount of closeness meant a great deal to Douglas. The owner moved away as Douglas turned to thank him. Lester winked again.

"Sap," he whispered, happily. "If he'd've refused us, we would have jumped him."

"He seems pretty tough."

"One against two doesn't go," Lester recited, solemnly. "Why weren't you at the party?"

"Too tired."

"Too snooty, more like."

"No, not that, Lester. What have I got to be snooty about in front of that lot?"

"Exactly. So you were scared then."

"Scared?"

"I don't mean scared." With the pomposity of a man on the verge of toppling into catatonic drunkenness, Lester searched throughout his vocabulary. "Worried," he announced. "Worried you wouldn't make an impression."

"I don't know what you're on about."

"Yes you do. You do." Lester paused, drank deeply, nodded deeply. "You do."

"O.K. I do. Now then. What do you want?"

"Do you remember when we used to pinch apples?"

"Yes."

"You were worried then."

"I was. But I still came along."

"You still came along. I'll grant you that. But you were worried."

"To be totally honest, Lester, I was worried when I was with *you* because you talked about it so much I knew that Mother would get to know. When I took my own gang I was often so unworried I look back with amazement."

"Why?"

"Because I'm the worrying kind. And I'm law abiding."

"I'm not."

"I know."

"Your father was very good to me." Lester tippled a critically large Jack Daniels into his glass. Once that was inside him, Douglas knew, he would be deep in the alcoholic swamp. Lester held up the glass and glared at it, like some Norseman seeking to challenge it to do its worst. "Very good," he repeated, but before he took a gulp, Douglas arrested his arm.

"If we're going to talk, let's talk now." Douglas paused. "Before you get paralytic."

239

Unexpectedly, Lester saw the sense of a remark which in other circumstances and times he would have regarded as the very peak of provocation.

"My father was a bloody washout," he said. Then, unusually for him, he added, in confidence, "If he was my bloody father. You know what my mother is."

Everybody in the Tallentire family knew what Lester's mother was but, even in the late Seventies, the word did not pass their lips.

"Our Aileen's done well," Lester said, rather lugubriously. He had taken no notice of his younger sister when she was a plump, bespectacled, put upon, asthmatic and doleful child. Now that she had emerged from that sad and unpromising chrysalis as a thoughtful, educated woman, who even had not unrealizable ambitions to stand for Parliament, Lester would still have ignored her, but for the fact that she had married Harry. "I didn't think she'd manage to get hold of somebody like Harry," he said. "Now *he's* a good lad."

The implication was clear.

Was it happening all over the world, Douglas wondered. Were couples from Chicago who found themselves in Delhi discussing their back street adolescent adventures in the windy city? Were friends from Valparaiso who had met up in Leningrad talking about the days of their youth? Were students from the Sorbonne now become artists in L.A. mulling over the nights on the Left Bank? Very likely. The further we move from our past, the more eagerly we seize on the chances to revisit it. Not surprisingly. It is most of what we have.

"Lester," Douglas said, patiently. "I'm very tired. You said it was urgent. What is it?"

Over Lester's face came a look of such ill-fitting cunning that Douglas' heart sank. He had suspected that Lester was about to try to pull a dirty one: alas, it seemed that he was right. Douglas took a glum pull at his rye.

"Merlin hasn't signed his contract yet," Lester began.

"That's right."

"So—technically, technically—the thing isn't on the up and up, it isn't legal. Not yet."

"Technically you are right."

"It puts us all in an awkward position," Lester said craftily. Douglas groaned. Lester was encouraged. "I'm sorry to put it over on you, my own cousin, but it's every man for himself in this life. Agreed?" Douglas said nothing. "And you won't suffer. I'll see to it that you don't suffer. I'll guarantee that, Douglas, for old times' sake."

"What are you suggesting?" Douglas wanted it over with but for Lester this was a moment to be cherished.

"You see," Lester said, with just sufficient remaining wisdom to refrain from sinking any more spirits, "Merlin and me's built up this 'thing'. Don't get me wrong. It's nothing personal. Nothing personal. It's just that—you know," and here he became confidential, even bashful, and Douglas felt a genuine lurch of sympathy for him, "some of those songs he sang tonight—the new ones—they came out of things I told him. I couldn't tell you *how*, exactly. I couldn't put my finger on it. But they do. It could be worked out. You see. And he needs that, you see. I mean," Lester took a sip, "when I met up with him again—you know—he was just coming out of being a wreck. He'd had one of these full scale depressions. He was bumbling around. He was raving with all sorts of political stuff and messages in his songs. I've *heard* those tapes. They're terrible—what he did when he was in his depressions. But from the first time he met me—BINGO!—that was it— BINGO!—he got cracking again on the real stuff, the real hot stuff, the stuff that makes a bloody fortune. And he got thinner. Did you see him tonight? Never looked better. Looks after himself. We went to a gym together. It was in Holland Park. There was this madman ..."

"What's this leading up to?" Douglas asked.

"I'm sorry to say this, old pal, but we won't release the film."

Lester sat back like a gangster in a movie and indeed might well have thought himself half there, with the beefy, aproned barman swabbing out the place, the chairs upended on the tables, the occasional mellifluous yodel of a police car racing up First Avenue, the Manhattan adventure just four or five yards away.

"You mean he won't sign."

"Not for the B.B.C. Why should he? This has turned out to be the biggest thing since—" Lester was no longer capable of completing such a sentence. "That's Showbiz," he concluded.

"And what do you propose to do?" Douglas heard the ice in his voice. "Although the contract is not signed there is after all a firm gentleman's agreement. I expect that would carry some weight if it came to a legal battle."

"Oh Douglas." Lester laid a sympathetic hand on his cousin's arm. "Don't come the hard man. We can always beat your lawyers to pulp. What we want is a deal."

"I'm listening."

"We want to buy all the stuff from you—we'll pay a fair price, we'll have our people work it all out—we want *you*," Lester said, graciously, "yes, we want *you*—and then we'll market the film in our own way. Look at it from our point of view. You have all that stuff. Nobody else has it. Nobody else has ever had as much stuff on Merlin in the history of the world. It's the hottest property this century. And what does he get out of it? A lousy what is it—honourable—?"

"Nominal."

"Nominal fee. And what do you get out of it? Not much more. And what about me? Sweet F.A. So we can all get rich for once and it's O.K. for the B.B.C., we'll let them have a television deal some time."

"You must do what you want but I'm having nothing to do with it," Douglas said.

"You could make a fortune. And a name. Who cares—who cares in America who directs an English TV thing? But *this*—this could make you. I've thought it all out. Listen to Lester, kid."

"I have listened. And I'm going back to the hotel."

"Think it over?"

"It won't work, Lester. I won't play. I'll advise the B.B.C. to keep hold of the material. You'll get nothing out of it."

"You wouldn't fuck it all up, would you?"

Douglas waited for that moment or two until he was certain that Lester would take in the full implications of his reply.

"Yes. If you tried it on, I'd fuck it up."

Lester hoisted himself up, drew back his arm, lunged forward and was clipped on the jaw by the barman, who then caught him as he fell, cold.

"Here," he said to Douglas. "Take him away. He's *your* pal. Get out, the both of you. Crazy English."

Douglas dragged Lester out onto the pavement, propped him up, in a sitting position, against the wall.

Lester drowsily woke up.

"One question," Douglas said, kneeling beside him. "Are you listening?"

"Yes."

"Have you sorted all this out with Merlin?"

"Merlin and me," Lester declared, eyes wide open, mind about to snap tight shut, "are like *that!*"

He held out two fingers, clearly wanting to cross them to show the rapport, the kinship, the link between himself and Raven, but he was too far gone and the fingers remained in the Churchill position as Lester crashed into inner darkness.

Poor sod, Douglas thought, you don't even know that your great pal has decided to dump you. Thus has spoken the Raven. Douglas looked around for a yellow cab to haul his cousin across the dark rock of a city to a bed.

# 4
# Love and Marriage

When Douglas rang to tell her that he would have to stay on in New York for a few days because of the extended length of the project, Mary calmly replied that it was perfectly all right, assured him that John was about to go north to his grandparents perfectly happily, asked one or two questions about the concert and about Lester, was bright with a gobbet or two of gossip, sounded cheerful and busy, put the phone down and collapsed.

It was so unfair. She had made so many efforts and fought so many battles—yet it did not seem to be working. She despised herself for her dependence. For, even though Douglas was (at her request) not living with her, his absence in the U.S.A. pointed up how much she needed to know that he was, somehow, in a nearby zone she could retreat to when necessary. In touch. They had become—or, bitterly, she conceded, *she* had become—like one of those insects totally dependent on the immensely intimate workings of a single and delicate plant for survival: when the plant suffered, she did; when it died, she died. The plant—which had become both intricate and delicate—was her marriage to Douglas.

For, now that she had had time to think—and it seemed to Mary that she had time to do nothing else, so remorselessly did analysis and continuing analysis of her marriage pound through her mind—she saw how many, how often contradictory, how complicated and how perilous were the demands they had made on the marriage.

Yet, with all the early illusions contradicted and the attempt at an older cynicism seen to fail, Mary had discovered, in her time alone, that it was still that monstrous, useless, unsatisfactory, twisted marriage which gave her sustenance. For all its painfulness and humiliations, its deceits, shortcomings, distortions and barrenness, it was what made her live, she now found. And she wanted to be free of it. Yet a kind, thoughtful and perfectly reasonable and understandable telephone call from Douglas—the separated husband, the villain who, confusingly and unjustly, seemed to be more stable and more cheerful than she was—sent her into weak tears and turmoil.

John went to Cumbria by bus the next day and Mary telephoned Mike. Whatever happened—whether Douglas came back or not, whether she met someone else or not, whatever happened, she had to find a way to live her life without this marriage. It would have to be cast away. She needed to grow for herself and for that she needed help. The effort which went into telephoning Mike confirmed her in her determination. She hesitated and feared it and found excuses against it for some hours—confirming the very state she knew she had to get out of. He came round that evening.

When she saw him, she wished she had not invited him. Not because he was unwelcome in himself but because he would need attention and she had none to spare from herself. He stood on her doorstep like an unbidden guest and it was with a weary effort of will that she asked him in. She had made only the merest preparations for his coming: previously she would have taken care to duff the cushions, re-set anything which was out of true, put on the side lamps, do that last minute tidying up which she could do with so much flair and which clearly indicated that expectation had been keen and warm. Mike noticed this and felt the chill of neglect beginning to settle on the place. A dirty glass, a mug half full of coffee, two ashtrays teeming with butts, the "Guardian" strewn on the floor. And Mary herself, he thought, looked unwell. Undoubtedly thinner, her face white, her luscious hair drawn back for convenience and lack lustre. She did not ask him whether he wanted a cup of coffee but immediately held up the bottle of scotch and poured out two stiff ones.

They sat under the uncosy glare of the main light.

Mike was sitting in the chair which had been—still was—Douglas' favourite. An undistinguished but comfortable chair—she had seen him there so often: even though the place was different and the purpose of taking the flat had been to wipe out such associations—the chair mesmerized her.

245

"You seem a bit down."

"I'm sorry?"

"You seem rather down."

Mary let the repeated remark fall between them. She stood up.

"This is silly," she said, "but would you change—chairs? Oh God!"

Mike instantly understood what had led up to the request and felt drained of hope. She was in bad shape. He moved to another chair.

"It's terrible," she said.

"I thought you were doing well," Mike replied. "On your own. As you said last time."

"I thought I was. But it won't go away." Still standing, looking, poor love, Mike thought, as forlorn as he could ever imagine her looking, she held her head with both hands for a minute and then rejected the gesture as too melodramatic. "It just grows inside my head. Really. Like something growing, heavier and heavier. I keep thinking of it being a solid object, sitting there, weighing me down, dragging everything into itself, sucking on all my energy. And it's to do with loss or missing him or—I don't know. But I feel that there's nothing else except this terrible lump. The rest of me . . . never mind. I can't think about anything else. It seems I can't talk about anything else."

"You have to talk it out, I suppose," Mike said.

"Do you?"

"That's what they say. Maybe they're right. Or perhaps you need a complete change. They say that as well. Get out of yourself."

"I shouldn't have asked you round. I'm boring. People who are jilted are boring, aren't they?"

"I thought it was you who did the jilting."

"That's the strange thing. I can't seem to accept that. Even though it's true."

Again she paused and Mike let her drift into what he now saw was the beginning of a habit of reverie. Until now he had been Mr Nice and Scrupulous and Honourable until his teeth ached. Had a Senate Committee investigated his conduct they would

246

have given him a sheet so clean it could have been used in a soap powder ad. Mary sat down, nervously, on the edge of the seat of the chair he had just abandoned.

"Mary," he said, "I think I may be in love with you. I think you could return it, eventually. Why don't we try?"

"Try."

"Yes."

She looked startled. Then she considered what he had said.

"You mean we should go to bed."

"Sooner or later."

"What would that prove?"

"That's not a question that can be answered."

"I couldn't—Douglas—I haven't. Ever." She spoke as if short of breath.

"At least we could go off somewhere for a few days. Leave this place. Leave London. Leave England. Get out."

"I'd like that."

"We could go to Paris. Tomorrow afternoon. For a long weekend."

"Paris. It sounds so old-fashioned."

"It's still a good place to go."

"We went once—Douglas . . . Are you serious?"

"Yes. We could catch the afternoon flight. I know a little hotel just off St Germain. You'd enjoy it."

"What if I didn't? What about you?"

"I'd see Paris."

"I don't know. I've never been unfaithful."

"That is not a condition. Although I intend to be irresistible! No, Mary. Let's get out. You and me. Not because you need it, or I want it, but to do something together. You and me. See what happens."

"I want to." Mary found herself weeping again and did not stop it. "I want to go somewhere else. I want to, I truly want to lose this burden of Douglas. I want to want to go to bed with—you—I must, in a way, if I'm to have any chance. You don't mind that, do you? I have to. I have to be somebody on my own. But I don't know what that is. Oh God, why is it like this?"

"Paris?"

Mary paused and then turned her head into the chair and answered him loudly.

"Yes," she said. "Yes. Yes."

(2)

Most people you worked for, Hilda had concluded, were a pain in the neck. Her boss in the film institute was typical. He was terrified of *his* boss and that governed him. When his boss threw a tantrum or demanded an explanation or passed on a grouse or a complaint he had received from *his* boss, then down it came to Hilda. She was angered at how strongly the hierarchical system based itself on shows of power and displays of fear. Surely, she thought, in the late twentieth century, and in such a milk-and-water little endeavour as this, there ought to be a feeling of ease about authority. After all, it mattered very little in terms of the work being done and it was generally acknowledged that some of the more technically (on the salary and promotion scale) junior employees did the most important work. And the work was in that apparently easy-going area somewhere between journalism, scholarship and the media where mateyness and democratic attitudes were rigorously *de rigueur*. Here there were practically no distinctions made through dress or accent or background. Here the notion of one man one equal voice (and one woman one slightly more than equal voice, at the moment, with the heightened awareness of women's rights) was taken for gospel. Here the old notions of structures of authority were daily challenged in long theoretical talks, and always decisively dismissed. Here was the all-equal society.

Yet, there was no doubt about it, Hilda thought, underneath that casual, chatty brotherhood was a rigid little power complex based on the traditional territorial premises. And that day, at the office, had been like a bad-joke day with her boss, on the run from his boss, relieving his anxiety and attempting to dissolve his fear by snapping at her and correcting her—in short, bullying her. At six thirty she invented a migraine and left. Her boss stayed on for another two hours, vainly hoping for an encouraging word from *his* boss, who always worked late.

248

Hilda decided to walk back some of the way. It was a fine summer evening and if she chose her streets cleverly she could pass through various garden squares, along streets with lovely shops in them, and come to the park at the perfect hour, the very end of the afternoon, before dusk began to gather. She had learnt to gather together such mundane treats and spend them carefully.

For something to do, she guessed. For a distraction.

The park was full of distractions and, Hilda suspected, just as full of people seeking them. Old men sitting on benches, sometimes smiling into an unfocused middle distance: old ladies, often with their bags of crumbs or nuts for the ducks and squirrels: solitary young people walking purposefully in a circle, looking for that big explosive meeting which would ignite their lives: she, "Lovely young(ish) woman likes films, music—all types—and books. Enjoys walking and talking. Seeks man, preferably 35–40, similar." And they would meet in a place like this—an anonymous cafeteria beside a boating lake, she with a "blue scarf", he with a "green tie" and instantly fall silent . . . It was not much use attempting to deride that sort of thing. She was very near it now and she felt ashamed.

It was difficult to bear, this shame, and even to remind herself of it gave her a stab in the brain which felt physical. She felt abandoned and rejected and humiliated.

She had been aware of the young man for some time. He had trailed her along the edge of the Serpentine as ineptly as a reluctant comic detective. He was, she thought, ridiculously young. When she turned her attention to him, she found herself rapidly spurred to imagining what he would do, what she might do. She might take him up, the Older Woman, the great layby lady of literature, the initiator of young heroes, the woman of worldly experience, teaching and moulding the virgin young, making a man of him, watching him grow and then turning him gently out into the wide world, now equipped to conquer it, herself to retreat gracefully with the wound gallantly born, perhaps to find consolation with some old flame most fortunately rediscovered. Or he could be so stoppered and pent with sexual frustration that he would awkwardly edge her into a lonely spot here in the park and fall on her, tooth and nail, insatiable. Or she would remind him of his older sister, or old girl friend, with luck, or his mother, who had died young, and they would play a scene of tender reminiscence over lagers in the metropolitan dusk until, melancholy slaked, they would ease away into the great city with hearts assuaged and a light but permanent sweet memory traced on their minds. Or she could use him. She could not be certain whether she truly missed sex or merely missed the feeling of its being always possible. Sometimes, though, she felt as ravenous as a hungry vixen. Her mind seemed to howl out for touch, contact, penetration, fondling. The loneliness of the flesh would infect her like a stinging rash. Anybody, she thought, would serve.

Yet that passed away. Another, harder fury remained: her seemingly ineradicable commitment to Douglas.

She walked over the bridge to the octagonal shaped bar with its conical glass roofs and uninviting interior. She *was* thirsty. A quick glance reassured her that the young man had stuck to his self-appointed task. She went into the bar, feeling suddenly dispossessed, as she always did when she went into a strange pub alone. The young man came up to the bar beside her. He was, Hilda could sense, almost completely knotted up with anxiety. It was the barman who undid the puzzle.

"If you sit at one of the tables," he said, in an Irish accent and not too kindly, "somebody'll come across and get your order."

By assuming they were together he helped Hilda to decide—what the hell—why not talk to a stranger for once? They sat down uncomfortably at the uncomfortable tables.

"My name's Hilda," she said.

"David," he muttered. Same initial, she thought and then thought—Oh God! "David," he repeated and then, as if remembering an ancient custom, he held out his right hand. Hilda took it. They shook, solemnly.

She felt like his mother.

But he had, after all, had the gall to—hunt her down? Something like that.

"Can I try to guess what you do?" she asked.

"Yes." His face cleared. Her attitude reassured him. He was not with a looney. And already he could feel that she was nice.

250

She certainly looked better close up, he decided, with the well weighed appraisal of his nineteen years. A bit too thin, maybe, and strained looking—but he did not mind that: it was her eyes, full of cheerfulness and—he hoped—promise. And her breasts, he decided—breasts were his nightly dream comforters—were much better close up. The sort you could reach out for and hold one in each hand and feel soft and firm and a delicious handful. He took his eyes off them—Hilda was wearing a thin summer dress with a shapely satin bra underneath—only when she coughed.

"Student?"

"Yes."

"That was easy." She smiled at him. He relaxed a little and his eyes dropped back to her breasts, where they landed like jump jets on target. "What do you study?"

"Er," reluctantly he drew up his irises and found it was possible to enjoy the sight of her face: he hesitated. "Engineering."

"Yes?" The barman reappeared beside them as a waiter, notebook in hand, pencil hovering, eyes scanning the twilit park for some excitement.

"I'll—what do you want?" David asked.

"Half of bitter, please," Hilda said.

"Half of bitter and—" David paused, "another half of bitter."

"Two halves of bitter!" The scorn was unmistakable. Perhaps he had dreams of running a cocktail bar with pink gins and champagne cocktails, with daiquiris and whisky sours, with all the verbal and alcoholic paraphernalia of the sunset crowd. Instead he was stuck in a glasshouse in Hyde Park serving halves of bitter to quite ordinary people.

"He thinks we're not good enough for him," Hilda said, happily. She was sure of herself now. She would chat, pay for her own drink, and then, soon, walk across the park to catch a tube.

David began to emerge from the shock of shyness which had hit him at the moment of what he now began to think of as his success. He had clicked!

"Do you make a habit of following women around in the park?" Hilda asked, amusedly.

251

"No." David blushed and then was vehement. "Certainly not."

"Only one or two."

"Why do you ask?"

"Because I want to know," Hilda said, calmly. "Do you?" She paused. "Or am I the *first*?"

She was afraid he would sulk: and then it would be really boring. To avert that, she smiled encouragingly.

"No," he admitted, having weighed the odds. "You're not the first."

"Clicked before?"

"Two halves of bitter!" A small dish of nuts accompanied the two halves of beer and the waiter rolled his eyes in despair as David's right hand leapt out automatically to grab a fistful. While he was grubbing in his hand, Hilda produced a pound note and the waiter took it.

"No," David gurgled, through a mass of salted peanuts. "No! It's me. I'll pay."

Frantically his knobbly hands swooped towards his trouser pockets. He was wearing no jacket and the trousers were accompanied by an open-necked orange shirt which he clearly considered dashing; the trouser pockets proving useless, he assaulted the two bulging pockets which breasted the front of the shirt. Buttons got in the way. Fingers were unable to discriminate between coins and pens and a trove of mini-junk.

By the time he had uncovered a pound note, Hilda and the waiter had completed the transaction.

"You must let me pay," he said.

"Why should you? I'm earning a wage. Your grant can't be very big. Cheers."

She held up the glass and sipped at the warm beer.

"It's very kind of you." He took a running gulp at the bitter and all but finished it off in one.

"So," Hilda said, to tease out the few minutes she would give him, "what happens with these Other Women?"

"There haven't been any," he said. "I've—tried. I'll admit that. And once or twice—but if a woman's on her own in a park maybe she's looking for companionship, just like a man. She could be. It's not a sin to ask." Again his eyes dropped to her breasts and the breasts warmed a little under his longing scrutiny. His defensive explanation had brought some animation to a face until now characterized by an intense shy wariness. He's good looking, Hilda thought, with surprise: why should he be tailing women in the park?

"Why do you do it?" she asked. "I would've thought you could have managed a girlfriend easily enough."

"It's not that easy," he replied, promptly, and then pulled back from the confession which, Hilda realized, was there to be delivered. So that was it. She was to be Mother Confessor. She relaxed a little and finished her drink. He took the hint and, after some rather frantic semaphore, indicated to the superior Irishman that the same again was required. Almost half-past eight, Hilda was thinking, stay here for about another twenty minutes, walk to the bus, trundle home by about quarter to ten, have a bath, eat a little, sink a couple of Valiums and hope for the best. Usually she took more care to organize her evenings against the kind of drifting she had indulged in this evening: it allowed too much thought, it built up regret, it signified emptiness. So she had taken a way out by taking on, as it were, this very tentative adventurer. Yet he only had part of her attention. She feared that she was beginning another of those phases where she would be drawn into an obsessive preoccupation with Douglas, with what had been, what might have been, what could be. She had beaten it off until now but she was not sure she could continue to do so.

"Good luck," she said and raised the stubby glass to the boy in front of her. He grinned rather confidently and offered her a cigarette.

"So," Hilda persisted, seeing in this line of enquiry the only interesting talk they could have, "you don't find it easy to get girlfriends."

David scowled and did not reply. Hilda ignored this reaction.

"Is it hard," she asked, genuinely, "studying engineering?"

"You have to work at it," he said, rather grimly. "And they call the place you do it in—a Polytechnic, while all the fancy boys and—women—who do any old Arts subject that anybody could do with a bit of flannel—they all go to Universities. I'm doing it and then getting out to somewhere else where engineers

253

are thought of as something a bit more than mechanics. Even my own mother thinks that I'm studying to be a superior garage repair man. Yes, it's *very* hard. You have a lot of theory to keep up with and the practical is bloody difficult because the facilities are so second rate. The money goes on the useful citizens who are studying sociology or the Novel or the Philosophy of whatever."

Hilda's attention was engaged. The undisguised bitterness, the feeling of having to struggle against Them who had it easy: the way in which, as it often seemed to her, by some determination of history in this country, those who did the essential work were made to feel inferior—all this found an echo in her own life.

"You seem rather upset by it," she said and went on, blind but sure. "Had it something to do with why you lost your girlfriend?"

"Maybe." He paused and looked past her—out to the park now sprinkled with lights in the soft city dark. "How did you guess?"

"I don't know," Hilda lied. She knew very well; there was about him that shorn and forlorn appearance which precisely reflected her own condition. She waited.

"It wasn't the engineering," David began, almost reluctantly, "although it *could* have been the Polytechnic, a bit. No, it wasn't even that. When it came down to it, I read more books and listen to more records and certainly go to more movies than the rest of them. There's a gang of us," he explained, "most of us came to London for one reason and another and we stuck together. Until—Anne and I—split."

"When was that?"

"A month or so—a month ago exactly."

For the "exactly" her heart went out to him. He was intent now and openly unhappy. "I didn't want to see any of them, somehow," he said, and again his eyes dropped to her breasts but now the Pavlovian lusting had receded. He was no longer in the character of someone with his eye on a quick grope. The character had not suited him anyway. But frustration and unhappiness had exercised their usual distorting influence. Added to which, he had his fantasies, like all adolescents, and

254

when the opportunity arose it was hard not to try it out. He looked up. "Anne and I had been going together for three years, you see. At school. We'd been around Europe together. We weren't engaged but that was just because our lot don't get engaged. She went off with my best friend. My best friend," he repeated, as if it were the first time in the world such a thing had happened and incomprehensible. The repetition was to re-assure Hilda that she was hearing correctly. It seemed to David that it was the most unexpected thing in the world.

"It often happens like that," Hilda said.

"Your best friend?"

"Yes."

"I don't believe it." He drank some more bitter and indicated the offer of another round. Hilda shook her head. "Anyway," he concluded, withdrawing from the brink of full and true confessions, "he—my best friend—and her—Anne—they still knock around with the gang. As if nothing had happened. I can't—well. I can't go around with them pretending nothing's happened, can I? I can't see her there with him when she was with me a month ago. It isn't as if I've stopped just because she's stopped. You can't hide your feelings, can you? And so—"

So many chords had been struck in Hilda by this recital, and by its clear implications, that she felt quite hemmed in. But she helped him out again.

"You come to the park."

"Yes."

"Well," she finished her drink, "I'll have to be going now."

"Can I—we were just starting."

"I think it's better not."

"Where are you going?"

"To catch a bus."

"I've got a motorbike. It looks a bit old fashioned, I put it together myself, but it works well enough."

"I'm sure it does." Why could fifteen years not drop off her, like an old skin? Why could she not be meeting this boy-man as prepared as he was to begin something and with enough hope to see it resolved? Why were the meetings in her life always with the right men at the wrong time? "But I'll stick to the bus."

255

"What's your address? Can I phone you?"

He jumped up as she left the table and worried her to the door. They went out side by side and the air seemed to restore David, or rather to make him pull back to his earlier persona. His flirtatiousness momentarily asserted itself. He made a clumsy grab at Hilda. She evaded it easily and looked directly into his face.

"Why *do* you prowl around here?"

"You wouldn't understand."

"I might." In the dusk he looked fragile. His inept honesty reminded her of Douglas: perhaps, she thought, Douglas had been this fragile once, this lost in the city. "Where do you come from?" she asked, abruptly.

"Near Bristol. A little town called Thornbury."

"I see. A stranger here. And your best friend—I'm sorry but I'm curious—is he an Arts student?"

"English. Wants to do sociology."

"You shouldn't prowl around here, you know. Somebody might take you up on it, or panic and cause trouble. Either way isn't much of a life."

They were walking now, Hilda keeping a deliberately steady pace.

"What else can I do?"

"There's bound to be somebody you meet around the Polytechnic, isn't there? Or—don't you have clubs?"

"The Poly's full of men. The only decent clubs are sports clubs. We all live too spread out in the suburbs to get together much."

"Well," Hilda advised, lightly, "give it up for a while."

"I got used to it," David groaned lugubriously. "It isn't simple to give it up. I think I'll go mad if there isn't a woman to talk to. Or . . ." He left it at that. Then took up the theme again as Hilda remained silent. "I can't get interested in anybody."

"Except in a park."

"Yes." The darkness now as they went along the road, which wound, country fashion, through the trees, and the relief he felt with Hilda emboldened him. "*You* noticed me quite early on. You could have signalled that you weren't at all interested. You could have signalled that you were offended. You could've scared me off. Why didn't you?"

There was no reply Hilda could make which would not further implicate them. She decided to cut out. They would never see each other again: it had been brief, let it be a brief mistake.

Again David made a clumsy lunge for her but this time he caught her and pressed her tightly against himself uttering a little moan. Hilda wrenched herself away and, as he came back at her, she raised her hand.

"I'll scream, David, and you'll be sorry. You're right. I did encourage you—but that wasn't an invitation to rape or to a lifetime's companionship. It was the sort of thing a lonely person does without even beginning to reckon up the consequences. Now it's over. You go your way, I'll go mine. If you try anything on, I'll yell."

One or two cars swung comfortably around the bends in the road. The mild air had attracted a number of evening strollers to the park. David glanced around, apprehensively, fearing that his behaviour might already have prompted repercussions.

"I'm sorry," he said, "you've been very nice."

Hilda nodded. She felt overcome by a dizzying weariness. What had she got herself into? How could she have been so idle?

David still walked alongside her but she said no more until she reached the park gates.

"My bus-stop's over there," she said.

"Are you sure?" He sounded so sweet, she thought, so tender and companionable. "Really sure? I'm not—like that."

"Goodbye."

She held out her hand: he took it. She turned and walked away firmly, without looking back.

At the bus-stop she glanced across and saw him still watching. Then he turned and raced away. She guessed that he just might be going for his motorbike so that he could follow the bus. She waited until he was well out of sight and then walked along towards the Underground.

The weariness she had felt increasingly over the past few weeks had been exacerbated by the encounter. It could have

257

been poignant, she thought, had she wanted to make it so, or even passionate. Women could submit to being prey in a big city: there were always hunters at large, timid though most of them were. And there would always be young men who would like advice and unfussy sex and security. There were legitimate bachelors on the go, too: she had met one or two at the occasions organized for her by one of her friends: and there was the legion of married men, more intriguing, generally, partly because they *were* married.

As she walked the last few yards to the flat and then went into the usual routine, it was the forbidden subject which crashed in on her. Douglas.

She broke her rule. As if in a daze she went to the phone, dialled his home—Mary's flat, where she thought he was now newly housed and settled—and waited. The sound of his voice would be enough. Just the "Hello". She would put down the receiver immediately.

No one answered.

(3)

Joseph had finished in the garden, or rather—he had done enough. You were never, he would say to Betty most sternly, especially when she was asking for help, you were never finished in a garden.

It was still light. The evening was warm, truly warm, with no edgy little breeze to take the pleasantness off it. And clear. The sort of evening when you could see down to Skiddaw and the fells in the south and clear across to Criffel and Scotland in the north.

He had courted Betty, he remembered, on evenings like this. Walking through the Show Fields along the River Wiza. Other couples, old and young, doing the same as them, on a summer evening in the Thirties. Nobody very well off—a chief cashier, a schoolteacher, a chief clerk perhaps being the elite: mostly working people like Betty and himself in their second best, perambulating beside the meandering stream as formally and tranquilly now, in his memory, as if they had been doing a minuet in a costume drama.

258

As Joseph put away his tools in the tiny shed, which he kept strictly tidy, he felt a spasm of love for that past. It was the death of his father which had encouraged his turn to the past. To his surprise, he had found himself thinking of his childhood, remembering the old man when he had been strong and hopeful and young in the other world of Britain which clung around him at Joseph's birth: the late Victorian and Edwardian age which had marked his father as if he had been a foreigner. Perhaps we each have our age and, as time goes by, become increasingly foreign to the changing world. Old John's world had altogether gone by the time he died: he must have wondered which planet he was on, sometimes.

He came around to look at the garden. Even John would have been proud of it. Harry still did much of the heavy work, of course, but the laying out and the caring for the plants and blooms was Joseph's care. He took out a cigarette and allowed himself a stroll about, bending to pluck out a minute weed here, nip off a dead leaf there. Life had certainly ended up by giving him a very good deal.

A strong feeling of gratitude surged into him on this benign summer's evening. His carpings fell away. Gone the gripe about those who did no work and those who did not know how to govern and those who were too stupid to run a football team and the councillors who were too foolish to run a fish shop and the whole dreadful world which was generally a sitting duck for the disparaging darts of Joseph and his philosophical cronies. It was not, he had to admit on a night like this, too bad.

The feeling gathered impetus. The past seemed a fine sheltered place which he could visit at will. He had spent much of his life with his nose pressed to the present. This realization of the past was like being given a new kingdom. And it rose like a tide and brought benefits into the life he lived now. He had never thought he would own a house—and such a decent, well appointed place with the garage and the garden, the central heating, the pleasant furniture, and all the knick-knacks of that bit of superfluous wealth. Nor that he would be able to have such an agreeable retirement in financial terms. The pension, plus all his small savings, together with what he got for his part-time job, kept him in very adequate comfort. His health was not so very good but not so very bad either. There were the cronies to keep interest in the world's ways alive and ticking. And there was Betty, looking after him. A full measure of contentment flooded out of his recollections and burst the banks of his usual domestic inactivity.

"Betty, Betty," he began to call as he went back to the house. It was a habit that was rooted now. Whenever he wanted anything of Betty, he would begin to call out her name— although she might be at the other end of the bungalow— and continue to do so until he came across her. He did not realize how old it made him sound—but then, he had no false vanities about age.

Betty was playing whist with young John, who had grown bored of helping his grandfather in the garden when all that needed to be done was so small and finicky. For a moment Joseph stood and enjoyed the cosy sight.

He announced his news as if heralding the principal event in a Greek drama.

"It's a lovely night for a walk," he said, and, as if expecting applause, added, "Let's up and off."

Betty had been thinking exactly the same herself and indeed she had been toying with the idea of persuading John to come with her. Just in time she caught Joseph's eye, saw the anxiety lest the request be turned down, and sensed that here was a time to drop her guard.

"Isn't that a good idea?" she said to John. "Just wash your face and put your blazer on and we'll be off."

"Along the river," Joseph put in, emphatically, as if playing a trump.

"John likes the river," Betty said, "don't you?"

John smiled and nodded. There was something a bit comical about the old pair, he thought, but he basked in their attention and liked them too much to let cruel or critical thoughts colour his love for them. He left the room for the unnecessary wash.

"He's coming on," Joseph said, expansively, as Betty tidied up the cards. "He's twice the lad he was at Christmas." He paused. "You would've thought it would've upset him— *then*—you know. I put it down to your influence as much as anybody's."

260

"Mary's very good," Betty said, closing further argument. "Where did he put that card box?"

"Here, mother," Joseph spotted it and all but trotted over to hand it to her. When he did so, he gave her an awkward hug. Betty looked up at him in some surprise.

"What's that for?"

"I felt like it," Joseph replied, skittishly, and the more she scrutinized him, the jollier he became. In the twilight he looked a bit like a goblin, she thought, his large red nose, the thin hair tufted up with cream, the dodging gestures. "Can't a man embrace his wife?"

"What do you want?"

"Do I have to want something?"

"Yes."

"Look." Joseph, rather dashed, stopped dancing about and spread out his hands like a salesman. "Believe me—I don't want anything. That's the point. I'm very well off. That's what I've been thinking."

"I see." Betty smiled to herself as she got up. She had sensed his mood and needed no more explanations but it amused her to tease him a little and this she did as they got ready to go out.

"You walk in the middle," Joseph said to John. "No. Walk beside your grandmother on that side and I'll be on this side."

"Like two detectives with a suspect," Betty said.

"You always take things the wrong way."

"I'm worried about your grandad's sudden urge to walk," Betty said to John and winked. "Do you think he wants to get us out of the house for some reason?"

"I've *told* you. It's the perfect night for a walk. I've told you."

Others had had the same thought. The three fields alongside the river were strewn with evening walkers. Everybody nodded a greeting at everyone else. There was a mood of satisfied amiability.

"It's just like old times, isn't it?" Joseph rejoiced. Betty nodded. She had become used to percolating all her experience into a private chamber of her mind. Sharing with Joseph had long since fallen into disuse and even when he articulated her own feelings accurately, as he did now, she found it hard to empathize with him. Yet it might still be possible.

261

"Your grandmother and me used to do our courting along this river," Joseph announced to John, who rather stiffly took in the information. But he was pleased to be told it, Joseph could tell.

"She was a real beauty then," he said.

"Don't listen to him," Betty said to John, but not sharply. "Your grandfather always exaggerates."

"Often enough we hadn't a penny in our pockets," he went on, enthusiastically. "And I'm speaking about old pennies. There were farthings, then, you know. I expect they teach you that in History. Things were marked up in farthings—$3\frac{3}{4}$d, $2\frac{1}{4}$d."

"He'll be thinking we've just walked off the Ark," Betty said, warmed, to her surprise, by Joseph's nostalgia.

"There seemed to be a lot of fine evenings then," he went on, encouraged to become lyrical. "Sometimes we would get our bikes out and go down to Silloth for a swim. Buy some fish and chips and then ride back—by moonlight."

"Goodness me, Joseph, the lad'll think we were daft! Moonlight!"

"We did!" Joseph maintained, stoutly and truthfully, and then burst into song: "By the light—tum ti tum, tum ti tum, of the sil-very moon—tum ti tum, tum ti tum—I heard this tune—tum ti tum, tum ti tum—Da da di da in June—"

"Those aren't the words."

"It doesn't matter. Do you think I would have made a pop singer, John?"

John grinned and Betty's heart skipped that the boy should be capable of looking so happy. Joseph was forever teasing him about pop music, which John studied fanatically and debated studiously with great expertise.

They had gone down the West Road and headed south through the fields. Joseph continued his chatting and teasing of them both. People greeted each other cheerfully; the fields were lush and dry; the hills guarding the Lake District were clear as cut-outs against the slowly darkening sky. When they came into the last field, the river swung away from the path, and John broke away to follow it along the bank, leaving his grandparents together on the path in unaccustomed companionship.

262

"You've helped that boy a lot," Joseph said.

"He's a brave little lad. He takes some getting to know. But when you get through to him, he has all sorts of things about him. He's a bit like your father."

"I think he's going to be very clever," Joseph predicted, rather solemnly.

"That doesn't matter as long as he's happy. Cleverness doesn't do much for you in the end." She was thinking of Douglas: it pained her to think of him, lost, as she saw it, out of true with everything that mattered.

"You mean our Douglas?"

"Of course not. He's done well. But *she's* done really well. Mary. Much better than I would have guessed. She's really given that boy what he needed. He isn't the same person he was at Christmas. I admire her for that."

"Do you think . . .?"

"I don't think about it." She glanced over at John, who was going along the bank like a bloodhound, peering into the river uninterruptedly. "We can only do so much. He needs his father."

"It happens all the time nowadays," Joseph said, trying to assuage her anxiety. "Not only in the papers. Everywhere."

"That doesn't make it any better for the children, does it?"

For some moments they walked along silently. But Joseph's euphoria would not be dashed.

"You know," he tumbled over the following words, determined to get them out, afraid that Betty would laugh and puncture his sentiment, "I've been thinking. When you get older you're supposed to get wiser—that's what they said. And I always thought that, alongside that, things got worse for you personally—that's why my own father was so reluctant to give up work. He was frightened of the workhouse still and so am I, to a certain extent. Though things are better than I could have imagined. But I don't feel any wiser. I think I know nothing at all. It's as if I've just got all the, you know, daft bits of me sorted out and what I should be doing is settling down to a life of learning things. I'm sure I would have enjoyed that. I would have enjoyed being a village schoolmaster, you know. You

263

could have contributed something then. And there would have been time for thinking about things. What have I thought about? There's all this life to think about—what have I done about thinking about it? And mostly what I read is the newspapers. There are all those Great Books. I haven't read the majority of them. I never will now. Why have I been so stupid?" He paused. Impressed by the emphatic nature of his delivery, Betty avoided his eyes and appeared to be listening intently. "It strikes you though, doesn't it? And it all seems to add up on one or two times in your life—like tonight. Or when I took you home to meet my family for the first time. Or the day I came back out of the forces. Or when Douglas or Harry did a particular thing. It doesn't worry me, you understand, although I think that if I was cleverer it would. But I just can't make head nor tail out of it." He took a deep breath. "I'm glad we've managed to batter through together anyway. That's something."

Betty nodded. She knew he was reaching out and she would not repulse him. Perhaps there had always been a companionship between them which busyness had obscured. John had filled the gap of need: the church work enabled her to keep busy and feel tolerably useful. Between those two poles she had constructed a life, over the past few months, which had enabled her to see above the aimless despair which had begun to claim her. Sensitive to others always, she recognized that Joseph was asking for help. He had never wanted it before. She glanced at him. He was a little embarrassed by his speech and had turned away, ostensibly to watch John. He wanted to be looked after, Betty thought. He would never admit it but that was the sum of it.

"It's turning rather cooler," she said. "We should be getting back."

Joseph nodded and shouted out to John, who trailed across reluctantly.

"I saw two trout," he said.

"That place used to be full of trout," Joseph boasted. "Fresh river and sea trout. I've seen sea trout up as far as the bottom of the fields. We used to watch them jumping. It was one of the loveliest sights I've ever seen in my life. Those salmon trout struggling upstream to lay their eggs, you know. It's an amazing thing how they know and how they won't give up."

"I'd like to see them," John said, enviously. "I'd really like to."

"Right," Joseph promised. "Charlie Allardyce'll know where to look. I'll get onto him and we'll have a look-see. Mind you—you have to be patient."

"I don't mind that," the boy replied. "I just want to see them jump."

"How about a fishing rod for your birthday?" Joseph asked, struck with inspiration.

"Oh—smashing! *Smashing!*" John slipped his arm around that of his grandfather and hugged it tightly. "That's *exactly* what I want. *Exactly*." He imitated a Dalek's voice. "You — read — my — mind — you — will — not — be — exterminated."

"That was *good*," Joseph said. "*Very* good. You could be a mimic. Your dad was a good mimic. He could take off anybody in the town."

"When he was my age?"

"Yes. About then."

"What else did he do?" John spoke eagerly.

"Well," Joseph adjusted himself and decided that there was everything to be gained from telling the boy as much as he could remember. As he chatted on, John visibly squirmed with delight and then darted in with further questions to pinpoint exactly what Douglas had done, what age he had been, what others had thought of it and what they had thought of him.

The conversation went on until they were back in their street. They had walked past two of the big new estates which now encircled the town and drew the residential life out of it, and along a road full of the older cottages and small houses which Betty had known from her childhood. There wasn't a lane or alley in the place that did not bring back an image. Down that track had lived a man who bred donkeys and she had gone there with a friend one summer evening, like this, to see if they could borrow one for a carnival. Yes, he had said, if you can ride one. And the donkey had thrashed about like a bucking bronco.

Further on was the sandpit to which, audaciously, she had sneaked off one afternoon while at the primary school and later been found having the time of her life building a house in sand. There was a mission hall up the steps and the two rather grand houses with orchards the boys would steal from, and the little red-brick infants' school, like something out of a child's pop-up play book.

The images were sad, but they carried consolations. Perhaps it was better to go entirely away and just break off. Perhaps all this just dragged you down, was more of a dead weight than a ballast. She did not know. It was what she had, that was all.

As they turned into the street, Joseph, aware that some kind of domestic spell had been kindly cast over the three of them, was loath to break it. Yet the itch to return to his routine proved too compelling to resist.

"I think," he said, looking earnestly at his watch, "yes. I think they'll all be wondering where I've got to."

"In the pub?" John asked, innocently enough.

"That's where we meet, yes. For convenience's sake as much as anything else. They don't have clubs and such like in Thurston. And the Reading Room closed long ago."

"When did you ever go to the Reading Room?" Betty asked, innocently.

"We could always afford our own newspaper. But the point is made."

He hovered, edgy as a schoolboy seeking permission to leave the class. Betty smiled. She was glad he had his friends.

"What are you waiting for, then?" she asked, knowing the answer. He wanted her approval. "Give them all my regards." To pin it home, she added, "Thank George Marrs for the eggs. They were lovely. John knew they were different right away."

"I will." Joseph was very happy. "I'll do just that. There's nothing to beat farm eggs. And," he tousled John's hair, "I'll bring you a bottle of pop and a packet of crisps. Anything I can get you?" To Betty.

She shook her head. He beamed at her, turned, almost pirouetted, and puttered away down the tranquil street to his den in The Crown where the world would be shredded and reconstituted.

266

"Grandad likes the pub, doesn't he?"

"Men have to have some enjoyment," Betty said. "He doesn't fare too badly."

"Will he really get me a fishing rod?"

"I'll see he does."

"Who'll teach me to fish?" He paused. "I don't think Dad can, do you?"

"He was never patient enough. Your grandad'll find somebody. He knows all sorts of people. Don't worry."

John nodded, reassured, and linked arms with her. She liked that very much.

The telephone rang just a couple of minutes after they got into the house. It was Douglas.

He spent a long time talking with John and, although Betty tried to keep her eyes averted, so as not to intrude, she could not help but hear. John had been clipped in his speech, even laconic to begin with, but soon he was laughing and asking questions about the height of the skyscrapers, the lifts in the Empire State Building and the sounds on the police cars. She was relieved that he could still be so warm with Douglas. One of her worst fears was that Douglas would get separated from his son.

"He wants to say hello to you now," John said and handed over the telephone. "There was some sort of mix up at the airport and he flew back in a *Concorde*. A *Concorde*!" The boy danced about the room, clapping his hands.

"You seem to have hit the jackpot there," Betty said to Douglas. "I've never seen him so full of himself."

"He sounds very well," said Douglas. "Thank you."

"His mother's worked wonders," Betty replied grimly. She was caught in a fix. She loved to talk to Douglas and was happy just to hear him "prattle on", as she called it. But she disapproved of what he was doing. She had tried to stay on the sidelines but John had brought her into Mary's camp and, although she would never admit that out loud, it certainly coloured her behaviour and, as now, slipped into her conversation without her being able to stop it.

"She has," Douglas agreed. It would help his mother, he knew, if he had told her that he was trying to repair his

267

marriage. But the information was too sensitive and perhaps the fear of failure was too great.

"Did you have a good time in America?"

"Very. I like it there. There's nothing depressing about—not that I see, anyway."

"What was the weather like?"

"O.K. I think. Yes. Fine."

"It's been beautiful here. John might have the starting of a tan."

"I went," Douglas searched among his souvenirs with a certain desperation, "I went up the second highest building in the world for dinner."

"The second highest?"

"Yes." Douglas laughed. "The highest's in Chicago." He swallowed his laughter. "While I was having dinner, helicopters flew past—underneath."

"I see."

"It's a marvellous city—New York."

"There's that new song about it."

"How's Dad?"

"Bearing up. Are you managing to look after yourself?" She was convinced he was living with the other woman but maintained her fiction that he was living alone: which he was. And in need of care and attention. Which he also was, though she was certain the other woman pandered to his smallest wish.

"Not too bad," he said. A glance around the dismal, littered hallway of his rooming house confirmed the accuracy of his downbeat diagnosis.

"Will you be getting up here some time?"

"I thought of coming up tomorrow and then bringing John back."

"That would be very nice for him. He would like that."

"I'll catch an early train. See you."

"Yes."

He put the phone down. She held onto it for a while. It was indecent the way her heart had leapt, physically seemed to somersault, at his news.

"Your father's coming up tomorrow to see you," she said, steadily, to John. "You can tell him all about the fishing."

## 4

Douglas had just decided to go to Cumbria on the spur of the moment. It was a good decision, though, he felt it. And he would stick to it.

He dialled Hilda's number. There had been a message left at his office and two left here. She answered immediately.

"I wanted to talk to you, that's all," she answered, in response to his first question. "I've wanted to talk to you for weeks. I know I asked you not to—but suddenly it all seemed rather silly. You can ring off if you want. Do you?"

"Don't be daft." He paused. It had been an effort to repress thoughts of Hilda and to prevent himself from ringing her up: he had made it under the impression that it was the best way, an impression which had grown firmer with time. And there had been some compensation: a feeling of simplicity entering his affairs, the sense of a single direction possible. Now it was all as it had been.

"You sound—well, nothing at all—shall I say taken aback?"

Hilda's voice danced mischievously down the phone and Douglas could see her eyes brimming with amusement at the correctly intuited assessment of his reaction.

"It is rather a turn up. After the Heavy Letter. I thought that was me executed, slam, head off, caput."

"It was. I meant every word of it—when I wrote it."

"Thanks."

"Well, you must admit it was a shitty thing to do to tell me you were going back to your wife. Although I notice you've kept your flat on. Still need an escape hatch?"

"Something like that."

"Don't we sound cross!"

"Do I?"

"Don't you want to see me then?"

"Of course."

"You don't sound very enthusiastic. When?"

"I'm going north tomorrow."

"What about tonight? Now."

"What can I say?"

269

"You could say no. But that would be silly because I know you want to see me too. So it's yes. Where?" She hesitated only fractionally. "Our usual place? Three quarters of an hour?"

"O.K. See you."

"Don't sound so glum. You'll love it!"

Hilda put down the receiver and Douglas went back into his room.

He had ceased to like it. The bareness and ugliness of the place depressed him now.

Once again he read the letter which Mary had left for him "To Await Arrival".

Dear Douglas,

John is with your mother. She's pleased to have him there, I'm certain of that, so there's no question of imposing. She assured me that she was well and could cope. As for John, he's delighted to go. He likes it up there. I think he may end up preferring the country.

I've gone away for a few days with a friend. I don't quite know how much or how little you have any right to be told. At this stage we've decided "least said soonest mended"—although that isn't quite what I mean. What I mean is the less said the better. I am very tired and need the holiday which I hope this will turn out to be.

I've done a lot of thinking while you've been away and I want you to know that I really did appreciate what you were trying to do, even though I might criticize the way you went about it and the assumptions you base your decisions on. (grammar!)

There's part of me that will always love you—I never thought I would write that sentence to *anyone*, let alone you, but there we are. At this moment, though, I have no idea how strong that is, or how important it is. I don't know how much it means to either of us.

What I do know is that I am very tired and need a break. I hope you enjoyed yours.

Love,<br>Mary.

*"We've decided"*! That was what got him. Not only was there a man, and a man who swanned in large as life when he was three thousand miles away across the Atlantic Ocean, the man had the bare face to involve himself in discussions with Mary about *him*! It was intolerable. He metaphorically clapped his hands to his ears to shut out the imagined tittle-tattle and chit-chat about whether they should tell Douglas this, when they should tell Douglas that. The idea of being talked about in that way made him angry. There was nothing he could do. He presumed she had left an address with a friend of hers, in case of emergencies: he had intended to ask John if he had an address for his mother, but pride had forbidden it. Had he asked that night—he would have been given the small hotel in Paris, the address he was given the next day when he talked with John and could no longer contain his jealousy. *"We've* decided"!

He ripped up the letter—into four—and then put the small pile on his dressing table. Perhaps if he read it later he would see more in it.

As far as he could tell, Mary had never been unfaithful to him.

Did it matter?

Of course it mattered! It stung and wounded him as if he had been unblemished. There is no fair accounting of emotions. He wanted to disable the masculine component of *"We've* decided" and win back Mary.

And yet, although this outburst of emotions did occur, it did not sweep away the complications and ambiguities of feeling. Rather, it added more intensity to what existed.

As he went towards the pub to meet Hilda, he realized how little of the solution—if there ever could be one—was in his hands. And yet with his whole spirit he longed for a solution.

The pub was on the edge of Covent Garden, still beamed and poky, still the sort of place in which you might call for a hot poker to ram into a pint of ale. Oak settles, a bar laden with good food, and, on such a warm summer's evening as this, packed out.

Hilda was already there. Douglas shrugged at her across the crowded room and she nodded and came across.

271

"The trouble is," he said, as they picked their way over the bodies sprawled up and down the pavement outside the two bars, "that all the decent pubs are full and if we find an empty pub it's bound to be rotten."

"We could go and eat," Hilda said. "Restaurants are easier for talking."

Douglas was still rather jet-lagged—he had only flown in that morning—and his meal-count was completely askew. All he knew was that he did not want to eat.

"Let's try Paganini's," he said.

This was one of several fashionable, expensive and reasonably good restaurants which had opened in Covent Garden since the market had moved. The whole place was inexorably escalating towards an in-town Hampstead, more-fun-than-Chelsea area. Douglas had heard Raven recommend Paganini's.

It was almost full—a good sign at that time of night—and the head waiter was an efficient young man who made no fuss, led them to a quietish table, took the drinks order and left Douglas with the impression that the drinks themselves might already be on the way. The decor was baroque pop but not offensive: Paganini himself figured in various prints and articles about the place. The only naff note, as it were, was that the menu was shaped like a violin. Still, clean table cloths and napkins and glasses, two good Pimms when they came, a menu not absurdly long and full of sensible promises such as, "Vegetables fresh from the market daily" and, "Fish absolutely guaranteed fresh daily"—not bad. It would set him back about twenty-five to thirty pounds.

"It's as if we'd never parted," Hilda said, rather uncertainly. Her vulnerable nervousness turned Douglas' confused feelings towards protectiveness. She was, he thought, defenceless and he had contributed to that.

"Cheers."

The Pimms slaked the dusty summer thirst. Hilda was nowhere near as self-possessed as she had been on the telephone. She looked thinner, Douglas saw, and fraught: she kept flicking out a hand towards his, seeking a reassuring contact.

"I thought, I'll phone, I might as *well* phone. It seemed

272

stupid not to. And you would have phoned if I hadn't." She gave him the opportunity to confirm this and he smiled, which did the trick. She reached out for his hand and held it firmly. "You see. It would have been one of us. We think alike. We *are* alike."

Douglas took note of the wildness which was not far from the surface of her talk and again it was her weakness which drew out his affection.

They ordered cold vichysoisse, and turbot.

Hilda glanced about her rapidly, nervously, as if pecking the air, as if reassuring herself that things were as they had been. Douglas, who had ordered hock, pulled too deeply at the chilled white wine and felt that warning chute of coarseness down his sternum which told him he was slowly toppling into exhaustion.

"I like this place," Hilda said and sipped very tentatively at the glass. They smiled at each other and held hands like honeymooners.

The fact was, Douglas reflected, that he kept falling in love. There you were. In a society so highly tuned to monogamy—and one in which the rules for breaking the rules were strict, and punishable in law and pocket—this inherently amiable characteristic was a liability. Because he meant love, not lust: not generally; not any more. And love meant worry. Or, its other face, responsibility. But such responsibility brought immediate complications, since it led to insoluble contradictions. How, for example, could he follow through his love and responsibility to Hilda and Mary simultaneously, without short-changing one or both of them?

Two bottles of wine later, over sensibly large cups of coffee, Douglas at last focused properly on Hilda. He was aware that they had gossiped. He had passed on chit-chat about Merlin Raven: everyone was interested in Raven. And Hilda had called up their few mutual friends to spin out an appearance of community. It had been agreeable, happy, the two of them harmoniously in touch, connected.

"Well," Douglas said. "Here we are."

"Yes." Hilda smiled a little over brightly. She had relaxed but clearly he wanted to talk seriously about their future and she did not. She sensed his decision before he had spoken it and

273

tried to snap and perpetuate the present moment. If you tried, she now thought, if you really tried, you could find a way of living in the present without pain.

"I thought, you see, after your letter," he started out, rather helplessly, "that it was over. For us."

"You sound as if you wanted it to be."

"You know I don't," Douglas defended himself weakly, although in fact he meant what he said.

"I do know that." Her hand covered his and her eyes sought out his glance. "I'm sorry. I'm nervy, that's all."

"There's something I have to say. And I want it to be as honest as I can make it."

"You look terribly tired all of a sudden."

"Jet lag. Booze. And being honest." He grinned. "Hilda—listen. I can't keep going as we did. I don't know why. In its hectic way it worked. Maybe we'll all miss it and be the poorer for it. But I've had it."

It was as if Hilda's nightmare had suddenly risen up before her.

The silence between them had to be broken.

"So you've found married life gives you all you need then," Hilda said.

"That isn't it. I'm not living with Mary. She doesn't want me back. But the point is that I want to go back and I can't any longer split myself in two. We can see each other but we can't sleep together."

"Why not?"

"I don't know. Maybe it should be the other way round. We should sleep together but not see each other. That makes sense at least. It's just that if I'm going to keep things together and have some sort of coherence in my head, then I have to have everything in the same place. Splitting sex is like splitting an atom inside myself—bang! Everything scatters all over the place, destroyed. I don't know why. It's crappy and creepy in a way, but there it is."

"You misunderstood. I meant—why will she not have you back?"

"There's another fella. No. I'm sure it's not that—although there *is* another fella. She wants some air, too."

"I can't understand you."

"No?" The waiter had brought a third bottle of wine and the bill. Douglas was by now pouring down the wine like beer on a hot afternoon.

"No. You say you love me. You needn't say it actually, I know you do. And Mary doesn't want you back. And yet you still won't come and live with me." Hilda's brows furrowed—Douglas, all but drunk, was careful to notice that the word was properly applied. They furrowed.

"It makes no sense," he agreed.

"That's a cop out."

"I agree." He sank a glass of the cool wine and reached for the truth. "You say you love me and you know I love you. I don't know what love is. That is to say, I know what I want it to be but it isn't that or rather it can't be that. So I don't know what it is. I don't know what weight it carries. I know what passion is—we had that, we still have it and not only in bed. I think I know what eroticism is: this meal could have been erotic if you had not been so tense and I had not been so tired. And then there's the awful gap—love: after that I know what duty is—a bit too late—and the same goes for responsibility—again too late. But *love*—love—I'll have to do without that now."

"That's a terrible thing to say!"

Hilda was poised like a tigress threatened. He loved her when she was so intense, so devoted to an idea. Here she was defending Love as if it were her young.

"It's a tired thing to say."

"It's your own fault you're tired. Some people are *really* tired—with blooming hard work. Your 'tired' is self-indulgence."

"True, oh queen. True enough."

She smiled, confident now. "I don't think you know what you're saying, to be honest. If you want to know what I think, it's that everything's finished between you and Mary but you don't want to admit it. I'm sure you will admit it. You're in a transition period now, that's all."

"No, I'm not. I mean what I say."

"In that case tell me you don't love me."

"It doesn't follow."

275

"Oh yes it does," Hilda said, almost laughing now, enjoying having him cornered. "Tell me you don't love me."

"It's meaningless." And it's not the point, he thought.

"If it's meaningless say it then."

"You know I can't."

"Well, as long as you can't," she said, steadily, "I'm not going away. If you want me to vanish, just say that and I will. I've sat in my flat for nights on end, thinking I was doing something useful, I was helping you to clear up your life, taking a burden away from you, giving Mary and John an opportunity. It wasn't much consolation but it made sense of a kind. And then I began to do weird things—I'll tell you about them sometime!—and I thought—I *know*—he still loves me—whatever you say, you can't think of a better word. And if he still loves me and I certainly still love him—what am I doing alone? So I phoned. And here we are."

"Yes." Douglas still had clarity of thought, slow as it might be. "But I still mean what I said. *See*—yes. Sleep—no."

"You look as if you could sleep for a week. My place?"

"I'm going to see John." With difficulty, Douglas found and delivered his Barclaycard.

"I thought you weren't with Mary."

"Neither is he. He's with my mother. There's a sleeper I can catch."

"Where are your things?"

"Things? I can buy them up there. About time I had a batch of new things anyway. New razor thing; new toothbrush thing; new trousers and shirt thing. Advert for Oxfam. Cheers." He drained the glass and poured out a last satisfying measure. Hilda had stopped drinking long ago.

The bill came to over thirty pounds with the tip.

As they walked along the pavement, his arm affectionately, and for reasons of support, around Hilda's shoulder, Douglas incanted a favourite sum.

"Thirty pounds," he said, "was as much as my grandfather earned in his first *year* of employment—eighty-two hours a week. And thirty pounds was almost a year's wages for my father when he started although he got his keep thrown in—no, six months, six months. He was a boots boy. And thirty pounds

276

has just slid into our organs on wined skids. Besides which, consider the starving half of the globe, about whom my more sober friends would consider it a blasphemy for me to speak in this condition: a family in the starving half of the globe could live for a year on that thirty quid. Now what sense is there in all that? Bewilderment, guilt and finally a lack of real concern. That's all. Isn't it?"

The air had spun him into drunkenness and Hilda loaded him into a taxi and, conscientiously—for John, she realized, had to be looked after—ushered him to Euston, bought his ticket and took him to the train. It was rather disconcerting how sober and perfectly self-possessed he appeared. Even when he spoke one or two words to the ticket collector the words were neither slurred nor were they nonsense.

She took him into his compartment and they kissed each other very warmly. Douglas was in the narrow bed within a few moments. His head swirled like snow in one of those tiny crystal balls. His brain seemed like a swing and sway backwards and forwards inside the stretched tent of his skull. His throat was parched. His head began to ache.

"I wanted to be a vicar," he said, abruptly, loudly. "But I couldn't believe in God. I saw eternity as two parallel lines and they never met. It used to drive me nearly mad when I was trying to get to sleep. They just kept on travelling into space."

The train jolted away. Some sort of unconsciousness descended.

Hilda stood until the train had drawn out of the station and then she turned and walked along the concrete and up the barren slipway to the gate. The main hall was like a dosshouse, students mainly, she guessed, apparently snug in their sleeping bags, between trains or holidays or lives. She envied them their licensed summer carefreeness.

Outside, London felt almost balmy. She decided to walk some of the way. She felt secure again now and she wanted to relish it. The big black city with streamers of lights and wayward strollers was just the place to savour this reconciliation.

They were playing the Eton Boating Song. Emma paused to make absolutely certain, but there was no doubt about it. In Regent's Park on a Sunday afternoon, English fleecy clouds, sunny as the weather in a rattling Wodehouse story, full of large young men in boats and pretty girls in frocks and less, strewn with ageing bodies in ageing dresses hitched up to the bare white knee for the rays of heat, infiltrated by weary-faced foreigners seeking a respite from sightseeing and collapsing contentedly onto the crew-cut lawns (no charge) patrolled by invisible park wardens and speckled by one or two gentle loonies and snoring afternoon drunks and many dogs, not to mention the famous ducks and children with ice creams and courting couples curdling their breath together obliviously, the all perspiring band in bottle green uniforms were playing the Eton Boating Song.

Emma smiled soppily. She liked to be back in London. She had come up on a very early train and gone to see her old landlady, who had a curious tale about someone who must have been Lester threatening to return and terrorize her—Emma had reassured the old lady and made a promise to herself to tick off Lester for being so wicked, although the landlady was a bigoted and prejudiced old . . . she was still a person. Then she had dropped in at the Laughing Duck and, Luck! met up with several of the gang, who oohed and aahed at her new slimness, at her post-natal "completeness", at her country freshness, and stood her gins and It. She drank only a couple and thoroughly enjoyed the tasty talk of Andrew doing well in that Granada series about the waiter, you know the one, yes, *that* one, well, Andrew was the chef, not very much to say, not anything so far, but in *every* episode, imagine the fees if it gets sold abroad! And Pris, who'd got into the National, really, the National, *Pris*, it was unbelievable and you couldn't call it the old hello-hello, not with the director *she* was working with, my dear. And Alex and Annie, always rather intense, joined a co-operative company, touring North Wales with a show about pre-revolutionary Siam (was it called that now?) anyway—*very*, you know, *intense*, voting on everything and no laughs and everybody writes the script and a tidy Arts Council subsidy, thank you very much. And did she know . . . ?

She had loved it all. Loved them for their generous gossip, loved the crowded, hemmed-in little pub, loved the stroll down towards the park. It had been a boy, almost three months old now—and the birth of the child had secured Emma as nothing else in the world could have done. Her parents had been perfect bricks. They could not be kind enough or helpful enough. Indeed, her mother swore it had given her a new lease of life and her father seemed not the slightest bit perturbed by any fear of censure from his parishioners. For three months, the four of them had been as contented as a Beatrix Potter happy family. But it would pass soon, she saw that with the clarity nowadays second nature to her. And she still loved Lester.

Needs found ways. She had heard of Douglas' involvement with Merlin Raven, contacted him at the B.B.C. and managed to engineer a phone call to coincide with a visit Lester was making to Douglas' office. Douglas was an efficient accomplice. Emma had worked out a firm proposition: would he meet her the following Sunday afternoon in Regent's Park about three o'clock near the band? No strings, no scenes, no heavy number, just a chance for a chat. Lester had agreed.

He was there before her. She could scarcely believe it and took care to take her time before going over to him. He sat, pale and sadly she thought. Dark shoes and socks, dark trousers, a white shirt wide open at the neck, his jacket on the grass behind him to be used as a pillow. He was smoking, puffing too quickly, once again, without doubt, out of luck. Emma stood there and, stupid though it was, tried to will good fortune into him, to irradiate him with good fortune. Nothing had changed in her feelings. But her will was stronger and she had a strategy. There was the child now.

At first Lester wondered who it was, this slim, sexy looking woman, very "upper" in a large straw hat with a purple ribbon round it and a basket under her arm like Cherry Ripe, coming waving across the lawn towards him, the dress fluttering erotically against her figure, long hair blowing about her face: like some posh bird in an ad., he thought. And it was all for him. Without knowing why, Lester stood up. That gesture was the

279

first to indicate an almost subliminal awareness on his part of the indisputable superiority of her external condition. She sank into his arms and pressed herself hard against him. It was the best thing that had happened to Lester for quite a while.

When they had sat down, she took out the picnic immediately—she had not eaten lunch and Lester was always a couple of meals adrift. Her mother had packed a white cloth which she spread on the grass and loaded with fruit—home grown punnets of raspberries and strawberries; two pies, one chicken, one veal; freshly baked bread, local cheese, home grown tomatoes and rather unsuccessful lettuce, but plenty of it, large and numerous radishes and an apple cake. She had bought four cans of beer in the pub.

"There," she said. "I'm famished."

Lester flicked open a can of beer and sank half of it. Then he fell to. The food was first class and sitting on the grass eating it made conversation difficult, which suited him very well as he was suffering from a confused invasion of thoughts and impressions. He was touched that she should be so thoughtful as to bring all this along for both of them and particularly moved that there should not only be beer, but his favourite label. He was a little daunted by her attractiveness. Emma had been the big fattie, the friendly Dunlopillo in a tight night spot, the nice but really, *be serious*, handy bit for emergencies, convenient in trouble. Now she was a looker. There was no doubt about it. He had watched the men swivelling their craniums as she had floated across the grass towards him and he too had taken a keen hard look at what they were noticing. It was very good stuff.

It was also worrying. If she had changed so much outside, perhaps she had changed inside. He had turned up—although he would have denied it—because he wanted to be with someone who thought he was great and who made him feel at least a bit better than average. He had been dumped, though not nastily and with a little paper handshake, by Raven and although Douglas tried his best to pretend he was useful, it was clear to Lester that his cousin could get on perfectly well without him. Besides which, he still felt sore at being outmanoeuvred and out-drunk in New York. In short, he was back where he had started before meeting Raven. He felt lost.

Emma's bounding puppy-dog affection would be just the pick-up he needed, he had thought. Now he was faced by this very desirable, young-looking female. He waited for her to make the moves.

To occupy the time, he took up the book which Emma had brought with her to protect her against what she had more than half suspected would be an empty and embarrassingly solitary afternoon.

"'Our Mutual Friend'," he read, "by Charles Dickens. Any good?"

"Yes," Emma returned, carefully. One of the things she admired but feared in Lester was his ability to make her cast off all pretentiousness. She came clean with him and felt safer for it.

"I read some of Charles Dickens at school," he said. "I quite liked it. Then the films. Fagin. Mr Pickwick. They were all right. Are you going to read it right through?"

"Yes."

Lester nodded and eased up on the food. He had satisfied the pangs provoked by the sight of such a tasty spread and satiation, plus a feeling that he had been gobbling in rather an adolescent manner, caused him to change pace. As was his custom, he lit up a cigarette to accompany the last part of the meal, and managed, in that act, to disguise (he thought) a burp.

"I expect you talk about books in your house," he said, mildly curious.

"Sometimes," Emma admitted. "But they're such big readers that they would rather be reading than talking about it."

"I used to read a bit," Lester offered. "In Liverpool. When I was hanging around the bands rehearsing. Ever heard of a writer called Maclean? Something like that."

Emma thought she had—was he not the man who wrote adventure stories? But was it Maclean? Somehow that didn't sound right. She played safe.

"No."

"You should get hold of one. I couldn't stand Agatha Christie."

"I quite enjoy her," Emma said, stoutly, faithful to the hours of escape into her mysteries.

"She's crap," Lester said, concluding the literary discussion. "If you want a detective you have to go to the pictures. The Americans have got all the detectives." He paused. "I suppose you could get used to reading if there was nothing else to do," he conceded, out of affection. He sounded very doubtful.

Emma smiled and handed him another can of beer. Her attention had been taken by a small child—about eighteen months—naked but for a pair of briefs, toddling backwards and forwards with the index fingers of both hands placed firmly in its navel. She began to watch the performance, which resembled the entranced dance of a witch doctor, as the almost naked child stomped across the grass in patterns known only to itself. Lester caught the intensity of Emma and in a moment of inspiration found a way to repay her for bringing along the meal.

"I suppose you have a photo of it?" he enquired, rather coyly.

Emma blushed deeply. She nodded and took out a small black photo-wallet which she had prepared. It contained two photographs. One of herself and the baby, one of the baby on its own. Inside the wallet was her name, address and telephone number. She handed it over to Lester, who stared at it dutifully.

"It's a boy," Emma explained.

"Good. He looks like Edward G. Robinson. Or a Chinese."

"He looks like you."

"Does he?"

"When he relaxes."

"What have you called him?"

"I thought I'd talk to you about that."

"Harry," Lester said. "Call him Harry. That's a good name. And give him a middle name. You never know when he could need it."

"Henry Tallentire," she said.

"Tallentire?"

"Only if you agree. It doesn't mean anything. I mean, I'm not going to claim anything from you."

"I see."

He snapped the wallet shut and held it out for her.

"You can keep that," she said. "I'd like you to keep it."

Lester nodded understandingly.

This time they relaxed together. He stretched back for a snooze. Emma lazily began to gather in some of the debris and continued to enjoy the park. It was so docile here. The unhurting sun, the grass easy on the feet, people in deck chairs, apparently untroubled, white shirts, vivid summer skirts and dresses, children scampering about, the band playing—was that Elgar? Yes. She was boning up on her music, too. It had already become a greater passion than literature. She had discovered that her father had been left an immense record collection by a friendly parishioner, and that, complemented by B.B.C. Radio Three, had directed her towards a lavish pleasure ground of music and performances. It *was* Elgar. "Enigma Variations." A simple one to guess, but you had to start somewhere. The listeners offered up a discreet spattering of applause, the same polite yet grateful yet unshowy clapping which trickled across the land at this time on a Sunday afternoon, around bandstands in parks and on promenades, at village cricket matches, at horse jumping competitions, at small tennis clubs and on bowling greens, as the English led their sabbatical sporting life at leisure and warm, for a change. Lester was asleep. Emma sneaked a look at her own photograph of—Harry? Harry it was, a perfect name! She was already missing the child! Shameful. She ought to be more liberated than that.

She read her book a while and thought about Lizzie Hexham.

She was gathering her strength. There was a proposition she wanted to put to Lester. She had little doubt it would be rejected, but she had worked it out with some care and would state it, whatever happened.

Eventually he woke up, smiled beatifically at her, shivered and lit up.

"Lester," she plunged in. "I'm moving back to London. The parents are very good but I want to be in London. Daddy—my father," she corrected herself—"Daddy" had always irritated him beyond reason, she had forgotten that, "has a friend—another vicar—in North Ken. and he'll let me have what used to be the housekeeper's flat very cheap. It's fantastically lucky. There's a crèche in the Church Hall next door and I'm going to help run it so I can earn something *and* look after— Harry at the same time. Now—the address is in that wallet I gave you. If you want to come along any time ..."

"A vicarage?"

"Yes," she whispered.

Lester unbent magisterially to ask, "What's a crèche?"

Emma explained.

"The kid'll be O.K. there? They need a lot of looking after, you know."

She reassured him.

"Sounds as if you landed on your feet," he said.

"How was New York?" she asked, in the same spirit of congratulation. "That Merlin Raven deal seems super—I mean, very good."

"Yea?" Lester looked at her as if she alone were responsible for what was to follow. "It's all over. He's a shit."

Emma was silent. She saw that yet again Lester had been used and then dropped. She wanted to cradle him and protect him from all this. She made a move but retreated at his stiffening "Keep Off". She hated Merlin Raven.

"They're all shits, aren't they?" Lester added, somehow exonerating her and putting them on the same side. "What are you doing tonight?" he asked.

She had managed to get a ticket for a concert at the Festival Hall. Rudolf Serkin. A tremendous treat—so sure had she been that, even if Lester had turned up, he would flit before the evening. She had planned to go to the concert and then catch what was called "the milk train" back, to be there for the baby in the morning.

"Nothing," she said.

"I've got to see this man about a new group. These punks! They want to do it with a light show now, as if we weren't all doing that in the Sixties. They say we're all past it—you know that? Somebody said that Raven and his lot were 'dinosaurs'. But the new guys just haven't got it. They've got the mouth and all the writers love them because they're supposed to be talking about the new generation—but who cares? The bloody tunes are no good. And the arrangements! And the playing! I tell you—I'm thinking of getting out and going into something quieter. A friend of mine's got a betting shop over your way—where you'll be—North Ken.—he says I can work in with him. Not work *for* him, more of a, sort of, partner."

"That sounds," Emma hesitated, conscious that she was walking on a stack of broken glass, "useful."

"Exactly. Useful. Could be."

Lester got to his feet and looked down on her. She was very very fanciable, he thought. But, he also thought, I've done her enough damage.

"I'm a bit short," he said, "or I'd—you know. But I've got the address." He waved the wallet at her. "I'll see you all right."

"I can—thank you."

Emma suddenly felt the pressure of tears. It was too sudden for her to hold them back. Lester squatted down beside her and talked quietly and intensely.

"Look, Emma. You've made yourself into a lovely bird. You've got looks and connections. You don't want me. You think you do now but in a few months—no. There's nothing I can give you that'll do you any good. I'll send money for the nipper if I get hold of any. That's gospel. But now I'm going to do you a big favour—and vanish. Tara."

She clutched at him but he sprang to his feet and set off rapidly through the deckchairs and sunbathers and running children. Emma wanted to follow him but knew that he would hate her for it and be cruel on that account. She tried to weep unseen.

The band played Airs from Gilbert and Sullivan.

(6)

It was surprising how soon you got used to it, Harry thought. When Aileen's pregnancy had first begun to make her look noticeably different, then Harry's pleasure and awe and, occasionally, alarm, had made him treat her as if she *were* indeed different. She laughed at the cloudburst of courtesy which showered antique attentions on her. But Harry was unable to prevent himself from leaping to open doors which were often already ajar, puff up cushions already sufficiently comfortable, make unwanted cups of tea, do domestic jobs which had been done previously and generally behave as though his wife had turned into a monster of fragility. Aileen lapped it up. And she was a little sad when his attentions began to fall off. He was just as loving—he would never, she thought happily and securely, be anything less than that: and he was still careful of her. But the fuss died down as he got used to the bulk which grew inside her. He got used to it, as she did. There were two or three months, towards the end, when it seemed as if she had been heavily pregnant all the days of her life: she could recall times without the pregnancy, of course, but they were so insubstantial compared with the solid, growing, undeniable fact of another life taking its course and shape inside her own. While, to Harry, the whole experience had so much importance that the rest of his life rearranged itself as no more than a preparation for this time—when he would incontestably root himself in the world, and join onto it by starting his own family. He wanted a large family. There seemed to him no better stake in life.

But even that profound satisfaction became absorbed and now he was fast asleep, just before dawn on a summer's morning, a Sunday, with Aileen beside him, on her back, the swell of the belly now enormous, concentrating hard. Was this a cramp or were these the first real pains? There they came again. She glanced at the electric alarm clock beside the bed. It had a second hand on it: she had put it there specifically for this moment, so that she could check on the timings. There it came again.

It was a strange moment. So, she thought, this is the time. I'm going to have a child, really to have it. It will come out of me and be itself. How very strange, she thought, in that dreamy moment which might not have lasted more than a second but which spread across her mind like a film. Some great yearning in her was appeased. There would be another human being.

Yes. The pains were definitely in the first stage. There was no panic. She knew what she had to do. She had attended the classes and Harry too had put a gallant determination before his embarrassment and done his bit. He was squeamish about her. Aileen knew that, and he had told her that he did not want to make a fool of himself or to mess things up by passing out or doing something stupid in the delivery room. The arrangement was that he could walk out if he felt that he could not take it. She had assured him that this would be all right: in fact she had helped him all the way along by saying that it might be better for her, too—because she would be worried about him! She tapped lightly on his naked back. He made no move. She looked at him in the dusky light. There was a peaceful honesty about his sleeping face which moved her greatly.

"Harry. *Harry*."

"Yes?"

"I think you'd better get the ambulance."

"I see."

It was like a double take in a corny movie. As banal as that. He turned over to steal a few extra seconds of sleep: there was a pause: and then he shot up like an electrified hare and glared at her, mouth wide open, eyes startled full awake.

"Don't panic!" he said.

"I'm O.K." Aileen felt a giggle ripple through her and somehow, comfortably, it joined itself into a pang which satisfied her, this time, like a physical relief.

"Well don't!" Harry was transfixed. "That's all!"

"Ambulance."

"Right away."

He hurled back the sheets and made for the door. Then, naked, he whirled around, came back and tucked the sheets over her.

"Keep warm," he said, still shocked. "You *must* keep warm."

"Thank you," Aileen said, gently.

"I'll get the ambulance."

Harry turned and dashed straight into her dressing table. Brushes, combs, bangles, bracelets, necklaces and perfume bottles jumped and jangled on the jarred surface.

"Sorry," he said, turning to her and bowing. Then he spun around, headed for the door at top speed and banged his foot on the leg of a chair.

Aileen burrowed under the sheets and let the laughter run up and down her body like a massage as he hopped around the room.

"An ambulance!" he said and limped out as quickly as he could.

A sense of calm must have been transmitted by the telephone operator for though Harry returned at top speed, thundering through the flat like a horse let out of the stables after a month's confinement, he was no longer quite as mind-glazed.

"Tea?" he asked. "No," he answered, before she could. "I'd better get dressed. *You'd* better get dressed. *No*. Dressing gown. That'll do. Yes. Where's my other sock?"

As Aileen levered herself out of bed she saw Harry, naked but for one black sock, crawling about the floor.

"I've lost my sock," he said, helplessly.

"You can't have done."

"I *have*. I've lost it. It was here and now it's gone."

"I'll help you."

She got down on her knees and began to travel the floor systematically in search of the sock. Harry shifted about like a pointer dog, his bare bum bobbing up and down before Aileen's eyes. Suddenly he jumped up.

"It's got to be *some*where!" He stood almost at attention. "I came in as usual. I put my shirt there—there it is. My trousers there—see—there they are. My slippers are there—*there*—yes. My underpants are—"

"Harry. Could you help me up?"

"One second. One second! *Got* it! Leg of trouser."

He made as if to launch an assault on his trousers and then spun around. Aileen, half-laughing, half-groaning, was on her hands and knees swaying from side to side.

"Oh damn!" Harry said. "I'm sorry."

The blatant evidence of his thoughtlessness cut through the nerves and restored him at once.

He helped her up. Put on her dressing gown. Saw her through to the living room where he settled her before making a cup of tea. The ambulance had to come from Carlisle, eleven miles away.

The rest of that morning was so clear and yet so hallucinatory that it seemed to inhabit a time zone of its own. The ambulance eventually arrived and they went through the deserted town along the empty familiar road to Carlisle and into the Infirmary.

288

Everyone was very calm. Everyone knew what to do, making Harry feel that he too knew what to do.

They were left alone in a delivery room. The pangs had eased off. Harry sat in the corner, watching.

It would take about eight hours, they said.

The room was so very bare. A bed which seemed to be made out of aluminium. His plain chair. A white bedside table. Aileen somehow scientifically displayed. Harry felt shy and tried desperately to think of something to say.

"I'm glad you're here," Aileen said, and smiled at him. "I would've been lonely on my own."

"It *is* a bit bare, isn't it?" he replied, politely. "I expect it's for hygienic purposes."

"Yes," Aileen grinned at him. "Come and give us a kiss then, before the shouting and the heaving starts."

Obediently he went across and kissed her forehead. It was a little damp. Her face had broadened during the pregnancy but she had still taken care to resist a return of the fat which had plagued her childhood so painfully.

"I'll stay," Harry said.

"You needn't."

"I couldn't leave now."

The pains began to come more regularly. Aileen shouted out. The chief nurse, a good-looking young local girl, was a little embarrassed by the shouting. As if Aileen were talking loudly in church. She asked her not to, it could upset others in the hospital. Aileen ignored her and yelled again as the pains gripped her and the calculations went through the window. The child was waiting to be born now.

Harry was decked out in a white coat, and a face mask. Stood beside the oxygen and was shown how to put the mask on Aileen's face. Helped her with the counting. Found himself joining in what became a concerted commentary of reassurance, command, instruction, congratulation, push, *push*, well done, and again, longer, there we are, push, relax now, it's O.K., oxygen, she grabbed the oxygen mask from his hands and here they came again—*puuush! puuush*—and again—and that was good, another one—no, you *must*, you must, come on, another one, wait a moment, and—yes—*puuuush*—I can see the head—yes! It's nearly there—the other two nurses flanked the midwife with towels and gleaming bowls and watched Harry, who was as calm and sensible as could be and totally unaware that tears were streaming down his face and *puuush*, again! Again! *Again*! It's—*again*! You *must*!

The child slid out as comfortably as someone coming down a banana slide, just slid out; Harry felt the tension go out of both of them—it was there—a girl—she was born—Aileen was fine—the rest was uncomplicated—they wiped the baby quickly and handed it up to Aileen, who looked radiantly brisk and totally delighted with herself.

Harry looked at the two of them. Mother and child. His. Well.

"She's lovely," Aileen said, and he nodded, unable to find words.

(7)

It was Mary who had made the decision and she held to it now. After those few days in Paris, Mike had wanted Douglas to be told. It was intolerable, he said, to work with Douglas and hide this from him: it appeared cowardly and deceitful. Neither these nor other arguments budged her. She wanted it to be kept secret and again, though Douglas had pushed her hard, she had not given in.

"Why are you so mysterious?" he asked. "I come around to see you the day after you come back from your trip and clearly you've had a good time—"

"There's no need to sound so bitter about that," Mary said.

"Perhaps not." Douglas wanted to let it drop but there was something about her persistence which goaded him on. "I would have thought that it was a good time to tell the truth," he added drily.

"Listen to you!" Mary's indignation was immediate and ferocious. "Your lies wore us out."

"Do you really think that?"

"Yes, I do."

"Yes." Douglas paused. "Although you could argue that if I hadn't lied it would have come to this much sooner. Sometimes lies can staunch something or keep something going until a new skin grows. Sometimes they're a way to survive. Like mould."

"But what's left after them isn't worth having."

"There is that," Douglas agreed. "But you could argue—I think I would—that lying is, in its way, a declaration of—affection, even of love, in that you are prepared to be deceitful and run the risks of that—most importantly the risk to yourself—myself. Because lies hurt the liar most."

"You are unbelievable!" she said.

"It's true, though," Douglas protested his case the more cheerfully for her comment. "It imposes a burden on you when you lie. Its effect on the liar is probably as bad as, if not worse than, its effect on the lie-ee. It twists up your sense of reality."

"How you must have suffered!"

"I did. As a matter of fact."

"Why didn't you stop?"

"I did."

"Eventually."

"Yes."

"And now you tell no lies."

"No."

"So I'm not worth lying for now?"

"Touché."

"Are you still seeing that woman?"

"Yes."

"Do you—sleep with her?"

"No." Douglas paused only fractionally. "And you?"

"I'm not going to tell you, Douglas. Sorry."

"You have."

"Please."

"You have." He said it colourlessly. "I've just registered it. Of course you have." He paused. "Christ."

During the pause, Douglas felt as if a great deal of himself was simply draining away. Of course she had slept with him. *"We've decided."* Yes. And of course there was nothing he was in a position to say about it. But the idea of her loyalty, her purity—that was the word he would use—of all that he had both taken for granted and admired in her suddenly gone—that seemed to Douglas the worst outcome of his own behaviour. For she had cherished her own fidelity greatly, he knew that: now that was gone.

Yet, at almost the same time, the beginnings of two other responses were felt. Firstly, he realized that his reaction, given his own behaviour, was a nauseating mixture of hypocrisy, prudery and ancient male chauvinism: what was sauce for the gander was not to be sauce for the goose. Secondly, he was relieved. Quite simply, it evened the score—it entitled them to meet on equal terms again—to be, in fact, as they had been when they had first met: about equally experienced, equally prepared to say "pass" to the other's previous affairs. Yet this was a perception of future balm: at that moment, Douglas was nonplussed.

"There we are then," he said, to fill a gap.

Mary smiled. For a moment he reverted to the boyish bafflement she remembered from their first few months together. But she quickly checked herself. She had decided on a policy and was determined to stick to it.

"Yes," she said, "there we are."

She stood up and put on the light. They were in her flat, in the living room, which, to Douglas, was both uncannily similar to and at the same time different from their living room in the old place. It was sprucer than the old place. He liked that. He liked everything about it: the colours, the arrangement of the furniture and the few rugs and pictures and books, the neatness, the lack of fussiness.

"I'm sick of that place I live in," he said.

"I thought you liked it. What was it you called it? A *cell*. That was it. Like a *monk*! Yes." She smiled.

"Oh God," he groaned. "I believe I did. It sounds just like me. Yes. Well. It's a dump."

"What will you do?"

"Move in here?"

"You said that without any conviction at all," Mary observed, gravely.

"I know."

"Do you really want to?"

"I think so."

292

"You still *see* that other woman, you said. Why don't you move in with her?"

"I don't want to."

"Poor old Douglas."

"Not so very poor." He stood up. "O.K. You want me to go."

"Do you want to?"

"This, my dear, is how people drive each other bats."

Douglas walked across to Mary, took her by the shoulders, looked at her firmly and kissed her.

"I'll go now," he said. "I'll be back on Saturday for John. I'm taking him to see Spurs."

For a second, Douglas would have sworn that Mary was genuinely reluctant to let him go. But that could not be the case. He went to the door.

"John's been telling me all about your taking him fishing in Thurston," Mary said. "I didn't know you could fish."

"I couldn't. I made it up as I went along."

"He had a lovely time."

"He's a lovely kid. I like being with him. With your permission I intend to indulge that."

"That's fine."

"Good. Well. Back to the cell."

"Thanks for coming round."

"Thanks for the snack."

"It wasn't much."

"It was great."

"Goodnight then."

"Goodnight."

He went. Mary sat down and thought as calmly as she could. There was real hope that she would get through. No doubt about it. She felt hopeful for the first time all year. Douglas was helping her. He was better for her now than he had been for years, she thought.

# 5
# A Matter of Conscience

It took a lot of working out. Harry felt that he needed to clear a
space in his life, so that he could sit down and think through all
the possible and probable consequences. But there was so little
time. The dispute was by now an urgent matter, seemingly
possessed of its own dynamic, which pushed and pressed it
along at a rate far more rapid than most of the participants
wanted or could assimilate. And Harry was very nearly in the
middle of it.

There had rarely been such a strong display of political
feeling in Thurston. The bye-election campaign was already
under way—itself reasonably exciting, given the tight balance
between the main political parties and the emotional polarization which had crept up on people, until masses of voters who
would have described themselves as fairly detached now
seethed with one or another fast-breeding resentment. The
media were in an orgy of verbal overkill on the desperate social,
economic and moral short-term and long-term straits Britain
was in. The lash of blame provoked shouts and whispers up and
down the island. And in Thurston the factory had on its hands
its first serious industrial dispute.

Harry still could not quite believe it was happening. That was
the first thing. He had appreciated, for example, Aileen's
interest in politics and he would spar with her now and then
when he thought she was speaking jargon or what he thought of
as unrealistic theories. But it was part of her life, just as rugby
was part of his life, and in the exchange market of marriage he
saw them as about evenly weighted. Of course, he would concede, her interest was more serious than his: but that did not
really bother him, nor did it dent his general opinion that Aileen
had her Politics and he had his Rugby and it was a Good Thing

because it gave them something to be independent about. He had been perturbed lately by the passion of some of her statements—but, there again, she was somebody who felt strongly and knew her own mind and he admired that in her. Yet he was relieved—and honest enough to admit it—when the birth of their daughter persuaded her not to fight the bye-election. She still worked at it, taking the child with her, carrying the burden lightly, adding provision of crèches at work-places and tax relief on home-helps who released women for work to her long list of special causes.

Harry supported her in the sense that he listened when she was tired, helped when she needed it, was, in politics as in peace, the reliable, straightforward, honest man she had spotted and wanted. She was aware, though, that he was by no means completely in agreement with her politics. She would not go so far as to think him a Tory, even less a Liberal, but there was in him a deeply obstinate complex of convictions which often opposed her position. He admired, above all, independence of mind, spirit and action in causes he held to be just. He put loyalty to his friends and family before all but the most fundamental principles and even those would be challenged in the name of his family. Politics took second place.

Like much of the rest of the country, the workers at Thurston's principal factory—which directly supported well over half the work force in the town and indirectly propped up much of the rest—were in a deadlocked dispute. It seemed endemic at the beginning of that autumn. Disputes about pay differentials, about manning, about bonus payments, new machinery, comparability rates and studies, about production targets; management-union disputes, union-union disputes, internal union disputes—all of them lumped together by much of the media and variously dubbed as "madness", "suicide" and "the end of Britain". The reaction was uniformly extreme: the solution, too, was uniform: strikes and picket lines. Instant industrial heroes and victims and martyrs were pulped into prominence.

Harry could become one of these, Aileen feared. So did he. He hated fuss. Like Betty. He avoided the least personal display. Now, to his profound embarrassment, distaste and dislike, he was the town's talking point. What would he do, they asked, would he cross the picket line?

When he had gone to the factory, Harry had taken on the job of shop steward to a small union, A.P.E.X. It was poorly represented within the works and that in itself had eased Harry into it and then helped him take on the job. He allowed himself to be persuaded because this small branch of a small union happened to include a couple of men he played rugby with, the less well-heeled members of the team, local men born and bred, irresistible to Harry. There was the clear idea around that the last in had to do the dirty job of being shop steward and it was in that compliant spirit that he had taken it on.

He resisted the, to him, over-persistent and over-angry approach from the shop steward of T.A.S.S., a union which served an overlapping number of workers but gained power far in excess of its numbers through its association with one of the biggest unions in the country, the A.U.E.W. As far as Harry was concerned, the T.A.S.S. man took himself too seriously and made too many threatening noises. It was now this man who was using Harry and, in the process, nailing him.

Both unions had gone on strike against the management's plan to introduce new machinery which would, the unions claimed, bring about intolerable redundancies. Harry had joined the strike reluctantly. Although his was one of the jobs directly threatened, he could not convince himself that a wish to improve the long-term efficiency and competitiveness of the place deserved to be met with such a blank reaction. But he came out. Other unions in the factory joined in. The place was empty. Over a thousand men were idle. The emptiness and wasted feel of the factory lay on the little town like a dead whale on the shore. There was ugliness on the picket lines—but as yet it was mimetic. As if Thurston men, having seen the television newsreels, were determined to show that they could be no less tough.

The real ugliness in that period—in Harry's opinion— concerned the threat to a man called Fletcher.

Joseph Fletcher was about ten years older than Harry; married, with four children; a pigeon fancier, with his loft along Bird-Cage Walk where he would go every evening and potter about with the pigeons or work away at the allotment, which sat beside the loft. He had never been a union man for the reason, simple as he saw it, that he did not agree with them. He did not agree with the management either, he would add, but you had to work for somebody. He had been in the army and fought in the Korean War, from which he had brought back a medal for bravery and the unshakeable conviction that *They*—i.e. *all* big institutions, bosses, unions, politicians, newspapers—*They* —were all to be looked at thoroughly sceptically and avoided if at all possible.

He thought that the strike was foolish, said so, and, despite unpleasant scenes, crossed the picket line. Harry had been on the line two or three times when Fletcher had gone over it, and, justified though he thought the union's case was, he was ashamed of the bullying taunts and threats which met the man at the gate. And impressed by Fletcher's apparent disdain.

Things had become much worse though, in Harry's opinion, when some of the wilder members of the strike committee —they denied it, but no one was in any doubt—raided Fletcher's pigeon loft and wrung the necks of all his prize racing pigeons, as well as trampling over all his vegetables. Harry had been on the gate the morning after, and he was not the only one who tried to sympathize when the man came down, alone, claiming, as he saw it, his right to go into work. Fletcher ignored them all.

Yet, despite the sympathy for Fletcher, which grew from that incident, there were still those who insisted that as soon as they did get back to work, they would operate a rigidly closed shop and Fletcher would have to go. If he did not join the union he would lose his job, and the way things were going in the district, he would find it very difficult indeed to find a job anywhere else.

In the talk over this—and there was a lot of time for talk as the management and the unions engaged in a face-to-face test of strength, aping the two super-powers—Harry came down firmly on Fletcher's side. He believed in trades unionism and saw the merits in the closed shop: but he thought that there had to be more flexibility built into it. It was not enough that the

297

only allowable reason for objecting to being in a union was to do with conscience. Nor was it tolerable that if a man were to be spurned by the union, or even to spurn the union, he should be in a position of such weakness that his ability to gain a livelihood anywhere at all would be threatened. It seemed to Harry that for the sake of a little sense and humanity and decency a whole system was being allowed to become potentially dictatorial. He was aware, in these discussions, that the shop steward of T.A.S.S., who was wholly for the closed shop, wasted no chance to get in a dig at him.

The strike began to disturb the town. It was, after all, a one-factory town. Rumours began to move around: that it would be cheaper for the management to close down the Thurston factory altogether and concentrate on their branches in Lancashire; that they had in fact engineered the strike in order to do just this; that redundancy payment lists had been spotted in someone's car; that the top management were about to sell their houses and move south to the nearest sister-factory. People grew very worried. The Thirties depression was not erased from memory and it was not a town with any tradition of strikes, nor with any confidence in the value of its product. As in a lot of small places, there were a substantial number who thought that they were lucky to be well employed at all.

Then A.P.E.X. settled nationally. In theory, Harry and his few members could return to work. A substantial part of the work force wanted them to do that—though they would not admit it—because there was a general feeling that, once a breach was made, the factory would gradually settle all round. The T.A.S.S. shop steward, though, made an issue of it. If Harry went back, he said, then he, Harry, would be totally and personally responsible for breaking solidarity at a time when negotiations were reaching a very favourable conclusion. Although everyone knew this last boast to be a lie, they were apprehensive. Solidarity mattered. Pickets had politicized them. Harry was on his own—public opinion for him, picket opinion against him.

But Harry's union contained two men—one a cousin of Joseph Fletcher's, the other a friend of his. They had been sickened by the inhumanity shown him and were not prepared

298

to let themselves be pushed around, as they saw it, by a union which had always bullied them, rarely supported them and was, once again, trying to lean on them.

A.P.E.X. *could* go back. Members had already returned in other plants in other parts of the country. The men were willing to follow Harry's lead. Within a day the local and national newspapers were onto it, people in the town were chivvying and persuading him wherever he went, the T.A.S.S. steward was sending an unremitting number of warnings and Aileen and himself were seriously at odds.

(2)

"It's very simple," Aileen said stonily. "Will you or will you not cross the picket line?"

"Put like that, there's no argument," Douglas said. "He's explained the position in some detail, Aileen, have a heart. It's much more complicated than that."

"Not in the final analysis," she said.

There was a resolute piety about her which made Douglas want to shake her. There she was, ironing nappies as if engaged on work of the highest worth, unimpeachable in her maternal fortress, now doubly impregnable by virtue of this inflexible call to workers' solidarity.

"It's nothing *like* as simple as you think," Douglas added, irritably.

"What have you got to do with it?"

"I asked him round to talk it over," Harry protested. "Let's not fall out among ourselves."

"He can't answer," Aileen retorted.

"The same question could be asked of you," Douglas said. "Although you rely on us not to be so ungallant as to ask it. *We're* talking—you and me—but Harry has to share the question."

"If he crossed the picket lines now—two days before the bye-election—it would be worth a thousand Labour votes to the Tories."

"Aileen," Douglas said, fully in control of himself now, "there are scarcely a thousand Labour votes available around

299

here. This area's so Tory the Queen couldn't get in as a Labour candidate."

"It's the principle."

"And I don't know that you're right. O.K. I haven't done as much canvassing as you have—I certainly haven't done as much as I would have done if *you'd* been standing—but what I've heard convinces me that party lines are blurred on this. Even if it's useful or right to think of it in terms of party advantage—and I think it's neither—then you're wrong. *Most* people want the strike to be over. Even most of those on *strike* want it to be over by now. The real argument's over the ways and means."

"And Harry supplies both," Aileen said, sharply.

"That's not fair." Harry was ruffled and showing it. There was not enough time for him to think it through for himself. Wherever he went, other people gave him their opinions and their views. "I'm concerned with what *I* think is right and with what the members of *our* union want."

"You've never thought much of the strike anyway."

"As a matter of fact I haven't," Harry said. "But I went along with it. And I've been made redundant once already in my working life, Aileen, so it wasn't as if I was ignorant of the consequences. I just think you can't beat progress."

"But that isn't the issue here and now." Douglas cut in quickly to forestall the environmentalist anti-growth tirade which he saw that Aileen was about to unleash. Besides, he hated to see these two unhappy with each other.

"If you cross the picket lines you'll be doing what the management wants," Aileen said. "That ought to stop you for a start."

"But why?" Harry asked. "If what we want is the same as what they want—why should that stop us?"

Aileen merely stamped the iron harder on the nappy and, with an effort, held her tongue.

"For what it's worth, I think he would be perfectly justified in going back," Douglas said.

"For what it's worth I think your opinion in this matter is irrelevant," Aileen said, much more crossly than she had intended. The tiredness from the child, the tension of the election and, on top of it, this strike, in which she saw Harry spreadeagled in the middle of interests far more knowing and manipulative than himself—it was all too much for her.

"Well, I'll be off in a minute so never worry," Douglas said. "But there's one more thing. If Harry's members vote to go back tomorrow morning, he has no alternative but to lead them back."

"They've said they would take his guidance!" Aileen almost wailed out this piece of information which, in a perverse way, made her proud that Harry had become the repository of so much trust. But she was convinced that he was not up to it.

"Your trouble," Douglas said, as his parting shot, "your trouble, Aileen—and it has been ever since you got yourself into politics—is that you think that nobody else has a mind of their own. You're a bit arrogant."

She looked at him intently and then blushed. Glanced at Harry, whose embarrassment confirmed her fear that he agreed with what Douglas had said.

"I just don't want Harry to get hurt," she said. "They'll blame it all on him. They'll say he broke the strike. The next time there's trouble, then T.A.S.S. will go round saying how weak Harry was. That's what that lot *wants*. And what if the others *don't* settle and go in with him? Besides which, you can call me arrogant if you like and maybe the unions aren't a hundred per cent right but I'd rather be on their side in any struggle and that's that!"

All three of them recognized that she was about to cry.

"I said I'd be back before John went to bed," Douglas said.

"Walk him back," Aileen suggested to Harry. "I'd like to finish these and then I want to do some envelopes."

"You're tired."

"There's only two more days."

"O.K."

The two men, brought up as brothers, unlike in so many ways, walked through the deserted late-night streets of the small town.

"John looks better these days," Harry said.

"He likes coming up here. That big holiday in summer really brought him out. And I like to be up here with him at half-term. He's good company. He's teaching me to fish."

"And ... is Mary well?"

"She seems fine." Douglas had kept a firm silence about his private life. "What'll you do?"

"I expect I'll advise them to go back. We have the meeting first thing tomorrow morning. But I'm not settled in my own mind. There's something I should do. But I don't know what it is. I'll have to sleep on it."

"What if Aileen's right and they don't follow you—the other unions?"

"We'll have to wait and see. Anyway, Douglas, you can't guarantee the future, can you? All you can do is be careful to do the best you can at the time."

"Is that the answer to everything?"

"I've no idea," Harry replied, and laughed. "I can't imagine you fishing."

"I can't imagine you still playing rugby."

"Every Saturday."

"John's a hard teacher. Tells me off if I make a bad cast."

"He's coming on well. How do you find—" Harry had always had difficulty in saying "parents" or "mother and father", much less "mam and dad" before Douglas.

"Mother's a lot perkier. The church seems to have given her a new life, if that isn't blasphemous. She seems to be busy all day. And Dad's mellowing. I'll be out for a drink with him later—in The Crown?"

"I'd like to, but I'd better not."

"He's better in the pub than at home."

"Most of us are."

"True." Douglas paused. "I think the world of Aileen, you know. I suppose we're all a bit anxious about this business. But she's quite somebody, isn't she?"

"She is," Harry said. He needed no reassurance about his wife.

When they reached the bungalow he would not be tempted in. Betty came to the door to talk to him "as if he was one of those canvassers", she said. They chatted about the baby and

302

then John came to show him his new rod and finally Harry turned to go and went the long way round, working out his plan. He thought he knew what to do.

(3)

The next morning Harry was up early. He went down to Bird-Cage Walk. This was the old path alongside the town's minor stream and it was here that the pigeon men had one of their settlements. Joe Fletcher was working away steadily as he did for an hour every morning before work. The destruction of his loft had not set him back for more than a few days: he had immediately invested in some new pigeons and was already beginning to have hopes of them.

He was a nimble man, Joe, handy with everything, twinkle-eyed, lean, nothing mean or shifty or at all self-serving about him. The sort of stalwart man Harry could just see winning a medal and then totally refusing to talk about it.

"What's this, then?" he said. "We're up early."

"I'd like a word, Joe, if you have a minute."

Harry was standing at the gate of the allotment: Joe, in the half-light of an autumn dawn, was some yards away, on the porch of his loft.

"Come on in, then," Joe said. "Come in."

The gates were made of planks and wire netting well cobbled together. In fact the entire allotment revealed a variety of dependent skills and a wide range of materials from rubber tyres to kitchen doors, bicycle wheels, buckets, window frames, anything and everything used ingeniously to provide comfort for pigeons or repose for vegetables.

"Not interested in pigeons, are you, Harry?"

"No."

"Pity. I can't make me mind up about this one here. Looks to me like such a beauty I can't understand why they let me have it. Fellow from Maryport. I didn't ask any of the Thurston fellows in case they got themselves embarrassed and worried to death about having anything to do with me."

There was a very awkward silence.

303

"I'd be surprised if you didn't feel bitter," Harry said.

"Not bitter." Joe held the bird firmly and stroked it gently with his thumb. It cooed contentedly, "Mad, though."

"Yes."

"And I'm not taking it lying down either." Joe spoke evenly—without bitterness but with emphasis. "I've a good idea who was in among these birds of mine. And I'll catch up with those fine gentlemen one night and then we'll see whose feathers will fly. They'll not get away with it."

"I'm—we're going back," Harry said. "That's what I'm advising them this morning."

"You should never have come out."

"I think the fears were justified," Harry said, doggedly fair. "There had been no consultation about the machinery: there was no preparation—nothing. The unions were right to strike."

"You don't believe that. A lot of you don't. You just go along."

"I think there's a lot wrong with the union and with what it does," Harry said. "But I think the best thing to do is to try to change it from inside. Not to stand aside."

"Like me, you mean?"

"Yes. Although I think you have the right to. But yes—you should join the union. It could do with people like you."

"Is that what you came to say?"

"It is."

"Well, I'll be buggered!"

Joe threw the bird up into the air and watched it swoop into the sky.

"I thought you were coming to offer sympathy or something in that line."

"I did that before."

"You did."

"And you ignored it. I don't blame you."

"You don't like these bloody union men, do you, Harry? Look at them! Look who they are! All the arse-lickers and ferrets—you don't belong there, do you?"

"I hope not. Anyway, that's unfair."

"Well then. Tell them to drop dead."

304

"It's too late. I'm in it now. And, funnily enough, I see the meaning of it now."

"You see more than I do then."

"Well." Harry's throat was a little constricted: he was apprehensive of the tone of nobility which might be creeping into his voice. "The union has screwed you up. They could screw me up. If that's going to happen, I'd rather be in than out. I'd rather be trying to do something to change it."

"Good luck to you."

"I'd feel a lot happier if you were on my side—if you can put it like that."

"I'm against all the union men—all of them." Joe's fierceness felt so final that Harry was about to give up. It was a good exit line. He could say he had tried his best. Say to whom? To that part of himself which in some way had found an equation between applying himself to the task of getting Joseph Fletcher into a union and advising his own members to cross the picket lines and return to work. In that equation was the beginning of the new self-respect he would need, he now sensed quite clearly, were he to keep his head in the turbulence of the union conflicts.

"You're wrong to be against us," Harry said. "It serves you nothing to be against us. You can make us all feel small—like you did—but that doesn't do much in the end."

"What does?"

"Decent people sticking up for what they think is right."

"That's a mouthful."

"It is." Harry hesitated, as if reprimanded. Then he went on, "I'm sure we could get you into our union."

"Come off it, Harry, I *hate* the buggers."

"You know the fellows in A.P.E.X. down there. You can't hate them."

"It isn't them. It isn't you. It's the whole thing."

"The whole thing *is* them and me. That's the point."

Harry arrived at this clarity of conclusion by the accident of argument but, having done so, he experienced an enormous relief. That was it. That was his case.

"Don't you *see*!" he exclaimed. "If we get together and make it something that *we* think is O.K.—then it won't be able to do

305

the things you object to. It's only people, Joe. There's no point in pretending it isn't. They're not monsters or dictators. I'm a shop steward and if that doesn't make you laugh, what does?"

Joe did laugh and gripped Harry's shoulder affectionately. He liked the man. He had followed what he had to say with increasing interest and even, he noticed, keenness. There was a limit to the amount of dynamic you could wrest from an isolated position—however self-justified you felt. Perhaps there would be something in going in with Harry: certainly its surprise value alone would be a tonic!

"You talk a lot of rubbish but I'll walk to the factory with you," Joe said.

Harry knew that something had caught; a grappling hook had lodged itself. He would work at it. He had made a breach.

"You don't mind being seen with a scab then?" Joe asked, as they turned out of the lane and went towards the pickets at the factory gate. The baying was already to be heard.

"They'll be calling *me* that in about half an hour," Harry said. "But they'll be wrong."

"Daft, isn't it?" Joe grinned. "The thing to be at, you know, on a morning like this, is out on the Solway doing a bit of flounder fishing. That would be the real life. Agreed?"

"Agreed!" Harry said, emphatically, as the two men, in step, came up to the massed picket lines.

(4)

Very late that night, Joseph and Douglas managed to extricate themselves from the depths of conversation, alcohol, intimacy and philosophy which had enwrapped and enraptured them in the snug bar of The Crown. Closing time had come and, fair enough, the landlord had closed the dor and locked them in. An ease and amplitude had descended on the privileged late-stayers and the central topic had been Harry's crossing of the picket lines. Contrary to the opinion which had thought that the issue was over and empty of further present passion, there had been violent scenes. Harry had come out of it more badly even than Aileen had feared. The local Tory press declared him a hero (mentioning how loyal an employee he had been of theirs before his, unmentioned, redundancy) and it was evident that T.A.S.S. and the Tories between them had used him to their best advantage.

Douglas had gone round to see them but, oddly or miraculously, he had no idea which, Aileen and Harry and the child were apparently in a state of calm and happiness. They talked about the incidents at the factory gate. Aileen, now the die was cast, surprised herself by being totally and firmly pro-Harry. Her theories fell into place behind her loyalty and love. Douglas was both moved and relieved.

Now Douglas and his father stood outside Joseph's house in a friendly, conspiratorial, boozy mood which broke down the barriers raised by so many years of different experiences and expectations; a mood in which they felt amicably towards each other and indeed as father and son. They had been talking about Harry and Joseph had been waiting for the opportunity to link this with a homily he had long thought it his duty to deliver.

"The thing about Harry," he said, in a low voice, as they stood under the street light in the sleeping town, "is that, now that he's made his mind up, there's nothing'll change it. Not if he thinks it's right." Joseph's tendency to be lyrical about those he saw as heroes was on the rampage again, Douglas could see that. But he agreed with him in this case and encouraged him by his swaying affirmation, "Yes", "That's right" and "That's Harry."

"If he thinks it's right—well then—that's that. That's that."

"That's right," Douglas said.

"And they'll be surprised," Joseph said. "He'll surprise them all because now he's got his teeth into it he'll find out all about the bloody unions and, you take my word for it, he'll be hard to beat at the game. You take my word for it, he'll be mustard. They think he's a bumpkin now but just wait, they won't do him down. And that's because he's clear in his conscience."

"Yes. Agreed," Douglas said. God, he was tired. A sleep, then back to London with John. Where was Mary tonight? With her bloke? Didn't bear thinking about. Listen. Father.

"That's what gives him the basic strength, you see. Now

307

then. I like Mary. I always have liked her. I think the world of her. Do you see what I mean?"

"No."

"Yes you do." Joseph smiled and in the half-light Douglas realized how very *like* his father he was. He had seen the same moony smile plastered across his own face late at night or early in the morning, as it encountered a mirror on its way from booze to bed. Was that his course? To become more and more like his father? What, then, was the man like? "Yes you do. Now then. None of my business. Haven't said a thing. Your mother's upset, of course, but she keeps it in and she gets on the telephone to Mary. And there's John between them. No, it's you. You're our son, after all. We worry about you, you know—now don't look like that—we do. It's a matter of conscience. Is it clear? There's nothing can buy a clear conscience. Harry has one. Worth all the money in the world, believe me—and I've had my failings. We all have. That's the point. That's what I wanted to say. If your conscience is clear—that's all right."

Douglas looked at him. In such a very short time they would all be dead, all the actors of the day. It was all so very strange.

"Thank you," he said. "I appreciate that."

They went in quietly and woke up Betty and John within seconds.

# 6
# London Lives

## 1

As the calendar burrowed into autumn and London dug itself
into the end of the year, Douglas, on an evening in late October,
felt that the place was alive and home. The trips to Cumbria had
convinced him that, if ever there were to come a day when he
would be able to go back full time to the countryside which held
his roots, then that time was in a future as yet unhinted at. He
was not capable of drawing enough from the countryside now.
It would be easy to say that the time had passed when a writer
could successfully isolate himself within a rural community—but Douglas knew that, even as he thought thus,
there would be someone in some remote place contradicting
him by turning out fine work. No, the fault was in himself—if it
could be called a fault—and the fact that he *did* think of it as a
fault revealed his quasi-religious respect for the superior
authority of rural life. Rural knowledge was still thought to be
somehow "better", rural pastimes and pursuits somehow
"purer", rural friendships more enduring and enriching, the
pulse of rural life itself more direct and insistent on the bare
earth than on the bare pavement. Nature was nurture.

There was something in that, he thought, but the necessities
which drove him now were urban. Even in the country he had
no escape from the global city. He was no farmer, no real
working countryman. He loved the country, and particularly all
his home part of it, and he liked to go back there and could feel
alive in isolation there more comfortably than anywhere in the
world. But it was here in the city that he could be all that he
wanted to be. In the hard shock of late autumn when the parks
rotted with dead leaves and the metropolis culled the world for
films and music and shows to add to the compost of pleasure;
when new night clubs opened, full of garish promises, and

Parliaments came back from an unmourned and immense absence, just as full of promises; when gossip columnists dug up the plots which would see them through the winter and television shows breezed out into the air claiming attention; when the drinkers stayed a bit longer in the pubs, rather than face the colder road home, and double-decker buses twinkled and rollocked magically through the dark streets and suburbs; when the West End seemed to speak with tom-toms from discos, strip clubs, clip joints, casinos, drinking clubs, late night stores, porno stores, family stores, delis, cafés, restaurants and private bars; this time of autumn seemed to Douglas rich indeed in the possibilities round and about him.

It was as if he stood in the middle of a tamed and humanized jungle, full of fruits and surprises, full of extraordinary transmutations and wild configurations—all the twisted and perverse developments of civilization squashed and deformed and intertwined together in this brick and concrete growth, thicketed with buildings of every kind. Here, in the middle of a giant city, the wonder of the human enterprise really came into its own: there were these deformities, these grotesque specialities, these apparently insupportable people and institutions and shops and gatherings and events—and yet they all lived, they all found accommodation in and out of the government buildings and the factories, the flyovers and museums and airports, the banks and offices and sewers, the markets and schools and homes. In this metropolis, the impact of the most generalized and the most particular, the plainest and the most perverse, the most boring and the most titillating, the dullest and the most stimulating, the lousiest, meanest, most squalid and nastiest, and the noblest, finest, most altruistic and best was there to be felt and seen and experienced every day.

And sometimes, as on this day, Douglas could imagine the whole range of it flowing through him as vibrantly as any natural impulses, as firmly as any feeling he had ever gathered in from watching a phenomenon of nature. This mouldering, dusk-filled metropolis, with its cross-cultures and dreams, its instant excitements and long disappointments, this baggage train for a hundred armies was where he could breathe most fully now: and he loved it. The question was—how to live in it.

## 2

"I'm seeing him again tomorrow," Mike said. "We're talking over the rough-cut of the Raven thing and then there's some party. He wants to eat afterwards. And talk about you, I think. He's scarcely mentioned you for weeks but I don't know how much longer he can keep it in. And if he does talk directly about you—I shall have to say something."

"Why?" Mary asked the question although she already knew the answer. Indeed it was so obvious that she was ashamed of herself. But she waited for an answer.

"Because it would be silly and hypocritical not to. As it is, I fail to see who is benefiting from this secrecy."

"I am, I think."

"And would you want me to lie to his face?"

"You needn't put it like that."

"Come on, Mary."

He was soft on her, and she exploited it, yet neither of them suffered from that. They had found a gentle, yielding friendship which gave them a lot. Mike wanted more from it than Mary but he was too wise and too schooled in disappointment to risk losing all by attempting to seize all. They were in her flat, late at night, John in bed, a bottle of wine half drunk beside them in the side-lit, dusky, cosy room; and music. She had found much consolation in music.

"How is he these days?" she asked him, as she was always asking him.

"You see him as often as I do."

"He puts on an act for me."

"Don't we all."

"Don't be silly." She smiled. She liked Mike more and more. He was so unfussed, so completed, far from the restless stretching and testing and wriggling with his fate which made Douglas, in her eyes, both fretful and disturbing.

"He's better than I've seen him for ages, as a matter of fact," Mike said. "This film on Raven is a winner, but it's very tricky work—copyright problems, Equity and M.U. problems. He had a problem with the sound on one of the mikes at the concert, his editor's playing up, the old footage he needs isn't coming through as fast as he needs it—the logistics would drive most of my other producers round the bend and Douglas just sails through it all. He's very good at his job. *And* he's back reviewing regularly and doing that World Service programme and, so he says, thinking of writing something else. In those terms he seems to me to be better than he has been all year."

"Sometimes he looks dreadful."

"So I notice."

"It isn't drink."

"No. He's cracked that. Although he still drinks hard."

"Well?"

"It could be living in that wardrobe of his and subsisting on B.B.C. canteen fodder. It could be the outward and visible sign of inward stress." Mike paused. "Or he could be missing you."

"He has his other woman."

"That's none of my business and you know it."

"He told me that someone wanted him to go to Hollywood and do a script," Mary said. "Somebody who'd heard of the—the story he's just written—"

"—'Death of a Friend'," Mike said.

"Yes. Just heard of it and wanted Douglas to transfer it to the desert in America. He said the producer thought that the idea was 'just sensational'—that was his word—and it would go down wonderfully well in America. He was going to read Douglas' book and then come back with a proper offer."

"In a way I hope he doesn't make an offer," Mike said. "I think half of Douglas' problem is that he moves from one job to another so fast he can't fix a focus on what's important."

"He's always been unwilling to stay in one place for long," Mary said. "However good the conditions. He's always had this itch to prove that he's his own boss and that he doesn't need anybody. He's quite obsessed about his independence."

"That's all very well up to a point. After that it can start to work against you."

"You should've known him when he was younger!" Mary said. "You would have thought he could have taken on everything and anything. It was like living with an army rolled into one man. He was so bold; and so funny."

"You're much better these days," Mike said, eventually.

"Some of that's thanks to you." She did feel better. Frail at times, but safely past the demoralizing anxiety which had beset her in the first months of separation.

"I'm going to tell him about us, whether he asks or not," Mike said and drained his glass. "He's probably guessed anyway."

"As long as you tell him everything," Mary said. "The whole truth. That's important."

## (3)

Lester liked the back streets. They reminded him of Thurston when he was a boy. There were shops selling all sorts of bits of things, run down shops, shops which were mini-factories, shops supervised by men in ancient overcoats and a carapace of gruffness, shops where you could buy junk or metal or old hardware or wholesale lavatory pans or bargain bundles of wall paper or pre-revolutionary hosiery or pets and pet food. It was a homely little area, this west part of London, and Lester was settling into it not too badly.

He worked for a man called Latchford who owned several betting shops in that area. Lester had come across him at a party after a night at the All-In Wrestling with Merlin, in that brief period when he had been Merlin's pal about town. Lester had been in an expansive mood and included Latchford in the circle which was instantly phalanx-formed about Merlin. Latchford's red-head had been impressed and Lester had been given one of those "any time I can be of service" routines which had turned into something more substantial that same week when Lester had again run across him and again done him a small favour.

Working in the west of London while cutting the film—Douglas' editing rooms were in Hammersmith—he had bumped into Latchford—on purpose this time—and mentioned that he could do with something part time. He wanted to "look into" the bookie business, get a bit of experience, nothing like being paid while you learnt, yes, Merlin was very well, never better, old Merlin.

At first Lester had managed to play it well. Douglas had eked out his attachment to the project and he went regularly to the cutting rooms where, in the pokiest place he had ever been in, seemingly miles of black snaky liquorice celluloid spooled and swarmed all over hand-cranked machines before being cut out with a fancy razor blade and pasted together with sellotape. You could do anything with the stuff, Lester thought, disgustedly. You could make anybody look anything you liked by chopping it about. The same man could look a brain-box or a fully paid up idiot—it just depended how you played about with it. You could take a bit from here and another bit from there and pretend they came from the same place: you could find bits where he completely contradicted himself: you could cut out all the bits that were real but made him look like the creep he often was; you could put music under it and make it ten times more exciting or stuff other bits in from other people and make it seem deep: it was all a con, Lester saw that, and he was disgusted. He wanted films to be real.

But he stuck it out for the experience and also, it had to be confessed, for the increasingly forlorn hope of picking up the contact with Merlin again through Douglas. But Douglas didn't seem to care about Merlin. He seemed untouched by any consideration of what Merlin might do for him. Lester was baffled. It was not as if Douglas was doing all that well—not on the surface anyway. He lived in a single room, even smaller than Lester's own; he dressed with no great style; he seemed to organize what was left of his life after work around visits to Mary and outings with John. Nothing to write home about there. There was no push or go about him, Lester thought angrily. Still, he seemed to have a certain amount of luck and so Lester kept going to the cutting rooms and then walking back, ferreting around those little scabby streets he liked, and able for quite a while to give the impression he wanted to give: of someone looking over the business for his long-term project, not *really* concerned with the weekly wage he was lifting.

The wage kept him together. The work, too, though Lester

would not admit it, was enjoyable. He liked being in the gambling business and he liked having to do with horses and dogs and the sporting fraternity. He knew where he was in the world. He could call the odds and argue the toss with the best of them—so he boasted to Douglas, and it was true enough. As the weeks went on he began to entertain the beginnings of an ambition both sane and reasonably realistic. He would like to get a little stake together, he thought, and open a bookie's business, somewhere in the country—not in Cumbria, where he was known, somewhere he'd never been. Then he would go to the race meetings and set up his board and shout out the odds, he could be part of the crowd, he could watch the races, get to know some of the jockeys and owners, be a *real* part of that world, not the glorified typist and telephone operator you were here in London. As often happens, he had invented a convenient lie about his real intentions, but the lie had contained much of what he wished to be truth: and now he was adopting it as his ambition. Yes. He would not want to admit it yet—they would all laugh at him—what a come-down from Personal Confidant of Merlin Raven, Rock Group Manager and Associate Film Director. But the attraction of the notion had grappled itself into his mind and whenever he tugged against it he felt the pull of its power. He wanted to be a bookie.

He began to take a proper interest in the business. He asked questions. He was indeed the man who had just come in to pick up the way things worked before branching out on his own. But a curious thing happened. When he had been "playing" at it, and while he was still haloed by newness and the background presence of the phenomenally rich Raven—he had been treated well. Now that his interest was real; now that his enquiries were in earnest; now that he made notes and turned up early and stayed late—he spread unease. There was worry. A fear of possible aggravation entered the heads of the three other men who worked in the shop: it was as if Lester were casing the joint, or an informer. They alerted Latchford.

Latchford was on his guard. He dabbled in misdirected motor cars, kept an interest in a club in Fulham not best known for its clean record, employed heavies from time to time, shifted the odd few crates off the odd lorry, could always find you a real fox fur for less than a quarter the asking price, or get you a genuine Cartier watch for a song: there were connections with Amsterdam and Heathrow Airport. Latchford was a smart boy.

He waited until the place had closed and invited Lester on his own into the back room for a drink. Very civil, Lester thought, teach the others a bit of a lesson, been less than welcoming lately—not that it mattered much—he had just about got all the information he wanted. His thoughts were turning to a stake. He reckoned he needed about ten thousand pounds. It was a terrible amount of money to find. But it would set him up for life.

Lester had a lot of time for Latchford. He was about the same age, a little flabby, but only a little—tried to keep himself fit, you could see that. Dressed beautifully—three piece suits, craftily cut, the little gold chain across the almost-flat stomach, oh yes, the silk shirt and the very plushy tie, not too flashy; the beautiful boots—that thin Italian leather that cost a bomb. A gold chain around his wrist; three heavy rings—the real McCoy; hair always just washed; and always the cigar—not too big and showy but smelling perfect. And, parked on the pavement, the new Camargue with the new red-head patiently waiting inside. Latchford had made it all right, Lester thought. This was Britain working at its best. Here was an example of individual free enterprise and initiative—because Latchford's background in Fulham was every bit as poor and downtrodden as Lester's own. Fulham was maybe his one crucial advantage, Lester thought, inevitably comparing himself. Latchford had got to know the city, the ins and outs and twists and openings of the city. Lester had been left behind a bit there. But still, he would hand it to Latchford—more than to Douglas and more than to that sod Raven, who was some sort of freak—Latchford was the real inspiration.

"So how are we then, my son?" Latchford asked, offering Lester a cigar and pushing a can of beer his way. The small office was somehow made to seem tiny and shabby, Lester thought, by the glamorous presence of Latchford. There was something about the man, Lester could see that, which spelt POWER. He was a man worth sticking close by, was old Latchford. He was going places on the inside track.

"Very well, Ray, not bad at all," Lester replied, easily adopting the appropriate tone—oh yes, he still had the touch.

"And our friend Merlin? How's our friend Merlin?"

Latchford hadn't asked him to sit down and so he remained standing. Odd as that seemed, on reflection, it never occurred to Lester to question it at the time. Latchford sat in a tilted-back chair with his feet crossed on the desk in front of him—like one of the ministers in the House of Commons.

"Merlin's great," Lester affirmed. "Matter of fact, he was telling me only the other day that he was feeling better than he's felt for a long time. A very long time."

"Glad to hear it." Latchford lit his cigar and did not pass over his lighter to Lester. "The guy's a ravin' genius. Best in the world. That's what I admire. *The* very *best*." He puffed out the pedigree grey smoke dreamily. "And loaded as a ten ton truck."

"Loaded?" Lester confirmed, just a shade bitterly. "You've said it."

"What—what does your friend Merlin think of your working for me?"

"Great. He thinks it's great. He understands, Merlin, about when you want to set up a few things for yourself. He thinks it's great."

"He going in with you?"

"We haven't got round to talking about it yet." Lester's mouth was becoming dry—he could not understand it. He took a deep and noisy swig from the can of beer. That was better.

"Does he know you've been a naughty boy?" Latchford asked, very quietly.

"What's that?"

"I've heard one little bird singing out in Soho and another little bird in Brixton: and then somebody was telling me you'd done a bit in Her Majesty's."

"That was years ago," Lester said. "I was just a kid."

"I wouldn't be the man to hold a person's past against them," Latchford said fairly. "But you put me in a very difficult position."

"Why's that?"

"Don't you see? My business is very delicate. My business

317

is very, very delicate. There's a lot of funny people wants to know things that I would sooner they did not know. So why are you taking notes and numbers like Kojak with his tail up?"

"I told you. I want to learn. I want to start my own business."

"Yea? With Merlin Raven's money behind you? Don't make me laugh, Lester my son. You're working for somebody, aren't you? Who is it?"

"Look." Lester involuntarily glanced at the glass door behind him. Two men were leaning against it. "Honest, Ray, I'm working for myself."

"Who you gonna sell it to?"

"What?"

"The information."

"What information?"

"Don't try to be bloody clever with me, you little ponce!" Latchford jumped to his feet and the two men came into the room. "You're working for Abbot, aren't you?"

"Look. It's a mistake. I don't know what's happening. Here." He dug in his pockets. "Look at what I wrote down. Look at it. It's just tips—about rents and how you get a licence and fixing odds. Who would be interested in that?"

"That's my question. And I've got the answer. What made you think you'd get away with it?"

"It's for me. I want to start up—" One of the men chopped him on the back of the neck. Lester stumbled forward and Latchford kicked him violently in the groin and then pulled him up by his hair before smashing him in the face with his three-ringed fist. The three men slugged him around between them. They stopped before he was badly beaten.

"I'm going to be nice to you," Latchford said, standing over Lester, who was curled up on the floor vaguely trying to protect his face and his genitals. "They'll drop you off round Kingston by-pass so you can have some time to think things over away from the big city. And, listen! If anything happens to me that I can trace back to you, you'll be in at Tilbury with a block of cement up to your knees. Right? Right."

It was something Mary had thought about for weeks now. The imminent encounter between Mike and Douglas made it more urgent. In order to calm herself down, she rehearsed what she would say several times and, even in the rehearsing, felt nervous. She had tried to examine her motives for wanting to make this phone call but shied away from her own conclusions. It was enough that the impulse had endured for so long.

She decided to do it at the end of the afternoon. She would be in from school, the day's work behind her; John would be in his bedroom, supposedly getting on with his homework; Hilda, presumably, would be at the office and less pressed than at other times in the day.

Mary picked up the phone and dialled the number, as if she were embarking on an illicit gamble. She was put through to Hilda directly.

"This is Mary Tallentire here," she heard a fairly firm, even voice say. "Douglas' wife."

"Oh yes." Hilda was taken completely by surprise. She glanced around the empty office as if hoping someone would be there to give her an excuse not to talk. But what was she afraid of?

"I've been meaning to phone you up for a long time," Mary said, repeating a well rehearsed line: but where did it lead to? Her tongue was dry, mind wiped of thought.

"Yes," said Hilda, into the silence.

"I think it might be an idea for us to meet," Mary said, jumping three stages, to come immediately to her intention.

"What good would that do?"

"I don't know." Mary was trying to fit a face and a personality around this edgy, defensive voice. There were no clues. "But I think it would be more honest."

"I can't think of anything we have to say to each other," Hilda replied.

"Oh, I'm sure there would be plenty to talk about."

"But on what basis?" Hilda asked.

"What do you mean?"

"I mean—why do you want to?"

It seemed to Mary at that moment that she had been right to make the telephone call. Hilda's question seemed to signal some uncertainty. Mary's confidence, hard fought for, over the year, sometimes desperately lacking, was sure enough of itself to feel able to pass on.

"It's demeaning if we don't," Mary said. "Can't you see?"

"Demeaning to whom?"

"Both of us. It's saying—we accept that—Douglas—can come and go and keep us apart from each other while critically important decisions are being made for all our lives. I talk to him. He talks to you, I'm sure. Why shouldn't we talk?"

"It sounds very logical," Hilda admitted, rather truculently. "But I still can't see why we *have* to do it."

Hilda's sense of privacy was offended. Apart from a complex of what she would have called "natural" reasons for not wanting to see Mary, there was a reluctance bred out of a deep class-feeling. Mary's voice and manner came over to her as coolly middle class: and, to that extent, privileged and, in what she said, patronizing. After all, Mary held all the cards—what was she on about? Moreover, Hilda did not subscribe to the notion that everything ought to be in the open. She could not bear to discuss her love for Douglas with anybody. It seemed totally at odds with the mystery and uniqueness of the affair. She resented Mary's assumption that it could be discussed like a shopping list. What she felt for Douglas and what, she was still sure, Douglas felt for her, was secret and thrilling; it bound them together sexually and mystically, it existed apart from other people, it was able to survive even the competition of a marriage and a misdirected puritan conscience. Mary, typically, Hilda thought, would be unaware of all that. Her background had no respect for secrets and sex because it had no understanding of them. Her ideal was to "talk everything out", as if talking things out could even approach a solution to any real problem.

In Hilda's world and, she thought, in Douglas', due to a great number of factors, from environment through to tradition, the primacy of fine but inarticulate feelings was acknowledged. In Mary's world, Hilda suspected, if fine feelings could not be proved in dogged discussion then they did not count. Mary stood for that sort of good sense about emotions which Hilda considered to be evidence of having no emotions worth bothering about. Hilda's deep reluctance to engage in conversation seemed to Mary to be evidence of insecurity and panic.

"What can we lose?" Mary asked.

"That isn't the point," Hilda replied. "I think we could lose quite a lot." She smiled. "Our tempers for a start! But the real point is—what would we gain from it? I can't see anything."

"It wouldn't be this hole-in-the-corner business."

"It never has been. Not for us anyway," Hilda retorted.

"Hasn't it?"

Neither of them spoke for a few moments.

"It just seems so undignified," Mary said. "It's as if we're not really interested in having a say in our lives."

"I have my say."

"Do you?"

Again the silence. Mary made a last effort.

"It's quite easy to score points," Mary said. "I could do it myself. I could say that Douglas wants to come back here—I'm sure you know that. I could point out that he is not with you even though I have given him every chance . . ." she paused, "and even provocation. But there would be nothing gained from all that. I don't seem to be able to get through to you, but my only point is to try to lead a decent life. I don't want to let things pass by, unquestioned and unanswered, any more. I don't want to be just told things or faced with *faits accomplis*. I want to take things carefully. That's all. I thought it might help if we talked."

Hilda was touched by this, but her mind had been made up and she stuck with it. She was terrified of meeting Mary. She was afraid she might be drawn to sympathize with her. Then where would she be? There was a time when trenches had to be dug, when battle-lines had to be drawn, when enemies had to be named and cultivated. She *wanted* Douglas, for God's sake!

"I'm sorry," Hilda said. And then, "I can't see the point," she lied.

She would not be the first to put down the phone.

"I'm sorry too," Mary replied: and put down the phone. She was trembling.

## 5

"It must certainly remind them of home," Douglas said.

The walls were plastered with travel posters of Greece and Cyprus. Ethnic vessels swung from the ceiling and clambered over the walls. The waiters sang out in Greek to each other and the menus were as big and as closely printed as Greek newspapers. And there was a plastic bouzouki in the background.

"There's a stage when something's so wholeheartedly—bad taste if you like—that it works. I like it here."

"Ouzo?"

"Or retsina."

"Both," Douglas decided. "Let's avoid any argument on a night like this."

"You seem better than I've seen you for months," Mike said.

"I feel it. I don't know why."

"So what are you going to do next?" Mike asked eventually, after they had gossiped for a while.

"The Raven isn't finished yet. We can't clear that early stuff of Raven in Paris, which is a damned nuisance. And the record company's suddenly decided to be very evasive about the old tour footage we were promised. I suspect Raven's moved onto something else and stopped co-operating."

"Do you see him still?"

"No."

"Why not?"

"I always felt rather uncomfortable with him," Douglas said. Then, "Lester. Is there any way you can swing a job his way?"

"Not again. We've helped him once already, Douglas."

"I saw him the other day. He's fallen flat on his face again." Douglas smiled. "I shouldn't laugh, but he does seem to walk into hammerings like Tom in 'Tom and Jerry'. If there's a loose plank, Lester'll step on it and whap! it'll flatten his nose; if there's a large pane of glass, Lester'll walk straight through it and look at you in his rags and bloody cuts as if to say, 'nobody told me about it.' But this time he seems to have lost all his bounce. There's a woman in the equation somewhere, but he keeps quiet about that."

"What can I get him that he would want?"

"I don't know. Some sort of offer—just to give him the reassurance that there's a job somewhere. I think he's come to the end of his resources. Raven kicked him out, you know. Sooner or later everybody seems to have kicked Lester out."

"That's a bit sentimental," Mike said. "Lester begs to be kicked out."

"True." Douglas motioned for another carafe of retsina. "Perhaps."

"I thought you were easing up on the booze."

"In a manner of speaking. Another, please. Thanks." He chewed at the tough lamb. "So? Any chance? He needs a job. He *got* us the Raven project, you know."

"It's where to fit him in where his pride's not hurt and then how to get him a job at all. He isn't the most employable man around, is he?"

"I thought a location driver," Douglas suggested. "He could always pretend he was just filling in until something better came up. It would get him out and about and on the set so that he could get to know everybody and do this and that. Could you try?"

"I'll talk to him." Mike said. "Then I'll see what I can do. Perhaps it could work. I'll try." He paused. Douglas clearly wanted more than that. "We should manage something."

"Thanks." Douglas nodded. "Good."

"And what about you? Are you still keen on that regionalism idea or will you take on the interviews?"

Mike had suggested that Douglas interview a dozen contemporaries—in films, the theatre, politics, businesses, show biz, the universities and sport—and make documentary portraits, rather like the Raven film, in the attempt to talk sensibly to someone about their work and show the world they lived in.

"I've been thinking that it would be very nice to come in to the B.B.C. full time," Douglas said. "It must take a lot off your mind to have a regular wage coming in and regular work lined up."

323

"I can understand the need for security," Mike said. "Had it myself. It's a lot easier on the inside of these institutions. You still torment yourself, don't you?"

"The days of the freelance ..." Douglas intoned: but his glance at Mike was waiting for a different response, "... are over. Are they not?"

"Like other independent operators, we're told," Mike said. There was a tightness about his throat. So. The truth was already out, was it? What was needed now was for it to be faced up to. "Maybe the odds are that in fifty or a hundred years we'll all be safely tucked inside big institutions or organizations or corporations. And we'll have to make our lives revolve around that."

"Like the mediaeval church," Douglas said, "or the feudal system ... Except ours will have a corporate head and a state policy."

"That seems to be the picture."

"And that leaves Mary," Douglas said.

There was a pause.

"When did you know?" Mike asked.

"Just a few days ago. We were in your office. It clicked. So there we are."

"I wanted to tell you much earlier."

"I know." ("*We* decided"!) "I'm still trying to work out what I feel. It's very complicated, having a friend involved with a wife you've no rights over, except most likely you're still in love with her."

"Are you?"

"Perhaps. It's become no more than a slogan," Douglas said. "I'm amazed to discover that I'm not withering away due to lack of sex. Long ago I thought I would waste away in a week if I slipped for a day. Now it seems to matter so much less." Douglas drank some more. "I trust it's a phase I'll pass through quickly. It's like the less than startling discovery that I have no career-ambition—except to do these regional programmes, that is. I've thought a lot more about them, Mike. In Cumbria, we could show the Bewcastle cross and the thirteenth-century gargoyles and features of landscape together with the menhirs and Wordsworth's verse—that would give you a new notion of

324

the quiddity of Cumbria, for example—done all over the place, it would arrest that sort of depressing acceptance that our time is past and we're all herding ourselves gently into the asylum of institutional post-democracy. I find it painful to talk about Mary. What about you?"

"I can't think what you'd want to hear."

"You've slept together?"

"Yes." Mike hesitated. "In Paris. Not since. I think she was rather ashamed of doing it." He spoke with difficulty. "There was something wilful about it—not quite as if she were getting her own back—more—I've thought about it a lot—more as if she no longer wanted to have such an advantage over you and so she was determined to betray you physically. That's what I thought."

Douglas began to experience the peculiarly intense pleasure of talking to a man who loved the same woman as he loved.

"That sounds like her," he said. "On the other hand, it's an explanation I'm likely to welcome, aren't I?"

"If you want to live with her again."

"She must have told you that I asked her."

"She didn't think you sounded convinced. And then there's—whoever it is, you see."

"Hilda. Yes. There's Hilda."

"Mary minds about her a lot."

"So I understand." Douglas sat back while the dishes were cleared away. He ordered some more to drink. "By sitting down and trying to work out the best and right thing to do, I seem to have arrived at a state of impotence. All round. What are *you* going to do?"

"I'm afraid that depends on you."

"On her."

"On her. If it didn't happen to be you," Mike said, "I wouldn't let you have a look in." The fury and determination were undisguised.

The wine came.

"Cheers."

"Cheers," said Douglas, raising his glass.

They drank, and talked of other things until the restaurant closed.

## 6

Lester had not noticed her and yet she was sure that he had come there on purpose to seek her out. What other reason could there be for his hanging around a small, run-down shopping parade in North Kensington? Emma stopped and turned her back on him to look into the window of a shop which sold junk clothes. She had just popped out to buy some candles and turnips for the Hallowe'en party they were planning for the evening. It was to be an attempt to bring together the different sections of the community served by the church and the vicarage. The children would come first of all, and then, later, churchgoers and those who used the social enquiry service set up by the enterprising vicar. A mixture of races and temperaments; poor whites, generally, and "upwardly striving" to be mobile blacks. There would be other friends there too, those who came within the nexus of help and aid existing in the parish, and it was here that Emma was in difficulties.

There was a young social worker, an Adventure Playground and Child Care Leader called Mark, who had liked her and whom, in turn, she was beginning to like. Mark was the son of a Harley Street psychiatrist. He had been to Bryanston—a rather liberal public school—and then gone to Art College where he had taken drugs, dropped out, been salvaged by a community group and turned into a devoted helper of others. Emma felt so easy with him, sisterly and at home. They made private jokes about "The Wind In The Willows" and Toad. Mark would be there—spectacularly tall, slim, shockingly blond bedraggled hair, blue-grey eyes, now innocent, now shrewd, in most respects like a guardsman, but dressed casually, almost to the point of seeming a dosser. And charming.

Emma turned from Lester, then, in the street, because there was now a choice and a decision. Mark had asked her to go out for a bite to eat after the festivities that evening and she had not only agreed, she had revealed to both of them that she was looking forward to it. And now there was Lester. She glanced around quickly. Yes. Looking awful. He only seemed to come to her when he had nowhere else on earth to go, she thought, and then she checked the irritation. That was unfair. In one sense he did so because that was what she asked for. She turned from the window full of soiled skirts and worn shirts and half-bald coats and baggy grubby trousers and made for him. She would ask for something different now.

Lester smiled broadly. He had seen her pause and hesitate and, far from making him concerned, he had enjoyed it. It showed that he had an impact still. As she walked over to him he rocked on his heels and glanced about him like a mangy but cocky terrier sniffing the air.

"You look terrible," she said.

That was not what he had expected.

"I haven't heard from you for months," she said.

"There you go," he answered, lamely.

Although the Parade was run down, it was busy enough and it tended to be full of slow moving shoppers—old people carefully costing and comparing the vegetables from shop to shop; all ages slowly fingering the cheap knock-down SALE! SALE! furniture and the kitchen and bathroom bargains, the five-pound televisions and one-pound radios. The Parade was one of those places in London which was the last stop and prop before destitution and the dustbin. This busyness distracted Lester. And Emma, who looked better than ever and decidedly "classy" in a waisted wine-coloured velvet coat, a white crocheted scarf and dark brown boots, seemed in no mood for the acquiescent understanding he had come to rely on.

"What do you think I feel like when you just disappear?" she asked. One or two people lingered a little longer in anticipation of a good row. "You just walk off and there I am—expected to pick myself up and get on with it without the slightest help from you."

"I never promised anything."

"That's certainly true. But it doesn't excuse you."

Lester did not reply: he could not, in truth, understand the connection between his promising nothing and this not excusing him. And he wanted no public row.

"Is there nowhere we could have a cup of coffee?"

"I've got to get some things for our Hallowe'en party—I'm

327

only supposed to be out for ten minutes," Emma fretted. She was rigorously conscientious about her duties.

"Well, if that's the way it is, I'll bugger off."

"Don't be silly."

Emma considered for a moment or two and then sorted it out.

"There's something called DINING ROOMS just down there on the left. I'll see you there in a few minutes. I just have to buy a couple of things and then I can drop them off and come back."

"Don't put yourself out."

"What happened to you?" She reached out and lightly touched his left cheekbone, which had a bruised lump on it.

"A fracture. I fell."

"I'll just be a few minutes."

"I could come back with you if you wanted," Lester said, quietly. "If you wanted."

"It would be less disruptive if we met outside the Centre."

She nodded and left him. He watched her with some apprehension. She had made him feel as shabby as he knew that he looked. The deterioration in his appearance upset Lester, but he no longer had the nerve to steal. Or the guts—that was how he put it to himself. He was in a worse position than he had been at about the same time last year when he had sought out Emma for refuge and then gone north for the New Year. And now she seemed to be turning on him.

The DINING ROOMS were blank, shabby and already half full, half way through the morning. There were long, refectory-type tables and cheap wooden chairs. The counter at the far end announced SELF SERVICE, but signally failed to encourage it. Perhaps the much advertised SOUPS would be hot and filling and redeem the place; the mug of stewed tea and fly-catching sticky bun looked grim. The place was full of solitary people, it seemed, mostly old women staring into space.

Emma swept into it like a fairy in a fairy tale. The whole place lightened. Some of the old ladies nodded and greeted her. She seemed to know most of them by sight or by name.

"Well," she said, sat opposite him, both her hands warming on the large white mug of coffee, "it's nice to see you."

Lester grinned warily. But she meant it. She had taken the opportunity of a few minutes on her own to "get a grip on herself".

"I can remember going to a Hallowe'en do once," Lester said, "that'll be your candles and turnips, won't it?"

"Yes."

"It was at the Catholic church. In Thurston. They have nuns there. They ran a youth club—you hadn't got to be a Catholic to join, but it was mainly the Catholic lads. They used to have a football team and what they called an athletics team."

"You were good at that, weren't you?"

"Yes, I was. And they had this party. Hallowe'en. Candles and turnips." As he talked, the bruised defensiveness seemed to leave his face and once again Emma recognized the vulnerable/tough man she had fallen in love with. It was no use pretending that anything had changed. "I liked that. Mind you, I had to nick mine from somebody. But they put the lights out. All those turnip faces lit up on the inside. Amazing what you remember, isn't it?"

"Why don't you come to our party this evening?"

"I'm too old, Emma."

"I'd like you to meet some of the kids," she said. "Some of them are very good athletes, I'm sure—especially the West Indians. They've been looking for someone to start a sports group."

"An athletics team," Lester corrected her.

"Exactly. The man who looks after the kids has so much else on his plate he can't get round to it. But he says," Emma went on, improvising effortlessly, lying without a qualm, "that if somebody who knew something could get hold of those kids they could be sensational."

"You just have to look around," Lester said. "John Conteh, Maurice Hope, Viv Anderson, Cyrille Regis, Laurie Cunningham—they've got the talent." He paused. "And they're hungry for it. I was hungry for it. But I got caught up in the pro-game. In running. They never forgive you for that. That's what did it for me. A few measly quid when I was a kid."

"What about having a look at them?" Emma pressed her

case. Lester was hooked. She herself was amazed at the aptness of this impromptu inspiration. Of course—such a job would be ideal for Lester and he might even be good at it. In her imagination, the mutual benefits expanded to a bountiful shower of success all round.

"I would quite like that," Lester said. "Knocking them into shape. Of course, I wouldn't want any money for it. But I'd need facilities."

"I'm sure we could find a school that would lend us its gym. And there's St Luke's, which has a football pitch—it's not grass, it's under the motorway—but I think Mark said something about a running track being measured out."

"Mark who?"

"Mark James. He's the social worker in charge of children in this area."

"I wouldn't want any interference."

"I'm sure he wouldn't want to interfere."

"This is where the champions of tomorrow come from," Lester said, looking around at the old, tired faces. "It's from places like this that the Greats come. Yes. I'd like that."

"Good." Emma bit her tongue. She must not over-sell it or he would be suspicious. Yet it giggled in her mind. It was such a good idea—the salvation of Lester! The making of the two of them! The focus for many of the boys she saw so aimless now. He *would* sort them out, she was sure.

"Mary will be there tonight as well," she said. "Mary Tallentire. Douglas' wife."

"What for?"

"She used to do voluntary teaching around here. She gave up in the summer but she still keeps in touch. They say that she was very good. The committee wanted her to come."

"She's O.K., Mary," Lester said. He had scarcely taken a moment's notice of her in his life, but he wanted to extend a proprietorial hand.

"I must be off now." Emma was careful to be brisk.

Lester wanted to ask if he could move in with her. In his vision of the scene they were to have played, Emma was going to beg him to move in with her and he would have accepted, eventually—apparently unwillingly—to please her, retaining all his independence. Now that she was leaving he felt bereft. Her companionship, even in that brief time, had emphasized how isolated he now was.

"I'll walk you back."

"Thank you."

Those who saw them walking together through the crumbling inner city streets thought, "There goes that nice helpful girl from the Centre with another of her Good Causes." Emma thought, "I'll leave Mark a note at the enquiry office, putting off tonight's supper, so that Lester won't be embarrassed if he stays on." Lester thought, "A squad of athletes. That would be the job. I'll turn them into world beaters. They would have to do as I say, though. They would have to work—no skiving, no short cuts, no selling short. *My* rules. World-beaters!"

"How's little Harry?" he asked. The question had just popped into his head.

"*Lovely!*" Emma said—and she leaned over and kissed him.

I could do a lot worse than get married, Lester decided, and took Emma's arm.

(7)

Douglas wondered at what point he ought to tell him. As they sat facing each other he kept thinking: surely he knows; how can he not know? How can he assume I don't remember? What's he playing at? But Alfie Javitt just kept on playing. He was the film producer who owed Douglas £2,500: the man who had begun as a teenager with a fruit and flower stall and stormed up, comic hero fashion, through the tumbling Sixties to become a bright British export to the U.S. of A., where his Beatle association had boosted him into a circuit vampire-greedy for new blood. He was shrewd, fast talking, eccentric, cocksure, original, loud mouthed and full of total confidence about "the audience", "the ordinary joe", "the guy who pays for his seat in Kansas City and Wakefield" *and*, equally important, he fancied himself as a trend-spotter. "The mini-skirt is here to stay," "Jeans are on the way out, but *out*," "Health foods—forget it," "Science Fiction will never work in the big-time movies"—that kind of thing. His career had been hit and miss, rich and bust, up and down, never in or out for long.

The place at which he called the meeting was also a little disconcerting, as far as Douglas was concerned. It was in the middle of Mayfair, in a pretty street full of splendid early Victorian houses, once the town houses of the rich and racy members of English society; now offices. It was here, in this very room, that Douglas had got his first film script in the late 1960s. Paid £2,000, which was a sackful of gold then (although the going rate was at least ten times as much), and embarked on some months of a refined torment which drew out the most contradictory feelings: excitement at being in the dream machine which had blotted up so many fantastical hours of his youth, anxiety over how to do the job, bewilderment at the discovery that no one else seemed to know either, guilt at the money involved and the money talked about and the money promised and the nouveau richness of the fat-cat life of heavy lunches, heavier dinners, private cinemas, heated swimming pools, Swiss accounts and spoilt stars; disdain for the vulgarity of the operation, accreting contempt for the manners, attitudes and brains of those involved, a reluctant acknowledgement that there were Big Top Barnum skills and energies he did not possess, self-disgust at not waking up to and taking advantage of the conclusion that he was being asked to be a lieutenant in a war run by caricature colonels and mutton-headed generals, and, finally—and this was what had caused him to pull back from and out of the industry—he had found not only no satisfaction in the work but, powerfully, there had been a cold physical sensation in his stomach for weeks, as if he had contravened some basic rule within his own scheme of things and was thereby frozen out and discarded by a better and more useful self. But he remembered the room very well.

It had not changed at all, he thought. The over-large desk, the swivel chair, the two long black leather chesterfields, the yellow grassy Wilton carpet, wall to wall, the fine Victorian bookcase full of unread lengths of classics in calf, novels and biographies and stories "bought" (in a larger than usual sense) by the producer. There was still the huge photograph of Manhattan at night on the one wall and, on the other, the large blow-up of W. C. Fields holding a hand of poker close to his cunning face. And, scattered here and there, the chunky rich junk which could be found in the surrounding shops: heavy glass and gold, like ashtrays, a monstrous dice, a gargantuan paper-clip, the smaller necessities and toys of life inflated to ponderous proportions, giving an overall effect of striving for an effect which was never revealed or arrived at.

Alfie—he liked to be known by the matey diminutive—Alfie would have maintained that he was light years away from the dinosaurs of Hollywood who had inhabited this office before him. There was a brief period in the Sixties when, frightened by the competition of television in the States and in the self-constructed throes of a death agony on the Hollywood lots, several producers had shifted to Europe, further attracted by the low labour costs, the tales of permissiveness along the King's Road and a desperate search for a source of new energy to fuel the cranky monster on the West Coast. The man who had employed Douglas had been just such a dinosaur. Out of Central Europe, by way of deals and twists and turns and luck and one-reelers and "B" features and accidental deaths and meetings and then pots of gold and more gold. A loud, funny, bullying, ignorant, enjoyable, fat-faced, devious, generous, cunning, careless, big-bummed papa figure, who modelled himself on so many different picture heroes—now Big Daddy, now Wyatt Earp, now the Gent, now the Industrial Bum, now Svengali, now Napoleon—that he ended up spending most of his time outmanoeuvring himself with various opposed parties whom he thought he was playing off against each other. Working with him was like being in a very small bathtub with a gigantic manic, roistering dwarf.

Alfie would have described himself as "cool", new style, no flashy clothes—well, not *seeming* flashy, expensive on the sly. He would also have seen himself as the low profile laid back, relaxed operator, who knew the pedals on the organ. Cultural names, at which his predecessor in the swivel chair had jibbed like an unbroken horse, would slide easily across the large desk which, for some reason, had a piece of glass covering it. Douglas could not work out why. The desk was a reproduction. And

333

Alfie knew the in-groups: talk of trouble at the National Theatre, manoeuvres at the A.L.P., new production outfits being set up by the television companies—he would know the connections.

It took Douglas about ten minutes to work out that the old game had not changed an iota. Alfie, too, was a reproduction.

"I read your story by accident, to tell you the truth," Alfie said, smoking a thin but costly cigar, his Gucci boots firmly and coolly on the table showing off his deeply casual Molton Street cords and lumberjack shirt, for which he had paid a lumberjack's monthly wages. "Your agent had tried to sell me the usual spy-story crap." He smiled indulgently. "That's all *passé*. Spy stories are finished. What they want now—over in the Coast—is something with a bit of depth. They're looking for unusual properties they can get their teeth into. There's actors over there hungry for stretching. They've got to be stretched. They've made the money—they've got the fame and riches—you know—Jack and Robert and Richard and Al—and there are hundreds more where they came from, believe me, the Coast is crowded out with great actors. *Great* actors. Great *film* actors. On the screen. And they've got the directors. The very best. *Very* best. And *do* they know the medium? You should hear them talk, Douglas, it would amaze you, the details they go into. It amazes me, I don't mind admitting it. When you get Francis and George and—*and* the others in a room, it's like being at a fucking University, I kid you not. The *detail*. But what they have a crying need for is the story: the script: the idea: the basics. Not a *plot*! I'm not talking to you about a *plot*! That's out. Plots are finished. It's the thing itself. The Whole Thing. That's what matters. That's what grabbed me about your story 'Death of a Friend'—what a title! What an Eighties title! I tell you there are grown up men on the Coast who would sit down and weep for a title like that! I mean the title *in itself as a title* is ace. Ace. *As a title!* And the story. That *man*! What you do with him! It's brilliant. On his own. In that wood. I can see it. I can see them all wanting it. Talk about an acting role. A *role*! All it needs is to be written as a script."

"What about my £2,500?" Douglas thought. Not yet?

"What I would like to do is this," Alfie said. "I could get

up-front money here, no problem, on the title alone. But why get jerks involved? I'm going to the Coast tomorrow. I want to take that story and be in a position to set it up over there. You could come out and work on the first draft—paid in dollars, useful—I'd rather do that than set anything up here."

"You want a free option."

"Free? What's free? There's a lot needs to be done to it."

"I agree."

"Do you know what I think?" Alfie said, ruminatively, letting the creative juices squeeze through. "I think the reason he takes to the woods should be Vietnam."

"Vietnam?"

"It's the hottest thing in Hollywood now. Three years ago you couldn't touch it. Now you've got that Jane Fonda movie, you've got 'The Deerhunter', you've got 'Apocalypse' and 'Dog Soldiers'. If he's been in Vietnam you'll get Jack, Richard, Al, De Niro—any of them just waiting to get their hands on it. Just watch them. Vietnam is the business."

"In that case it would be a totally different story."

"Not totally, Douglas. Totally's going too far. I think of it as giving it recognizable motivation."

"The whole point is that the man goes to the woods for reasons neither he nor I can explain."

"That's the problem. That's perfect in a story—and, I repeat, I love the story. But in a film—motivation is the name of it. Motivation is what makes it work. We're aware of that now."

"What if the Vietnam thing is over?" Douglas asked, keeping a straight face.

"That's one of the things I want to suss out."

"I see."

"He could've been a terrorist."

"A terrorist?"

"Before he took to the woods. You need some heavy in-cut or flashback stuff for motivation."

"I see. An American terrorist."

"They have them, believe me. They have everything over there. You name it."

"Why don't we just scrap it and start from the beginning?"

"But I love the story. I've told you. The story and the title."

"They're a property?"

"You've beaten me to the post, Douglas. You've thought it through. Correct. It's a property. There are very few properties on the market now. I know that. I think I could sell this one Big. And to the right people."

"And then I would come out and change it entirely and script it."

"*With* a director," Alfie said by way of making the deal even more attractive. "With a very good director, hopefully. Working side by side at your elbow."

Douglas took a breath.

"The last thing I did for you, Alfie. A while back. I'm still owed on it."

"Money?"

"Yes."

"I don't believe it. I never owe." Alfie swung his feet off the table self-righteously and stood up, patently deeply concerned. "There must have been a mistake."

"£2,500."

"I mean a mistake—mistake. Look. I'll get onto the accountants." He shook his young head sadly. "These guys. You have to tell them everything. I mean, a simple payment. And peanuts! But, I can see, it's the principle." Douglas thought of the better flat £2,500 would enable him to rent: peanuts could taste good. "So what do you say?" Alfie asked.

"About the money?"

"That'll be through in a couple of days. Believe me. My mistake. About the property?"

"The story means a lot to me."

"Exactly. That's its strength. That's its strength. It means a lot to you. That's a very English thing. I understand it. You can feel it."

Douglas had enjoyed the bouncing around with Alfie and he was by now sufficiently in control of himself to realize that, while Alfie was not proposing anything alluring at the moment, there could be the seeds of a film project in his plans to ride around Hollywood waving the story around. There could even be interest from an intelligent actor or director. The story would be published eventually and have its own life. This was something else. There could be the fun of working in Holly-wood for a short spell and, possibly, a wad of money which would bankroll him for six months—a year. It would be prissy to jib. The film could be thought of as having nothing to do with the story. Yet, before he gave it the nod, he acknowledged a passing sadness. Alan Jackson's death the inspiration for an Oscar-nominated performance by one of the new, tough American actors. Aware of the sentimentality of the gesture, he nevertheless made it.

"I'll need some time to think about it," Douglas said.

"Two days."

"O.K."

(8)

It was going to take him a long time to digest the implications of what Mary had said to him. Mike was glad that the rest of the day and the evening were full of work.

Mike sat on the jury which judged the best television of the year—in several categories, documentary, drama, light enter-tainment, the best actor, best actress, best factual series and so on. Mike had gradually been prevailed on to take more and more of an interest in this and eventually he had discovered that he was hooked. He found it a genuine stimulant to sit through such a selection of what was generally high quality stuff. The unexpected pleasure he had gained since his return to British television was just this wealth of work. He liked to enjoy the double satisfaction of seeing programmes and films over which so much care and intelligence had been spent, while knowing that they would be broadcast equally to practically every house in the land.

But tonight he was simply glad it was there—for occupation.

They were showing plays. Mike had seen most of them on transmission, which made it easy for him to watch them this time with half a mind, while he slowly absorbed the news and in effect, the ultimatum—though that was too threatening a word. Mary had simply stated her policy. It was unfair and ironic in several ways—not least of which was the fact that it was through Mike that she had regained sufficient strength, confidence and composure to make such a decision. But that was the least of it.

The plays went past: a drama-musical by Dennis Potter, an amoral rock-romp by Howard Schuman, a comedy of provincial manners by Alan Bennett—these and other of Douglas' contemporaries, Mike realized . . . What was the picture of the country that emerged from these works, he wondered. If, as was claimed, some of the best dramatists were writing some of their best plays for television and if, as they would likely claim, they were writing about the society they lived in—then it was not a bad piece of litmus paper, this videotape and celluloid. So. A fondness for the past, particularly the near past, something obsessive about the revisions and recapitulations of recent history, as if trying to discover what could be readjusted in order to release the present from the obsessive spell. The last fifty years came onto the screen again and again, in war and peace, rage and riches, despair and idle indulgence, politics and comedy, in bleakness and in wealth, as if the writers were saying—"We are them, look, see, they are us, aren't they? Are they? Are they?" Then you would have to admit the continued prevalence of a wry, ingrown sense of humour which got a laugh out of constipation and cocks, sexual ambiguities and social conventions—and this at all levels of class and sophistication, even within those works which strove to avoid it. There was the overall impression of a society, wealthy or quixotic, that could put so much talent into this form. A lack of passion, too, though melodrama often went on the rampage. A fondness for "character", even when the most urgent and political notions of the day were informing the piece. A nice sense of style: a strong feeling for place: a seemingly bottomless well of good actors, working hard and skilfully to the camera: a powerful air of work well rounded and completed. Nothing here for moaning or gnashing of teeth. At the most, an undefined apprehension.

The judges exchanged a few notes. The final assessments would be made in an afternoon meeting in the next fortnight. Mike declined to join a couple of the others for a quick meal.

He walked back to his flat, through Piccadilly and up into Soho—both still crowded—and onto his own pleasantly anonymous patch. He had heard that it was now being considered fashionable (what wasn't?). As long as the rents kept sane.

The flat was very cold. He had forgotten to switch on the heating. It was too late to bother now. He picked up the post—it always arrived after he had left for work—and went through into the living room. There was a small electric fire: he turned that on and poured himself a scotch. It still did not seem comfortable. He glanced around critically. There was not much furniture, but the place could not be called bare. There were books all over the place, and magazines and newspapers. One or two framed posters and prints were on the walls. He rarely gave the look of the place a thought: it was serviced and a woman came in twice a week to make sure it was clean and tidy. Mike was neat. Yet . . . it felt very empty—almost as empty as it had felt when he had first moved into it and left his family.

It was odd, he thought, having maintained and brought up a family at this distance—though no odder than a sailor in former years, or any traveller. When he had made the split, then it had been done carefully and well, but it had also seemed the best thing to do. And his wife and daughter had survived, even thriven. So had he.

But now there was a lack felt keenly. Over the past few months he had found that his friendship with Mary had opened up the potential of love. There was something erotic in meeting her, in being with her, in eating together, the fixing of small things; something which gave warmth and comfort to everything. In unseen ways he had come to want that, to assuage the lack of it which he had not noticed for many years.

She had made it clear that although she wanted to see him—she would not yet live with him. Despite what had happened. And this flat, which had seemed a refuge from one relationship, now seemed like a prison cell in which he would have to serve out his term without any real certainty.

For he knew that to force it would be to lose her. She was bound on a course of her own and as yet had no energy to share. He could only wait.

(9)

Douglas realized that time was up. The jokey phrase was deadly accurate. Mary had changed and he did not know in which direction that had taken her.

It was she who had asked him out. They had gone—the three of them—to a pleasant and calm little pizza house in Chalk Farm. Then Mary had invited him back to her place. Douglas was wary and took care. He concentrated on John. The two of them got on so much better now. Douglas had worked at it, and the first results of that were almost embarrassingly rich. John was happier, chirpier, he had found something to care about—fishing—which allowed him to feel independent. Being alone with his mother had rallied his sense of responsibility, while Douglas' new attentiveness had raised his self-estimation.

"He's a *lot* better," Mary said, when John finally disappeared into his bedroom. "I think your mother's helped him such a lot. So have you."

"You're his mother."

"He was in a bad way, poor boy," Mary said, plumping cushions, as she appeared to be setting the room for a scene. A tender enough scene, by the look of it, side lights, coffee on the bubble, an already opened bottle of red wine brought out with two glasses. "There. That looks fine, don't you think?"

"How old is this wine?" Douglas asked, feeling a spike of jealousy, for the true question he was quite obviously asking was—"Did you and Mike crack this bottle?"

"Mike and I had a glass this lunchtime," she said.

"A busy day."

"Half-term. We teachers have to fit things in when we can."

"We learners never learn that." He poured out two full glasses. "I feel," he said, "a significant moment coming on. Am I right?"

"Right," Mary said. Her tone was not solemn but it was rather sober, he noticed, carrying neither reprimand nor, particularly, any warning. Douglas had settled down in the settee beside the drink. Mary took her glass and went to the armchair which was generally his.

"You look very lovely," Douglas said. He raised his glass. "You're slimmer and it suits you. Your hair's started to look shiny as it used to when we first met. You look great."

"Thank you." She smiled. "You could do with cutting back on the drink a little. The chin," she said.

340

"Which one?"

"Do you remember back in the cottage last New Year?"

"Yes."

"I was thinking about it today. Although it was horrible and tense—you were exhausted *and* drunk *and* full of all your worst 'am I coming or going' symptoms—there was something about that."

"'Have this one on the house,'" Douglas quoted.

"Yes." She laughed. "And you did."

"I remember. On the mat."

He poured himself some more wine. There was knowing someone through living with them. There was all that store of just knowing them so intensely well from ten thousand observations and unknown perceptions. There was the capacity to make the finest adjustments of rhythm and mood, he thought, to let yourself be becalmed in a zoneless time, where there were just the two of you, the systole and diastole, to and fro, backwards and forwards, yin and yang, until the convergence. There was this ability to draw up from the well of commitment a deep calm, a sensuous understanding; mutual comprehension and peace. Douglas felt it lap about him.

"I'm pregnant," Mary said.

Douglas was very still. Something stopped and ended, he thought. Or perhaps nothing happened. There was this peculiar no-time. Undeniable. He waited for her to wind back, the words to return into her mouth, to be unspoken, for this not to have happened at all. It was so odd.

"I see," he said, after what seemed a very long time. Then he cleared his throat, which had become clogged and constricted. "I see," he repeated.

"It's early," Mary said, quietly. "I could get rid of it. But at my age—we talked about this, in fact I began to talk about it in the cottage—it isn't easy. We proved that."

"We—" He was going to say, "We never really tried."

"I did," she said. "But nothing happened. This could be a last chance. Anyway. I'm not risking anything; I want to have the child."

"Mike, of course."

"Yes."

It was only now that Douglas began to notice that what he had thought of as sobriety was in fact very stern determination.

"Christ," he said. He did not know what he felt. Her announcement had scooped out his normal responses and simply flung them away. But he felt it incumbent on him to keep a conversation alive. "What did he have to say?"

"He was pleased," Mary answered. "A bit surprised." She spoke on carefully. "We did it when we were in Paris for that holiday. Not since."

"Can I ask why not?"

"I don't know whether I love him," Mary said.

"How can you know a thing like that?" Douglas asked, and it seemed to him that a true answer to that question would solve the puzzle which seemed to him still at the centre of most things.

"I know it," she said. "Perhaps because I knew that I loved you."

"But you're having his child."

"Our child. My child. A child. Yes."

"I don't know what to say, Mary. What do you expect me to say?"

"I'm pleased about it—" she glanced at her belly. Without any suggestion of rancour, she went on, "Of course, you couldn't be expected to be. Not yet."

"Yet?" Douglas checked his own sharpness. But the sharpness was a superficial reaction. Jealousy had dissolved. Perhaps he had ceased to have any feelings for her at all.

"I think it must be terrible for you if you really don't know what love is," Mary said. "If you've really lost that; if you've really locked that off. But you love Betty, don't you? And John?"

"Of course. But there's no choice in that. It's where there's a choice that it seems meaningless."

"That's blasphemy," Mary said, and her voice was firm. "Where there's the choice is when it's most important."

"What does Mike have to say?"

"He wants us to get a divorce so that he and I can get married."

"I really don't know what to say."

342

"You don't have to say anything. It's a lot to take in." Mary held out her glass. "Could you pour me one, please?"

Douglas filled her glass.

"I ought to be yelling 'What a bloody mess!' and stomping about in a regressed and unjust but sincere war dance about my rights and your tartiness and your—sluttishness!" The word had an unintended accusing force.

"You slept with Hilda, didn't you?"

"Yes. But we were careful."

"I thought I'd been careful. It was an accident."

"I don't believe in that sort of accident."

"That's what Mike said."

"Sod Mike." Douglas glared at her. "I'm having no part of any bloody *ménage à trois*, you know. If we get together, it's you and me. He can have access or whatever, but I'm not living in a bloody little commune."

"I wouldn't want that, either." Mary paused. "I spoke to Hilda."

"What for?"

"I thought we should meet."

"Why?"

"To talk."

"Well?"

"Do you still sleep together?"

"No."

There was a long silence.

"It just seems very strange," Douglas said, finally. "That so much time and energy should go into who lives with whom."

"You think there are more important things?"

"Yes."

"Perhaps. It's very convenient to think that."

Douglas poured himself the rest of the bottle: Mary had indicated she wanted no more.

"So, after all that's happened, the old way would have been the best. One man, one wife," Douglas said.

"I think so."

"It was never that I didn't like you. Or even fell out of love with you."

343

"I know that now."

"It's so simple. Like self-destruction is a simple way to prove free will. I just wanted so much. I thought that with so much choice it was wrong to waste opportunities," Douglas said.

"You have no more choice than your grandfather had," Mary said. "That's your delusion."

"Opportunity?"

"He could have skipped off or opted out too."

"So I've been mistaken all along."

"In my opinion, yes," Mary said, carefully. "I once said I respected you for it. I don't now. There are commitments, not choices."

"So where do we go from here?"

"Well," Mary took a deep breath, "*we* don't go on anywhere. It's over, our living together. In one way I think you've played it gently and well, over the last year. You've been reliable where I needed it and helpful when I needed it. Given that you were not living with me, you couldn't have been much better. But there's absolutely no way at all in which we could ever live together again. None. I couldn't bear it."

Douglas took some time to digest that. Eventually, he nodded.

"Mike?"

"I think so. I hope so. But not for a while. I'm so weak at the moment. I have a chance to be on my own and get stronger on my own. I want to take it."

"Do you really think that most of what I've been saying and trying to do this last year has been a waste of time?"

"Not a waste of time, no. I'm sure you're sincere about it all."

"But mistaken."

"Yes. And," Mary added, carefully, "it's got very little to do with life as it's lived. All your worrying about being honest and truthful and loyal and believing in this but not in that and so on. Life's making the best of what you find. And that's to do with things that never seem to impinge on your 'world-view'. I mean things like putting up shelves or changing nappies or putting up with bad times. And, most of all, thinking about other people. It's all very well going around having thoughts on death! You could've spared an extra thought for our life."

344

"If I let you get away with that, I'd be betraying everything I believe in. It's easy to chop down those who try to take a view."

"Or to puncture those who are inflated?"

"I believe it's important to think life through. Even if you make a mess of it. There's an army of those who have failed. Better be with them than your 'making the best of it' brigade—heads down and anything for a quiet life. No thanks."

"We disagree, then. I think you've been hiding from the real facts with all your larger anxieties."

"It's got to be worth something."

"So you say."

"Perhaps you think there's no point at all in questions or answers. Let only professionally qualified people ask them. The rest of us should just get on and 'make the best of it'."

"I never thought you weren't sincere," Mary said.

"I've suspected myself regularly. I've thought I was manipulating you, me, her, them, anyone to get what I wanted."

"But you never knew what you wanted."

"That was the point!" Douglas said and they both laughed. "Don't you see?"

"Yes and no."

"Perfect," he said, feeling more warmly towards her than he had done for months.

"No it isn't," Mary continued, gravely. "Our marriage is over, Douglas. Fourteen years. It's over now. And you still don't seem to me to be facing up to it. You are upset. I can see that. You worry about John and fuss over me, I can see that. You cope very well. You write a story—Mike says it's the best thing you've done. You make this television film; you carry on with your reviewing and sell a house and get a flat and God knows what else. You cope. And I admire that. I see the strain. But what you don't do is see that our marriage has been just disintegrating."

"Maybe I saw that and decided to look the other way. Maybe I couldn't bear the sight. Maybe I thought that if I didn't look, it would go away and everything would end up happily ever after."

"Yes. Perhaps."

"Perhaps all that's been going on in my head about death has been no more than a transference. What really upset me was the death of us. Does that make any sense?" Douglas knew that, if ever in his life he was telling the truth and needed to be believed, it was now. If Mary, who knew him so well, failed to see when he had reached the bottom of his own pit of evasions and ambiguities and self-deceits, if his wife would not accept that indeed his year had been shaken and disturbed by the terrible fact of an empty marriage yawning before him, if she would not take this offering of honesty—then he was truly lost. He had so sliced through his self-confidence; he had alternately lashed and indulged himself; he had screwed up every move he made for so long that, to use the biblical phrase which often came to mind, "there was no health in him". And the salt had lost its savour. And the appetite had sickened. She had to believe him.

She said nothing.

"I love you," Douglas said, dry throated, slow, bending all his will to it. "I always will, I think, because I once did. But, the truth is," he licked his lips and forced the words through, "this last year, I've been trying all I could, not to admit to hating you. Not because of you. Not entirely. Our marriage was over, and neither of us wanted to see it. You wouldn't because of John, most probably. I wouldn't because to me the end of the marriage was the end of the world. It was shame and failure and my eternal guilt and not being able to look anybody in the eye again and spoiling John's chances of domestic security and condemning us to bitterness against each other. And it was letting parents down, giving in, joining the quitters; all that. But there was this hatred that I wouldn't even acknowledge to myself. I've chopped it out of my mind so much that it's never been articulated until now. But now I can see that it was there. All the time. I hated you as much as I'd loved you."

"Why didn't you let it out? It might have helped."

"Yes. Perhaps. Or it could have been destructive. In many ways I wanted us to go on. You know that. Not just for convenience. But because of the pain of not going on. Oh—I know I

346

was exhilarated in those first few weeks, when I left the house. So were you, in a way. That was just to do with newness. It wasn't callous. But after that there was pain. I kept transferring it. I kept thinking it was to do with death: I kept suffocating it under that blanket expression. I put it in the story. Maybe in the film."

"Why?"

"I don't know. I suppose I didn't want to face up to it. But to admit to such a hatred would have prevented us from acting. Don't you see?"

"You mean it would have torn us apart."

"Yes. If I'd let it rise up it would have—I don't know. It would have wounded you and me so badly we could have bled to death. So maybe those useless, unrealistic thoughts you so convincingly disparage served a purpose beyond themselves: maybe they were the thousand and one strings and thin ropes that bound down this Gulliver of—feeling—which could have trampled over everything and crushed all about us."

"You should've let it out."

"No." Douglas felt deeply tired and sadder than he could remember since their daughter's death. "No. It would have spared nothing, you see. It would have stripped both of us bare. It would have said how loathsome and profoundly unlikeable each of us finds the other because it would have called on those parts—perhaps they are in everyone—which simply observe and draw on the weaknesses found in any close relationship. These are things about me you can't stand, and vice versa. If that hatred had been released it would have ignited all that and the flames would have burnt us to ashes."

"Instead of which I feel as much as a stone," Mary said.

"But you're still intact. And there's John—he's intact." He paused. "And Mike came along."

"What if he hadn't? Would you have stayed?"

"I wouldn't have gone."

"You left me long ago, Douglas," Mary said, taking yet another cigarette. "Long ago," she repeated. "You're right— you didn't face up to it—but neither did I. I let myself live, knowing that I was not loved. Loved! Not even wanted half the

347

time, and the other half merely tolerated and only that with great efforts on all sides. There came a time when I should have rebelled against that and I didn't and the time passed. So where did that leave me? It wasn't John so much I ran away to, as work. All the extra teaching, and the voluntary overtime. You didn't know that side of me. 'Good old Mary'll do it.' And good old Mary did. If you became a monster, it was because I was a sucker. But the truth isn't so dramatic. Both of us believe in love and we fell out of it. And we couldn't accept that for several years. Finally it dawned on us and still we didn't accept it and acted as if it simply was not true. But it is true. I will always love you, too, Douglas: but the you I love is not the man in front of me now. And you don't love me, today, as I am. We've avoided stirring up the hatred against each other. Let's not sentimental- ize the love. It's no more than a scar now. Maybe an honourable scar, but a scar."

There was silence for a while.

"So it *is* over."

"Yes. It is."

"It seems so very odd. I keep thinking that. Just ending."

"Will you go to Hilda?"

"No. I think not. Like you—I feel no use to anybody at the moment. Are we right?"

"Yes. I think so." Mary, too, was weary: and yet, for a little while longer, probably for the last time in this last mood of their married life, she, like Douglas, wanted to stay.

"Things can change," Douglas said. "Look at my own parents. At one time I would have said that they had got so used to living apart from each other's real feelings that they had become no more than two people who shared a house and a certain number of past experiences. Now they seem to have come together—just this year—and they seem to be getting closer all the time. So things can change. And maybe they weren't ever all that far apart, just hidden from each other by the screens of busyness and fatigue and just getting through life that surround us all. I remember my father saying once that *his* father, Old John, had once said he was always too tired to talk to his wife. We've had those chances—but there have been other barriers. And perhaps ..."

348

"No, Douglas. You left me. And I let you go. That's what happened."

"But why?"

"That's either a whole history or a mystery. We met," Mary said and quite suddenly in her mind's eye she "saw" that first time: he looked so young, then, so eager and brimful of life—and the vision checked her, a treacherous view: she went on. "Now we've parted."

"John?"

"He's been better since we split. Everybody says that. And you're better to him now than you have been for years."

"I'll take him out tomorrow morning."

"Not in the morning. He's going over to the Heath fishing in the morning."

"On his own?"

"There's a few of them. I've been there. It's nice," Mary said. "It's very nice. They bring their little stools and their sandwiches and flasks and sit down beside the ponds, lost to the world. He loves it. He's quite safe."

"I'll come after lunch then."

"Yes."

Douglas stood up. It was very late. He could have slept where he dropped.

"You know, I came here fully expecting to stay."

"The night?"

"No. For ever."

"Did you?"

"I thought so."

"And now."

"I must guiltily steal away."

"Guilty, eh? In case you betray someone else by sleeping with your wife?"

"Not only that."

"Well." Mary stood up. "No doubt there'll be less happy nights than this."

"I'll go, then," Douglas said.

"Yes." Mary paused. "Goodnight."

Douglas stepped forward to kiss her but she stepped back. He did not insist. She closed the door very quietly behind him.

Outside he stood on the edge of the pavement for some time. It was as if he were still held to what was inside that flat. Quite unmistakably he felt bound to it, even lashed to it and he felt that he had to strain and pull and burst through this feeling in order to leave the spot. There was so much to leave. Wife. Child. Past. Tragedy. Past. Happiness. What would happen to that immense portion of shared life?

They had been part of each other for so long, swept in and out of each other's fantasies and pleasures and illnesses and delights and nightmares. Yes, it was no exaggeration: he felt bound to the place. He was breaking the most serious promise he had made.

From deep within the room, where he could not possibly see her, she watched him and knew why he paused, for she too felt too rooted in their relationship to want to move away and rip open the body of life they had formed together.

So, for some minutes, they stood, as close-bound as ever in their lives they had been, until finally, wearily, Douglas began to walk away. Mary let him go out of sight, out of sound, before dry-eyed, she went to her bed and crawled under the covers without undressing.

As he trudged through the dark and empty city, Douglas found that he was weeping. It did not last very long, but long enough for him to sense the regret and remorse which could well accompany many more of his solitary hours. Yet he walked on.

Tried to think of simple plans to staunch this spring of unhappiness which, released now after months, perhaps even years, of self-deceit, spilled into his mind steadily, without, as yet, either hint or promise of relief or peace. Must write to the man and accept the film offer: must buy John an aluminium rod: must write to parents, let them know how much I appreciate them—never do:—must check that Mike has got a job for Lester: must get better flat.

But these were flimsy defences, soon worn down by the relentless surge of unhappiness.

He walked to assuage it. He walked to tire himself. He walked to seek the comfort of activity. The streets were clear.

Not until dawn did he turn towards his room, his cell, and

begin the final stretch. The city began to show signs of its life and complexity. The street lights were dimmed by the lightness of the dawn and, before Douglas reached his place, they had been turned off.

Douglas needed a new line now, to set him off again into this different life. What had Mary said? Commitment. Yes. But if he had been a fool to think the world his kingdom, then the fool had seen his folly and the folly still lived. Yes, there was a kingdom he could look for, but no longer in himself. Self had been blighted in some explicable but most profound passion to survive. Now he was free. Free? Freer.

To be of some use to those he could help. Perhaps even to risk resurrecting the ideals of younger days and in some way trying to forget himself in the greater demands of others. Yes?

Inside the room, he was too tired to undress and he fell on the bed. It was sad to sleep alone. Once he had been afraid of it. As a child. And in the dark. Spells to beat off the evil spirits which so surrounded the bed . . . and prayers . . .?

"Thy Kingdom come, Thy will be done."


( 10 )

John got up quietly, so as not to disturb his mother.

His clothes were neatly laid out over a chair beside his bed. He had practised with his eyes closed so that he could, if necessary, dress in the dark. He did not want to draw the curtains because of the harsh sound they made.

The sandwiches were neatly parcelled: the flask stood beside them like a sentry. He put them carefully in his bag with the bait and the hooks and the flies and the tin of worms, carefully aerated. His grandfather had given him the tin—an ancient two-ounce Capstan tobacco tin.

He went out quietly. The rod and the camp-stool were behind the door. Soon he was through the streets and onto the Heath. He knew the short cuts now.

As he trekked up Parliament Hill the sun began to come up behind him. On the top of the hill he paused not a moment to look over the waking city. St Paul's, the parks, the Surrey hills, London. He was intent on his day's occupation.

351

Down the hill to the bridge which divided the two ponds. His heart lurched, happily. He was the first there. He could take his pick.

John chose his territory carefully and set up camp. He looked around briefly at the trees, the Heath beyond, the grand big houses backing onto the water. Then he made his first cast of the day. It was just about perfect.